4 80

CRITICAL ACCLAIM FOR
LYNN ABBEY

"[Lynn Abbey's novels] make fantasy worth reading."   —*Booklist*

"Lynn Abbey is a talented fantasy author comfortable in many different Fantasy worlds. She populates her books with strong women characters with magic talents."   —Suite101.com

"Lynn Abbey has . . . a knack for historical fantasy, and her protagonists display an unusual complexity and grittiness . . ."
                                    —*The Encyclopedia of Fantasy*

D1051370

FANTASY TITLES
Published by ibooks, inc.:

Black Unicorn
by Tanith Lee

Nightwings
by Robert Silverberg

Changeling
by Roger Zelazny

Swords and Deviltry
Book 1 of the Adventures of
Fafhrd and the Gray Mouser
by Fritz Leiber

Fantasy: The Best of 2001
Robert Silverberg & Karen Haber, Editors

Roger Zelazny's
The Dawn of Amber
by John Gregory Betancourt

UNICORN & DRAGON™

LYNN ABBEY

Illustrated by
ROBERT GOULD

ibooks
new york
www.ibooks.net

DISTRIBUTED BY SIMON & SCHUSTER, INC.

A Publication of ibooks, inc.

Copyright © 1987 by
Byron Preiss Visual Publications, Inc.
Illustrations copyright © 1987 by
Byron Preiss Visual Publications, Inc.
Unicorn & Dragon is a trademark of
Byron Preiss Visual Publications, Inc.

An ibooks, inc. Book
Published by arrangement with
Byron Preiss Visual Publications, Inc.

All rights reserved, including the right to reproduce this book
or portions thereof in any form whatsoever.

Distributed by Simon & Schuster, Inc.
1230 Avenue of the Americas, New York, NY 10020

ibooks, inc.
24 West 25th Street
New York, NY 10010

The ibooks World Wide Web Site Address is:
http://www.ibooks.net

ISBN 0-7434-5821-4
First ibooks, inc. printing February 2003
10 9 8 7 6 5 4 3 2 1

Edited by David M. Harris
Book design by Alex Jay
Cover art by Robert Gould
Cover design by j. vita

Printed in the U.S.A.

To my parents,
who have always believed in me

UNICORN & DRAGON ™

he wolves were howling. Their unworldly chorus echoed from the hills behind him through the looming forests either side of the narrow trail. Stephen reined his horse, Sulwyn, to a halt and bellowed his uncle's war cry back at them into the moonlight.

"Tor-wor-den!"

Now it was his own voice that echoed through the wintry air; the wolves fell silent. The young man was relieved but not deceived. The pack hadn't broken from the hunt. They were still watching him and they would, barring a miracle he did not truly expect, attack sometime in the long hours before dawn light.

Rewrapping the reins around his numb fingers, Stephen clapped his heels to the horse's flanks. Sulwyn blew an icy mist from his nostrils and started walking, his iron-shod hooves crunching through the light blanket of snow.

Their task had seemed so simple at the beginning: take a message to Duke William's man at the channel port of Pevensey; get it there in less than six days and ride in the company of Torworden's veteran campaigners. It had seemed so simple that his uncle and guardian, Jean Beauleyas, had consented to let him carry the carved silver case.

The initial disaster had struck near noon of their second day. The ground had been frozen since the middle of November, but snow had not yet completely obscured the contours of the road. They had been moving along at a trot that kept both man and beast's blood flowing. Stephen had been in the front, abreast of Ranulf, the only one of his uncle's ruffians he called his friend, when Baldwin's horse had screamed in terror and pain. Snow and shadow had concealed a small sinkhole.

It was over by the time he got Sulwyn reined around:

1

Baldwin's great chestnut horse lay on its side, blood and gore already showing around the shattered bones of its right foreleg. And Baldwin lay beneath the horse.

Ranulf slit the horse's throat at once, but God's law forbade such mercy to a man. While Stephen and another young squire struggled with the blood-spooked horses, the men put their shoulders to the carcass and, with much effort, freed their companion.

Baldwin's leg had been as twisted and bloody as his horse's; he shrieked and fell unconscious when Ranulf gently probed the injury. Stephen felt a sick ache in his own knees as Ranulf swiftly lashed Baldwin's sword scabbard and leg together. There were few things that put a more decisive end to a man's campaigning than the weight of his own horse landing on him.

"You'll take him back to Torworden," Ranulf had announced. "The lad and I will take the message on to Pevensey."

The other men agreed and made a litter for the injured Baldwin before he regained consciousness. It was a measure of Beauleyas's temper that they had waited for Ranulf, who had his own lands across the Channel and, therefore, some other place in which to escape Jean's wrath, to order them to help Baldwin rather than abandon him at the side of the road.

The trail wound out of the forest. Sulwyn climbed to the top of the first ridge and halted, waiting for his master's command. Stephen blinked in the bright moonlight and sought the dark shadow of the road. He found it, meandering toward another finger of the forest, as did the wolves as well, their shaggy coats pricked with silver as they paced along a not-very-distant ridge.

Reciting prayers he had not said since early childhood, Stephen urged Sulwyn to a ground-eating walk and wondered if the wolves were more likely to attack in the open or under the cover of the forest. The wild openness of these Saxon kingdoms was nothing like the civilized countryside of his childhood home in the Loire Valley.

He had been knighted, a bit prematurely perhaps, before crossing the Channel to join his uncle. He was supposed to be above fear, but he distrusted every inch of Wessex and its every inhabitant as well. Not for the first time he wished that Ranulf, who'd spent ten years here already, still rode by his side.

If their first catastrophe had been an act of God, the second, just after sunrise yesterday, had been the treachery of men. He and Ranulf had barely ridden the ground's chill from their bones when the outlaws had dropped from the very trees around them. They had weighted nets and bows—not powerful Norman bows, but sturdy enough to send an arrow deep into an unarmored man—and they vastly outnumbered Stephen and Ranulf.

Still, they were mounted knights and these were Saxon-scum brigands. Stephen moved to unsheathe his long-sword, but Ranulf had butted his weapon into Sulwyn's flank and sent the dark bay thundering out of the ambush before Stephen or the brigands had a chance to react.

"Get on with it, lad," Ranulf had shouted to him. "I'll see you again in heaven or hell!"

Stephen had not meant to obey. Hauling back violently on the reins, he heeled Sulwyn around as quickly as possible and brought him back to the edge of a clearing above the fight, fully intending to charge headlong into the fray. But Ranulf was down with an arrow through his throat. Two of the murderers were already brawling over his sword and the brigand leader—at least, Stephen assumed it was the leader—was trying to mount Ranulf's skittish horse. While he sat gaping, one of the others spotted him and launched an arrow that sliced through the dumb-struck youth's shoulder.

The wound, which burned like fire, was the first Stephen had ever taken from an enemy. His careful education in martial attitudes demanded vengeance for an injury and disregarded pain as unmanly. He longed to charge at them, sword flashing, but the Norman stars were rising because they could compromise with their honor. He wrenched the arrow free and tucked it into the saddle padding; then, after fixing a good image of their leader in his mind, he made his way back to the road. He had obligations to his uncle and to Ranulf—vengeance would come at another, more propitious time.

Alone, with the message removed from its ornate case and carefully folded amid the layers of his hose, Stephen hurried in what he hoped was Pevensey's direction. He prayed for Ranulf's soul, vengeance on the brigands, clear weather, and, once the sun had set and the howling had begun, deliverance from the wolves.

The men of Torworden had jested about a Saxon manor some distance to the southeast. Like all Saxons, Godfrey Hafwynder was caught between the anarchy of the heirless king's last illness and the bastard duke of Normandy, unable to choose between them. His uncle's men would not have deigned to pass a night under his roof, but Stephen, aware that the wolves were matching his pace along the ridge, was not so proud.

A Saxon road forked to the south near the White Dragon, an immense and ancient beast carved into the chalk ridges. With the moonlight and the snow it was more of a black dragon, but the young man welcomed the sight of it and the crude crossroads marker. If the ancient road Stephen had been following was little more than a pair of ox tracks, then Hafwynder Way was barely a shallow ditch scraped through the topsoil. Despite the wolves' howling, the young man was forced to hold Sulwyn to a slow walk; Baldwin's fate was still fresh in his mind.

It was inevitable, though, that his slow pace would draw the beasts in closer. While the palfrey placed hoof after cautious hoof through the crusted snow, Stephen fumbled beneath his cloak to free his sword. He was dressed for warmth, not fighting. The heavy fur-lined mantle trapped his arms and hid the clasp on his scabbard. Uttering an oath for which he would eventually have to do penance, he heaved the material back from his left shoulder. The sudden movement opened the almost-forgotten arrow wound. He felt a searing pain as frigid air touched warm blood.

It was some moments before he was settled again with the cloak properly lapped over his chest and his right hand well gripped around the hilt. Forcing himself to relax against the cold and take note of the terrain Sulwyn crossed, he realized, with a start, that the wolves had fallen silent. Daring to thank God for a miracle, he glanced back into the moonlight and saw a wolf pacing along not a hundred steps behind him.

Perhaps it saw the look of terror on his face, for it chose that moment to throw its head high and howl. The answering chorus, erupting from the brush on both sides of the road, told Stephen he had been encircled and ambushed. There was no higher ground to which he could scramble, nor even a wider clearing from which to make his defense. There was nothing to be done except fling open the cloak, draw the sword, and hope to make a good end for himself.

The wolves were on him before he could pray or think of anything else, a dozen or more of the shaggy beasts spewing out of the forest with steam rising from their bared fangs. Bellowing his own battle cry in reflexive response, Stephen brandished the yard-long knight's sword and brought the edge down onto the spine of the foremost wolf.

It died with a night-rending shriek; if they had continued to come at him singly he could have dispatched them with ease. But they were wolves, and their hereditary strength was the pack. Stephen had one clean stroke and the chance to draw a dagger with his left hand, but nothing more. The beasts leaped at him and his horse, their jaws snapping loudly when the fangs missed their mark. Sulwyn trumpeted and plunged and, though he was no destrier trained to complement a knight's skills in battle, his iron-shod hooves thudded home more than once. But not often enough.

Jaws that could snap the shinbone of an ox locked around Stephen's ankle. His foot came free from the stirrup as the wolf sank back on its haunches, contracting its powerful neck muscles. The young knight felt himself shaken from the saddle; only by dropping the dagger and grabbing a handful of Sulwyn's mane did he resist the wolf's strength. By then, though, he'd gotten the sword above his head. The jaws spasmed, then relaxed, when he sliced downward.

Another leaped and scrabbled for balance atop Sulwyn's broad hindquarters. The palfrey screamed and clenched the bit in lockjaw panic while Stephen, his left-hand dagger gone, struck the wolf's fangs with his bare fist. He felt the fetid breath on his neck and heard the clasp-chain of his cloak clink against the beast's teeth.

Stiff-fingered, he swung blind, and, by God's grace, thrust his forefinger into the wolf's eye. It went rigid in a heartbeat and slid toward the ground, tangled in his cloak. The clasp-chain tightened across Stephen's throat, choking him, then snapped as the wolf and his cloak hit the ground.

Then the wolves retreated, growling, whining, and snuffling at the bodies of their maimed, cooling comrades. Stephen gulped the icy air and struggled to keep his sword arm from trembling as he groped blindly through the saddlebags for another short knife.

A howl came from behind. He commended his soul to God and the saints, but before he could shout his own war cry the wolves began to melt back into the brush and trees. Breathless and disbelieving, Stephen did not dare the silence for some long moments. Sulwyn's plaintive sigh broke the enchantment. After wiping the blade against his leggings, he slid it back into the scabbard with a loud snap.

"We're alive, Sul!" he gasped, leaning forward. "We're still alive!"

He patted the bay's neck as he had done thousands of times before, but Sulwyn shied from his touch, throwing his head back and whickering anxiously. Stephen felt the liquid warmth soak through the thin wool of his glove.

His own leg was throbbing where the wolf had seized it, and his left arm was numb from the shoulder down, but a knight was taught to regard his battle possessions more highly than his own well-being. Stephen thought of dismounting to retrieve his cloak and tend Sulwyn's injuries, then reluctantly dismissed the idea. Once afoot he would never be able to remount. Already shivering, and with his horse's injuries weighing heavily on his mind, he had no choice but to go onward.

Safety, if there was such a thing in midwinter Wessex, lay some distance ahead at the manor of Godfrey Hafwynder. Stephen pressed his calves against the horse's flanks, and forced himself to ignore both Sulwyn's whicker and the pain that lanced from ankle to shoulder.

8

omebody came to the gates in the middle of the night," Alison announced as soon as her eyes were open. "I dreamt he was covered all over with snow and ice, and his eyes glowed red like a dragon's!"

She shook her sister's shoulder and threw the bed curtains open. The outer room was scarcely brighter than the bedstead had been, but considerably colder. With a half-suppressed shiver, Alison grabbed her woolen chemise from the dressing-pole suspended above the pillows and pulled it over her shoulders. Its thick softness would eventually warm her, but for the moment there was no escaping the cold if she wanted to satisfy her gnawing curiosity. She pressed her hands and ear to the stones of the hearth chimney while her breath came in small, white puffs.

Her sister flailed drowsily at the draperies, trying to find some last pocket of warmth amid the rumpled bed linens. But it was too late; the coldest night of the coldest winter in memory had won its final victory. Tightening her face for the effort, Wildecent sat up and opened her eyes.

"There'll be ice in the garderobe, again," she complained, drawing the wolf-fur that served as their topmost blanket close around her face. Like Alison, Wildecent couldn't imagine a room that remained warm in winter, other than the kitchen, but Hafwynder Manor's new tower was worse than most, and nothing could make the sight of a crust of ice in the washbasin reassuring.

"His horse collapsed just inside the gates, and they thought he'd do the same before they could get him into the Hall. Leofric says he might be from the North, from Northumbria or maybe even Scotland, but Bethanil says he's got the look of a foreigner to him . . ."

Alison pressed harder against the stones, as if by her

closeness to them she could absorb what happened in the farthest reaches of Hafwynder Manor—which she could. Her talent for empathy and understanding had been noted many years before, and had been carefully nurtured since then, though her teacher would have objected strongly to its use to satisfy simple curiosity.

"She thinks he's from *France*—and gentle-born as well!"

Wildecent twisted an errant lock of dark hair around her ear, then thrust one foot tentatively into the chill air. She had received identical, arcane instruction alongside Alison, but all she got from the hearth stones was the heavy poker, which she used to good effect first on the slumbering coals and then on the iced-over shutters. The wood parted with a shower of snow and ice.

"There's no dead horse in the yard," she countered. "It was a dream, Alison. Just a dream. There's nothing at all out there except another foot of snow."

"Leofric went through his belongings—" Alison stepped back from the wall, a look of surprise and indignation on her face as a cold blast from the window lifted her chemise. "Wildecent, how could you?"

"I wanted to see for myself," her sister replied simply as she tried to hook the claw through an iron ring, now that her own curiosity was sated.

It took both of them grappling with the poker to bring the heavy wooden planks together again. They needed more teamwork to crank up the lid on the huge cope chest and remove a double armful of clean clothes. By the time they had dressed in two layers of hose, an extra chemise, undertunic, robe, and all the other garments necessary before a gentlewoman could leave her sleeping quarters, the dream and the missing dead horse had vanished from their conversation.

The young women lived in the latest addition to the collection of earthworks, walls, and partially reconstructed ruins that Godfrey Hafwynder called, with great pride, Hafwynder Manor.

If the king's favorites from Normandy were going to build themselves rectangular towers, then he would have one, too. He spared no expense and hired stonemasons from across the Channel, who had grudgingly rearranged stones hauled from an ancient, abandoned Roman villa, then covered it all, inside and out, with a gritty plaster. The plaster left a pale film of dust on everything within the stockade and had proclaimed Godfrey's desire to be innovative rather than any preference for the Normandy-raised king, Edward, over the heirs of the locally powerful Anglo-Scandinavian Godwinson family.

Wildecent and Alison, who were kept properly ignorant of Wessex's growing anarchy as childless and saintly King Edward's reign moved toward its tragic ending, knew only that the stonemasons had returned to France before completing the archways that were to connect the new tower with the hall and the kitchens. Godfrey had been forced to rely on local workers who, awed by the solidity of the plastered walls, had built an enclosed tunnel and stairway that promised security in a siege and was as inviting as a tomb in the meantime. It was also the only way out of their bedroom.

As always, Alison, the taller, bolder, and more confident of the pair, led the way, her fingers brushing lightly along the cold stones. Wildecent, her skirts gripped in both hands and one shoulder rasping against the outer wall, followed silently, counting each downward step until she reached the twenty-seventh where, since it was past dawn, light from the hearth fire in the kitchens illuminated the last three steps.

Godfrey said the dark-haired woman-child was short-sighted, as if her failure to see targets at the far end of a field were sufficient excuse for her timidity. But the stairway was pitch dark, Wildecent reminded herself. Short sight had nothing to do with it; not even a night-sighted cat could have seen anything between its walls. In the months they had slept in the tower she had never known the stones to settle overnight or a servant to leave some deadly object midway between top and bottom; the passageway had always been the same. But she never quite trusted the darkness, and Alison always reached the kitchen, and breakfast, a few moments before she did.

"Do they know who he is yet?" Alison asked Bethanil, the cook, as she helped herself to a steaming bowl of porridge, unmindful of the baleful stare she earned from Wildecent, who was still concealed by the tunnel.

The kitchens were set well apart from the rest of the predominantly wooden manor buildings because of the ever-present danger of fire. Only the tower tunnel, which could not burn, connected directly to the squat dome-roofed building. The hearth, set under the center of the dome, could roast a whole boar; smaller ovens were set into alcove walls. In the summer the heat was oppressive and the area shunned by those who could avoid it, but in winter it was the true gathering place for the forty-odd people of Godfrey's household.

This morning did seem a bit different, Wildecent conceded as she put her foot on the warm, redbrick floor, though she was not yet quite ready to believe her sister's wild dream. Only a handful of servingmen and -women had gathered on the benches, sipping broth at the end of their early morning labors.

"Know who *who* is?" Bethanil replied without looking up from her kettles.

"The man who came to the gates last night—who else? Do half-dead men normally ride up to our gates—"

"They made enough noise getting him in," Wildecent

interrupted, her fingers clenched around and pulling on one of Alison's long, blond braids.

Not everyone on the manor knew what Godfrey's sister-by-marriage, the Lady Ygurna, taught them each day while they worked in the solar room turning fleece into yarn, cloth, and clothing for the entire household, but many suspected it had nothing to do with a God-fearing Christian education. And none at all would have approved had they guessed it contained such tricks as pulling a man's thoughts through the wall he stood beside.

"That one," Leofric grumbled. He had finished the morning chores in the stables and had been napping by the bread ovens until Alison had fastened her curiosity on him. "He's hardly more a man than you two are women. His Lordship put him in his own bed for thawing. Even woke the Lady Ygurna to bandage him and dose him with a dollop of cyder as well. Suspect as he'll sleep until sundown.

"Couldn't get a word of sense out of him, nowise. No telling where he'd been or why'd he'd be out alone on such a night with no cloak and such wounds about him. There's a storytellin' there, for sure—"

"And his horse? Did wolves get it? Was it dying?"

"Alison!" Wildecent pleaded, tugging on the braid.

"Now, there's a thing," the hostler continued, sitting forward on his stool. "It's got a gash from neck to belly an' more on its legs. Wolf marks for sure, an' more besides. As if the lad'd swung his sword wild more'n once. I'm thinkin' it should go to the block rather than the stables, when the youngster gets himself away from Lord Hafwynder. 'Sulwyn,' he says an' goes arse-over-kettle to get himself between me an' the poor beast. Can't understand another word he says, but the lord guesses he won't get the lad out of the cold 'til he sees the beast in the stables an' tells me, loud an' clear, to get the gut and needle.

"So he takes the lad inside, finally, an' I'm working 'til dawn. 'Twas a good piece of horseflesh, though." Leofric hawked and spat into the central hearth for emphasis. "Got that hot Moorish blood in its veins. Too fine a beast to belong to a dew-eared boy like that. Ought to have his hide tanned for ridin' it so hot an' bloodied. If'n it and his fancy clothes do truly belong to him. Been smoke seen risin' above the trees—outlaws down from the Danelaw. Been honest men driven outside the law for the leather in that saddle alone.

"Don't know as his babble were Norse or not, but it weren't English."

"So is the horse still alive? Did you save it from the wolves?" Alison persisted.

Wildecent scarcely heard her sister's repeated question. It was winter, and the hard times that always accompanied that season had driven men beyond the law before. Still, Leofric's musings were the first she'd heard about outlaws banding in the great forests above the hall. Stockades and torches could keep natural wolves at bay, but were less effective against the human kind, which could ravage a manor in a single afternoon.

She had begun to wonder what precautions would be taken when Godfrey Hafwynder himself pushed open the outer door.

"Stables!" Leofric shouted, getting to his feet.

"What about them, man?" Godfrey replied.

The hostler's face settled into a puzzled frown. "The strange lad's horse, sir," Leofric explained as his hands twisted through his belt. "Its wounds— I don't know, I just thought . . ." His voice trailed off as he sorted through a pile of homespun cloaks.

"If it was alive when you saw it last, then, like as not, it's still alive now. No need to be braving the cold."

"I'd have your leave, my lord," the hostler persisted. "It's in my mind now and not likely to go away until I see to it."

Godfrey shrugged good-naturedly as Leofric scurried out the door. He had a reputation as a fair and reasonable master, but such displays of conscientiousness were not the rule, even on a well-run manor. Hafwynder was not alone in watching the hostler disappear toward the stables, which was just as well, since they all missed Wildecent's condemning glower and Alison's innocent smile.

"If any man can save that animal, it'll be Leofric," Godfrey mused aloud as he gave a cursory examination to the kettles simmering in the hearth. "If nothing else, I wouldn't mind putting it to a few of my mares."

"Won't it be gone by spring?" Alison asked. "I mean, the stranger, the one who rode the horse last night—won't he take it with him when he leaves?"

"There's not a secret can be kept within these walls," her father replied with a laugh, not seeming to suspect how true his words actually were. "But it's not likely, to my mind, that either will be going very far for some time. They were both nigh to frozen, and bloodied to boot, when Alfwine heard them outside the gate." He gave his daughter an affectionate embrace. "Your Lady Aunt Ygurna was awake until dawn seeing to poultices and medicines. She'll be tired today and needing your cooperation, not your curiosity."

Wildecent left her bowl on the sideboard and received a similar greeting. "But it was wolves, then? Real wolves—not outlaws?" she asked.

His smile fading, Hafwynder patted her on the cheek. Because of her small, almost delicate features and her all-consuming caution, Wildecent was usually treated as the younger of the two women, though she was, in fact, some months older. He sat down on one of the benches and balanced her across his thigh so she could look straight into his eyes.

"Are you worried about outlaws and bandits?"

She hesitated a moment before answering. Godfrey cherished all the womenfolk of his manor, respecting their rights and indulging their whims, but he was not so enlightened as to discuss the masculine subjects of politics and war with them. The doubts that gnawed at Wildecent's mind had been placed there by inference and interpretation of conversations never meant for her hearing. Meeting his unsuspecting gaze, she felt her heart pounding in her throat.

"Earl Tostig himself was declared an outlaw and banished from his office in Northumbria. The king has sent messages across the channel asking for men to support his cause—"

"Where do you hear such things?" Hafwynder demanded, his posture stiffening as he pushed her upright and away from him.

Wildecent shoved her trembling hands into the folds of her robe but did not lower her eyes. She was spared, however, from Godfrey's rage by another voice from the bench behind her.

"She listens more closely than you, my lord."

"Say you again?" Hafwynder demanded, shoving Wildecent aside as if she were no more than one of his dogs.

Thorkel Longsword made only the barest acknowledgment of his lord's question; he set his eating knife to one side of his trencher. "I said: a woman-child knows enough to realize that those outlaws in the hills and forests above us are not there by accident or despair."

The others in the kitchen, whether they were housecarls

charged with personal loyalty to Hafwynder and the defense of the manor or simply servants and slaves, watched the contest of wills with discreet fascination. Thorkel had attached himself to Hafwynder's entourage several years earlier, but he had never forsworn his first loyalties.

There were those, primarily Saxons like Godfrey, who privately believed that a Norseman, even one whose mother had been born in England, gave his allegiance only to war and the old pagan gods, regardless of whatever other oaths he might have given. Not that Hafwynder suspected the huge Viking with the shaggy, blond hair and ice-cold eyes of treason, but he felt the challenge and knew it needed answering.

"I have given my oaths to the king and Earl Harold of Wessex. I do not need to involve myself in private quarrels that do not concern me."

"But if they need you to stand on one side of the river or the other—does that not involve you, my lord? And if you will not choose of your own, will they not compel you? The king invites his Norman cronies to raise a tower not two days' ride from here—this is not the first time a rightful Saxon earl has been exiled and outlawed by your *saintly* king.

"There was an arrow tucked in that lad's saddle—a single arrow with blue and gray fletchings. What would you say to that, my Lord?"

"Outlaws," Godfrey replied in a voice that did not carry the full weight of his conviction. "Outlaws carrying arrows stolen from Earl Harold. But not the earl or his men, nor his brother, Earl Tostig, and certainly not the king. They would not dare . . . ."

The Norsemen might be comfortable in a world where loyalty, honor, and power were bought with blood; so might their near cousins—for all their newfound civilization—the Normans; but not Godfrey. It had been five

17

hundred years or more since the Saxons had raised a conquering army, and the once warlike tribes now were more comfortable with the rule of law than with the rule of might.

"They will dare, my lord. They will," Thorkel averred softly.

And Godfrey, sensing that time and events were sweeping him aside, let the statement stand unanswered.

"They were *wolves!*" Alison protested when the heavy silence became unbearable. "He was attacked by wolves—not robbers, or outlaws, or Normans."

The blond Viking stared at her as if she had suddenly appeared from the hearth fire. "Aye," he agreed in the slow, hard voice of authority. "Driven to this hall by wolves. Now tell me, why would such a young man, a foreign young man at that, be out riding alone on a such a night?"

"He . . . he . . ."

Wildecent watched a familiar vagueness come over her sister's face. Ygurna had explained the rudiments of scrying and prophecy, stressing the necessity of the proper invocations. It was dangerous for the seer to proceed without the proper rituals and even more dangerous to plunge into prophecy in the middle of a kitchen. Watching her sister's eyes glaze over, she prayed that Thorkel's command had triggered an involuntary response and not that Alison's wild curiosity had gotten the better of her judgment. Either way, Wildecent knew she could not allow her sister to speak.

Focusing her voice to sound as much like Ygurna as possible, she looked directly into Alison's eyes. "It isn't important. It's not worth considering," she commanded. "Leofric said he was a foreigner. He was simply lost. Who knows how long the wolves had been following him, or how far?"

"No," Alison replied, her voice flat and distant. "He wasn't—"

"Alison!" Wildecent fairly lunged for her sister's arm and gave it a violent pinch that succeeded in bringing awareness to those wide blue eyes.

They glowered at each other: Wildecent appalled that, willingly or not, Alison had been baited into testing those talents that Lady Ygurna said were sacred and that she herself so profoundly lacked; Alison because she had felt the elusive tingle of magic weaving about her and was not at all grateful to have it ripped away. Still, neither was aware of how they both appeared until Godfrey's voice cut into their awareness.

"Enough of this!" he shouted, the anger and frustration he could not direct toward Thorkel coming to rest on the young women. "It's bad enough that there is an unconscious man of unknown origin or destination lying in my bed and that my own housecarls raise treasonous questions under my very roof, but I will not have the two of you squalling like bitch cats!"

It was accepted, if not admired, that the lord of the manor had the right to discipline or maintain his property in whatever way he saw fit. And while the king's *witan* was specific regarding a woman's right to be not-property and Godfrey was known to be an even-tempered, indulgent father, still the rage in his eye brought outright fear to both young women. They instantly set aside their differences.

"We're sorry, Father," they said with one voice.

"Then begone with you both. There's women's work, surely, to be done in the solar, and no need for you to be interfering with the thoughts of men!"

Thankful for the reprieve, if not the tone of its delivery, the young women, Alison in the lead as always, hurried through the doors to the solar without pausing to find their cloaks.

he solar was the oldest bower-building within the manor stockade. Though its outer walls were patched and its tiled roof had long since been replaced with thatching, the faded outlines of a Roman festival painting could still be seen above the wainscoting. The mosaic floor, which showed a stiff-armed, flowing-haired woman presenting a bouquet of flowers to a charging bull, was unlike anything else in the shire around and was invariably shown, with great pride, to all Godfrey's guests. But the most remarkable aspect of the floor, the one which the two young women appreciated most on this frigid morning, was that it concealed a still-functioning hypocaust.

Charcoal and dried wood were set to burning in a small furnace beneath the floor and, before the sisters had had time to discuss and resolve their differences, fingers of warmth were reaching out along well-known patterns in the mosaic. Stools and benches had been left around the warmest stones and a new window, carefully glazed with a dozen irregular ovals of glass, had been cut into the body of a Roman matron to provide the light necessary for the important work which went on here.

Bags of fleece, hand looms, wool in every stage of work were neatly arrayed on all the shelves and racks, but Wildecent ignored them and the wedge of cheese she had brought with her from the kitchen.

"Gods, demons, and all the saints, Wildecent—what's bothering you?" Alison demanded good-naturedly as she loosened one waist-length braid and set about repairing the damage her sister had done to it. "This is the first halfway exciting thing that's happened this whole, dreary winter. I'd think you'd be a little bit curious, too."

"You were prying again."

"Not really, just asking questions."

"And when Thorkel asked *you* about the wolves and the stranger? What was that all about? It's not as if our lady aunt hasn't told you often enough. Thank God in his heaven that *she* wasn't there to see you!"

Alison let the braid drop into her lap. She hadn't intended to slip into the poorly defined realms of magic and prophecy as deeply as she had, and she was well aware of how her mentor would react if she learned of the error. Lady Ygurna had come to Hafwynder Manor when her older sister married Godfrey. She had remained after her sister's childbed death following the birth of Godfrey's daughter Alison. She had easily assumed the duties of mother and chatelaine; Hafwynder Manor was unimaginable without her stern, slender presence.

"It got away from me for a moment, that's all. No damage done. It's not as if anything happened—you saw to that for me."

There was a hint of gratefulness and apology in Alison's tone, but not enough to deter Wildecent's complaints or concerns.

"What do you mean, nothing happened! Leofric goes charging off to the stables on a fool's errand—on an errand *you* left rattling around in his head. And Thorkel. Don't you think he was looking at you with your eyes all glazed over? Thorkel Longsword—he still pours blood on his sword runes. Chicken's blood, maybe, but you know what it means. He's not one to have suspecting anything, and I'll wager he suspects something by now."

"You sound just like her," Alison complained in return. Whatever doubts she might have felt about her behavior were fast disappearing in the irritation of being reminded about it. "I'd know if anyone suspected anything."

"How?"

The blond girl shrugged and stared at the window. There really were no words to describe what her talents told her. Lady Ygurna had her rituals and explanations, of course, but Alison had long since realized her aunt was often describing things she had never felt. Her own talent was stronger, wilder, than anything in the older woman's pat phrases.

She had been on her own in the uncharted realms of magic since the first manifestation of her womanhood. Now, some four years later, she accepted the knowledge that no one—neither family, friends, nor teachers—understood what went on in her mind.

"Well," she began slowly, "maybe he suspects something, but it's not anything focused and it's not anything that . . . that leans against me."

Wildecent shook her head. "He doesn't have to suspect *you*," she explained softly. "All any of them have to do is suspect *something*. Once they start that, and they start talking to each other . . . They aren't fools, you know. They'll have priests and bishops in here so fast, not even our lord father's stature as reeve for the shire will protect us—"

"I'll know," Alison injected sharply. "*I'll* suspect something myself. And once that happens . . . well, they can't keep any secrets from me."

The dark-haired girl turned away and took up a partially spun coil of fleece, ending a conversation neither wished to continue. "Then just be careful, sister," she added as an afterthought.

Her education had not included any of the scholarly disciplines of logic and philosophy; still, Wildecent's nature, over the years, had given her considerable experience in the pathways of orderly thought. She knew the simplest explanation was generally the best one. And the simplest explanation of Leofric's reaction to Alison was that the horse-handler both resented and feared the authority implied by her insistent questions. Both girls were, after all, wards of Godfrey Hafwynder, and Godfrey's pleasure, or the lack of it, was the definition of justice for the old indentured servant.

That was the simplest explanation, and Wildecent had rejected it.

It was not that she knew that the hostler or the Viking, Thorkel, had actually discerned the pressure of Alison's curiosity against their inner thoughts; most likely they were as head-blind to magic as she herself was. But their intrigued expressions proclaimed that they knew something unusual was afoot. And for the ordinary man, the unusual was synonymous with magic.

Besides—and this was her biggest hesitation—for all Alison's demonstrated abilities, the blond young woman was simply not as powerful as she imagined herself to be. Wildecent knew there were thoughts she had kept hidden from her sister's talent; memories over which she had constructed lies that Alison blithely accepted. And if she—who was shortsighted and had no talent—could hide her secret thoughts, so could anyone else.

As Wildecent's reasoning led her to remember that she kept certain memories concealed from her sister and everyone else, those hidden thoughts and emotions burst into life within her. The unspun yarn slipped through her fingers as she drifted back toward the time when she had not lived at Hafwynder Manor; when Alison had not been her sister.

These memories were poorly focused images of a castle—a true castle, with stone walls throughout—far more active than Godfrey's out-of-the-way homestead. A mist of treachery clung to the memories, obscuring the faces Wildecent wished most to remember. One event, though, shone with a crystal clarity that never failed to bring the fear and emptiness back as if it had never been gone.

Giants, strange adults with rough accents and rougher manners, had come for her in the night. Wrapped in coarse blankets that rasped her skin rather than warmed it, she'd left the castle and begun a journey that had seemed endless to her childhood self although she guessed, now, that it had not lasted more than a month.

She had traveled alone, or at least without anyone she recognized from her life either at the mysterious castle or here at Hafwynder Manor—passed from the hands of one set of giants to the next, always bundled up and moved about on the darkest of nights. When she had been younger, everything about the journey had haunted her nightmares; now there was only one image beyond her control: a great white dragon chasing the giant who carried her on the back of his galloping horse. She could remember the intricate pattern of the giant's mail shirt, and she had seen the dragon many times since then.

Of course, she understood the dragon now—it had been carved into the side of a hill near the road that passed near Hafwynder Way and then went on to Cirencester. She'd seen it every year when Godfrey took his wards and his wools up to the cloth fair held under the protection of the great church there. It watched one full day of their travel, and she had made friends with it long ago. Still, in her nightmares, she would smell the sweating horse, feel its bone-pounding gallop, and see the silver-glinted beast rising through the trees behind her.

Whatever the memories were, whatever the nightmares meant, there had to be some truth to them, because Godfrey had flown into one of his rare fits of rage when she'd mentioned the story once, just before her sixth birthday, while he had entertained the king's for-

eign favorites. He'd thrashed her soundly, in front of the entire household, and locked her in the stable under-room for a week; there'd been no birthday feast—only stale bread and her tears.

Wildecent never mentioned the giants or the dragon again, nor did anyone else, not even Lady Ygurna, who tended to the welts and bruises, which had lasted far longer than her imprisonment. She had been born, her aunt told her gently, on the wrong side of the blankets, and if she valued her comfort she'd forget whatever she remembered about unfamiliar people and places. So she called Godfrey "father," and Alison "sister," and, except for infrequent, uncomfortable moments, had herself forgotten that her words were lies.

The white dragon was in Wildecent's mind just then, its eyes full of fire and its body glowing deathly pale. She extended her untalented self-control to its utmost limits to keep Alison from sensing it—Alison, whom she loved as if she truly were a sister but who stole a person's tenderest thoughts and scattered them like straw in a stable.

She came back to the present with a startled jump as the wool came away from her absentminded hands. Alison was beside her, deftly respinning the fleece to eliminate the slubs Wildecent's daydreaming had left behind.

"You look as if you've seen a ghost," Alison said gently as the spindle snapped taut and whistled.

"No, just remembering Thorkel and father. There'll be trouble there soon enough." Another lie, but she pushed it and wrapped it with sincerity until she almost believed it herself and the tension faded from Alison's face.

"You worry too much."

"And what would you possibly be worrying about on a beautiful day like this?" a third voice inquired from the doorway behind them.

The girls jumped and turned to face Lady Ygurna, the red flush of embarrassment more apparent on Alison but spreading across both girl's faces nonetheless. The tall, steel-haired woman was not without a sense of humor, though those who spent the greatest amount of time in her company might have preferred otherwise.

"The outlaws," said Wildecent; "The Viking's insolence," said Alison at the same time.

"And not the young man in the upper room? You surprise me very much." Lady Ygurna was smiling as she latched the door and hung her outer cloak on a peg. "No one in the kitchen would believe you, you know."

That smile, and intimate knowledge of how the older woman's temper truly showed itself, emboldened the girls.

"What's he like?" Alison asked.

"Well, that's rather hard to say since when he's not unconscious I haven't been able to understand a word he's said—"

"But he'll live; he'll get better, won't he?" Wildecent interrupted.

"I certainly haven't given him up yet. He's suffering from the cold and both kinds of wolves, but the injuries haven't joined forces against me."

Alison gave the spindle back to Wildecent and made room for Lady Ygurna on the bench beside them. "Both kinds of wolves?" she asked, clearly hoping for more detailed information than the men in the kitchen had been willing to provide.

"Aye, the men who live outside the king's law and the beasts whose only crime is that they live within God's. There was an arrow in that shoulder before the wolves attacked him. No wolf's fang could go so deep—and they tell me they found a bloody arrow under his saddle, besides."

"Then it is true that there are outlaws in the forests," Wildecent mused, as if only their teacher would give them the absolute truth. "What will Father do?"

Lady Ygurna shrugged and moved coals from one brazier to another with her bare fingers. "What he can. What he must. They were all very concerned about the arrow—its fletchings would proclaim it belongs to Earl Harold. Now, it could be the outlaws took it from Harold's men, or it could be that they're no outlaws at all but the earl's own men and that young man above the hall was no victim of circumstance to be receiving our medicines and pity.

"Lord Godfrey does not dare act alone on this. He'll leave tomorrow, once the sun's up, and visit with all the other landowners, and he'll hope my medicines will bring some sense to that boy's head while he's gone. Foreigner or not, we should be able to get some facts out of him. No doubt he was not riding for his own pleasure. My Lord Godfrey will need to know where he'd been and where he was headed. It's my own guess our greatest danger is not in the forests."

"What could be worse than outlaws and wolves?" Wildecent continued.

Ygurna ignored the question, busying herself dusting the mosaic bouquet. With a grunt she lifted the faded pink stones, revealing a narrow staircase that was of much more recent construction. Seated on the floor, her legs hanging in darkness, she gave her attention back to the waiting young women. She was no longer smiling.

"Any man may kill a wolf and receive a bounty for the fur. Any man who is inside the law may kill a man who is shut outside it. But it's past two months now that our Earl Harold and King Edward stand apart from Earl Tostig because of Northumbria. And while our king has fits and seizures that Norman, Duke William the Bastard, sits and

28

waits across the Channel. Your father must be very careful where he draws the law's line."

"Surely no one thinks that he . . . I mean, he's not an outlaw, is he?" Alison demanded hesitantly.

Ygurna gave her pupils an appraising look that sent Alison diving behind whatever defenses her particular talents could erect.

"He is a stranger with guest-right in Lord Godfrey's house because of his wounds; that's all you should know and all you dare think about," the older woman informed them as she descended into the hidden chamber below the hypocaust.

The sisters waited in silence until candlelight flickered in the darkness and their aunt could be heard collecting the various herb jars for the young man's medicines. Alison found her own spindle and settled close beside Wildecent so their conversation could not be overheard below.

"I wonder what made her get so suspicious?" she whispered.

"I thought you knew these things."

"Not with our lady aunt—"

Wildecent sniffed. Perhaps having no talent was not the complete end of the world. *She* wasn't at all puzzled. Alison had just turned sixteen. They were both well past the age where Godfrey could start thinking seriously about marriage offers and nigh upon the age where curiosity about the suitor he would ultimately select was presumed to be the only thought in their minds. And such an assumption would have been very nearly correct.

"He might be betrothed, or even married already. I think they marry young over there—if they're worth marrying at all," the dark-haired young woman said sagely.

"No. No, he couldn't be."

"Alison, you couldn't possibly *know* anything about that."

"I'll find out."

"You can't very well go upstairs and ask him, you know. He's unconscious and, besides, everyone says you can't understand him when he talks . . ." Wildecent's voice trailed off as she considered what her sister most likely intended to do. "No, you can't lean on him. He's gentle-born."

Alison grinned mischievously.

"You wouldn't! It wouldn't be right. Suppose he's *not* betrothed. Suppose he does stay here with us. Suppose our lord father does accept him, then what? Do you want to be *leaning* on your husband?"

"How else do you find out what men are thinking?"

Wildecent let her spindle clatter to the floor. Whatever the method—talent or dogged guesswork—women didn't stay informed by asking direct questions and their thoughts weren't appreciated by their menfolk if ever they were voiced. Maybe a woman could be powerful, as the king's mother, Emma, had been when he was younger, but if she was, she wouldn't be loved. Emma had died alone, abandoned, impoverished, and hated by her enemies and onetime allies alike. At sixteen it was hard to imagine dying, but it was just possible to imagine loneliness and to reject the paths that seemed to lead to it.

"If there's no other way— Could you actually lean on him while he's unconscious?"

Alison shrugged. "Maybe, if being unconscious is like being asleep and dreaming. Sometimes, well—maybe once or twice, I've felt dreams and changed them, a bit."

Wildecent's eyes widened involuntarily.

"Not yours, you goose. I—I didn't do it deliberately, just suddenly I was in a dream that wasn't my own and I made it *change*." Alison grinned self-consciously.

"Bethanil complained of a headache for three days afterward!"

"Then you'd have to be very careful. He's not well—"

"I'm not going to go crashing through his inner thoughts like a fire-breathing dragon, Wildecent."

"Then how, if not like a dragon? It's not as if you belonged there."

The blond girl stared off into nothing for a moment. "Like a unicorn," she decided. "Very beautiful and very magical, so he'll trust me if he knows I'm there."

Wildecent raised one eyebrow—a hard-practiced talent that her sister did not share and which, therefore, always amused and infuriated her. "And so he'll recognize you later?" she laughed.

Wildecent was spared from hearing her sister's reply by the mingled sounds of glass breaking and a woman's single, short sob of pain rising from the bolt-hole beneath the mosaic. This time the dark-haired girl moved first, leaving the fleece in a tangled lump as she hurried to peer through the opening.

"Are you all right?"

"Of course I'm all right!"

The reply was sharp-edged and ungrateful. Wildecent sat back on her knees as if slapped. Lady Ygurna never welcomed sympathy. Alison, who had remained hunched over her spindle, always sensed the older woman's spiny defenses whenever anything unexpected happened. She had learned to hold her compassion in reserve, as Wildecent would never do, so now she felt the hurts from both of them.

With a strip of linen wrapped around her hand, Lady Ygurna stomped up the stairway. One glance at her hard, gray eyes would have told Wildecent to get back to her spinning—if she had broken away from her own thoughts long enough to look up. Instead, dwelling on how unfair it was that her intentions were always misunderstood, she remained oblivious to the unfocused anger glaring down at her.

"If you've got nothing better to do than to sit on the floor, you can grind the comfrey and woundwort together, decoct it, and find another bottle in the storerooms to keep it in, since that young stranger's wounds will be needing more of it than I've got now."

Wildecent winced both from Ygurna's tone and from the thought of grinding the comfrey, which, for all its curative powers, invariably left her hands inflamed for days. There would be no use arguing with the older woman, not now when her lips were drawn into that thin, pale line.

She lowered her head and whispered the proper phrases of obedience to the floor. She would have continued to sit there, staring at nothing and contemplating her injuries, except Lady Ygurna was still bustling about gathering washed fleece for the bandages, and inactivity would only invite further reprimand. Collecting her dropped spindle and unspun wool with more care than was customary, Wildecent managed to stay busy until Lady Ygurna wrapped her cloak around her shoulders and headed back to the hall, whereupon she sank back onto the bench with a groaning sigh.

"I'll help you," Alison assured her.

"Why should we both get into trouble? No, you do the spinning—"

"It's not as if it was your fault, Wildecent. She's really upset about something—and not about wolves, medicines, or even injuries."

"So I learned—the hard way, as usual."

"Then what do you say? I'll help you grind the herbs, then you can help me spin. The same amount gets done, but neither of us has to work alone." Alison paused while

Wildecent considered the offer. "Truth now, it could just as easily have been me she scolded—it probably will be next time—and I'd expect you to share the work with me."

It wasn't exactly true: Alison was generally adept at avoiding Ygurna's displeasure; but it was close enough that Wildecent was able to accept the assistance.

hey applied the herbal plasters all that day
and the following morning as well without
breaking the young man's fever or wresting
him from the grip of delirium. Lord Hafwynder decided he could delay the visits to
his neighbors no longer and departed with a dozen
housecarls, all of them armed. Without him, his manor
fell into a fitful routine of waiting either for the lord to
return or for the ailing youth's condition to change.

As idleness was among the greater sins the Lady Ygurna
could imagine, and her own idleness the worst sin of all,
both Wildecent and Alison found their waiting time filled
with normally neglected chores and long hours watching
over their still-nameless patient. Three times a day Lady
Ygurna would change the bandages on his wounds and
reappraise his condition, always with the two girls beside
her.

It was late afternoon of the third day after his arrival
when a grim-faced Ygurna lifted her palm from his forehead and conceded that his fever was rising. His sable
brown hair stuck to his face in sweat-twisted spikes; his
cheeks and nose were marred by blisters where frostbitten
skin was starting to flake away. Both Wildecent and Alison
had acknowledged to each other that it was impossible to
guess whether he possessed any handsome qualities but
they reacted to their aunt's pessimism as if their heart's
love had been sentenced to death.

"I'm not giving up," the older woman assured them.
"Tonight we'll add wild clary to the drawing water and
see if that helps. Perhaps we can sweat the poisons and
fever out of him."

Alison, who had spent the afternoon in the sickroom,
slid her hand around his. His fingers, also blackened by

34

frostbite, were uncomfortably warm against her skin. "Why not now?" she demanded, as her aunt unknotted his shoulder bandage.

"Because clary's a moon plant," Wildecent explained in a rush. She might not have any inborn talents, but she applied herself diligently to any lesson that could be learned by logic and memory alone. This time her analysis had been insufficient; Lady Ygurna's tired face did not show a glimmer of approval. She plunged deeper into her memory; a brilliant flush crept across her face. "And— and—" she stammered, "because its use is not limited to drawing poisons and lowering fevers but is not favored for fetching lust to an unwilling husband!"

"Well done," Ygurna agreed, forcing a smile from her half-clenched jaw as she caught sight of the viscous, discolored matter clotting the bandage. "Hold the basin steady, please," she said, trying to keep the harshness out of her voice. "We're going to have to soak this off so we can examine the wound."

Wildecent brought the steaming basin of herb-infused water closer to the bed. The young man's face, where it was not marred by frostbite, had taken on a peaceful, otherworldly translucence. Every hour, their teacher said, their patient held his fever was another day he'd need to recover his strength—if he recovered at all.

Moments later Ygurna lifted the tainted wad of fleece and threw it into the chamber pot. The wound her movements revealed was an angry, swollen patch of flesh about the size of her palm. Surface lacerations from the wolf's fangs showed well-formed scabs on either side of the larger, weeping tear the youth had made pulling the arrow out. It was clear, to an experienced eye, that the arrow wound went deep into the muscular tissues and was creating a pocket for the dangerous poisons of both injuries.

It had always fallen to the women of this or any other

manor to tend the wounds and illnesses of their menfolk. And it fell equally to the oldest women of the manor to ensure that the daughters of her spirit and her flesh were prepared for their tasks. The two young women had been an active presence in the sickroom for several years and were affected neither by the sight of the wounds nor the naked body of the youth who bore them.

"You'll have to cut it open," Alison offered once she had seen the shining, almost black surface of the arrow wound.

"But the poisons aren't rising to the skin," her sister protested. "Cutting it now would only push the poison to his heart."

Alison probed the wound delicately with her finger, gauging its warmth and watching a trickle of watery blood ooze past her finger. "If you wait much longer it'll be too late."

They both looked to Lady Ygurna, who stared at the wound, biting on her lower lip. She encouraged them to make their opinions known, but the final decision when, or if, to drain the poisons from his shoulder would be hers and hers alone. They knew she had spent the past two nights sitting in this room, waiting, praying, for this young man to return to his senses but it would be many years before they understood the anguish such a vigil brought.

"Get the clary," she announced, not noticing whether Wildecent or Alison responded to the command.

An anxious girl, some years younger than Wildecent, returned with her to help grind the seeds into a paste, which they heated, then applied over the entire swollen area. His eyes opened wide when they pressed it firmly into the lacerations themselves. He gasped and muttered in his incomprehensible language, then, with a sigh that

36

shook his whole body, slipped back into a quieter unconsciousness.

"That ought to hold him for a while," Ygurna said as she tried another wad of herb-dampened fleece over the paste. She lifted and twisted the bedclothes so his shoulder was covered and his foot, supported by a straw-filled bolster, was exposed. "Now, let's have a look at where the wolves tried to eat this foreign whelp's foot."

"His name is Stephen," Alison announced softly.

Both Wildecent and Lady Ygurna stared at her in thoughtful silence; the scullery girl, sensing only that something unexpected had occurred, stared at Lady Ygurna. She bolted from the room when the mistress of the manor dismissed her with a quick nod of her head.

"How do you know that?" Lady Ygurna demanded.

"I heard it."

"That moan certainly didn't sound like 'Stephen' to me—"

Ygurna cut Wildecent short with a look. "You *heard* him say his name just now?"

Regretting the impulse already, Alison twisted her hands through the long fringes of her belt. "No . . . not just now. Not exactly."

"Then what, *exactly.*"

"Well, earlier, when I was alone with him— Well, he seemed restless for a moment and I . . . I thought it might be something important—"

"Keep going," Lady Ygurna urged while Wildecent hid her hands in the folds of her skirt and crossed her fingers to give her sister all the luck she'd need in the next few moments.

"Well, his name is Stephen."

Lady Ygurna gave Stephen's purple-mottled foot a cursory examination and then, deciding that her niece's revelations were far more important, pulled the blankets into place above it. "You don't mean that he said his name in a way that just anyone could understand, do you?"

Alison squirmed. "No, I felt it there, on the top of his memories. Stephen—*Étienne*—" she repeated, trying to duplicate the Languedoc lilt of his thoughts, so different from the Germanic inflections of English.

Her fingers squeezed so tight that they throbbed, Wildecent glanced from her aunt's impassive face to Alison's anxious one and wished she could join the scullery maid.

"You know you did something both foolish and dangerous," Ygurna began. "A strange man—a foreigner, and unconscious as well. Did you even think of the dangers? You could have fallen into his thoughts and never found your way out."

"There wasn't any danger," Alison insisted, twisting her voice into a whine. "I couldn't have fallen into his thoughts if I'd wanted to. Everything was smooth and hard, like glass, except for his name—and even that sank down again once he was quiet."

Alison wished she could have sank through the floor to a similar oblivion. The explanation that was supposed to reassure her aunt had, if anything, only gotten her more upset. Lady Ygurna repeated the same questions, pacing the length of the room with her skirts snapping about her legs as she went. Finally she stopped and studied Stephen with a look that mixed fear and hatred.

"Don't go near his thoughts again," she warned in a tone that admitted no argument.

"But—"

"Don't even think about it!"

"But Lady Aunt," Wildecent interrupted, "what's so terrible about learning his name? It doesn't seem to be such an awful mistake," she added, not daring to mention that names were the least of the things Alison had pulled

38

from people's thoughts without seeming to harm them or herself.

"He has been guarded," Lady Ygurna said reluctantly, as if the admission left a bad taste in her mouth. She looked at the young women and needed none of her own intuitive talents to guess what questions lay at the tops of their minds. "There are ways—until now I had only heard about them—but it is possible to place a shield between yourself and the rest of nature."

"Stephen?" Alison ventured.

Ygurna shook her head. Her shoulders sagged as she brushed the hair from Stephen's forehead. "No. It is also possible to place that shield around someone else—to defend them, perhaps, or to hide something within their thoughts."

"Then he *is* dangerous," Wildecent said with a disappointed sigh.

The older woman pressed her palm against his forehead, not seeking the measurement of his fever this time but the nature of his thoughts. She closed her eyes a moment then lifted her hand away. Without Alison's clues, she could not have perceived the hard, dark-edged shield lying just beneath the smooth surface of Stephen's unconscious mind and even with them she could not penetrate it. "I— I could not say."

Alison extended her own hand to duplicate her aunt's efforts but Ygurna's fingers locked over her wrist.

"Don't," she repeated. "Perhaps later, if your father thinks it's necessary. Whoever put that shield there will know, sooner or later, if it's been tampered with—and your mark will be on the tampering."

Alison blanched, giving Wildecent the understanding that the shield was thoroughly tampered with. She felt a tide of guilt as well, for though she had often wished to see her sister's limitations revealed she had never meant for it to happen in this way.

"Agatha can watch him, can't she?" Wildecent asked, indicating the doorway through which the scullery maid had vanished. "I don't think either of us want to stay here right now."

She took Alison's other hand and led her silently downstairs to the hall.

"He was unconscious," Alison explained, talking mostly to herself rather than her sister. "I've never leaned on anyone who was unconscious. I thought that was why it felt so strange."

Wildecent pulled a jumble of yarn and wooden plaques from a basket. She dropped one end in Alison's lap and wound the trailing strands of the other around her waist.

"I wouldn't worry about it. You've always said you'd know if someone leaned back on you, and our lady aunt wouldn't let anything truly bad happen."

Alison's shoulders rose, then slumped again as she went through the motions of wrapping her end of the belt-loom around her waist. An unfinished band of red and ocher embroidery stretched out between them.

"But *sorcery*, Wildecent," she said softly, giving the plaques a quarter turn and sliding the shuttle thread through the separated warp threads. "In His name and by all the saints—I didn't think it was sorcery!"

"So?"

Wildecent had heard of sorcery—and alchemy, thaumaturgy, conjury, and all the other names by which magic was known—and, since it was all as unattainable as the unnamed powers that Ygurna encouraged in Alison, gave the concept little more thought. She was surprised, therefore, by the look that flashed briefly across her sister's face.

"Sorcery's not natural," the other girl explained. "They use spells and draw power from themselves to create things

40

opposed to nature—like that shield in Stephen's thoughts."

"But you said you can't lean on Lady Ygurna either, didn't you?" Wildecent asked, not adding her own name to the challenge.

Alison sighed, letting the yarn go limp. "You can't understand." It was the first time she had ever openly acknowledged the differences between them. "Lady Ygurna—well, she's silvery and soft and isn't supposed to be touched, but with Stephen it was like cold, black glass. I thought it was because he was hurt. I felt like he hurt. I guess that's because someone put that shield in his mind. Having it there must hurt."

Keeping her head bowed, pretending to untangle a knot in the yarn, Wildecent wondered how much Alison had been taught when she herself had been sent to do some chores in a far corner of the manor. At the same time, she pondered the possible shape of her own thoughts and whether wanting protection would be enough for a non-magical person to create that protection. A shield, whether it was silvery or black, seemed like a useful thing to have in a world where your dearest friends and family had talents that, though they might be called natural, were beyond your imagination.

"Are you going to hold your end tight?" she demanded, giving the weaving a sharp tug.

Alison felt the change in her sister's thoughts like the breath of an icy wind. She bit her lower lip and retreated into her private memories. Long ago, when Wildecent had first come to the manor, Lady Ygurna had told her that they were, or would be, different, and that her new sister was head-blind to many of the things they could feel. So Wildecent's palpable hostility had never surprised her—after all, the rest of the world was simply ignorant, but this timid, dark-haired child of a different mother was actually blind.

She leaned back against the pull of the warp threads and pushed the shuttle back and forth by touch alone; the image of the pain her sister and Stephen must feel behind their walls had filled her own eyes with tears.

The sisters were not the only ones entrenched in their own thoughts as twilight filled the lofty room. Ygurna had taken only a few desultory stitches in the tunic she was making for Lord Godfrey's Twelfth Night gift. Two housecarls, fresh from a bitter-cold afternoon atop the tower lookout, were still warming their hands by the fire and had not taken up their usual game of draughts. Only Thorkel Longsword, in whose care Godfrey had left Hafwynder Manor, seemed unaffected by his lord's absence. He chanted a wordless tune to himself as he ran a whetstone along the edge of his sword.

The Saxon system had evolved a social tradition quite different from the notions of unquestioning loyalty embraced by Viking raiders and their descendants on the Normandy coast. Godfrey Hafwynder was the largest landowner in his district and thus the shire reeve for his lesser neighbors, standing between them and the great courts of the king and the frequently divided earls—but by tradition he was only the voice of their carefully argued consensus. And Hafwynder's portion of Wessex, which had been spared the worst of the Norse raiding over the past several generations, was inordinately proud of its adherence to tradition.

The simple truth, as Thorkel silently saw it, was that, despite their pride and their traditions, Hafwynder and his neighbors much preferred to gather in a congenial hall to discuss a matter of urgency rather than to do anything about it. They had traveled a long, twisted road since their ancestors had terrorized the Roman-Britons.

It was in subtle and not fully conscious acknowledgment of this that Godfrey had entrusted the well-being of Hafwynder Manor to Thorkel while he pursued hallowed traditions. The dour Norseman had no use for equitable discussion, but kept a disciplined handful of housecarls patrolling the manor's borders and an alert lookout team within the guard-porch over the stockade gate.

Thorkel kept to himself by the pit-hearth in the great hall, like a spider at the center of its web, listening to everything and keeping his thoughts to himself. He felt the women's concern as the darkness deepened without word from Godfrey, just as he felt the housecarls' knowledge that, with their reduced numbers, they would be unable to defend the manor from any organized assault. But, as there was nothing he could do for any of them, he kept his attention fixed on the slow perfection of the sword edge.

Bethanil came through a curtained doorway, puffing under the weight of a large food tray.

"Food, my lady," she announced with a trace of annoyance in her voice, "since you did not seem to be coming down to my kitchens to eat it."

Lady Ygurna glanced from the tray to the high, canted windows. The strain of the past few days showed in her face; her strength came from her personality, not her rail-thin body. She swept the unfinished tunic off the table.

"Set it down, Bethanil. I'll see to the serving. Take the housecarls with you to the kitchen."

"As you wish, my lady," the woman agreed pleasantly enough, though Lady Ygurna knew the cook had hoped to remain through the meal, listening to their conversations and reporting to the other retainers who did not have the right to eat in the hall with Godfrey absent. She met Ygurna's dark-circled eyes for only an instant, then retreated after the housecarls, making sure she closed the door loudly behind her.

"You will join us?" Ygurna directed the question toward the hearth; the whetstone did not waver in its rhythm.

They were very similar, these two restrained and frequently disapproving persons, and they had displayed a cordial dislike of each other from the moment Godfrey had brought the Norseman into his household.

Thorkel pushed the whetstone down the edge of the blade. The *skree-rip* of stone against metal filled the entire chamber. Alison and Wildecent leaned closer together as they unwound the belt-loom, fearing another outburst of quiet hostility.

Then the Viking laid the sword and stone on the floor beside him. "The honing must be equal on both sides of the blade," he informed no one in particular as he stood up.

"Do you expect to need your sword tonight?" Alison asked. The tension of Godfrey's continued absence was a palpable force and one which she strove consciously to lessen.

"One never knows. There was smoke rising to the northwest again this morning."

"But those hills are more than a day's ride away—you said so yourself yesterday when they first saw the smoke," she persisted.

"Aye, true enough." Thorkel hollowed an oval out of his trencher-bread and filled it with stew. He maintained a cautious cordiality with Hafwynder's young women, as if they might see the wisdom of his positions and influence their father and guardian. "But think on it a moment. How big must that outlaw camp be? How bold its leader that he proclaims himself with such a bonfire?"

Both girls' eyes widened as they considered this possibility.

Ygurna set her trencher on the table. "Enough of that! I'll not have you scaring them half to death. We don't even know it *is* an outlaw camp."

"And what else is it likely to be?" Thorkel retorted, looking at her for the first time since joining them at the table. "None of the shire's people live up there. Surely not the four-footed wolves?"

Alison caught the look that passed between her aunt and the Norseman. Reflexively, she measured it in her mind, hoping to gauge what sort of comment might best calm them both but was spared the need to say anything when the tower lookout shouted an alarm.

Thorkel dropped his trencher to the floor in his haste to grab his sword en route to the door. Wildecent and Alison stared at their aunt, fear glistening in their faces, but Lady Ygurna's eyes were closed and she was smiling.

"Thank the Lord and the Lady," she whispered, referring to the elder gods of the bolt-hole beneath the hypocaust. "He's come home safe to take care of all this."

e attacked the holy brothers at my chapel of Saint Cuthbert!'' Godfrey exclaimed as he swept into his hall closely followed by the women, Thorkel, and three of the now homeless clergymen, two of whom were limping badly.

"Calls himself the Black Wolf and *dares* to attack God's men at their prayers and drive them into the forest!"

Lord Hafwynder had built the little chapel after his wife died and paid the livings of the small community that dwelt there doing whatever it was that clergymen were supposed to do to keep his manor and his people on the right side of God. It was difficult to tell from his rantings if he was more outraged that the chapel had been attacked or that the surviving brothers were unable to perform their ordained, and paid for, tasks.

He landed in his high-backed chair by the fire-pit with an audible thud and, having stretched his legs out straight in front of him, gripped the dragon's head armrests tightly. It was Alison's turn to dart from the shadows and wrestle with his heavy riding boots while Wildecent stood close with his softer, and warmer, house boots. A trickle of water ran from his melting mustache across his corn-silk beard and onto his tunic.

"I told them all—Edmund Saex, Beorth, Cynsige, even Offa's horse-face widow, Ealdgith, and all the rest of them that it was intolerable, and they just sat there and mumbled that it was a bishop's right and duty to protect the Church. Cowards—the damned lot of them!"

The clergymen warming themselves by the fire looked at Godfrey and hastily made the sign of the Cross, but Thorkel, who'd voiced the same opinion many times himself, smiled broadly for the first time in many days.

"I suppose, then, that accounts for the smoke we've seen rising to the north of here. This Black Wolf's made the chapel his base. With a good roof over his head and the good brothers' food stores, I shouldn't doubt he plans to stay the whole winter," the Viking said thoughtfully.

"Nay, sir," one of the injured brothers interrupted. "We did overturn the casks and set the cellar on fire ourselves—"

"You destroyed the wine and food I provided!"

"It was Father Ralf's idea, my Lord Hafwynder," young Brother Alfred added quickly, making the sign of the Cross again for Father Ralf, their spiritual leader, who had died of his wounds in the forest.

"Damned Norman foreigner," Godfrey muttered, away from the brethren's hearing. He maintained the chapel but he had not, to his dismay, been able to control whom the bishop put there. He grabbed the beaker of heated wine Lady Ygurna held out to him and drained it.

Thorkel laid a restraining hand on his lord's shoulder. "The tactic has its merits," he said, not bothering to add the usual honorifics. "Without provisions they will have to maraud through the countryside. Eventually your peers will find reason to bring him to justice."

"But he'll come here first!" Godfrey protested.

"Then we must be prepared to defeat him *ourselves*, my lord."

Godfrey held out the empty beaker and rested his forehead against his other hand.

"What of the other wolves, the ones that attacked our guest and his horse," Lady Ygurna inquired as she poured the wine, thinking it was time to change the course of the discussion, but her brother-by-marriage merely shook his head and spoke to the palm of his hand.

"We saw tracks across the snow and Beorth admitted they'd attacked his sheep byre not four night's past.

They're ready for a hunt—but not deep into the forest where they might find the Black Wolf and *his* pack, and not a one of them willing to give a lamb or goat to draw them in close!

"We are paralyzed," Godfrey admitted, looking at his family and close retainers with red-rimmed eyes. "Our king will die childless and heirless; our earls make cause against each other, and not even the presence of wolves and outlaws in the forests can bring the men of this shire together." He sipped loudly from the beaker.

"Father Ralf said we must pray for deliverance," Brother Alfred advised and received dark looks from the entire household.

Hafwynder lurched to his feet; the heated and spiced wine, coming at the end of a hard and hungry day, was already having an effect on him. "I'll be damned to Hell before I'll pray for his *Norman* deliverance!" he roared at the brethren, who were too stunned to react to his blasphemy.

He turned his back to them and took an unsteady step or two to the table where the forgotten stew sat congealing. It had never been his habit to slip so quickly into drunkenness or rage, though both seemed to come easily these days. Father Ralf had been a pious man with a healthy measure of humor to take the sting out of his cross-Channel accent. He deserved sincere mourning, but Godfrey, reaching within himself, found no compassion.

With a burst of helpless anger that astounded him as much as it frightened his silent audience, he swept the unappealing food onto the rush-covered floor. In a frozen moment—the bowl, the bread, and the gravy caught at the top of their arc—he found some connection to the people he loved: he was grateful that his foolish gesture

48

was not going to land on the tunic Lady Ygurna had put so much time and effort into.

He should have married her after her sister, his wife, had died; should have appealed to king and church to have the laws against consanguineous marriages set aside. But no, it was probably just as well—though she had been a handsome woman back then—for he had not done well by his wives. He would be fifty-two this coming April. The little cemetery in a nearby grove was the final home for several generations of Hafwynders. His parents and grandparents were buried there; his siblings and his three wives . . . each grave marked by a weathered wooden cross. Nine of his children were buried there as well; none had lived more than a month, and he could no longer remember all their names. There was only Alison whom he loved as life itself, though that love was tainted by the memories of what he had lost.

In the end it all came down to Alison. He could have faced the decadence and destruction of his Saxon heritage with a certain degree of irony if not for her, because he secretly agreed with Thorkel and had accepted the Viking's service to hear the very words he could not bring himself to say. But she was young and her life, unless it were snuffed out, would last well into the night beyond Wessex.

He'd need to provide for her—to get her a husband who knew his way along survival's twisted paths. At first he had considered Thorkel, but he could not imagine his daughter happy with a dour man twenty years her senior. He kept his eyes open as he went about his business in the shire and on his periodic visits to the king or earl's court. There were eligible young men by the score, but the only ones he judged likely to survive the coming conflagration were those with their roots in Normandy.

It didn't take a prophet to see what would happen to

his race once it accepted the Normans as kings, conquerors, or bed partners: their energy was daunting, their arrogance all the more unbearable because it was justified. Yes, he could provide for his daughter—but only at the cost of everything else he held dear.

There was movement off to his side; Wildecent knelt and silently gathered the worst of the soiled rushes along with the broken trencher-bread. Her hair was loose and concealed her face, and her thoughts, behind a sable curtain. Balancing the mess across one thigh, she stirred the rushes to cover the bare stones; then, without glancing up at him, she stood and threw the garbage onto the fire where, in the moments before it charred, it filled the hall with a pleasing aroma.

Not for the first time, Godfrey wondered who her parents truly had been and what misfortunes had compelled them to send their child into exile. The three gold *mancuses*, promised annually for her keep, had arrived for two years only, and the old moneylender from Winchester who had forwarded them was ten years in his grave, taking whatever he had known with him.

She was a strange whelp: quiet and shy, not meant for the hearty society of the West Saxon halls. The six heavy gold coins he kept for her would have bought a place in a reputable convent, where everyone from Lady Ygurna to Father Ralf said she belonged, but she was Alison's friend, and gave his golden daughter the love he could not. So he'd let it be known she was his own blood, raised in his hall and to be dowered the same as Alison.

There had been a handful of offers from solid burghers wanting a comely lass for their declining years, even one from a besotted young knight who'd met her during the king's progress through the shire two summers past and declared her shadowy ways were worth more than any title or fortune. Godfrey would have accepted any of

Wildecent's suitors, but he could not decide who Alison should marry, and he would see his daughter safely married before his ward.

Concern for the young women had effectively blunted Lord Hafwynder's raging emotions. He was on the verge of turning around to apologize for his outburst when one of the brothers created a disruption of his own by fainting into the fire pit.

"A hand here, my lord," Thorkel called.

Lord Hafwynder lent his strength to getting the quivering man, by far the weightiest of the displaced clergymen, onto a hastily erected trestle table; then he stood to one side, feeling more useless than the guests, who could at least throw themselves into their prayers, as Lady Ygurna took command.

Without regard for ceremony or propriety, Lady Ygurna got the little knife from her embroidery basket and hacked through the brother's homespun robes. A liverish contusion spread over half the man's chest. Godfrey, who knew as much about the causes of such injuries as his sister-by-marriage knew about their healing, guessed three or more ribs were broken and cursed that he had not examined them himself when he found them.

"Go to the solar," she told Alison. "Get a two-ell bandage and the clary paste you made earlier—"

"But Stephen—"

"No questions. Get it and bring it here. And you, Wildecent, to the kitchens and have Bethanil set a kettle on the fire."

Both girls raced past Hafwynder while he deciphered the exchange, finally remembering the unconscious foreigner he'd left upstairs.

"Stephen?" he inquired, taking position on the opposite side of the trestle.

Lady Ygurna gave him a dark look that said *later* and turned her attention to the remaining brethren.

"What other surprises have you brought with you?" she demanded. "Off with those robes. I'll have a look at the lot of you!"

"But my *lady!*" Brother Alfred protested, a blush rising from his neck to his tonsure.

"See what your friend's false modesty's gotten him."

Thorkel gave one of his rare laughs. "There isn't a man within hunting distance who hasn't faced our lady's appraising eye. It's your wounds that interest her, nothing more." Brother Alfred's face became a flaming scarlet.

"Enough! If you must be helpful go out to the bowers and see if one of the men has an extra leather belt I can use to hold the bandage tight."

Still chuckling, the Viking left the hall, passing Alison in the doorway as he did.

"Tell your father about *Stephen,*" Lady Ygurna said as she took the bowl and bundle of cloth. Alison blinked back tears as disapproval echoed in her mind.

She told her story carefully, knowing that her aunt was listening, no matter how occupied she seemed to be. She dared not claim that he was out of his delirium or that he had set aside his incomprehensible speech, and *Stephen* was a name more common on the eastern shore of the Channel.

"A Norman lad chasing across the countryside," Godfrey mused when she'd finished spinning her tale. "And no one looking for him or even having heard of him."

"Like as not, they don't suspect he's been run to ground," Thorkel suggested as he returned to the hall. He gave the heavy straps slung over his arm to Lady Ygurna, then rubbed the blood back into his hands over the fire before responding to his lord's questioning stare.

"Think on it. You'd be out searching for that horse alone—unless you were well aware it was gone and weren't expecting to see it back for a good while—let's say, at least the time that's past since you took him in."

Godfrey pushed sandy-colored hair off his brow. "No. No, Thorkel, I can't accept that. A lone youth, a stranger to these parts, sent out deliberately on a journey in December. For anything important enough to justify a courier like that, I'd want a more experienced man."

And because not even Thorkel could imagine the circumstances that had separated Stephen from the five men who'd left Torworden with him, speculation died.

The women washed and bandaged the brothers' injuries, working until the moon had set and both Thorkel and Godfrey had begun snoring loudly. They listened to the brothers bemoan the loss of their water clock to the marauders and their inability to determine the proper hour for matins, then they carried their bandages, bowls, and herbs up the stairs to Stephen's room. The girl Agatha, whom Ygurna had left watching him, snored more loudly than the lord of the manor. They woke her, none too gently, and sent her to her pallet at the foot of Lady Ygurna's bed.

"His color seems better," Alison said hopefully as her aunt turned back the bedcovers.

The bandages had not shifted since the afternoon, nor did they show the dark stains of blood and infection. Ygurna's hand shook when she reached out to touch the linen knot at his shoulder.

"Perhaps we don't need to do anything now? If he's sleeping comfortably there's no sense to disturbing him," Alison continued, her concern for the young man tempered by concern for her aunt and her own exhaustion.

Lady Ygurna signaled her agreement not by answering, but by replacing the bedcovers. She leaned back against the stone wall, her eyes closed and her arms wrapped tightly against her sides as if they hurt. Alison caught her sister's eye; they nodded to each other.

"We can watch him tonight," Wildecent suggested. "Agatha left her blanket behind and there're sure to be some left downstairs. The brothers won't be comfortable unless they're cold as well."

Ygurna managed a weak smile as she pushed herself back from the wall. Her place was here, or in the hall below, but the clergymen had each other; this one was resting more peacefully than he had since they'd first carried him in from the courtyard, and there *was* a crablike pain in her gut that none of her herbs would touch. She slipped across the gallery to her own room moments after the girls went down to the hall to gather blankets.

"She doesn't look well herself," Wildecent whispered as they climbed back up, a double armload of coarse wool between them.

"She's not."

The dark-haired girl stopped short. There was a certainty—a finality—to her sister's words that frightened her. "How do you know?" she whispered after a moment. "Did she tell you?"

Alison held her silence until they were into the room and the door tightly closed behind them. "No one's supposed to know—and, no, I haven't leaned on her. I told you that I can't do that. It's just that she's been getting thinner since autumn. She just pushes the food around; I don't think she's eaten a full meal since the ground froze. If it weren't she herself you know what she'd be saying."

"That tincture of poppy she bought from the alchemist in Cirencester is half gone," Wildecent said dully.

"Then you knew, too. Why ask me?"

"I thought you'd tell me I was wrong."

They said nothing as they gathered the rushes into a layer against the inside wall and spread the blankets over them. Later, huddled together for warmth, with the brazier glowing a dull red but bringing neither light nor heat into the small room, Wildecent voiced her fears: "He'll have to marry again . . ."

"Or find husbands for us," Alison replied lightly.

"For you."

"Don't be a goose. Father isn't going to send you to a nunnery someplace. He's said we are the same to him. I won't marry a man who doesn't understand that—and neither will you. We'll stay here and share Hafwynder Manor."

"Sisters can't stay together once they're grown."

"Lady Ygurna stayed with my mother," Alison retorted as if that settled the matter.

"Lady Ygurna never married. Men must have their own land; they cannot share."

Alison sighed. It was like her sister to find the dark shadows across any path. Life could be different; it could be *made* to be different in the worst case—although her head-blind sister couldn't understand that, of course. Still, as Alison thought over the weddings and betrothals in the shire, Wildecent had a point. Blood ties were vastly stronger than the simple bonds of marriage.

"Brothers," she stated after a few more moments of thought. "What we'll need is brothers."

"What good would they do us? They couldn't even defend their chapel!"

The rushes crackled as Alison fought a bad outburst of the giggles. "Not God's brothers—real brothers. If we were to marry brothers, then we could all live here."

"The church has laws against that.'

"Oh bother," Alison grumbled, pulling the blankets over her head. "All it takes is a little gold for all the

Church's laws to vanish. You don't even want to try! Maybe Stephen has a brother—and if he doesn't, there're bound to be others. Try thinking of something cheerful for a change!"

"Maybe Lady Ygurna will get better."

ildecent was sleeping soundly when Alison awoke and wriggled out of their mound of blankets. The lord's bedroom had only one outside wall, and that one faced opposite the prevailing winds of the valley, so she did not see her breath as she undid the length of twine that had kept her chemise from riding up her thighs while she slept. The marginally warmer air, however, did not compensate for a night spent on the spiky rushes and unyielding floorboards. There didn't seem to be a part of her body that wasn't aching or numb.

Holding her arms above her head, Alison took several deep breaths and heard the sinews along her spine snap into place. Pleased by what a little stretching had accomplished, she threw herself into a series of twists and turns that produced an alarming symphony from her joints. She had settled into whirling her arms in countercircles when she realized she had an audience watching her from her father's bed.

He said a few words in his own language before giving her an amused smile that brought color boiling up her neck.

"You've no right to look at me like that," she protested, but he just laughed and went on smiling.

Propriety and concern for a man who had spent several days not far from death's door told her both to awaken her sister and to seek out Lady Ygurna, but his dark, unreadable eyes held her attention instead. Belatedly checking the laces of her chemise, she edged closer to the bed. He caught her hand when she reached for the blanket covering his shoulder.

"Well, I'm glad you're feeling better." She pressed the

forefinger of her free hand against a nerve in his wrist and twisted loose. "But I've got to look at that shoulder."

The faintly superior grin passed from his face to hers as he studied the tiny red mark her finger had left on his skin and she satisfied herself that the bandages were unchanged from the previous night. Stephen rubbed at the spot and studied her with somewhat increased respect.

"I am Lord Hafwynder's daughter. His *daughter*—I'll wager you've that much understanding of English. You'll mind your manners, if you've got any, and if you don't there's men down below who'll be glad of the opportunity to teach you."

Stephen nodded and pulled the blankets up again. "Where am I?" he asked, his words slow and heavily accented.

"You're in Lord Godfrey Hafwynder's bed, that's where you are. Lord Godfrey's my father and the shire reeve—not the king's reeve, mind you, but the shire reeve."

The language she called English rasped his ears and hovered beyond his understanding, which had been far from perfect. At Torworden even the churls had a smattering of Norman French and were encouraged to speak the language of their masters rather than the other way around. Stephen recognized the name *Hafwynder,* which surfaced repeatedly in her rapid speech, and guessed that, though he remembered little of the final stages of the journey, he'd come safely to the Saxon manor.

"How long?" he asked, holding up his hand to get her attention but not daring to touch her again. She gave him a short answer and he wished he'd paid a bit more attention to the conversations his uncle's churls had among themselves. He held up one finger and told her the proper word for one, then repeated the gesture for two, three, four and five. She said something in her own language and held up five fingers; he closed his eyes as the weight of failure came to rest.

He hadn't read the message his uncle had given him, not even when he'd transferred it from its valuable case, but it must have been important and it should have been delivered before this morning. The throbbing in his shoulder would be nothing compared to what he'd feel when his uncle was through with him. Jean Beauleyas's wrath, when he learned that Duke William's men had sailed for Normandy without that piece of parchment, would be formidable. It might have been wiser to be eaten by wolves or freeze to death at the side of the road.

Alison felt a pang of terror when his eyes closed and did not reopen. His question had been simple enough, a common one among men who'd lost their wits to their injuries. She didn't believe it was her answer that set him back, but he showed no response when she spoke his name and did not try to break free when she grasped his wrist.

"Wildecent! Wake up!"

"I'm awake. What's wrong with him?"

Alison turned to see her sister kicking free of the blankets. "I don't know. He asked how long he'd been here, then he went like this."

"Were you leaning on him?"

While her sister sputtered denials, Wildecent poured a glass of cyder and sniffed it cautiously. The ewer had been on the sideboard since Stephen had been brought into the room, but winter had done a fair job of keeping it drinkable. Pushing her sister aside, she shoved the aromatic spirits under his nose and prepared to wrestle him to a sitting position.

"His shoulder!" Alison protested.

"Then help me."

But there was no need. The strong, aromatic cyder and

the tickle of Wildecent's hair across his face got Stephen to open his eyes. He took the beaker in his own hands and sat without anyone's help.

He remembered the gossip now: there were two daughters here; the heiress and an acknowledged by-blow. The sturdy blond one who looked as if she could swing a knight's sword was probably the heiress; the Saxons set a woman's *weregeld* as equal to one ox and seemed content to equate the two in other ways as well. The other one, the one who looked more frightened than indignant, would be the bastard. Her dark hair and pale skin were more to his taste. He smiled at her; she retreated a half step.

He told her, as he had told her half sister, that she was a pretty sight for a sick man's eyes. But unlike her sister, who'd blushed with embarrassment, the darker girl relaxed and returned his smile.

It was not that Wildecent understood his words—not completely, anyway—but they had a musical lilt to them and conjured up warm, secure sensations. The mist-shrouded faces in her memory glowed clearer for a moment. She heard that same lilt in their voices.

"Merci," she replied softly, then occupied herself folding the blankets.

Alison watched all this with little amusement. She hadn't seen Wildecent's face, but she hadn't needed to—although she couldn't imagine how head-blind Wildecent had managed to find a word to make Stephen smile. A rapport had been born between them, or, at least, something had happened on Stephen's side of the short exchange, and Alison found herself grappling with the unfamiliar pangs of jealousy.

She *was* the prettier of the two sisters; everyone in the shire had said so in so many words—they said precious little about Wildecent, whose exotic appearance was presumed to come from her unfortunate, wayward mother. It had been easy, then, for Alison to compliment Wildecent's flawless, ivory skin; her night black hair and gold-amber eyes. But now this foreigner, with flaky spots on his cheeks from frostbite and a glasslike shield over his mind, had the clear audacity to prefer shy, mousy Wildecent.

Clearly something had gone awry with his first impressions of them—something Alison felt duty-bound to correct. Wildecent already had all the blankets under her arm; it would make sense, since she was ready to leave the room, to send her off in search of their aunt.

"We shouldn't both leave him alone," Alison began, "so you can tell Lady Ygurna he's better—and maybe see what Bethanil's got hanging over the hearth. I'll bet he's hungry."

Wildecent mumbled a reply and left, leaving the door open behind her.

Alison got the ewer of cyder and, on the pretext of filling his beaker, approached the bed. She took Lady Ygurna's warnings about sorcery seriously, but not personally; she couldn't imagine the power that had placed the barrier in Stephen's mind, but she had felt his name despite it and was confident that she could plant her own image on its surface without betraying anyone. Physical contact would help; she allowed their fingertips to touch while he held the beaker.

The shield was not so apparent when he was awake and healthy. Alison leaned gently against it and sank into the upper layer of his thoughts. It was one thing to find the answer to a specific question or to tell if someone wasn't saying what he was thinking, but unstructured thoughts, especially couched in a language she didn't understand, were beyond her comprehension.

She needed to sing a silent song about friendship,

honor, beauty, and love to lure the answers she wanted to the surface. A memory bounded toward her like an excited puppy; Alison let it surround her and slid within it.

There was a kite-shield over their left arm and a heavy sword held high in their right hand. The figure looming over them wielded a two-handed sword and glowered like death itself—but, or so the memory claimed, he was a man they trusted and revered. The swords were wrapped, their edges blunted with rawhide, but the blow Stephen deflected with his shield stunned Alison and would have given him a fair bruise if it had landed. Reeling and no longer in control of the unfolding memory, Alison felt him pivot the sword in his wrist and snap it downward against his partner's momentarily undefended neck.

The older man went spinning to the ground with a shout that was laughter mixed with real pain. Stephen held his guard a few moments longer, then dropped his weapons to one side and extended his hand.

"Well done, lad," the man said, grasping Stephen's hand and jumping to his feet—or at least that's what the words meant within the memory.

"Indeed. It's no small honor to get behind Drago's defense."

Stephen had not heard the other man approach; the focus of the memory changed. Alison felt a flood of Stephen's satisfaction as they turned and greeted a man in his early twenties. This man, dressed in somber colors and conveying a worldly air, was Stephen's friend and a man he would have emulated, if he'd been able.

"I'm glad you came down to watch, Ambrose," Stephen remembered saying. "I know you've been busy."

"I thought today might be the day you laid the big

fellow in the mud.'' He put an arm over Stephen's shoulder and led him away from the practice ground.

Alison had called for certain emotions and had received an understanding of friendship among men that she had not suspected before—but it wasn't the information she wanted. Separating herself, she changed the silent song and waited until another memory floated by.

The meadow filled with flowers, sunlight and gentle breezes; it seemed to go on forever and had a dreamlike quality that made Alison suspect she had stumbled upon something that was not so much a memory as an elaborate, oft-repeated fantasy. The girl appeared from nowhere and was running lightly through the grass, her hair and robes streaming out behind her. The hair, of course, was sooty black.

When Stephen started to run after her, she glanced over her shoulder and gave him a look that sent shivers down Alison's immaterial spine. The woman bore only a superficial resemblance to Wildecent but her hair alone was enough to explain the attraction, so Alison leaned on the image and the hair turned to gold like her own.

The girl ran true and fast, but Stephen was the stronger and was soon right behind her. He whipped his cloak around in front of them and caught a handful of her hair. They fell to the ground gracefully and without pain—which convinced Alison that she partook of a fantasy—then he wrapped his arms around her and kissed her full on the mouth.

Alison pushed away from the image, not caring that her shocked sensibilities sent ripples far below the idle thoughts upon which she'd been spying.

What's happening? What— Who are you? How are you here?
The questions—Stephen's questions—buffeted Alison

63

from one unpleasant image to another. The shield she had penetrated so easily heartbeats before threatened to trap her within the young man's mind. She remembered Lady Ygurna's warning that getting out of someone's memories was often much more difficult than getting in. Belatedly, she also remembered the rest of her aunt's warnings as well. She dodged the arrowlike questions and contrived to disguise herself, all the while seeking to flow through the shield and back to herself.

Wildecent found her cloak on the peg by the back door of the great hall. She had seen the interest in Stephen's eyes when he smiled at her and heard the tinge of jealousy in Alison's voice. If Alison thought she had devised a subtle way of being alone with the young man, so be it—she was just as glad to be looking for Lady Ygurna. No good was going to come of it if she was courted while Alison was ignored.

Not that she found the young man all that attractive. His smiles had come too quickly, and no honorable gentleman would approach an honorable gentlewoman before announcing his intentions to her kinfolk. Her mother might have been one to succumb to his advances, but *she* wasn't going to disgrace Lord Godfrey Hafwynder that way.

Still, Stephen's voice had been pleasant and his face, a fine-boned face like her own, stayed clear in her memory. Something about him seemed to provoke memories of her never-named, never-mentioned mother. Wildecent had thought of that mysterious woman more times since his arrival than she had in the previous three or more years—and they were not comfortable thoughts.

"Excuse me, Bethanil, is there porridge left and have you seen my lady aunt about this morning?"

Wildecent had gone to her aunt's chamber first and

found it unoccupied. Indeed, it had appeared that for all her exhaustion, her aunt had scarcely slept at all.

"Be enough for you hangin' on the spit, yonder," the cook replied, not looking up from her meat chopping.

"Not for me, thank you. I've got to find my aunt first, but for Stephen, the knight who's been ill in my lord father's bed these last days. He's himself this morning—though we still can't understand a word he says—and sure to be hungry."

The plump, round-faced woman laid her cleaver aside and inspected the hearth-pot herself. "What's in the pot might set well in his belly. But it's four days since he's had a proper meal and a youngun like that needs meat to fill the spaces between his bones. When you find your aunt ask if she'll see to putting an extra bit of venison in the covered pie for him."

"Have you seen my lady aunt, then? Is she in the solar?"

Bethanil shrugged and went back to her chopping. "The Lady Ygurna went out a while back, jingling the keys."

Wildecent considered taking a bowl of the honey-nut porridge upstairs, then, remembering Alison's desire to be alone with Stephen, decided that she'd find her aunt first. If Alison was slipping into temptation, let Lady Ygurna discover it and chastise her.

She ran across the courtyard to the solar but that room, like Lady Ygurna's bedroom, was cold and dark. Bethanil had mentioned the keys, though, and that made the storage bowers likely places to search. The little buildings where the fleece, grain, and farming tools were kept were deserted, their iron locks coated with unbroken ice.

With a glance back toward the empty window of her father's bedroom, Wildecent hurried back to the hall. Her father's more delicate wealth, his gold, goblets, finished clothing, and the like, was kept in locked chests in the upper rooms of the east side of the hall. If her aunt were

in one of those dusty rooms, then Wildecent had practically walked by her on the way to the kitchen. She slipped
through Bethanil's domain without being noticed.

The spiral stairway to the storerooms, like the tunnel
connecting her bedroom with the kitchens, played with
Wildecent's fear of dark, enclosed spaces. Normally she
would have climbed the open stairs that led past the bed-
chambers; this time she swallowed her nervousness, gathered her skirts, and raced upward as fast as Alison ever
did.

The candle-lamp was gone from its usual hook. Lady
Ygurna was probably in one of the rooms, but Wildecent
would have to search for her in the perpetual gloom of
the windowless hall. The first two rooms were empty, as
was the third. She was closing the door when she heard
the darkness cough.

It was unthinkable that the outlaws could have gotten
into their manor and reached the storerooms without an
alarm being raised, but Wildecent considered the possibility as she hesitated in the doorway.

"Wildecent, is that you, child?"

It was Lady Ygurna's voice, but raspy and short of
breath. Still fearing that unseen hands might grab her, the
dark-haired girl took one step across the threshold.

"The candle fell—"

The fear changed. It wasn't marauders anymore but the
sound of something dreadfully wrong with her aunt.
Dropping quickly to her knees, Wildecent patted her way
across the floor until the candle, chipped and separated
from its wood-and-iron holder, was beneath her fingers.
She got flint and steel from a pouch slung from her belt,
but her hands were shaking and it took many tries before
the spark caught on the wick.

Lady Ygurna slumped against a rack of boots, one arm
clutching her side. Quickly shoving the candle into its

holder, Wildecent offered her outstretched hands but, even having asked for help, her aunt was still reluctant to accept it.

"Don't look so worried," she scolded, leaning heavily on her niece's arm. "I was counting the cloth, fell against the boot rack, and had the wind knocked out of me."

Her sheaf of parchment accounts was lying on the floor beside, along with a quill and an overturned vial of ink—so she had been counting the cloth, but the rest seemed unlikely to Wildecent's eye. None of the boots had fallen—young Stephen's clothing and boots were still precariously balanced across the top of the rack—and Lady Ygurna was clutching the wrong side of her body to have fallen on the wooden rack. Wildecent tried her hand at the sort of calculated innocence Alison used to such advantage.

"But we don't usually count the cloth again until spring."

"I—I didn't want to wait."

Lady Ygurna shook herself free, choosing to lean against the wall and the doorway, rather than another person.

"Stephen was awake when we woke up. Alison's with him now."

"What? Since dawn then? Is he speaking clearly? Why didn't you tell me sooner?"

"I came looking for you; you weren't easy to find."

"Never mind that. Have you seen Lord Hafwynder? He must be told—and Longsword too, I suppose. They'll both want to question him."

"He's still using his strange language; we can't understand him."

Her aunt was sharper than her sister, even leaning against the doorway with pain in her eyes. She heard the catch in Wildecent's voice. "Neither of you?"

"No, my lady—not really, anyway. He moves his hands,

and some of his words sound a bit familiar. But he learned more from us, I fear, asking how long he'd been here, than we learned about him."

"And Alison?"

"You were very precise, my lady. I'm sure she hasn't forgotten," Wildecent said, her fingers crossed behind her back though she was reasonably confident that Alison wouldn't *forget* their aunt's warnings; she'd completely ignore them.

"Very well then. I'll find Lord Hafwynder; you go back to your sister."

"But your side, my lady. Wouldn't you be more comfortable—"

"Wildecent! Do not question my judgment!"

ear God in his Heaven! Alison!"

Wildecent's skirts swirled around her as she came to an abrupt stop in the doorway. Her sister and the stranger were as statues, their fingertips touching above the blankets, the cyder a stain across the linen. Stephen's eyes were closed; but for the rapid rise and fall of his chest, he, and Alison, might well have been dead. Certainly neither showed any response at all to Wildecent's panic.

Venturing a wide arc around the immobile pair, Wildecent saw that her sister's eyes had rolled back in her skull, and she was blinking as if she might fall into a fit. Without considering her courage—or lack of it—but fearing that some diabolic possession had crept upon them, Wildecent leaped between them, pushing Alison against the wall to break the physical contact between her and Stephen.

Alison's eyes closed gently, but her arm continued to point toward the bed until Wildecent pushed it down.

The legends of the saints and heroes were filled with brave men and women who faced the direst evils of the world without flinching, but Wildecent, who knew her sister would not prove totally innocent of this disaster and knew that no punishment would fail to touch her as well, confronted the unknown with angry frustration. The slap she laid across Alison's cheek held as much rage as compassion, and the tears that came quickly were for herself.

Alison's eyes came open for a moment, focusing on something far from the cramped bedroom, then shut again.

Wildecent was about to administer another jaw-jolting slap when Stephen's voice interrupted her. The young man's words were still many steps from grammatical English, but she understood them well enough.

"I don't know what happened," she snapped, whirling about to face him. "But if she's still like this when my lady aunt and my Lord Hafwynder come through that door, we won't be worth a black tin groat."

He shook his head. It was clear he hadn't understood every word, but Wildecent's hands were seldom still when she talked—despite Lady Ygurna's disciplinary efforts over the years—and Alison's slack expression told a story of its own.

"Hafwynder?" he inquired, nearly gagging on the Germanic consonants.

"My lord father!" Wildecent replied as she slapped Alison on the other cheek.

This time the blond girl recognized her sister, or at least acknowledged a living presence. "Dear God, help me," she whispered.

"I'm trying!" But the eyes were already closing again. "Alison! Come back here!"

Whatever continued to affect Alison had released Stephen. The young man's mind was clearer than it had been, but his first decisions did nothing to relieve Wildecent's panic. Muttering something about his shoes—perhaps he thought his elevated, bandaged foot was still shod—he attempted to throw aside his blankets and leave the bed. His injured shoulder, however, was not ready for the exertion and he flopped backward, missing the bolster pillow, with a pained sigh.

"Damn you!" Wildecent exclaimed, leaving her sister and rushing to set him right in the bed again before he succeeded in reopening his wounds and, more important, before her aunt arrived.

Stephen's gesture had revealed that he was, except for his bandages, stark naked beneath the blankets. Revealed to himself, that is, for Wildecent was both well aware and quite unimpressed by the fact. But suddenly modesty

71

wrapped itself around him and he was not about to be pushed about by any maiden nor release his death's grip on the skewed linens.

A feminine growl rumbled at the back of Wildecent's throat. She made a fist and shook it in front of the recalcitrant youth's nose. *"The way you were, if you please. And if you don't—"*

"Clothes," he implored; then, as he recited the articles of his wardrobe in his own language, a look of panic as potent as Wildecent's own spread across his face. *"Mes chausses!"*

His agitation rose precipitously; Wildecent found herself involuntarily edging away from the bed. With evident desperation, Stephen reached out and grabbed her skirts. He pulled her closer then twisted the cloth so her woolen stockings and house boots were visible. Well-bred young ladies did *not* display their legs to strangers; Wildecent was speechless with shock and shame.

But as much as she'd been unimpressed by his nakedness, he cared only for her sagging hose. *"Chausses,"* he repeated, pointing vigorously. *"Mes chausses?"*

He said other things as well—a sputtering torrent of words, enough of which made sense that Wildecent knew he wanted his clothes—most especially his hose—and he wanted them before he saw her father. Wildecent could understand that a guest whose status in the house was clouded might not wish to meet his host clad only in his skin but she guessed, as well, that there was something special about his stockings. And he wanted her to risk everything by bringing them to him.

"No." Wildecent shook her head and tugged her skirts free. "Tell him yourself."

She turned her back on him and returned to her sister, who appeared to be recovering. Alison looked up at the

72

sound of her name and this time there was no question that she recognized her sister.

"Oh, Wildecent—it was horrible!" she explained, closing cold hands over Wildecent's wrists.

"It will be worse when Lady Ygurna and our lord father get here if you're still drooling like an idiot."

Reflexively, Alison wiped her chin, which was not at all moist. "I couldn't get out. I didn't know where I was and"—she leaned closer to her sister to whisper—"*he* almost found me."

"Stephen? Oh, Alison, she told you not to lean. Now look what's happened—"

"Not Stephen . . . it wasn't him. He didn't put that shield there. It was the other one. I was so frightened."

Tears had begun to flow down Alison's cheeks; she rested her head against Wildecent's shoulder. Her sobs were soft, ladylike, and shook the length of her spine. Wildecent would gladly have given Alison her full attention and compassion but Stephen kept distracting her, and Stephen's distractions reminded her of those who would be coming to the room at any moment.

"You've got to compose yourself," Wildecent whispered. "I found Lady Ygurna—that's a story to itself—but she decided our lord father would have to see Stephen right away. They won't be long, I promise."

Alison finally grasped the significance of Wildecent's concern. She blotted her eyes on the underside of her sleeve. She took an unaided step toward the cyder on the sideboard but swayed unsteadily enough that Wildecent rushed to get an arm around her.

There was only one beaker and it lay on the bed beside Stephen. He guessed Wildecent's intention and, with it grasped in his good arm, held it out of her reach while he repeated his request for his clothing.

"What does he want?" Alison asked, venturing a cautious step closer to the bed.

"He wants his clothes and stockings."

Not wanting to risk reinjuring him and certainly not wishing to climb onto the mattress beside him, Wildecent had been reduced to frantic, but ineffective, jumps that brought her nowhere near her goal.

Alison was taller; her reach might have been enough, but simply raising her arm over her head brought a wave of dizziness. "We don't even know where his clothes are," she complained.

"We . . . do," her sister replied between jumps. "I saw them in the storeroom where I found—"

"Then get them, please?"

"Alison, I don't want to do anything *for* Stephen—not after what he did to you. And I certainly don't want to leave you alone in here with him."

"It was my fault, not his—as you've already told me—and I'm not going to do anything like that again for a long time. *Stephen* didn't hurt me. It wasn't him I found behind that shield. Oh please, Wildecent. I'd get them myself. I'll give you that set of embroidered bands father brought me from Westminster last summer . . ."

Wildecent was tempted. Lord Godfrey always brought them both presents when he returned from his frequent journeys to the king's court, but Wildecent's gift of rock candy had been swiftly reduced to fond memories.

"Stockings," Wildecent said to Stephen, lifting her skirts just far enough to reveal the loose-fitting blue cloth wrapped around her ankles. *"Chausses*—right?" He nodded, but did not offer her the cup. "Let her have some cyder."

She pointed to Alison as she backed toward the doorway. He tossed the beaker to the foot of the bed. Alison couldn't catch it, but it was within her reach. Wildecent smiled and came back into the room.

"No, you must get his stockings. You promised."

"I did no such thing."

"I thought you did and he thought you did. Either you promised or you deceived us both."

Making her little growling noises again, Wildecent headed back out the door.

The hall below was empty except for Agatha raking the ashes in the hearth—and she could be relied on not to notice anything occurring on the upper level unless someone held a knife to her throat. Wildecent scampered from the southern gallery, where Stephen was, to the one opposite. Taking the candle-lamp and hoping no one would notice its absence, she reached the wardrobe room and shut the door behind her.

With the boots and the heavy traveling cloak, Stephen's clothing made a large bundle—too large to carry with the candle-lamp as well. She eased the door open again with her elbow and slipped back into the gallery.

"Where's that priest?" her father was asking.

Wildecent squeezed back against the doorway, blowing out the candle as she did.

"In the bower building beyond the stables," Thorkel Longsword replied.

"Get him. Let him earn his keep if it's Latin or French that boy's speaking. And someone light that fire; it's cold as a witch's heart in here."

She heard his chair creak: at least he wasn't coming upstairs until Longsword returned with Brother Alfred. If he hadn't moved his chair, and he was alone, then she had a reprieve. It was just possible that the noisy floorboards of the gallery wouldn't betray her and that she could get back without being noticed.

The hall remained quiet. She hung the candle-lamp back

on its hook and studied the dark wood hallway that would take her behind her father's back—or right in front of his eyes. Then, reminding herself that no one had told her *not* to comply with Stephen's wishes, she took the first step.

He wasn't alone; and it wasn't he in his chair but her aunt, Lady Ygurna. They seemed caught in their conversation. Wildecent raced to the corner where, because of the private nature of the bedrooms, tapestries had been hung to obscure the view from the hall.

"Hurry!" she commanded, dumping the clothes in Stephen's lap. "Lady Ygurna and our lord father are downstairs waiting for Thorkel to return with that Brother Alfred."

"Did they see you?" Alison had recovered her composure and color. She had been sitting on a low stool but rose to pace steadily beside her sister as Stephen made a one-handed rubble of the carefully folded garments. Wildecent shook her head noncommittally and gave Stephen a nervous glance. The young man seemed interested only in shaking everything he had worn before arriving at the hall—not in wearing any of it.

He was still intent at his labors when the doorway darkened and the bedroom filled with Lord Hafwynder along with Thorkel Longsword, Lady Ygurna, and the hapless, panting Brother Alfred.

"I can see he's awake—but is his mind whole?" Godfrey asked, bringing all other activity in the crowded room to a halt.

At Torworden they mocked the unwarlike Saxons but, sitting naked in a strange bed and looking up at Godfrey, Thorkel, and Ygurna, Stephen had sudden doubts about that judgment. He was aware of his injuries as he had not been since coming to his senses shortly after dawn, and acutely aware of his vulnerability. The English words he'd picked up from the two girls vanished from his memory; he addressed Thorkel, who he took to be the lord of the hall, in his own language.

"Well, Brother?" Godfrey inquired.

"French, my lord. Not as Father Ralf—may his soul be already with God—spoke it, but like enough, I think."

"Then get on with it."

Brother Alfred made a poor translator and a worse interrogator but, little by little, Stephen's name and his relation to the Norman keep at Torworden was revealed.

"What was he doing out on the road in the middle of the night?" Thorkel added.

Brother Alfred looked to Hafwynder and, after receiving the lord's assent, put the question to Stephen. He listened to the response, then translated: "He says he was with a group of his uncle's knights. They were beset by misfortune and he was the only one left to continue their journey, on his uncle's behalf, to Pevensey."

"Why Pevensey?"

The question was conveyed and, so it seemed to Godfrey, the lad's eyes showed more white as he made his hasty reply.

"They were to deliver a message to a tavern by the port. He says he doesn't know the name of the man they were to meet nor the contents of the message, which, he says, has been lost," Brother Alfred repeated, careful to distance himself from the possibility that Stephen was lying.

Hafwynder was, however, inclined to believe the young man. He had not believed Stephen was traveling alone, and he would never have entrusted sensitive information to a raw youth. He had begun to relax when Thorkel leaned forward to pluck a thin silver cylinder from the blanket valleys.

"Lost?" the Viking inquired and had no need of Brother Alfred's services to make himself understood as he waved the message case in front of Stephen's face.

Stephen made a grab for the flashing silver. It was doubtful he could have moved faster than Longsword under the best of circumstances; swaddled in bandages and forced to use his parrying hand, he didn't have a prayer of success. Thorkel lifted the clasp and discovered the case was empty.

"A ruse?" he wondered aloud.

It was then that Godfrey remembered what he had only half seen from his hearth below: his dark-haired ward running along the gallery with this man's clothes bundled in her arms. He looked at the message case and the tumble of garments on the bed. Suppose at least part of the tale were true: if he had been the least of the men sent from Torworden and they *had* been beset along the way, then only a fool would have left the message in a silver gilt case.

"I think not," Hafwynder said slowly, still putting it together in his mind. "Help him look through those garments; check the seams, the hems and anywhere else a roll of parchment might be hidden."

Thorkel moved quickly to carry out his lord's command. For a moment it appeared that Stephen was going to make a physical objection, but he recognized in Longsword the same ruthless dedication that he'd seen in his uncle's men and released his stockings to the Viking's scarred hands. Wildecent, because she was the next closest to the bed, took a step forward to aid the search.

"A moment, Wildecent," her father said in a tone that was frightening for its measured softness.

"My lord father?" She faced him and bowed her head in obedience.

"Just now I glimpsed you bringing these garments from the storerooms; running, I might add, as if it were of some importance that this young man paw through them before I entered this room."

"I understood him to want his clothing before speaking to you."

"*Understood?* What gifts do you possess that you understand this foreigner's speech?"

Wildecent's pulse pounded in her ears and her legs felt like thin reeds bending in a storm. She looked to her aunt for advice or support, but her nearsightedness held any of the subtle signs of Lady Ygurna's emotions away from her, and Alison, pressed against the sideboard, was an equally unhelpful blur. The memory of that week in the stables under-room was strong in her mind as she answered.

"No gifts, my lord father," she said truthfully, offering a silent prayer that her sacrifice would be appreciated. "Only memories. It seems I have heard his tongue before, and hearing him I can understand a few words and phrases."

Her father's reaction to this speech was cut short by Longsword's snort of satisfaction. He'd found the vellum, a bit worse for the wear, smoothed within several layers of wool hose. The reading of inked words was nothing he'd ever aspired to; he handed the scrap to Lord Godfrey without a glance at its contents. But it was not in the clear Saxon script nor even in Latin. Lord Godfrey was compelled to hand it to Brother Alfred.

The brother squinted and peered, then shrugged and returned it. "Father Ralf wrote mostly in Latin, my lord," he apologized. "I seldom saw him write the Norman's language but, even so, I think this is some sort of cipher. The pattern of letters is like nothing I've ever seen before."

Lord Godfrey ran his hand through his silk-fine beard. Though it might be blasphemy, he was beginning to feel like the biblical Job, with obstacles thrown onto every step of his path. Of all the heritages he had imagined for his mysterious ward, Norman-French had been the least likely. What manner of Norman would send his child to an estate deep in Saxon Wessex? Not that he could afford to consider that now. He wasn't surprised that the message was in cipher: it had to be important to have been sent at all; its contents could only be treasonous and he had no way at all of unraveling it.

"Ask him what he knows of it," he said to Brother Alfred, whose translation was followed by an outpouring of slippery French from the boy.

"He still says he knows nothing of the contents; he'll swear to that on any saint's relics, he says. He wants you to send a messenger to Torworden, though, to let his uncle know what has happened."

Hafwynder shrugged. The Norman interloper would have to be notified sooner or later; as late as possible, if he had his way. Best to let the young man stew a bit—it might improve his memory. Putting his back to the bed, he directed his attention again to Wildecent.

"What did he tell you about this message?" he asked as her eyes grew wide with fright.

"Nothing, my lord father. He spoke of his clothes. His speech was longer, perhaps, but I did not understand it."

Godfrey believed her. Wildecent had never been bold enough to lie outright to his face—a virtue he did not grant his daughter Alison—but concern had flickered across the Frenchman's face while the dark-haired girl whispered her answer. He meant to take full advantage of any weakness Stephen displayed.

"I disbelieve you," he snarled in a tone that was sure to send one or two tears sliding down her face where the youth could see them. "Perhaps some time alone will improve your memory and illuminate your errors. Thorkel, lock her away from my sight."

There was a rare kind of courage in the timid girl, he observed as she shrugged away from Thorkel and led the way, with careful dignity, from the room. The fearless confronted danger without recognizing its power, but theirs was a lesser bravery.

ildecent found herself escorted to her own bedroom in the tower. Perhaps the Viking did not know about the dank room beneath the stables, or perhaps he felt some sympathy for the skirted figure who preceded him up the dark stairs. Whatever, he offered her no violence and said nothing as he drew the bolt into place.

She was grateful for the silence; had she tried to say anything her voice would have cracked and the perceived weight of injustice would have tumbled out of her. She was grateful, as well, for a familiar prison in which to brood upon her misfortunes. Wrapping herself in the wolf-fur blanket from the bed, she made a little bundle of herself between the cope chest and the wall and made no further effort to conceal her weeping.

I told the truth, she reminded herself and any saints who might be listening.

Surely Alison, at least, had known that. It would have been a simple thing for her sister to defend her; to say the few necessary words that would have cleared away their father's suspicion. But Alison, like the iron weathercock above the stables, never faced into the wind. Godfrey Hafwynder's rage had never flared more unexpectedly than it had in his bedroom, and Alison's lifelong trait had been to keep herself from hopeless conflicts.

Wildecent was, however, an obedient child. If her father thought that contemplation of her sins was in order, then she would reconsider what she had done to reduce herself to this state—even if she, at first, saw no fault in her behavior. Father Ralf, after all, frequently preached that men, and women, were blind to their weaknesses.

Her mind echoed with Stephen's voice, and, try as she might, she could unlock no secret meanings from his words. She did *try*—pressing deep into those dim memories of her infancy for words and phrases. There was nothing useful in those shadows; nothing except a disquieting conviction that there was something very wrong with her understanding of her mother.

For the woman who laughed with music and offered her honeyed fruit from her own plate could not have been a shameless whore. Wildecent had seen such women, and they did not wear gowns edged with fur nor decorate their hair with gold and jewels. Of course, that finery could be the trick of memory, just as the white dragon of her nightmares had proven to be nothing more than a chalk carving. But there was a man in her memories. A man who held her safe on the saddle in front of him while his horse pranced; a man she heard herself call 'Papa'; a man who looked nothing at all like Lord Godfrey Hafwynder.

By the time the light filtering through the shutters had turned amber, Wildecent had forced herself to remember that last night in her parents' castle with crystal clarity. It had been her mother, her face dirty and streaked with tears, who had awakened her and given her to mail-clad men who were not strangers but her father's companions, made strange by their grim faces.

"Take her to Isak in Saint Suzanne. He has the letters and the gold," her mother had said, tucking the furs tightly around her frightened daughter. "And hurry. My lord sore needs you with him."

For Wildecent, her legs growing stiff with cold, it was the day's final injustice: that in obeying the man she called her father, she had discovered the man she had once called "Papa," only to have him and her mother ripped away.

The amber light faded. A churning stomach and pounding headache reminded Wildecent, as if she managed to forget it otherwise, that she had never gotten breakfast and that, in the growing darkness, it was unlikely she was going to have any dinner either. Earlier in the afternoon she had believed her exile would end at suppertime when Alison, as was their winter custom, would come upstairs for another pair of stockings and a heavier cloak. No longer so certain, Wildecent stretched her cramped legs, searched in the darkness for a candle stub and wondered, as the night wind rattled the shutters, if this tower were not worse than the room below the stables.

She had found a candle and a handful of wrinkled berries from a forgotten autumn afternoon when the bolt rasped against the bar and her sister appeared in the doorway. They said nothing while Alison set her lamp on the cope chest and closed the door.

"I brought you a bran cake," Alison began, putting the light brown bread into her sister's hands. "I hid it under my skirt. Our lord father isn't so angry now—but he's still frightful upset. I didn't want to remind him. I'm sure he'll have forgotten everything by tomorrow, but not yet at dinnertime."

Wildecent devoured the roll, then licked each finger clean. "Forgotten but not forgiven," she said rhetorically. "What did Stephen say after I left?"

"He'd been attacked by both wolves and outlaws, as everyone believed, but first one of his party had his leg crushed when his horse fell on it, and so they'd divided themselves. It was Stephen and just one other; they made an attractive target. But Stephen was just acting squire to the others, it would seem. Father's agreed to send a messenger party to Torworden in the morning to let his uncle know he's here and safe."

"Our father is assured there's no treason, then?"

Alison hesitated before answering. "It could not be anything but treason," she explained. "A coded message to Pevensey, where William the Bastard pays half the citizens to do his spying? How could it be anything but

84

treason—if not against King Edward himself, then surely against Earl Harold and all the ealdormen of Wessex."

Abandoning her fingers, Wildecent stared at her sister. Alison had never cared about things that did not seem to affect her, and whatever had passed between the Norman youth and her, it had nothing to do with the politics of succession to the Saxon throne. The words had been put into her sister's head; they still suspected her.

"It would not be treason to inform their duke of our king's illness. It has been proclaimed in all the churches. We've been praying for his health these last few months." She made the statement into a question with her voice.

"No, but—"

Clearly Alison had been tutored, but not with any thoroughness.

"If Stephen was acting as squire to the others, though," Wildecent suggested—logic had always been her stronghold between them—"then there wouldn't be any suspicion of treason attached to him. He would only have been doing his duty to his knights—even if he *had* told me why he wanted his clothes—"

"He didn't, did he?" Alison interrupted to ask her own question—not one suggested to her by her elders.

"I was lucky I understood he wanted his forsaken clothes, or maybe unlucky. If I hadn't understood him at all, none of this would have happened."

Wildecent wiped her perfectly cleaned fingers against her skirts as her stomach, with a will of its own and a complete disbelief that a day's hunger could be exchanged for one bran cake, churned loudly.

"You didn't have any breakfast either," her sister remembered. "They've all retired for the night; we can sneak down to the kitchens and get something else."

"I don't think that'd be wise. Our lord father hasn't

given permission. I don't think he intended for me to go to bed with a full belly."

"It's all right, Wildecent. Trust me."

Wildecent had, in fact, no good reason to trust her sister at that moment. But the churning in her midsection was not susceptible to the subtleties of logic. Alison took the candle-lamp—because it was nighttime, not because the stairway was darker than usual—and led the way.

They raided the alcove where the cheese was kept in tight baskets and the bread was wrapped in slightly damp rags. The cats who hunted in Bethanil's domain and kept the larders free from vermin came to investigate the intruders. Alison gave them a cheese rind, then pulled a stool close by the banked hearth fire, which still gave a pleasant warmth.

"He stole those words from me," the blond girl said at length, as if confiding some great secret.

"Beg your pardon?" Wildecent dragged another stool over. She had taken a thin slice from each of four sausages hanging in the alcove and was far more interested in her appetite than her sister's confession.

"Stephen. He stole—well, maybe not stole, maybe overheard and learned—those words you understood when I was trying to get away."

Food, the few mouthfuls she had swallowed and the prospect of more, had restored Wildecent's equilibrium. She laughed gently at her sister's guilt. "Perhaps. Though I can scarcely imagine you struggling to get free and screaming about stockings."

"Don't jest. My whole mind was vulnerable then; anything could have slipped away. I'm sure Lady Ygurna suspects something. If I'd told them what happened—" Alison's hands fluttered helplessly in her lap. "I'd have had both our lord father and Lady Ygurna furious. They'd have beaten me or locked me away."

Wildecent sliced a chunk of cheese with a bit more vigor than she'd intended. The knife bit into her thumb—not seriously, but enough to tell her that her anger was rising again. She sucked on the small cut and did not point out that she herself *had* been locked away.

"You understand, don't you? The mysteries have to be protected. If I had said anything there, with Brother Alfred in the room—especially Brother Alfred—everything we believe in would have been compromised."

The cut no longer stung and had not bled. Wildecent let her hands fall to her lap. She wanted to say that she didn't really believe in any of the esoteric things their aunt talked about. She had to believe in her sister's talent, but she'd never felt the power of the earth beneath her feet nor the power of the moon above her head, and she would not have mourned the absence of the secret bolt-hole in the solar so long as the truly useful, truly nonmagical herbs and medicines were not lost. Years of compromise, however, and the lingering hope that she might yet experience the mysteries kept the strongest cynicism swallowed behind her lips.

"Certainly," she said with only the barest hesitation. "But there are other explanations. As it happens, I *did* understand his words, a few of them at least."

It was Alison's turn to glance up from the cheesecloth she was unraveling. "How could you?" she demanded.

"How does one understand anything at all? They were words that had meaning. I hadn't heard them for a long time, but they still had meaning and I remembered them." Wildecent watched her sister's eyes widen in the candlelight. "I took our lord father's advice and contemplated what I had heard. I think I'd understand even more now but, in truth, I *do* think that Stephen had rather more English after you'd leaned on him, though it's not the English I'm referring to."

"That's not possible," Alison protested. "You're not my sister—not really."

"I know that."

"No, not that. Lady Ygurna told me when we were alone below the solar, mixing more medicine for Stephen. It's not just our mothers who are different: we're not sisters at all."

"I know that, Alison."

It began to seep through Alison's mind then, that the surfaces she perceived, even with the aid of her inborn talents, were not always the surfaces of truth. She had never doubted the story her aunt had told her when Wildecent had first appeared at the hall; until this exact moment, she would have sworn on all the relics at nearby Saint Mared-Epon's Church that Wildecent believed the story, too.

Alison was not inclined to introspection. In moments of crisis she relied on her talents and those whom her talent told her to trust, but with Wildecent munching on her cheese Alison was left to puzzle things out on her own. And, since without the proper heritage the mysteries were unattainable, there could be only one possible explanation—

"You're Norman!"

Wildecent did not look up from her slivers of cheese. "I'm an orphan," she corrected, "I think. I don't remember it very well."

"You're Norman—just like them. No wonder you went along. You've got nothing to lose. What difference would treason against us Saxons mean to you!"

Carefully setting her knife to one side, Wildecent looked squarely into her sister's eyes. "At *your* urging, my dear sister. *You* were the one who was so certain there could be nothing wrong. God's blood, Alison, you were prowling around in his head! Why didn't you know it was going to be treason?''

"You're not my—" Alison cut her accusation short. She had felt her father's anxiety all afternoon and evening; overheard his arguments with Thorkel Longsword. She'd even listened to her aunt strip away the blood-bond between herself and Wildecent. She'd accepted their concerns and their suspicions without hesitation, she realized with some shame, despite her own certainty that Stephen was innocent.

Her talent was supposed to reveal the proper pathways. It was supposed to show her a way to move among people to make them smile at her and think that she brought peace and understanding with her. When it failed, when accommodating herself to the shape of everyone else's thoughts did not bring the pleasant warm feelings she craved, Alison's world threatened to collapse around her.

"There's no safe path," she whispered, unaware that her tumultuous thoughts were becoming vocal. "I'm sorry, but there's just no path at all—"

Wildecent nibbled through her small feast. She was aware of Alison's confusion—logically, if not intuitively or magically—and was content to leave her sister in a guilt-ridden mire. But if her decision to ignore Alison's murmuring was the product of a primitive desire for justice, it was not totally without compassion either.

While Alison moved through life governed by her own emotions and her mystical understanding of other's feelings, Wildecent had been content to wait quietly, watching and building a knowledge of patterns and habits. She learned their ways, while it was Alison's way to throw up gleaming walls of trusts and assumptions that shattered and were rebuilt with little lasting thought. In fact, as Wildecent understood things, her sister's beliefs glistened so brightly because they were always new, unlike her own, which were as dark and solid . . . as the walls of the castle where she had been born.

Wildecent considered the image a moment. It had a sense of truth, though she had never thought of it before and the walls of her memory were not that much different from the walls of that stout fortress.

She didn't belong here. In many ways that wasn't a surprise. Working through her memories had been rediscovery, rather than shining revelations. The notion that Lord Godfrey Hafwynder was her father had never been that important to her—perhaps she had never really believed that Alison's father had broken his vows to her mother.

Paradox reared its head: Alison *was* her sister; Godfrey Hafwynder *was* her father; and Lady Ygurna, who was truly only Alison's maternal aunt, *was* her mother. No amount of churning through dim memories could undo the last eleven years of her life. She could dream about that castle and those people she had named mother and father, but Hafwynder Manor was her only home. The anguish her five-year-old self had felt would be a pittance compared to what she would experience if, from this terrible day forward, her position here changed. Nothing—

Not even her real mother's smile . . .

Wildecent's thoughts went cold and hard. There was a weight against her thoughts, pushing her toward ideas she did not wish to consider, summoning images and memories that only hurt and added confusion. Something that pushed and made her thoughts seem strange and foreign—

Alison! Get out! Get out of my mind!

The weight yielded but did not vanish. What the outer world heard as a high-pitched trill became, in Wildecent's inner reality, a bellow of absolute rage. She sent forth a beast of her own imagining to drive the blue-eyed weight away and was not aware of launching herself from her stool as she did.

Alison tumbled backward before Wildecent touched her, extinguishing the candle with the sway of her skirts. Not even in the panic-stricken eternity while she had tried to get out of Stephen's shielded mind had she needed to face a physical as well as a mental challenge. She stopped leaning altogether and withdrew every tendril of curiosity she had ever spun around her sister, but it wasn't enough. Wildecent's wrath, once loosed, could not be restrained.

They rolled away from the hearth pummeling and tearing at each other. Wildecent had a fistful of Alison's hair and seemed likely to wrench it out when Alison's fingernails gouged across her face, just missing her eyes. They reversed their direction and came perilously, heedlessly close to the glowing embers; then Wildecent got both hands locked on Alison's shoulders and, despite her lesser stature, shoved the other woman onto her back.

Neither woman knew anything about fighting; neither thought to grab one of the hearth stones, pokers, nor even the knife that had fallen from Wildecent's skirts at the onset of her fury. Their heavy layers of skirts, tunics, and stockings not only protected them from many bruises but became quickly and completely entangled, so that as much energy went into freeing twisted sleeves as into scratching, tearing, slapping, or pulling.

There was pain, though, and had there been any light it would have revealed bloody scratches on both dirty faces. Their shouts and exclamations of rage dwindled down to ragged breaths as they struggled to continue a battle neither had the strength or skill to end.

Wildecent hauled herself upright, balancing on unsteady legs, listening for a sound—above her own gasping—that would tell her where Alison had gone. And Alison, who in trying to stand had given herself the hardest knock of the night against the underside of Bethanil's cutting table, wanted only to escape to the tower stairway. She pushed herself away from the table. Wildecent charged toward the sound of Alison's torn skirt dragging across the stones—and stunned herself in a collision with the massive table.

"Wili?" Alison gasped as Wildecent sighed and sank, in the darkness, to the floor. "Wili?" But she continued on her way to the stairs.

Lying on the floor, Wildecent heard her leave. The fight, as well as the wind, was gone from her. She listened to hear if Alison locked the door to their room and, when she didn't, slowly gathered her strength for the climb.

orning found both young women asleep with the curtained bed they usually shared standing empty. Alison was wrapped in her fur-lined travel cloak. She had draped herself against one side of the cope chest and slept with her head on her hands and a great bruise rising from her swollen lip. Wildecent slept against the opposite side of the chest, where she had left the wolf-fur blanket the evening before. Three ragged, blood-crusted scratches ran from her ear to her chin.

They awoke to the sound of Lady Ygurna shutting the door. By the looks on their faces, both were disoriented and ready to believe it had been a nightmare; then they felt their aches and each cast a furtive glance at the other before staring resolutely at their aunt. Lady Ygurna, who had climbed the stairs suspecting what she would actually find, controlled her desire to laugh at them by forcing her face into an even sterner mask.

"The common children of the borough have more sense than the two of you. Nay, harlots and slaves behave better."

She paused. Alison made an effort to untangle her hair and looked in disbelief at the many strands that came away in her fingers. Wildecent tried to sit up, but doubled over from the sharp pain along her breastbone. They still would not meet each other's eyes.

"Bethanil was in a fine state this morning, believing her hearths had been assaulted by demons and brigands during the night. The porridge was burned and tonight's stew promises to be worse. You know how Lord Hafwynder will feel about that."

"We're sorry," Alison said, than added: "I'm sorry."

"And I too."

93

They looked at each other, but the sight of bruises and cuts was too shameful to be endured. They went back to staring at the floor.

"That won't be enough. By rights I should have Leofric take a saddle strap to both of you, but that won't solve my problem. I don't want your father to be disturbed by your childishness. I would prefer to ignore the matter entirely, but you have done too good work on each other and on Bethanil's cooking to be denied. If he sees you, he will guess what has happened. You'll do your work in the solar and take meals in the kitchens for today at least."

The saddle strap was no idle threat. Though both young women remained downcast, they knew they were getting off lightly. Both knew to be suspicious of the reprieve, but only Alison was bold enough to mention it.

"Is my lord father already disturbed this morning?" she inquired with polite concern.

"He and Thorkel Longsword have been closeted with Brother Alfred since dawn. They are composing the message for Jean Beauleyas—Stephan's uncle and the lord at Torworden."

With the mention of Stephen's name, Alison's thoughts began to shift away from the previous evening. "And Stephen himself?" she asked, making a more determined effort to straighten her hair and gown.

"Better. If his bitten foot were on the other side he'd be hopping about with a crutch tucked under his arm. But there's no strength in his right arm and shoulder yet."

Wildecent also found thoughts of the young man distracting her from her other worries. She imagined the proud youth hobbling across the hall and imagined he'd become a difficult patient before he was fully recovered.

She gave a wan smile and a slight shake of her head to the thought.

"And what amuses you?" her aunt demanded.

"Nothing. No—only that I think he'll make a poor cripple. Once he's out of that bed we'll have the devil's time getting him back into it."

Suspicion flashed across her aunt's face, as if Lady Ygurna too believed that there was some unwholesome communication between her and Stephen. It brought back all the previous day's sense of injustice. Within the space of a heartbeat Wildecent resolved never to mention Stephen again in her conversation nor to let him run freely through her thoughts; then the suspicion vanished and her aunt was looking at them both with more ordinary displeasure.

"Now look what you've done. It's the reason I came down to the kitchens looking for you and I'd have forgotten it completely. Your lord father will have his own bedstead back. I said we'd get a pallet ready in the lower hall, but Thorkel Longsword, ever by your lord father's right hand, says the lad's not so thick with our language as he pretends; he ought not to be lying so close by Lord Hafwynder's hearth. Put him in the bowers with the housecarls and the servants, he says.

"But Lord Godfrey said he'd hear more gossip among the housecarls than he will near us, and this Norman uncle of his might take it poorly if he thinks we treat his ward less nobly than we would our Wessex neighbors."

"Then where will he go?" Alison asked.

Only the women and Lord Hafwynder had private rooms to which they could retreat and sleep. The housecarls and married servants slept in separate bowers, some of which were almost halls themselves while others were nothing more than windowless sheds. Slaves slept in the stables with the animals or in kitchen corners, where doubtless they had witnessed Alison and Wildecent's brawl in unquestioning silence. A few trusted men, like Thorkel Longsword, slept every night on a pallet in the great hall, within easy call of Lord Godfrey.

Guests slept in the hall as well, unless they were women or very ill. Even the homeless brethren of Saint Cuthbert's said their prayers behind temporary screens at the south end of the hall.

"We will clear one of the storerooms in the east gallery," Lady Ygurna explained. A grim smile spread across her face. "Moving the baskets from one place to another should be penance enough for whatever hurts you've caused each other.

"I'll be waiting for you." Lady Ygurna opened the door, then paused and turned to them again. "You needn't stop in the kitchens—as I said, Bethanil burned the porridge. You wouldn't enjoy eating it."

She shut the door quietly behind her.

Alison pushed herself to her feet and surveyed the huge blotches of soot on her skirt. The hem was loose in her right sleeve as well; a week's work of needlework dangled from a few frayed threads. She bound and knotted it carefully and offered her hand to Wildecent.

"I haven't felt this foolish since we fell through the roof of the chicken coop and all the hens got loose."

That spring day, many years ago, bloomed in Wildecent's memory. She started to laugh but her chest hurt too much. Whatever else she felt about her sister's talent—when it worked, when it was well targeted—it could banish doubt and gloom from her mind. Gripping Alison's offered hand tightly, she rose from the wolf-fur.

"I landed on my feet that time, not on the edge of the chopping block."

Her clothing was in much the same state as her sister's.

96

While Wildecent hobbled to the garderobe, where the washbasin and privy were secreted, Alison cranked open their wardrobe chest and went burrowing for fresh clothes. She was dressed in a long gown of dust-colored wool by the time Wildecent came around the corner again. There was a velvet-wrapped package in her hands.

"I promised," she said.

The velvet fell away as she extended her hand to reveal a narrow length of white cloth dotted with fanciful birds and flowers in jewellike colors. Wildecent took the embroidery as if it were a delicate, living thing.

"It's so beautiful."

"The deep colors will look better on you anyway."

Wildecent sat on the edge of the chest, lost in her thoughts, a fingertip tracing the silk stems as they twisted from bird to flower and back again.

"Come on. You'd better get dressed. Find something that already looks dirty if we're going to spend the day crawling about in the storerooms. There's something dun-colored down at the bottom."

After rewrapping the gift in its velvet and tucking it into the corner of the chest where she kept her most prized possessions, Wildecent hauled out a gown and overtunic. The gown had been made two years before; its hem brushed scandalously against the top of her ankles and it was tight across her breasts, but the tunic was loose enough and her house boots came halfway up her calves. She'd be decent enough for the storerooms.

They were midway down the stairs, surrounded by darkness, when Alison reached and took her sister's wrist.

"I won't lean on you again."

The movement and pressure on her wrist caught Wildecent off guard. Reflexively, she tugged her hand back.

"No, really," Alison insisted, gripping harder. "If you

don't want to tell me about . . . about what it was like before, then it's your secret. I won't lean, honestly."

Wildecent knew she should apologize for her own doubts and dark thoughts, but the words would not come. "I believe you" was all she could say in a tight, whispered voice.

"We're still sisters then? We could exchange blood. I've heard Thorkel and the housecarls talk about that. It's what the Vikings do before they go hosting. We could do that, and then it wouldn't matter," Alison continued enthusiastically. "We'd vow always to stay together, no matter what."

"Still sisters," Wildecent agreed with considerably less enthusiasm for any ritual that copied the Norsemen. She freed her wrist from Alison's fingers and followed the rest of the way in silence.

Their aunt had selected the storeroom to be cleared—a narrow, airless room that jutted out over the courtyard wallow where the pigs were kept. She had assembled a supply of baskets and sacks for the actual moving, but by the time the girls arrived in the gallery she was sitting on a box clutching her side again.

The older woman mastered whatever pain she endured. She supervised the packing and redistribution of the valuables, the sweetening of the room with fresh rushes and herbs and finally, well after midday, the fitting of an oiled sheet of parchment into the casement. The aromas from the kitchen vents and the sounds of the housecarls drawing their bowls in the hall below rose into the room. Lady Ygurna ignored them without apparent effort; not so the sisters.

"Just a small bowl—between the two of us?" Wildecent pleaded as they tightened the rope-net mattress for Stephen's new bed. The knot in her empty stomach was worse than the occasional ache across her chest.

"We'll have him in here first, then we'll see if there's anything left."

"It will have gone cold by then," Alison complained.

"Shhh," Wildecent whispered as they followed their aunt onto the gallery. "If you don't want any, I'll eat yours—clotted or not."

Alison grimaced and Lady Ygurna looked over her shoulder. The blond woman wisely decided against saying anything more.

Stephen wore his own tunic, bloodstained and torn at the shoulder as it was. He had been brought a washbasin; much of the gray, frostbitten skin had been scrubbed away. Brother Alfred had loaned him a small volume of saints' lives to fill the boring hours of his convalescence, but it lay unopened on the blankets beside him. He was staring at the translucent parchment when the women came into his room.

"You are to be moved across the way so the lord might have his own bedstead," the Lady Ygurna told him.

He looked at her, but it was plain he had not completely understood her meaning. Her aunt and her sister both looked at Wildecent, and Wildecent stared at her feet with her heart pounding.

"*Ah—Messir, tu . . . tu êtes,*" she began, pointing at Stephen, the bed and the partially visible gallery on the far side of the hall as she spoke.

This time Stephen understood, and with equally hesitant English stated his desire to *move* anywhere. Lady Ygurna and Alison understood as well.

"It's all that waving and pointing," Alison said with a laugh. "It's like the jugglers with their animals or the mummers who come at Twelfth Night."

Wildecent reddened. Traveling entertainers were not suitable persons for a young lady to be imitating. She was relieved, though—despite the embarrassment—to find that she was no longer openly suspected of intrigue and treason.

Stephen balanced on his good foot. He had spent a week in bed, half of that in a fevered delirium. His legs went wobbly, and he would have fallen had Alison not gotten an arm around him. In his homeland, which had a vastly different history than Saxon England, women were held to be dependent creatures, weaker not only in spirit but in body as well. He expected the Wessex lord and his knights to come through the door and carry him to the other room since, as the dizziness washed over him again, he knew he could not negotiate the distance himself.

But Saxon women, and their Celtic predecessors, had fought in the fields beside their men. They had gentled some over the generations, but not enough to call their menfolk when their own strength was adequate for the task. The young man yelped with surprise when Alison and Wildecent locked hands behind him and swept him into a basket made from their arms.

His ragged tunic, the only garment Stephen wore, barely covered his thighs. He twisted about in attempts to recover his decency and dignity until, in tones that needed no translation, all three women told him to be still. He was obedient while they walked along the gallery, but trust and courage deserted him when the girls, rather than carry him down one set of stairs and up the other, stepped out onto the walkway between the galleries that Wildecent had used to bring him his clothing. It was nothing more than two rough, wide planks balanced across the second-story beams of the hall, and his mind filled with every barbaric tale he'd ever heard about the English natives.

He knew better than to squirm; he closed his fists around whatever was nearest and prayed that God had not forgotten him. They had only a few feet more to transverse when Alison and Wildecent stopped short and cocked their heads.

"Horses," Alison confirmed. "A firm number of them, and running hard."

The girls moved faster then, dangerously fast in Stephen's opinion. He'd not close his eyes like a coward, but they were in the new room before he could draw another breath. They left him sitting in the bed and disappeared onto the gallery beyond his view.

He studied his new quarters. The fresh rushes and parchment window could not disguise the fact that this had never been a bedroom and, with its heavy, locking door, could easily become a prison. When he heard the large doors of the hall slam open and the galleries fill with the sounds of angry, outraged men he feared the worst. His battered foot shot pain up his leg as he swung it over the edge of the bed. He wished for his sword, both as a weapon and as something to lean on.

There were easily two dozen men in the great hall, stomping and slapping the ice from their clothes, shouting for not only Lord Hafwynder but for servants to stoke up the fires and bring pitchers of spiced ale. The sisters glanced at each other and, although they could easily have gotten the wood or the ale, they took a step back from the banister to surround themselves more completely with shadow. No more than half the men below were from the manor; the rest, the ones whose beards were the most ice-caked and whose voices roared the loudest, were from other noble homesteads in the shire.

Lord Godfrey Hafwynder entered his hall through the recessed back door. Thorkel was a half step behind him, and behind Thorkel came the rest of the housecarls, panting with the cold, for they had run straight from the bowers without their cloaks or heavy boots. Hafwynder climbed onto the seat of his chair—which was, in fact, primarily a speaking platform for these occasions and was not particularly comfortable for sitting. The great hall quieted, and a dark bear of a man from Edmund Saex's manor strode forward.

The news he bore was bad enough that he did not even attempt to couch it in skaldic poetry and hyperbole. Edmund's manor had been reduced to smoking timbers. They had come after dark and had breached the stockade before Edmund and his housecarls knew their danger. Saex had rallied his men and made a good fight, but they had been doomed by the losses they'd taken in the first moments of what became a blazing massacre. The dark man had seen his lord fall and lingered, despite Edmund's dying commands, to hear his lady and the other womenfolk carried off into the forests.

The hall was silent except for Saint Cuthbert's brethren behind their screens, who had already begun the prayers for the dead. In the east gallery Alison and Wildecent gripped each other's hand tightly: there was no fate worse than what had befallen the women of Edmund Saex's manor. Neither they, nor anyone else, took note when one of Lord Godfrey's men—a man called Tostig the Raven for his hair and sharp eyes—came to stand beside Edmund's man.

"It is not all told," the Raven said to his lord. "Whether before or after we do not know, but Godeshaft's cottage was taken as well."

A shout of pure anguish erupted behind Thorkel and a man not much older than Stephen pushed forward. "My wife! My mother . . . father! Dear God, my son!"

"Dead," Tostig said without meeting the fellow's eyes. "Your wife by her own hand when they came after her."

In time, perhaps, her courage might comfort him, but not now. He fell to his knees and set up a keening that brought the horror of what had happened within the hall itself. Thorkel whispered a command and another pair guided him away.

"They must be brought under the ax," Lord Godfrey announced, his voice strong though his face glistened with tears. "Do you ride with us?" he demanded of Saex's men.

The dark man shifted uneasily and brought forth a leather case. "We ride for Westminster and the king," he explained, drawing a blue-fletched arrow from the case. "It is like the other you showed us, but the man we captured was Northumbrian and, before he died, swore he was Earl Tostig's man."

This was Wessex, which had been a kingdom long before there'd been an English king. Loyalty flowed most naturally toward the family of the late Earl Godwin; it extended to the Norman-raised King Edward mostly because he'd had the sense to marry Godwin's daughter and make her queen. Treachery between Godwin's sons—Harold, now Earl of Wessex, and Tostig, who had been Earl of Northumbria until its lesser nobles revolted and forced the king to outlaw him—was the ultimate outrage in their hearts.

It pained Godfrey Hafwynder, as it had pained him since early autumn when the rupture between the brothers had occurred, but he was lord to his own first. With anarchy burning his cottages and slaying his people, he'd have to act alone.

"King Edward is dying," he shouted. "He was broken when the earls sided against each other. He rages and bites his tongue when the sons of Earl Godwin are mentioned to him." He waited until they stared at him before continuing. "I have seen it so," he said in a softer voice. "He cannot help us."

Lord Godfrey held his own men, but they had either traveled to Westminster with him or had heard from their fellows what the royal court was like this season. He had less luck with Edmund Saex's men, though they were clearly torn.

"We will appeal to the queen, then," the dark man said after a long hesitation. "Or we will ride until we find Earl Harold and learn the truth of this."

Godfrey cursed five hundred years of civilization. His ancestors would have hacked the beating hearts from the outlaws' breasts; his friends were a different breed.

"You'll find this shire in ashes when—if—you return," he warned. "Divided as we are, some thick-tongued Northumbrian devil will reduce the heart of Wessex to ashes not for politics, you lumbering fools, but because we make it tempting for them."

He skirted perilously close to treason then; some of his own men were growing uneasy. Longsword stepped forward, carefully brushing his lord's chair to get his attention.

"Let them go, my lord," he said in his deep voice that carried well without shouting. "The might of Wessex is not so reduced that we cannot ourselves do what must be done." He appealed to their pride with an outsider's accent and calmed the room with lies, though he could not keep Saex's men from leaving on their empty mission.

From the gallery the sisters watched their father step wearily down from his chair. They could no longer hear any one man's voice and were about to retreat for conversation themselves when a hand thrust between them and settled on Wildecent's shoulder.

"Say Jean Beauleyas has men."

"No," they hissed as one.

But Stephen was no longer their vulnerable patient. He hadn't understood every word—or even half the words—the Saxons had used, but he'd recognized that blue-fletched arrow.

"I go down myself."

He forced his injured foot to bear his weight. Pain added ten years to his face; the sisters had no doubt that he would do what he said.

second message was prepared with Stephen's help. Carefully worded, it could fall into anyone's hands without shedding light on Lord Hafwynder's troubled loyalties. And it would, Stephen assured them, release the knightly strength housed in Torworden. Godfrey sealed the parchment with an old personal seal rather than using the shire reeve's official seal, and slid it into the silver message case Stephen had carried with him.

It was late by then. Bethanil sent a platter of cold meats and several pitchers of warm ale to the great hall for Lord Hafwynder's pleasure. Tostig the Raven tried to lighten the mood with a skaldic tale of Wessex's better days. Even Thorkel Longsword unlimbered a pleasing voice for the drinking songs of his Viking fathers.

All to no avail. The hearth fire burned low. Housecarls carried Stephen to his storeroom bed; the women dosed his wounds and retreated to their quarters. Hafwynder Manor slipped into a fretful night's sleep.

At about the same time, a good day's ride to the northwest, Hafwynder's messengers bedded down for the night. They slept in lofts above their horses, for the inn that sheltered them was little more than a farmstead taking advantage of its closeness to the king's road. The farmer had recognized Lord Hafwynder's seal on the message the men carried, accepted their coins, and thrown an extra piece of mutton into the pot for them. But when they'd mentioned the outlaws and the fate of Saint Cuthbert's, the farmer and his family grew quiet and fearful.

It could have been the honest reaction of simple folk to threats against which they had no defense. But it could have been something else. Beneath their huddled cloaks the men wore their boots and their weapons. They posted a double watch and planned to be gone before dawn.

Another day's ride beyond the inn, in the stone tower that was Torworden Keep, a solitary man climbed to a barren room just below the roof. He wore a hooded gown of black silk cut in a vaguely Byzantine fashion. The wind pushed ice crystals across the map he spread on a rough-plank table. He brushed them away, unmindful of the cold, and bolted the only door to the room.

In silence he suspended a web of fine silver wire wrapped in red silk across the map and anchored it in the tower walls themselves. He placed candles at certain of the intersections and bonded others together with wax of various colors. From a gold chain around his neck he removed a tear-shaped crystal and set it in a bezel that rode along the wires. Then, with his basket of light completed, he unknotted an ordinary rope that hung beside the door. There was a wooden crash, and moonlight flooded down from the roof across the map.

Entering that moonlight, Ambrose, adept of arcane Eastern sciences and unordained deacon of the Roman Church, prepared to search for his friend Stephen. The silken wires surrounded his head like a crown. His extended fingers touched soft, black wax. Ice sparkled in the candlelight as he closed his eyes and dove deep within himself to invoke a power that owed nothing to God or nature, but called itself a mortal's will. His fine hair rose in a nimbus; his skin went numb to all sensations except those conveyed by the basket of light.

Stephen wasn't expected back from Pevensey for several days; no one else in Torworden suspected the mission had gone awry or that Ambrose was not in the tiny cell he had appropriated for his personal use. Not even Ambrose himself knew what had set the doubts in his head—only that he had begun the search four nights ago and the map yet remained blank.

The crystal began to vibrate, then to slide along the wires. Moonlight, entering at the broader end of the stone, was concentrated into a silver dot that wandered uncertainly across the parchment. Wind blew out one of the candles, but that was of no importance. Ambrose had achieved rapport with his machine and would search until success or moonset stopped him.

He had set the focus in Stephen's mind some ten years before—when he was a raw young man himself, freshly appointed to tutor the boy. Stephen had been a child of seven with boundless energy, ceaseless curiosity and a tendency to get lost that terrified his parents. Ambrose had rescued his pupil from bell towers and irate bulls for many years, until the boy had outgrown his wanderings— or perhaps his sense of direction had finally improved. But once set, the focus should burn so long as life flowed in Stephen's veins. Armed with the basket and the map, Ambrose was confident he could find his friend.

There was a brief resonance, a flicker of Stephen's thoughts, as there had been several times before. Enough to convince the adept that the search should be continued but not enough to burn the moonlight onto the map. He drew the tingling deeper into his body, perilously close to his beating heart, and pushed harder.

It was there: a steady rhythm of pulses beating against the basket of light, as distinctive as the sound of his voice or the swing of his sword. The crystal ceased vibrating; a silver pinpoint seared the parchment. Ambrose began to relax and noticed, as he did, that the focus had changed.

Ten years is a long time. Stephen had certainly changed; perhaps it meant nothing that the focus was not exactly as he had left it. But the moon remained high in the heavens. Moving by itself, the bezel rotated and the lance end of the crystal pointed at the moon.

Ah—an old woman. One of the elder ones hiding deep in Wessex?

Lady Ygurna tossed and moaned in her sleep. She threw the blankets to one side. The cold brought a measure of peace to her dreams, then she turned to face the creature made from light.

"Lord?" her dream-self whispered. Not the Lord Christ nor the Lord God, his father, but the ancient one, Cernunnos, whose name was ever in her thoughts though it never crossed her lips.

He faced her, his brilliance growing until she fell to her knees and hid her face behind her hands. She felt the eye of his mind upon her; the cold reached to her bones and she grew afraid.

What have you here?

Ygurna brought forth the boxes of her memory—the inheritance passed in secret for not hundreds but thousands of years: before the Saxons, before the Romans. He was, after all, her god for whom she had waited a lifetime.

A Dancing Stone? the diety inquired. *Here? What star do you sight upon? What do you draw down?*

Knowledge was secret because it was power and danger both. It was passed along with suspicion and sanction. The stones belonged to Cernunnos; his blood had run through their meanders. Within Lady Ygurna the fear became fire; she raised her head and revealed her secrets.

What sort of Cernunnos could this be? The Winter Lord without horns? Without holly and mistletoe? No Winter Lord at all.

The light remained but its form changed. No longer

man-shaped, it manifested wings, claws and a spiraling tail. Gaping jaws parted to spew burning gold light.

"Ceridwen!" Lady Ygurna called—but it was a call without power. Her faith had been broken in the false god's light. She had only her own strength, and it had never been the old way to fight alone. Goddess and priestess had shared their power but no one had taught the priestess how to fight a raging god.

It was too late to learn. She hurled the fire back at him but it was weakly thrown and easily evaded. His fires burned the knowledge from her mind, shaming her worse than any mortal rape. Retreating, slowly and painfully, there was one last secret she strove to keep from him. He took that, too, without knowing its price.

You shall die, he said in an oddly compassionate voice as his light began to fade.

"I already knew that," she replied to the darkness.

A daughter. Somewhere near—a daughter of the spirit.

Alison embraced her pillow; the soft, worn linen caressed her cheek. She pulled it closer to her and her dreams, as they did so frequently of late, turned toward Stephen.

He was all brightness and light before her. If she had to have a husband, then it would be him. They would be happy together—with children and the wealth of Hafwynder Manor to support them.

Would you share everything with him? a voice she took for her own conscience asked.

"Of course," she replied without hesitation. "He will be my lord husband and I will love him as well as obey him."

He grew brighter with happiness and although she

III

could not see his face for the brilliance, she knew he was smiling.

Would you wait—or could you share everything with him now?

Since she knew the voice was her own conscience, there was no surprise that she understood its precise meaning. This was not a question of her chastity but of that secret inheritance she had from her mother. She considered a moment and realized that she was called upon, by her conscience, to do something about that unnatural, smooth shield clamped down over her beloved's thoughts.

Alison was not a healer, though Lady Ygurna had told her that the gift of healing had once been within the inheritance. Still, she had never perceived another living soul as she perceived Stephen's. The young man appeared before her; she was not afraid.

She walked toward him—that bouncing, floating movement that passes for walking in dreams where you have not given yourself the power of flight. Her arms extended to touch him and for a moment his radiance dazzled her eye. She felt the shield, though she could not see it, and guided by instinct alone, used her inheritance to reshape and dissolve it.

The shield was resilient, fighting back with a will of its own, but Alison had expected that. She bore down harder and it began to give way to natural but unique irregularities of conscience. The light flickered; she found herself in a viscous darkness far worse than she had experienced beneath Stephen's shield before. Alison lashed out and discovered a cool, blue light of her own that hung like spears and swords in the blackness.

Her light struck deep into some vital part of the darkness. It roared at her, a sound felt rather than heard, and closed in around her. Alison's lances held. The darkness tore and expelled her into another realm that was only as dark as the starlit sky.

Still dreaming, Alison contemplated the writhing emptiness that had been her radiant beloved. Her first efforts at healing could only be termed disastrous.

"I'll be back," Alison promised her conscience. "I'll make it right again—soon."

I'll see you in Hell came the reply, and, as darkness withdrew into itself, she began to wonder if it had been her conscience after all.

The basket of light shuddered. Light was gone from many of its interstices; the teardrop crystal careened wildly along the silken wires. There was barely enough strength in the waning moonlight to repair the damage. The crystal jerked its way through the web and swung slowly to point again at the moon.

One more. Another daughter, or a sister. Weaker, by all accounts. Perhaps even a serving wench . . .

Wildecent slept curled in a crescent, one hand clutching the edge of the mattress. The wolf-fur blanket was pulled high above her neck so only wisps of her hair and the tickle of the fur as she breathed would have betrayed her presence had there been light enough for any eyes to see her. Dreams, however, did not need eyes, and this one bore its own light.

She did not awaken, but she knew her mind too well to believe for an instant that this was something she had imagined.

"Alison?"

It did not answer but coalesced into a vaguely man-shaped bundle of light and sparkling energy. And though man-shaped could also be woman-shaped, she knew it was not her sister, nor anyone else she knew.

"You don't belong here." She contracted from a crescent to a sphere—the safest shape she could think of—and settled back at a greater distance to study it.

I seek a friend.

"I'm not a friend to the likes of you, dream-beast. You want my sister or someone like her. I'm head-blind." Wildecent addressed it with great confidence, not noting the paradox that the head-blind should not be bothered with such spiritual manifestations.

Is it your sister who tells you that you are head-blind? It cast a slur across the word *sister.*

"I do not need to be told what I am, spirit. I want nothing from your kind and magic save my own peace." She withdrew deeper into the sphere, determined to wait until it faded away. When some time—enough time, she hoped, though with dreams it was always difficult to be certain—had passed she rose to the surface of the sphere again.

You lie. You are, yourself, a seeker. I offer friendship.

It was less bright now, and more manlike with a face she might almost remember if she saw it again. It, or he, had leaned, as well, while she had been hidden for it radiated the truth of her inmost desires. There was little point in denying it.

"That wasn't fair," she accused.

Haven't they told you the secrets but not how to use them? Was that fair?

"I cannot use them. I may serve the mysteries but I cannot use them. I have already been honored." She repeated what Lady Ygurna and Alison had always said, though the words rang hollow and bitter.

The man of light laughed aloud. *Knowing is all the talent*

you need! Power comes in many forms. If you truly know the mysteries, I shall come and teach you.

He was fading and growing smaller. Wildecent did not mean to be tempted; did not wish to take the bait he dangled in front of her. She said nothing, but he saw into her heart in the moment that he vanished.

he tower bedroom was pitch dark. The thin slivers of moonlight that penetrated the shutters had vanished. Wildecent lay under the wolf-fur, shivering from something more than wintry cold. Her sister had whimpered twice, but the sounds of her breathing now were barely louder than the faint, icy breezes coming down from the forests.

Wildecent pulled the blanket up over her head and knotted her fingers in the long fur, but the trembling would not stop. There were new ideas in her head; new vantage points from which to see Alison and Lady Ygurna; new hope that the doors that had always been closed and triple-locked might yet open for her. And, for all that, the trembling just got worse, and the knot of fear in her stomach drew tighter until it seemed it would cut her in two.

Seeds fell on fertile ground, and Wildecent, not unwillingly—please God, his saints, his angels and all the pagan fairies to forgive her, not unwillingly—nurtured them. That face, with all its blurred features, burned in her memory, and she began to imagine what it would be like when she knew how to lean back.

Alison turned and muttered in her sleep as she tugged on the blanket that Wildecent had almost completely appropriated for herself.

"Even if she's not my sister," Wildecent murmured, not so much to God or his minions but to her own paralyzed conscience, "she has always been my friend." She made her fists unclench; the wolf-fur slid away from her shoulders.

The edge of the blanket tickled past her nose. She grabbed a corner before it disappeared completely. "It isn't fair," she complained. "Nothing's fair—and only God is perfect."

Alison mumbled again and twisted about until their shoulders were touching beneath the blanket. Wildecent relaxed and intended to go back to sleep herself, but sleep had become foreign to her. She imagined herself as a wise woman using the knowledge and power the stranger would awaken in her. She imagined herself seated in her father's chair explaining the mysteries to her sister and her aunt. She imagined herself with Stephen, dressed in magnificent furs and velvets, living in a castle that would make the king's new church at Westminster seem small by comparison. And nothing Wildecent imagined brought her one whit closer to sleep.

Much later, well aware that her flights of fancy had cost her a night's rest, Wildecent thrust her hand between the bed curtains and saw the gray dawn coming through the shutters.

It crossed her mind, even as she slid stealthily out of the bedstead and crept about the chilly room gathering her clothes, that she could have awakened Alison and shared the visions with her. Hadn't her sister, and even her aunt, always said it was only because she couldn't learn that they wouldn't teach her? Shouldn't they be glad with her that she had even *had* a mystic visitation and rejoice when they learned what she had been told? But she moved in silence and laced her boots on the landing after she had closed the bedroom door behind her.

She descended slowly, not through her usual distrust of the dark stairway but to conceal her approach from whoever might be breaking their fast in the kitchens. She needn't have worried. Only Bethanil and her drudges were awake. They moved about the hearths and carving blocks in dead-eyed habit, uninterested in which of their masters or mistresses was wandering about. Emboldened by their inattentiveness, Wildecent slipped behind a curtain and filled her sleeves with dried apples and berries.

In the summertime, when getting out of bed was not painful, restlessness had sometimes—once or twice, at least—dragged her away from the manor stockade in search of peace. She had ridden her pony bareback to the top of the grassy barrow behind the manor and watched the sun come into their valley. But today, with her thoughts bubbling as if they had their own source and energy, even if the ground weren't frozen and covered with snow, she would have been more foolish than restless to go beyond the stockade, where the outlaws roamed.

Hafwynder Manor offered community; there were relatively few private retreats within its walls—none at all for the housecarls, drudges, or their families—and most of those were too uncomfortable in this cold season. Wildecent began her search in the Roman room, which, with the manor still asleep, should be empty.

The room was dark but not quiet. Once Wildecent's eyes adjusted again to the darkness she could see the faint glow in the mosaic where light seeped up from the bolt-hole. She heard the sounds of glass clinking against glass and then the pain-filled wrack of Lady Ygurna's worsening cough. Freezing against the doorway, she resisted the impulse to run either toward or away from her aunt.

She's going to die. The realization was not a surprise. Lady Ygurna had taught her students too well; they both knew how to read the Crab's symptoms. Only Wildecent's inability to imagine the manor without her aunt had prevented her from seeing the obvious, but now, with the stranger's promises echoing in her mind, that cough's meaning was crystal clear.

Slipping the bolt quietly behind her, she made her way back across the courtyard. The kitchens were warm and filled with the lesser members of the household. Bethanil offered a bowl of piping hot porridge, which Wildecent refused. Wildecent lingered a few moments at the base of the tower stairway. Always in the past she and Alison had shared their deepest turmoil, but not this time. She opened the outer door and scurried along the cloister to the great hall and the sanctuary of the upper storerooms where, if one didn't mind dust or darkness, privacy could usually be found.

The door to the first storeroom was ajar. Wildecent had her hand on the latch to pull it shut before she remembered Stephen.

"Wildecent?"

The room was dark: there was only her silhouette in the doorway but he had recognized her.

"Are you all right?"

"Bored, with a shoulder that aches and a foot that's not my own. Come talk with me?"

She hesitated, her lusty fantasies of the previous night grating against the rules that governed a maiden's behavior. Stephen meant something to the spirit that had promised the mysteries to her, though it had never mentioned his name. The guilt rose up again, but Lady Ygurna was dying and the future would no longer resemble the past no matter how guilty or shamed she felt. Wildecent shut the door behind her.

Stephen's night lamp was long extinguished but in a box they had not moved to the next room there were tallow candles packed in straw and the chatelaine pouch hanging from her belt contained both flint and steel. She set the candle on the little table by the bed and sat on the candle box.

"You don't sound very foreign anymore," she commented, drawing her feet up under her skirts.

"I don't have a headache anymore, either. I have been at Torworden since the summer," he added, as if that was an explanation. "I know Latin, Danish and both the *langue d'oc* and *langue d'oïl*. This *English* of yours isn't so very difficult."

"She leaned on you, didn't she. That's how you know."

He was silent a moment. "Is that what you call it—what your sister did, I mean?"

Wildecent nodded. "What I call it, anyway. She wasn't supposed to. Lady Ygurna said it was dangerous because you've been protected."

"Protected? Jesus wept! I touch her hand and the next thing I know something is inside my head. What manner of protection would you call that?"

"You *knew* and you took something from her in return."

"You can't? I mean, you wouldn't know if your sister had touched your memories or had changed them in some way?"

It was Wildecent's turn to hesitate. "No," she admitted, and the silence lengthened.

"I think I like your ways better."

"My ways? I have no 'ways'."

Stephen laughed. "Your hands always move when you talk. I think I could understand what you said no matter what language you used."

His laughter burned. Self-consciously, Wildecent wedged her hands between her legs. She had come to the storerooms seeking privacy and, though she found Stephen a pleasant distraction, she didn't want to discuss herself, her sister, nor, certainly, anything resembling the mysteries with him. Her hands slipped free as words formed in her thoughts. She shoved them back and changed the subject.

"What's France like?" she asked.

"What France?" he replied, laughing again. "A weak,

mad Capetian king, a poor collection of churches and students in Paris? There's no real Frankish power anymore."

Wildecent felt her Wessex isolation and ignorance. Her hands slipped free again and she no longer tried to confine them. "Aren't the Normans French? Aren't you sworn to a French king? You speak French."

"No to the first and to the second as well. And no Norman is truly Frankish, though you Saxons seem unable to understand this. It's not a hundred years since my uncle's grandfather came hosting down from the Danish lands. The Capetian king gave Normandy to Rollo to keep the rest of the Vikings out of Paris—and so it remains to this day. What the Capetians think is of no importance to Normandy."

"Your uncle, the man at Torworden, he's a Norman— but you're not?" The dark-haired girl gave her own superior laugh. "That's close kinship whether through your mother or your father: you're Norman."

He lifted his hands in mock surrender. " 'Til this year I'd never seen Norman castle nor the Channel. I've always dwelled further south: Aquitaine, Angoulême, Provence. Now I'm in a foreign land with my uncle, but when Ambrose and I leave, I'll go back to make my own home."

Wildecent shuddered as if a cold draft had struck her back, though the tallow candle never flickered. Stephen did not seem to notice, but continued to explain life beyond the Channel.

"If I'm Norman, then maybe there's no Normandy, only places where Rollo's men and descendants have settled." He smiled at a private joke. "Marry their women, take their lands, their churches, and their languages too. Ambrose taught me Danish; no one in Normandy speaks it anymore. *Langue d'oc, langue d'oïl*—we speak whatever we hear. But you should understand that—I've heard you use both with me."

"I know nothing of these 'ocs' and 'oïls.' "

"But you've used them, and save for that priest I haven't heard anything but English spoken here."

"I was not born here," she told him simply, tucking her hands underneath her again.

"Where? Anjou? Poitou? Or in the north?"

"I don't know. I've always lived here, I just wasn't *born* here. You were babbling with your fever and I recognized some of the words, that's all." Her hands were already uncomfortable and his curiosity always pressed in directions she did not want to go. "I wish I hadn't," she snapped. "It's been nothing but trouble for me since you got here and set me listening and remembering."

He apologized, but Wildecent had retreated into herself and ignored him. The fruit tucked in her sleeves had begun to itch. Continuing to ignore him, she took a slice of apple and chewed it slowly.

Stephen fell silent and watched her. His recent life had been a near constant bustle of knightly training, lessons with Ambrose or the minutiae of service to his uncle, Beauleyas. His wounds were nearly mended, and his need for rest had vanished when he had hobbled down to Lord Godfrey and offered Torworden strength against the outlaws who had killed Normans as well as Saxons. Boredom did not begin to describe his mood as the apple smell wafted across the room.

"I think I'm starving," he called loudly enough to make her jump.

She affected not to hear him and he tried to imagine her thoughts. He gave up after a few moments. Ambrose, among others, taught that women didn't have thoughts that a man could understand. These women of Hafwynder Manor were like no others he had ever met, but the precept held true: he didn't understand them.

He was not completely ignorant of the distaff half of his

species, however. In the castles and courts where the embryonic *language d'oc* was spoken, flirtation was already becoming an art. That which Ambrose's vows prevented him from discussing with Stephen had already been explained, even demonstrated, to the young man several years earlier.

To be certain, the blond girl, the Saxon Alison who had boldly invaded his mind, was more fascinating—her face was superimposing itself on other memories of other women—but Wildecent was far easier to tease.

"I say: I think I'm starving. An apple, just one piece of your apple, fair Eve, will save me."

The candlelight glinted as her eyes glanced toward him behind the curtain of her dark hair. She swallowed and put another piece in her mouth.

"Wildecent, a piece, a single piece? Please? I am truly hungry."

She sighed and came over to the bed, within his grasp.

"I guess it's not your fault," she conceded, dropping the wrinkled discs into his hand.

They fell to the blanket as he moved with alarming speed to catch her wrist in a grip that, while not painful, Wildecent could not break. He began to sing.

Most of the poem was beyond Wildecent's childish understanding of any Frankish dialect but the few words she caught were enough to capture the bawdy sense of the lyric. Letting the rest of the fruit fall to the bed, she used her other hand against his encircling fingers, but hands agile enough to spin fine wool were not strong enough to loosen a knight's sword grip. Her ears burned with embarrassment; she begged him to stop as he began another verse.

"They'll hear you!" she exclaimed, tugging uselessly against him.

She'd heard Saxon ballads far coarser than his poem;

even sung them with everyone else in her father's great hall after the feasts, when mead and ale were flowing freely. She'd been alone with every man in the shire and with her sister poured bathwater over Godfrey's peers and their sons. But Stephen was breaking all the rules with his laughing eyes and gentle pressure against her skin.

"Haven't you caused me enough trouble?"

He abandoned the lyric, clasped his other hand around hers and brought her fingers to his lips. "You should smile more often, demoiselle," he whispered.

Wildecent's hand was free—it rested on his of *its* own will, if not *hers*—and she was smiling back at him. Swallowing hard, she jerked her hand back and fled the room. The ballads were filled with tales like this: a shy young woman, of gentle birth and innocence, snared and ruined by the laughing eyes of the strange guest. The stranger was always handsome and smooth-spoken, and the songs never ended happily.

She took the kitchen corner at a run and, thinking she saw Alison's blond braids near the hearth, bolted up the dark stairs to the privacy of her own bedroom. The door was closed behind her before she registered her sister's blue eyes staring at her from beside the clothes chest.

"What's the matter?"

"Everything!"

The word was out of her mouth before Wildecent could reconsider it and with its escape came the possibility that Alison would lean. Never before had there been so much swirling about in her mind that she didn't want to share with her sister. Still, Alison's talents tended to operate best on a person's surface thoughts and she might not lean at all if her curiosity were quickly satisfied. Wildecent fixed on the least of her problems, the one that had sent her scurrying back to this room in the first place.

The story emerged in staccato bursts that carefully dissembled and rearranged the actual events. "I couldn't sleep. I didn't want to wake you so I went to the store-rooms—"

"Stephen!" Alison was on her feet and pacing. "Has his fever returned? Was he ailing?"

"No, nothing like that. He's probably never felt better." Her tone shifted to a bitter sarcasm that Alison did not notice. "He said he was hungry. I'd got some fruit from the pantry and offered to share it with him. He *grabbed my wrist*, Alison, and held it while he sang—and then he *kissed* my hand!"

Wildecent had begun her tale with one hope: that her sister would believe that Stephen was the cause of all her anxiety. She hadn't had time to consider how Alison might react once she believed. The blond girl thumped down on the chest and began lacing her boots with a vengeance.

"He kissed you, you say? Just what sort of song did he sing?"

"I couldn't understand all the words but it seemed much as our men sing when they've been drinking mead by the hearth."

"Did he *mean* any of it?"

Alison's eyes had narrowed, her hands rested stiffly atop her hips when she stood up; belatedly, Wildecent realized her sister was not going to have any sympathy, only jealousy.

"How should I know?" she replied defensively.

"How should you not? He kissed your hand. Was it a jest or not? Was he smiling, laughing? How did you feel?"

Her own feelings about the matter were something Wildecent did not wish to examine herself, much less with Alison. "I— I was outraged. We've taken him in, healed his wounds and his gratitude is to compromise me!"

"You must have encouraged him," Alison concluded,

wrapping her cloak over her shoulders with a flourish. "He wouldn't have sung to you or kissed your hand if you hadn't been bold."

Wildecent recalled Stephen's claim that her sister's face was haunting him. You put yourself in his memories, she thought, more amazed than angry. You mean for him to think of no other, and there's no use telling you otherwise. Either I was bold or he betrayed you. You've set it so he has no other choice.

"I don't know what got into me," Wildecent explained, which was not truly a lie, though truth was no longer uppermost in her mind. "I was awake because I'd had a dream and from the dream I'd gotten . . . Well, I was thinking about Stephen."

These first threads of dissembling and evasion had a profound effect on Alison. The hardness melted from her face and she embraced her sister with a sad tenderness.

"You've been misused, Wili," the blond girl whispered.

The transformation was more than Wildecent had expected, more than anything her imagination could conjure. She rested her chin warily on Alison's shoulder and waited for such explanations as might be forthcoming.

"I had a dream, too," Alison confessed. "About Stephen. I saw that shield lying over him . . . and how it made him head-blind, like you. And I thought that I could cure him, and that maybe it wasn't a dream after all, but something else because there was another voice— a voice I mistook for my own heart's speech—saying I should. I went below the shield, like I did before—only without touching him or being rightly awake at all—and knew I could set things aright, but the voice attacked me.

"Oh, Wili, there's something terrible that's got hold of Stephen and when it couldn't bend me it reached for you."

Alison's arms tightened about Wildecent's shoulders and, with little hesitation, Wildecent responded in kind. The dark-haired girl could fit everything her sister said into thoughts and dreams even though she did not, could not, reach the same conclusions.

"You must be careful, Wildecent. Whoever, whatever, has involved itself with Stephen is very powerful and very dangerous. You should have a charm or a talisman to protect you but, Wili, we can't go to Lady Ygurna, so you'll just have to be very careful."

And with that, at least, Wildecent could wholeheartedly agree.

CHAPTER TWELVE

t was midnight three days later, and the huge bole of the Yule log had scarce burned through its heavy, black bark. Godfrey's prized high-backed chair had been pushed under the gallery and its place taken by a small altar upon which several candles burned around a brightly painted cross. It was Christmas Eve and though, because of the death of Father Ralf, there was no one to say the Mass, prayers would be repeated until dawn. Lord Hafwynder's entire household was there in the great hall and all of his cottagers as well, for the destruction of Godeshaft's home and the brutal murder of his family had convinced Lord Godfrey that his protection extended no further than the stout timber of his stockade.

They stood while they prayed, then knelt in the rushes when standing became too wearying. Lord Godfrey knelt in front of the altar with the homeless brothers of Saint Cuthbert's, the hearth fire warming his back. He would have much preferred being in bed or, if he was to pass another sleepless night, doing something useful—like whetting his sword or fletching his arrows. A night on his knees held no attraction.

Not that he wasn't a good Christian. He was as God-fearing a man as any of his neighbors. Hadn't he gone so far as to endow Saint Cuthbert's from his own purse in the first place, and hadn't he supplied the brethren and their priest with meat and ale? They prayed and he protected; it was—in his traditional opinion—the natural order of things. To be sure, he would not have passed this Yuletide night without a great log burning on his hearth, but he would certainly not have felt the need to be here before it with rivers of sweat coursing through the scratchy wool of his second-best tunic.

King Edward might think it seemly for a man to spend his time in devout contemplation and a chaste, monkish life, but Edward was a king, anointed with sacred oils like a priest, and hardly the model for an ordinary man like himself. Besides, Lord Godfrey mused while he should have been praying, where had prayer gotten King Edward? A married man with no children—with a virgin wife, if certain rumors were true—and a king about to leave his lands and subjects with no clear choice of heir.

So it was, while Brother Alfred led them through a seemingly endless cycle of Latin prayers, that Godfrey Hafwynder's thoughts took an uncharitable, very nearly unchristian, turn. He had good reason to begrudge his king and his saintly obsessions. Edmund Saex's men had passed the manor shortly before noon and their tidings had not been glad. King Edward, when he was not lost in his own mind or raving, spoke only of his great new church at Westminster, which was to be consecrated on December 28. He was too ill to sit on a horse, too ill to eat, too ill to consider the muddied succession, but not too ill to order the banners and parades to accompany the consecration.

The earls of England, and many lesser men, had gathered at Westminster, not for Christmas nor for the consecration of the church, but to watch the man who had been England's king for more than twenty years make an end of his life. Earl Harold, Earl of Wessex and Godfrey Hafwynder's liege lord, was at Westminster supposedly as Duke William of Normandy's oath-man to ensure that England's throne was delivered to the duke once Edward was dead. But Harold had sent a simple message to the Lord of Hafwynder Manor: *Hie yourself to Westminster. There will always be outlaws in winter; Edward dies but once. I need my oath-men beside me*.

Lord Hafwynder had exchanged harsh words with Earl

Harold's messenger. Treasonous words, perhaps, for Godfrey understood that Harold meant to take England for himself and not deliver it to the Normans. But as much as Lord Godfrey disliked the foreigners, he disliked oath-breakers even more. He hadn't proclaimed that his own oaths to Harold were null, but he hadn't hied himself to Westminster, either. He was staying right here behind his wooden stockade, protecting his lands and his household, because, like Edward, they could only die once. The Saxon lord's hope were now fixed to the northwest, to Torworden and such Norman might as it could provide.

Scratching the raw places along his spine, he got to his feet and glowered defiantly at the altar.

Lady Ygurna, who stood at his side, caught sight of the fire in his eyes and looked away. She had stood since the log was lit and would stand until dawn—partly because it was less painful but partly because this was her last Yule fire and she would not waver.

Her brother-in-law's argument with Edmund's men had been conducted in loud voices at the open gate of the stockade. There wasn't a man, woman, or child in the hall who didn't know every word that had been said, nor one who couldn't guess their lord's thoughts as his fists flexed by his sides.

She prayed for him, knowing he'd need all the prayers and luck he could get. Like her lord, though, Lady Ygurna stood vigil because it was expected of her and not through any deep religious conviction—not a *Christian* conviction, at any rate. The Yule log itself had been here before the Saxons, before Christ himself; it had been here when it was necessary to kindle a bonfire in darkest winter to remind the sun to begin its homeward journey to summer.

Lady Ygurna accepted that a god could have a child, a son, who would live among men, take their sins upon himself, and be their willing sacrifice. The Christian novelty was to say that it was necessary only once in the life of the world rather than once a year—or more often in bad times. The Latin did not bother her either, for she said her own prayers in the forgotten Celtic language of her mothers and grandmothers.

The dwindling threads of an almost vanished heritage had been woven through Lady Ygurna's life. In her own childhood Christian priests had fallen away from their vows. The Norse Vikings were reluctant to set aside their bloody beliefs for the god of meek priests who scattered before their axes. There had been signs of decadence and dissolution and a rebirth of hope within the hidden priesthood. The people of the land had begun to look for something else. Her sister's daughter was once destined to be a priestess of the highest order within a restored hierarchy.

But the Vikings accepted a religion they neither believed in nor respected, and the Normans, those same warriors her brother-in-law regarded with such suspicion, had embraced a newly reformed Christianity and sent it to England with Edward. Throughout Edward's long reign she had cherished a dwindling hope, but no longer. Her beliefs had failed her and she had failed them. She had betrayed her secrets to the demons of her dreams, and Alison would be lucky to find herself a strong husband.

Her people, the remnants of both the Celts and the romanized Britons, were going to vanish altogether along with their conquerors. A few tribes might endure in the hills of Wales or on the Cornish coasts, slipping closer to legendary Avalon and sunken Lyonesse with each season, but the Normans and the others of their ilk would recognize her people only by dancing stones and spirals—none of which they would know how to use safely.

Lady Ygurna's eyes misted with tears. The altar candles

took the form of the basket of light from her dreams. Her strength faltered and she reached for Lord Godfrey's arm as the altar bell chimed another hour's passage.

Lord Godfrey recoiled from her gray, emotionless face and her wide, terrified eyes.

"Enough!" he bellowed as Brother Alfred intoned the beginning of another cycle of prayers.

Heads came up slowly as the rest of the household roused from a trancelike state. Most were here because the lord and lady of the manor were here; few had paid Brother Alfred any attention, but all were instantly curious and exchanging excited glances with their neighbors.

"Enough of praying!" Lord Hafwynder stalked toward the gallery shadows, towing Lady Ygurna behind him and pushing her into his chair. "Or we'll be saying prayers for the dead!"

Brother Alfred clutched the bell in his fist; it gave a muted clanging as his hand shook. "My lord"—his voice went shrill with surprise—"it's the eve of our Savior's birth. We cannot hear the Mass, but we *must* recite the prayers."

"Go and recite them, then, in the stables where he was born, and let the women and children who wish to join you do so. But the men remain here."

The cleric's head bobbed up and down like a bird's but he scuttled back to the altar and whispered with his peers. "We cannot move the altar. It is you, my lord, who must leave this hall if you will not join us."

Disbelief was nearly audible as the men and women of Hafwynder Manor shared wide-eyed stares. It was unthinkable to put a lord out of his hall—it was a blood offense—yet Brother Alfred held his ground beside the altar and their lord was looking nervous. Even Alison and Wildecent linked their hands together for support in what figured to be a blasphemous confrontation.

132

But Lord Hafwynder backed down. "To the kitchens then, where there's food and ale and a hearth as warm as this one," he said in as polite a roar as his temper could manage. "Thorkel, Godeshaft—the rest of you—let's set about protecting these worshipers from themselves."

"Lord Godfrey," Lord Ygurna whispered from the chair. "It's passed now. Let the brothers go on with their service and prayers. It's only until dawn."

"Peace, woman!" her lord commanded. "My mind is made up. We've had enough of praying and thinking about the coming of God and his son. It's nigh time to prepare for the coming of those outlaws in the hills, or Earl Harold's men, or the Norman bastard William's men—or Earl Tostig's friends from Norway."

The litany of temporal powers arrayed against the manor and the kingdom got their attention and their silence; even Brother Alfred paused to make the sign of the cross. Lord Hafwynder pushed open the back door leading to the kitchens and disappeared through it without another glance over his shoulder. There was a moment of whispered hesitation; then the men, led by Thorkel Longsword, shouldered their way out of the crowd and followed their lord. Stephen hesitated a few moments longer, but was unable to stomach being the only man left with the clerics and women. Limping badly, but moving without cane or crutch or someone hovering at his side, he dragged himself out into the night air for the first time since his arrival at the manor.

Brother Alfred looked over his reduced flock and concealed whatever dismay he might have felt. He rang the bell again and took up the Latin chanting where it had been interrupted. The brothers' droning was louder now, with fewer bodies to absorb it, but whatever magic it had possessed was gone, as even Alfred himself was seen to glance away from the altar and toward the unopening door to the kitchens.

"Do you want to stay here?" Alison whispered when the bell had signaled the passage of another hour.

They stood alone now at the front of the household, looking past the Yule log to the altar. Not long after the men had left they'd heard a shuffling within the gallery shadows. Lady Ygurna had been carried, protesting softly each step of the way, from the hall. The young women had become their family's only presence before the clerics, the household, and God.

"No," Wildecent replied in a softer whisper, "but it's expected of us with our lord father and Lady Ygurna gone."

"Our lord father did not command that we remain here."

"Alison"—Wildecent wrung an extra syllable from her sister's name—"you know what he meant. Besides, it's Christ our Savior's vigil—we can't leave."

"We've never stood like this praying until dawn before. That's a priest's duty, not ours. Are you coming with me?"

"Everybody's watching us," the dark-haired girl whined, but she followed her sister from the hall all the same.

It was snowing. The flakes made little, angry hisses as they struck the torches set into the outer doorframe. Their house boots, made without wooden or leather soles, which had been adequate footwear on the packed snow, were soaked through after three steps. The young women burst through the kitchen door dancing from one cold foot to the other and totally unprepared for the sights that greeted them.

Lord Godfrey had commanded a barrel of ale from the cellars and his men, crowded among Bethanil's benches and tables, were already deep in enjoyment of it. Half a dozen men were standing on separate tables, each shouting his particular understanding of the treacheries and dangers ranged against them.

Alison, without the slightest intention of leaning, could feel their fear and their drunkenness. The sisters weren't the only women under the curved ceiling. Bethanil was there, guarding her drudges and her domain with ferret-bright eyes, but the ale had passed her way more than once. The cook pounded on her table as loudly as any man, and offered no protection to Lord Hafwynder's daughters. Stephen, who had secured himself a narrow bench along the back wall, saw them cowering in the doorway and beckoned them to share his perch.

"If King Edward's raving and our earl's too ambitious to come outside the Westminster gates," Lord Godfrey shouted, "we'll fight for ourselves, then, and the devil take the hindmost."

The men slammed cups and mugs against the tables and bellowed their approval.

A faceless voice rose above the rest and drew its own chorus: "We'll hunt them outlawed wolves ourselves—and keep their booty ourselves!"

Wildecent shrank back against the door. She wanted none of the smoky light at Stephen's side, nor even to risk the short dash to the tower stairways, and would have retreated to the great hall if Alison had not caught her wrist. To be sure, she had poured Lord Hafwynder's ale at gatherings far more raucous than this, but the smaller kitchen magnified their shouting and their words struck cold against her heart.

"An' what about that Norman pig, Bow-Legs-Ass? What's he done with our Raven, Tostig?" a slurring voice demanded.

Stephen's back stiffened. It was impossible to consider

Edward's succession without considering Normandy and its duke. He was still questioned, unpleasantly at times, about the message he had been carrying to Pevensey. Lord Hafwynder, Stephen thought, had finally come to believe he knew nothing of its contents or code—but that had been before this afternoon and the whispers of Earl Harold's ambitions.

Lord Godfrey's men were wound taut with fear and anxiety. They shouted ideas that would be treason if the wrong party came to the throne—or even if Edward recovered. They fed on their recklessness and, deep into the ale as they were, they would destroy a scapegoat if they found one. Still, Jean Beauleyas had Stephen's oath, and the young man made ready to defend his honor.

"There will be men. He will not refuse you."

"He's taken his Norman arse up to feast on our king's bones!" Another faceless voice; another chorus of agreement—no matter that they had just been complaining that Edward was both unable and unwilling to help them.

Sweat bloomed on Stephen's forehead as he faced the stares of these bearded, long-haired warriors. "Jean Beauleyas is a *miles* knight of Duke William. He will be here."

Stephen was not the only one who felt the sudden surge of Saxon distrust. It struck more forcibly against Alison, whose wild talent magnified its effect and who had never learned to defend herself from overwhelming emotion.

Wildecent felt her sister's grip go clammy and made a lunge for the dark tower stairway. She found herself tugging against dead weight. Lord Hafwynder shouted in support of Stephen's uncle, but the emotions in the kitchen did not change.

"I've got to get *away*," Alison protested.

The notion appealed to Wildecent. They left Stephen and their father to take care of themselves and escaped back into the cold midnight air. The steady falling snow

absorbed the kitchen noises and obscured the dome-roof as soon as they were a few yards away from it.

"The bolt-hole," Alison suggested, quickly recovering her strength and resuming her place as leader.

Rope guides had been strung between the major buildings within the stockade. With one hand on the rough fiber and the other firmly around her sister's wrist again, Alison pushed through the snow to the workroom. Men and women had lost their way on better nights than this and not been found until the morning—or not until spring.

She fumbled with the keys dangling from her belt until she realized the door was ringed with a thin band of light. Closing the door behind them, they stood on a section of the floor from which the mosaic had been long worn away and stamped feeling back into their feet. Neither of them heard Lady Ygurna ascend the ladder from the bolt-hole and when they did see her silhouetted and rising from the depths, they both squealed and gasped with shock.

"Went to the kitchens, didn't you?" their aunt observed with a dry chuckle. "That's the way it is with men, even the best of them. If their frenzy does not go berserk and feed on others, it lingers and feeds on their own minds.

"Come, the brazier's burning below. I can use your help, since you're here." She disappeared back into the warm glow of the bolt-hole.

Gathering their ice-sodden skirts, the young women followed carefully down the wooden ladder. The bolt-hole was about half the size of the upper workroom, with cluttered shelves, baskets, and a variety of piled chests making it seem considerably smaller. A U-shaped worktable dominated what space remained. Warmth came from three covered braziers beneath the table, light from oil lamps suspended from the ceiling above it. Both Alison and Wildecent took a swift inventory of the herbs and oils arrayed on the table.

"You expect there will be fighting, then?" Alison asked, grimacing as she sniffed the ragwort decoction her aunt had been simmering above one of the braziers. They steeped bandages in the reduced fluid and used them to bind wounds that could not immediately be cleaned or stitched.

"It's wisest to be prepared. I have not seen Lord Godfrey so distraught since you were a small child and our king sent the old earl, Godwin, into exile. Yes, I think there will be fighting, and I'm of better use here than sitting in my lord's chair listening to peace prayers."

She pushed another bundle of the foul-smelling roots toward Wildecent, who obediently went to the shelves for a wooden mortar. Lady Ygurna herself was using a black mortar and pestle that had been carved from a single, once-sacred stone. Its significance was not lost on the younger women.

If they only made medicines there would have been no need for the locked bolt-hole; they could just as easily have worked beside Bethanil in the kitchens. But they mixed poisons in that black stone dish, and other compounds whose purposes owed nothing to the rites going on in the great hall.

"Must we loose our own *berserkerang?*" Alison asked, examining the vial of green-black powder her aunt had just set aside.

"Not yet, my dear," Lady Ygurna replied, handing her a twine-tied bundle for grinding. "There's no harm to being prepared, but much to being overhasty." She tapped the contents of her mortar into a lop-edged mug and proceeded to drink the contents herself. "For now it keeps the Crab at bay."

It was the first time their aunt had mentioned her illness to them, and the words brought a silence to the bolt-hole that lasted until after dawn.

awn on Christmas morning in the year of our Lord 1065: a dust-colored glow along the eastern horizon reflecting off an unmarred expanse of snow fully a foot deeper than it had been when sunlight last vanished. The overhead sky was a few shades darker than the horizon, promising more snow eventually but able to contain its burdens for now. Plumes of smoke rose from the roof-vents of Hafwynder Manor, then quickly merged into the mottled gray sky. The smoke and a solitary figure pushing its way between two of the smaller buildings were the only signs of active habitation at this early hour of the morning.

Jean Beauleyas shifted in his saddle, relaxing his grip on the reins so his horse could lower its head and paw at the snow. He studied his destination with a second-nature professionalism. The two-story great hall near the center of the compound was built from brightly painted wood set above solid, mortar-and-stone walls. Its thatched roof was weighed down with snow and would burn slowly, if it burned at all. The stockade surrounding it and all the lesser buildings was well maintained, each timber stripped of bark and fire-sharpened to a point. A fast-moving stream flowed through the yard but there was at least one well near the kitchen so there would be little likelihood of the place succumbing to a siege.

Not that a siege would be ever be necessary. This Saxon, like so many others, had built his home for comfort and convenience and in full view of the forested ridge where Beauleyas assembled his men. When the time came, this English land would fall to Duke William like so much ripe fruit. He himself might even build a castle right here on this ridge. With a strong arm to hold it, this manor would be a worthy addition to any man's land.

"Is that saddle fixed yet?" he shouted, turning away from the prosperous, vulnerable valley. His long chain-mail hauberk jingled against the hard stirrup leathers.

"Indeed, my lord," the red-faced knight replied.

The standing knight needed a good push from two young squires to regain his now-repaired saddle. The mail offered protection from arrows and most lesser weapons. It was a wise precaution, but it slowed both men and horses and, as the broken buckle attested, put extra strain on their gear.

"Let's get on with it. I'd like to sit by a fire before the snow starts falling again."

The men heartily agreed. They'd welcomed the holy day in a gutted chapel that offered only the barest shelter from the cold and snow. The squires had been awake since midnight preparing armor, weapons, and a cold breakfast for their seniors, but even the knights, both sweating and shivering beneath their hauberks, had already put in a long morning. Following close behind their leader, some fifteen mounted men emerged from the forest at a confident pace.

The manor resisted the morning. Brother Alfred leaned against a wall, snoring contentedly. The Yulelog burned, tended diligently by a quiet sullen-faced youth, but the kitchen hearth was banked and Bethanil herself was still asleep, slumped against one of the housecarls. Even Thorkel Longsword was where he had landed some hours before dawn, a half-empty mug of ale balanced precariously on his thigh.

In the guard-porch built above the main gate of the stockade two young men huddled together for warmth. They had partaken of the first keg of ale but not of any of the later rounds, and had begrudged their fellows in bold terms throughout their watch, but now, as a dark shadow separated itself from the forest, they were the first of Lord Godfrey Hafwynder's men to give a sober shiver of fear.

While the youngest stood gape-mouthed in terror, the other staggered to the inside wall, where a flat piece of iron was suspended over the yard. He beat it with a mallet and raised a din that should have roused the dead.

"They hear us, Lord Jean," one of the knights remarked as the sound carried over the snow.

"Take care, then; shields up. There's no telling what these people will do when they see us."

Lord Godfrey lurched to his feet, unable to determine if the terrible racket came from within his own head or from someplace beyond it. His first thought, once he realized someone was beating on the gong, was to have the miscreant hung, but as he plunged his hands into the barrel of icy water by the door and splashed a handful into his uncooperative eyes, the truth cut through the dull ache in his head.

"Up, men!" he bellowed as his heart hammered blood. "They're at the gate and we've only God's mercy on our side."

Thorkel came to with a snort, the ale making an unsightly stain on his trousers. Others groaned and opened raw eyes as Lord Godfrey flung open the outer door. The early morning light cast no sharp shadows, but even so it was too much for some of the men who shoved their way to the snowbanks outside and a few who lacked the coordination to get that far.

Stephen climbed to his feet and had taken several wobbling steps toward the door before he remembered the bandages on his foot or felt its ache beneath the pounding in his head. It was the least of his problems, as the sour ale churned in his stomach. He barely reached the snow before his gut revolted and threatened to turn itself inside out.

"So you'll die with our good ale on your lips!" a house-carl slurred as he whacked Stephen between the shoulder blades. "You'll fight like the devil himself today."

The young man groaned and fell to his knees. He would have believed himself poisoned if the Saxons around him, having once relieved themselves, weren't getting to their feet and walking steadily to the armory, where Lord Godfrey was distributing heavy axes and swords to those men who did not possess their own weapons.

"You're somewhat green about the ears, young Norman," Thorkel said, rudely hoisting Stephen to his feet. "Be quick with your sword, child, or take your place with God's men in the hall."

A proud rage burned the fuzziness from Stephen's mind. He shrugged Thorkel's hand away and struck off for the hall at a run. "Dead drunk I'm worth two of you," he called back over his shoulder.

Thorkel brayed and slapped his hand against his legs. "You should live so long, young Norman!"

Stephen hit the hall door hard, slamming it back on its hinges. The brothers looked out from their huddle by the altar, as did the wide-eyed women and children who had fallen asleep in the rushes where they had prayed at the end of the vigil.

"What does it mean?" Brother Alfred asked.

"The outlaws," Stephen replied, slowing down as he mounted the spiral stairs to the gallery. "And vengeance!"

They'd given him a new boot to replace the one the wolves had destroyed. He threw the bandages into a corner and winced as he thrust his tender foot down through the unforgiving leather. Drawing the laces tight, he took a tentative step; the bruises screamed, but the leather added strength to his stride and pain was something he'd been taught to ignore. Buckling the sword above his hips, he headed back for the snow-covered yard.

The iron gong was still ringing. The lookouts above the gate were waving their arms and shouting to Lord Hafwynder, but with the noise and confusion their English was too garbled for Stephen's understanding. He judged, though, that there were still a few moments before the fighting would begin, moments he would spend in the stable readying Sulwyn.

Rapid exercise had either cured or completely numbed Stephen's ankle. He strode evenly along the stalls. His shoulder was another matter. The simple act of belting his sword had convinced him he'd be unable to swing the heavy blade with any strength. His weapons masters had been well aware that a knight could not always rely on his good arm; Stephen could fight left-handed when the occasion demanded. But left-handed and unarmored, he wanted the advantages only Sulwyn could give him.

He spotted his saddle and hurried toward the adjacent stall, which he supposed was Sulwyn's. The big bay welcomed him enthusiastically, but one glance at the scabbed and stitched band of skin curving from the horse's chest over his shoulder and then under his belly told Stephen everything. The Saxon hostler, Leofric, had worked a near miracle; but it would be spring before the horse could be asked to bear a man's weight.

Giving the horse an affectionate, but hasty, scratch along the nose, Stephen hurried back toward the yard. Perhaps he could use one of the unfamiliar, but lighter, Saxon shields on his weak right arm. He was looking for Lord Hafwynder or Thorkel Longsword when he spotted Alison, Wildecent, and their aunt emerging from an antique-style building.

They carried baskets and bundles of cloth for bandages and, like him, seemed to be looking for the lord of the manor.

"Take yourselves to the tower," Stephen informed them, pointing to the shuttered windows high above the yard. "Watch from there. This will not take long."

Stephen's crude command of English made him sound more confident than he felt. It was true though: whatever the outcome, the fight for Hafwynder Manor would be over quickly. There had been no time to prepare defenses, and from what Stephen could see, Lord Hafwynder commanded no more than three archers. The outlaws and the defenders would engage in a single melee, and then the women could either boil their medicines or, if they were wise and valued their honor, leap to their deaths from the windows.

He was relieved when, after a moment's conversation, the three did as they had been asked. The two younger women were deeply muddled into his thoughts. He would not have wanted to face an unknown enemy with concern for their safety dogging him. Then he heard Lord Hafwynder shouting orders and saw runners coming from the the end of the stockade enclosure with ladders. He hurried after them.

"Bar that door behind us," Lady Ygurna commanded once the three women had entered the chaos of the kitchens.

Bethanil, blotch-faced and far from her usual figure of calm authority, rushed to grab Lady Ygurna's arm.

"They've come to kill us all, just as they done to ealdorman Edmund an' his family, haven't they?"

The cook's beefy hands could have crushed Lady Ygurna's frail bones, but the older woman simply shook herself free. "Our men will defend us," she said coldly. "Now, *bar that door!*"

While Bethanil grappled with the heavy plank that had seldom, if ever, been set in its brackets across the door, Lady Ygurna swept the debris off one of the tables. "Start kettles and sharpen your knives," she commanded the drudges, who hastened to obey her. "Shutter those windows and clean up this unholy mess."

In the worst extreme the final stronghold of the manor would be here, in the kitchen, and not in the Norman-style tower or at the edge of a war ax. It was the women's domain, and with their cleavers, pots, and guile the outcome was by no means certain. Buried in Lady Ygurna's basket was a tightly stopped vial with enough black fluid in it to poison fifty men's ale. If the manor fell, its conquerors would not enjoy it for long.

"You two," Ygurna turned to the sisters, "up to the tower with you. Be my eyes and ears: watch what happens when men come to fighting."

Wildecent used the poker to free the shutters on all four sides of their tower bedroom. The room was soon as frigid as the yard, but they could see farther than the men on the guard-porch.

"God and all his saints protect us," Alison murmured from the shadows by the western window. "If those are wolf's-head outlaws, then surely we are doomed."

The mounted party was well separated from the forest now. Even Wildecent's nearsighted eyes could note the distinctive pattern and movement of fine mail hauberks. They'd imagined the outlaws to be desperate men—brutal, but tangibly inferior to Godfrey's housecarls. Now, with mail-clad riders moving in close formation behind their leader as the manor's defenders clambered up ladders to the narrow walkway that jutted out from the topmost lashings of the stockade, the truth seemed reversed, Hafwynder Manor was ill prepared and ill disciplined and the outlaws just rode slowly closer.

Finally the riders were in range. The three archers, kneeling in the protection of the covered guard-porch, loosed their arrows. It could not be said that Godfrey Hafwynder did not surround himself with competent warriors; each arrow found a mark, two in the mail-protected shoulder of the leader himself. But the hauberk did its work well and it was clear that the arrows, which were easily plucked and thrown aside, had not touched flesh.

A groan of dismay rose from the yard, then a second one when the archers reported that the outlaws had retreated beyond arrows' reach. The mounted men conferred with each other; then the leader and another, an unarmored man, separated and rode toward the gate.

"They've got our Raven," came the cry from the guardporch as Alison also whispered Tostig's name in the tower room.

Wildecent squinted her brows together. "They don't seem to have mistreated him," she said after a long moment's observation.

"They've made him their hostage."

"I think he's still wearing his sword."

"Don't be a goose—"

But Wildecent had correctly discerned a full scabbard at Tostig's side. Confusion reigned on the guard-porch until Godfrey himself was compelled to climb the ladder and survey the hillside for himself.

"Ho, the gate!" the mail-clad knight shouted. "Bring up Lord Hafwynder, if you dare."

"Release my man, if *you* dare," Godfrey replied.

The truth was clearer in the tower. Alison had begun to giggle while her father and the Norman still tilted and argued

148

with each other. "It is the Torworden Normans, I think, come as Stephen said they would," she told her sister.

"We're saved."

"We were never in any danger," Alison replied, latching the shutters and heading for the stairway. "Well, grab your cloak. Don't you want to meet them?"

By the time they had explained the unfolding comedy to their aunt and convinced that distrustful woman to unbar the kitchen door, the stockade gate was open and the strangers were riding into the yard. There were smiles and a few shouted greetings for Tostig and his companions' safe return, but the overall mood, as Alison led Wildecent through the men to her father's side, was one of restraint and awe.

King Edward's court had echoed with Norman accents since the king had returned from exile to take his crown some twenty years before, but the foreigners had seemed less conspicuous amid the large, stone halls their king favored. Here, surrounded by the smaller-scale hall and bowers of Hafwynder Manor, they looked like giants. They had not come on destriers, those fire-blooded horses whose mettle was so high they must be led, blindfolded, to the battleground, but the meanest of their palfreys was equal in size to Godfrey's best stallion and showed long, yellow teeth toward anything that crossed its shadow.

"Be welcome to Hafwynder Manor," Lord Godfrey said, deftly avoiding the palfrey's teeth and offering Beauleyas his hand and help in dismounting. "Forgive our not recognizing you. These are treacherous times."

"As well I know," Beauleyas replied once his feet were on the ground. He pulled the tight-fitting conical helmet from his head and pushed back the hood of his hauberk so that he might see and hear his counterpart clearly. "We too had no notion what might greet us—hence our own precautions." He shook his sleeve until the hauberk jingled.

"Surely my message, and Tostig himself—"

"Told me your household and land were in imminent danger. You see, my Lord Hafwynder, my eyes and ears at your king's court were well aware of these 'outlaws.' " Beauleyas brought a heavy arm down across Godfrey's shoulders with enough force to get his host moving toward the warmth of his hall. The two leaders were of a size, though it was apparent, from the ill-healed scar across Beauleyas's nose and the limp that made him lean ever so slightly on Godfrey as they walked, that the Norman had come to his leadership in war while Godfrey had been born to his in peace.

"That message of mine that you've got, I almost wish you could have broken its code. But not even Stephen— *Jesus wept!* My nephew, how is the lad? Where is he?"

As Hafwynder opened his mouth to answer, Stephen pushed himself into his uncle's path and dropped to one knee.

"Here, my lord. I failed you, my lord. Your message did not reach Pevensey. Ranulf died with a wolf's-head blue-fletched arrow in his throat." He lowered his head as if expecting a beheading strike from his uncle.

"They'll pay, lad," Beauleyas affirmed, offering Stephen his hand. "The Godwinson exile and his northern allies will pay the fullest price."

The Godwinson exile could only be Tostig, brother of Harold, Godfrey's earl here in Wessex. When Godwin himself had been alive, the family, rich in ambitious sons and daughters, had been united and successful in its pursuit of power; it had come to full nadir if Tostig was endowing outlaws to raid his brother's lands and oathmen. The Norman's words were hardly a surprise to Hafwynder and his men, but they brought a silence to the yard that even Beauleyas noticed.

"If you did not know even that," he said, returning to Godfrey's side and speaking more softly than was his custom, "then you will not have guessed at the rest. Have you a table in your hall where we may talk in peace?"

Numbly, fearing that his worst suspicions and more were about to be confirmed, Lord Godfrey nodded and continued toward his hall. He gave orders that his men should assist in quartering and stabling the Norman guests and that the women should begin heating bathwater for their noble guests. There was a palpable change in him, even though he led the way and acted the proper host, and though no one in the yard dared to mention it, it had not escaped their notice.

"We're more than saved," Wildecent corrected herself when she and Alison were the only two left not moving purposefully toward some task or another.

"They even *feel* big."

"Alison! You didn't try to lean on that Norman, did you?"

"I couldn't," the blond girl admitted in a tone that matched her father's.

Wildecent looked at her sister and knew, without asking unnecessary questions or bemoaning her lack of mystical talents, that Jean Beauleyas was not protected by some arcane shield that Alison would perceive as a challenge but, rather, that the Norman's mind was as commanding as his physical presence. "Come on," she said, beginning to feel the cold air of the yard through her tunic. "We'd better get to the kitchen before Lady Ygurna comes looking for us."

he bath was prepared with all due ceremony in a drape-door alcove off the kitchens. Water was heated in kettles and by
lowering hearth-baked loaf-stones into the
wooden tub. Spiced oils were swirled
through the water and one of Lord Hafwynder's tunics
was brought down in case Lord Beauleyas should prefer
not to don his own sweat-soaked clothes. But the fragrant
steam went unappreciated.

"You'd think the first thing he'd want is a bath," Alison complained, dangling her hands into the comfortable
liquid. "Our lord father would. So would everyone else,
but he'd rather sit in the hall and talk about *politics!*"

"Perhaps with his injured leg he thinks he could not
take a bath without assistance. He's had no wife for many
years, I've heard," Wildecent mused.

Lady Ygurna pushed the drapery back, thrusting her
head and shoulders into the alcove. "You've heard a few
too many things, I should think. If they don't want our
hospitality, then there's plenty else to be done. We'd
planned a Christmas feast half the size of the one we're
going to serve."

Alison got to her feet and wiped her hands on her skirt.
"What needs doing?"

"There's cloth for the tables. The others can set up the
trestles once the men have left the hall, but someone has
to go to the storerooms for the cloths and plates. They're
with the boxes we moved from Stephen's room, and I
don't have the time to go looking for them. And we'll
need another bushel of onions and peas to thicken the
pot. There's no time to send anyone into the forest, and
I'm not putting every piece of meat we've got hanging in
the cellar on the table for strangers."

The sisters exchanged knowing glances. Their aunt had conceived a hearty dislike for Jean Beauleyas and his men. She would never say so in exact words, but the sheer number of words and the no-argument tone of them got her meaning across. There was nothing to gain in giving Lady Ygurna's formless anger a target.

"I'll go up to the storerooms," Wildecent volunteered, already moving toward the drapery.

"Be quiet about it," her aunt cautioned. "No sense interrupting them and keeping them at it longer. We'll all work like slaves to get food to the tables by sundown as it is."

Wildecent nodded and slipped past her aunt. Alison shrugged her shoulders; usually her sister wasn't quick enough to choose the easier tasks.

"I suppose the onions will have to be chopped as well?"

"Yes, but I'll put Bethanil to that. Just choose a basketful and bring it up here. Then go out to the bolt-hole, get the black coffer, and take it to my room."

Alison felt an involuntary shiver race down her spine. The ancient wood box was one of her aunt's last secrets; Wildecent knew nothing of its existence, much less its power. It normally rested in the earth beneath the bolt-hole, and its emergence betokened a need for pure magic. Alison lowered her eyes and struggled to keep her excitement hidden within her heart as Lady Ygurna returned to her own tasks.

Every basket in the root cellar seemed partly filled with something that could not be easily added to another. Rather than waste her time looking for an empty one, Alison collected the onions in the folds of her apron and staggered up the stairs just before the cloth was certain to tear apart. She tumbled the gold-brown spheres into the basin beside a drudge who was about her own age. Sometimes she shared the work with these less fortunate girls, but today was not such a day. Ignoring the slow stare of disappointment that lodged between her shoulders, Alison fairly raced to the workrooms.

After carefully concealing the coffer in a sack of crude, undyed homespun, Alison rubbed her palms with mistletoe and headed, at a more dignified pace, for the great hall. The herb and the sack would keep anyone from noticing what she carried.

The hall was quiet. Beauleyas and her father were talking in soft voices that did not carry to the corners or the rafters, and the few men who sat near them were saying nothing at all. Alison thought the scuff of her house boots on the stairs was disconcertingly loud, but no one glanced her way and she slipped into her aunt's room confident that the mistletoe had worked and she had been invisible to eyes and memory.

She could not help but notice, as she set the wrapped coffer inside Lady Ygurna's wardrobe chest, that two rowan-tipped wands were laid upon the fine white cloth. Let the Normans come with their fine, great palfreys and their noisy hauberks; Hafwynder Manor would soon be protected in the time-honored ways that had always secured it against the folly of men.

Full of imagining, Alison returned to the gallery. The next door—the door to Stephen's room—was shut tight, but the one beyond it had been left open. She thought it likely that Wildecent, her arms full of embroidered cloth and serving plates, had been unable to close the door behind her. She had her hand on the latch, ready to do her sister a favor, when she realized the dark room was occupied.

"What are you doing there?" she demanded, catching the dim outline of her sister cowered down in the corner.

"Shhh!" Wildecent made a quick come-hither gesture with her hands. Many times Wildecent's curiosity had fastened upon something Alison could at best consider boring, at worst disgusting. The great hall storerooms were a far cry from the fish pond or the pig wallow, where the greater number of Wildecent's more dubious investigations had been carried out; nonetheless, Alison approached slowly and fell to her knees with great reluctance.

"What are—"

"*Shhh!*" Wildecent hissed, offering a metal goblet. "Listen."

Alison put the bell to the stones and her ear to the stem. The door to Stephen's room might be latched shut but the chamber was far from empty. Wildecent had, for once, stumbled upon something interesting.

"They are not heathen crones," Stephen was saying in a tone that implied he'd made the assertion more than once. "They use a Celtic rite, I think, though the brothers they're sheltering in the hall served a Cluniac priest. Their Christmas vigil was in proper Latin, for all that they had a Yulelog burning on the hearth." He conversed in a polyglot dialect that, though it included many words peculiar to the eastern shores of the Channel, was understood by both young women.

"Étienne. Étienne, how many times must I tell you to look beneath the surface?"

This second voice was unfamiliar and lacked both Norman sharpness and the light accent Stephen himself had from the southern kingdoms.

"I only see more of the surface."

"Extend yourself; reach into your memory. Has not some small thing, at least, about this manor struck you odd? In the moments when they thought you raving, were not strange things both said and done?"

Crouched by their goblets in the next storeroom, both young women cringed. Alison had gone tromping through his mind; that should be strange enough for a dozen men or manors. But Stephen hardly hesitated.

"Dear Ambrose, I *was* raving and I had wondrous dreams I should blame on the wolves that tried to eat me rather than the women who healed me. You have not seen Sulwyn; his wounds are stitched with black silk thread. Surely you don't think they witched my *horse?*"

"I don't know what to think, Étienne, but I warn you, there's something here we would best feed to those accursed outlaws if we cannot name and control it."

Now there was a silence on the other side of the wall.

"No," Stephen said, as if to assure himself. "My uncle would not have come all this way if he did not intend to defend this manor . . . and its people."

"I have warned him. I will warn him again."

"Then so will I. Your love of mystery has outstripped you, Ambrose. These Saxons are not broken peasants and animals, but neither are they crones and magi."

The sisters heard a sound that might have been a door opening. Without exchanging a word Wildecent blew out her lantern and both young women moved breathlessly through the dark. They crept silently into the shadows at the edge of the gallery, hoping to catch a glimpse of this Ambrose who was a friend and confidant to Stephen and suspected them of their deepest secrets. They saw the back of a man an inch or two taller than Stephen, though less powerfully built, then nothing as the two men disappeared down the stairs.

Stephen glanced over his shoulder and caught sight of a swirl of skirts retreating to the shadows. So they had been spying on him. He had suspected as much when he'd heard first one, then another person enter the storeroom beyond his own and not emerge. He found their curiosity amusing and typical of women, who were expected to be devious and less honorable than men. He did not think overmuch about what they might have heard.

He paused at the foot of the spiral stairway, watching his uncle lecture the Saxon lord and wondering if now was any sort of time for an interruption.

"Ho, Stephen . . . and Ambrose," Beauleyas called out, rendering Stephen's quandary pointless.

The men approached the hearth where the Yulelog was still burning. Other men from Torworden and the manor were sitting quietly on hastily assembled benches. They made no place for the newcomers, but left them to stand midway between the sworn men and the lords.

"Uncle?" Stephen began slowly.

"Glad to see you're getting about on your own. With what they've said here you were near enough a cripple." Jean extended his beringed hand toward Stephen but his attention was clearly on Ambrose. "They say it's begun to snow again. Just as you said it would. Can you say how much snow will fall by sunrise tomorrow?"

There was little change in Ambrose's demeanor. Only those who knew him well might have noted the slight tensing of the muscles in his neck or the brief moments when it seemed his eyes were focused elsewhere—someone who knew him well, or someone who had had encountered mystic and unexplained forces once or twice himself.

Lord Hafwynder drew his fingers slowly through his beard and shot a knowing glance toward Thorkel Longsword, who made an answering sign with a slight movement of one finger.

"There will be new snow to the depth of your knees, my lord," Ambrose replied respectfully. "There could be more."

"Then let us fervently hope that there will be more, shall we? Come, find yourselves stools and let me tell you what I've explained to Lord Godfrey."

The Norman's tone was bantering. Lord Hafwynder knew the true meaning of the exchange only because he'd felt the edges of Lady Ygurna's secrets often enough and knew when to turn a blind eye. He was in too deeply with the Normans now to question Beauleyas on anything so slight as mere morality or religion. He caught the questioning, challenging look in Longsword's eye and lowered his own brows; his man was calm-faced.

"It's time you knew what was in that message you carried, my boy," Beauleyas began once Stephen was seated beside him. "It's plain the old King Edward's dying. His succession oath was given many years ago, and confirmed by Harold over holy relics not two years past. But now Earl Harold and his viper-sister, Queen Edith, mean to put the oath by and set Harold on the throne."

Stephen nodded politely. He was too young to remember the mysterious visits to Normandy that Edward had made more than a decade before and, until earlier this year, his attentions had not been on the embroiled English-Norman succession but on the more civilized, but equally tumultuous, rivalries of central and southern France.

"Duke William will come to take what is his," the young man stated after a moment's silence. He knew of the duke's ambition and his pride; it seemed a safe enough reply.

"Aye, but it will take time. I've dispatched another courier with word of Harold's treachery. Even so, it is difficult to bring an army across the Channel in the winter—impossible, perhaps. By the time he gets here, it might not even be Harold whom he is facing on the field of honor. The old Earl Godwin bred treachery in all his sons and daughters, it seems. Harold and Edith set their plots on the neck of their brother Tostig, whom they sent in exile first to Normandy, then to Sweden.

"Duke William, either believing Tostig or underestimating Godwinson guile, did not put Tostig to the oath. Now Tostig claims the English throne himself, with the Norse king's aid, and means to see that neither Harold nor William can challenge him."

These Saxons and their allies were brutal gamesmen, without the subtlety of continental intriguers. Stephen pieced their plots together without much effort. "These outlaws then, the ones that beset us and have been ravaging the countryside—they're this Tostig's agents, then, and they mean to eat away at the countryside all winter."

Hafwynder blinked; it hadn't been so clear to him. Indeed, it still seemed quite unbelievable that Earl Tostig meant to destroy the Saxons loyal to King Edward's wishes, and even more unbelievable that both Edward and Harold had sworn holy oaths to Normandy. If his doubts and fears for his own people had not been building these last few years he would have dismissed it out of hand. As it was, he embraced it with the terrible glee of a man fighting his death battle.

"Is there not some danger here, then, my lord, if you've come down to Hafwynder Manor? Surely the wolf's-head outlaws were not blind to your movements?" Stephen asked, glancing from the Saxon to the Norman.

The hall rang with Jean Beauleyas's laughter. "Danger? Why of course, my boy. It's as much as throwing down the gauntlet at them. I might just as well have laid a trail to the gatehouse door."

The Saxons saw less humor in Beauleyas's assessment of the situation, but there was little doubt that the vicious band would quickly learn of Lord Hafwynder's guests and a ripe target would become irresistible.

"Ought we not return to Torworden, where you have all your knights and the strong walls of Torworden itself?" the young man asked.

Lord Jean's laughter stopped as abruptly as it had begun. His eyes grew as flinty as ever they did behind his shield or within his helmet. "I took oaths of both William and Edward for that land and its defense. This Saxon here is liege-loyal to his king—his *rightful* king, be that King Edward or his legitimate, sworn successor.

"Duke William's men do *not* abandon their sworn brethren."

Stephen sat straight on the stool as if he'd been struck. The bonds of fealty, whether sworn over holy relics or simply on a man's own honor, had been made clear to him since childhood. He had not considered, though, that the spiderweb nature of such oaths could bring his uncle out of the stronghold at Torworden and prevent him from returning to it.

Ambrose came to Stephen's rescue. "But my lord Beauleyas, this manor is indefensible!"

Lord Godfrey's men, led by Thorkel Longsword, stiffened and made to rise from their seats as the Norman lord's laughter began again with a loud, bitter snort.

"More the fool am I!" Jean declaimed, lofting his empty ale mug and illustrating how few years had passed since the Normans had been Vikings themselves. "This Tostig the Raven comes to my hall and tells me of his lord's danger and of the great stone tower setting right in the middle of the manor. Now how should I know that my Saxon host would build his stout little tower in the pit of a valley rather than on the ridge above it?"

Lord Hafwynder grew red across his pale face, which did not alleviate his men's anxiety a whit. "T'was built—"

"For comfort and beauty, like all your Saxon homes," Jean interrupted, lowering his mug and speaking in a more sympathetic tone. "Jesus wept, Hafwynder, the smoke rises straight to the hole and your doors fit square in the walls. I haven't been this comfortable since harvesting, and a man could live without meat or bread and only your ale to sustain him. Valley or not, your stockade's as tight as it should be, and no tower is a complete waste of stone."

"But how, my lord?" Stephen ventured.

Beauleyas passed another sidelong glance toward Ambrose. "Your tutor says it's going to snow heavy 'til dawn."

"The outlaws will be trapped in forests?"

"Nay, lad, they'll come as soon as the skies let them, but meanwhile we'll have made more stone from the snow itself."

Ambrose started forward on his stool, his composure broken by his understanding of what his lord demanded. "Stone from snow, my Lord Beauleyas!" he protested. "You know not what you ask."

The Norman lord took some amusement from the black-haired man's distress. He had no great liking and less trust for his nephew's mysterious companion, but he'd taken the man's oath and learned his measure in short order. There was some small satisfaction in seeing him acknowledge that there was something he did not believe he could do. "Restrain your fears, dear Ambrose," he said, tugging on Ambrose's fur-trimmed black sleeve. "It's only ice I mean—but as strong a stone as we'll need, and unburnable as well. Will we have enough snow to raise a white ring and ditch beyond the stockade?"

An answering grin spread across Ambrose's face as the winter-born fortifications came clear in his mind. "Aye, enough snow, my lord. And boiling water as well, to throw over the snow until it packs down and grows a heavy ice armor."

"Ha!" Beauleyas exclaimed, slapping Lord Godfrey on the shoulder. "I warned you he was a genius, did I not?

Your walls will be as slick as your fishpond when Ambrose has done with them. It's a better use for your great bathtubs than pouring perfumes over a fighting man's back!''

Lord Godfrey held his peace. Of Beauleyas's men, only Ambrose did not loudly proclaim his presence to a Saxon nose. But he could begin to envision the defenses these Normans planned, and though he would never have considered them himself, he suspected they'd work. "We could throw water on the stables and bowers as well,'' he suggested as the visions came clearer. ''They'll not fire an ice-covered wall or roof.''

Beauleyas pounded his shoulder again. "You learn quick, Saxon. You learn quick.''

he manor hummed with intense activity more appropriate for the height of the harvest or planting season than a holy day of winter. The bowers, which had absorbed the cottager families, were empty, as everyone was assigned some task, whether it be packing the snow as it fell, hauling the bitter-cold water from the stream or, for those who were luckiest, laboring in the kitchens where water was heated and pots of barley stew were always steaming.

The common folk had no vision of the tasks set before them, and the swirling snow, which blocked a body's sight like a wall at arm's length, offered them no opportunity for enlightenment. But the knights and housecarls observed the growth of their efforts and felt their spirits lift. Some five paces beyond the wooden posts of the stockade a man-high rampart had begun to emerge. Snow by the cartload and by the shovelful was heaped up, then battered upon and finally wet down with cauldrons of steaming water.

Tostig the Raven challenged two Torworden men to a race along the incomplete ridge. He gashed his nose in a fall on the way up, and fell a dozen times more before reaching the last of the iced-over portion. The Normans fared no better, and the project was proclaimed a success in a variety of dialects.

Stephen had volunteered to work on the rampart. He had a more personal grudge against the outlaws than many of the men, and a young man's need for vindication as well. But his blood spoke against him. It was one thing to risk the fingers and toes of the sworn men and common folk, and quite another to jeopardize a nobleman's heir.

"There's work to be done indoors," Beauleyas snapped.

"Women's work," Stephen muttered to himself as he headed, once again, for the busy kitchens.

It wasn't all women's work, he knew, watching as an iron-collared churl hauled another load of heated loaf-stones to the alcove, where the water was steaming. But what wasn't being done by women was being done by slaves—and that was even worse to contemplate. He stood there, convinced that all the Torworden men were laughing at him, until Ambrose came through the door behind him.

"Perhaps you'd consider helping me?"

If Stephen had had a friend throughout the chaotic years of his adolescence, that friend had been Ambrose. But this time Ambrose harkened to his uncle's orders and friendship wasn't enough. "I've no mind for parchment today," he snarled and turned away.

Ambrose caught the younger man's arm and held it fast. Though slightly built and educated to a point where even churchmen looked askance, Ambrose was no man to walk away from. His bundles contained a sword of fine Damascus metal that no man had been able to win fairly from him and no man had dared to steal.

"Ten days among these Saxons and you've grown distant, Étienne. If you won't help me, then at least give me your company. Your uncle won't be moved, you know."

"I belong out there with the men," Stephen said earnestly, but he'd stopped pulling away and was willing to follow Ambrose from the kitchens to the hall.

"I think you belong in the south of France, Étienne, and you do, too," the scholar said with a laugh as he opened the door. "I have prevailed upon the lords to give me the upper room of the tower—"

"That's where the sisters sleep."

"Ah, Lord Godfrey told me I would have to wait until

late this evening to move my belongings there. Very well, there are other things to do."

He turned and headed away from the hall to the nearly empty stables.

"I don't understand why we should have to move just because there're *Normans* here." Alison stood away from the tablecloth and surveyed her handiwork. "It's our room."

Lady Ygurna looked up from the small salt dishes she was filling. "You'll do as pleases your lord father . . . and it pleases your lord father that you should move into the great hall, where he is more certain of your safety."

"I thought the plan was that if it came to the worst, everyone would retreat to our tower?" Wildecent knew that was the plan, but some statements were better phrased as questions. She set the salt on the tablecloth, where it would be available to those of highest rank only.

"Perhaps, young lady, your lord father is worried about more than the outlaws. We have all the cottagers within the gate and those unwashed Normans as well. If you can't understand his concern, then perhaps we should lock the doors behind you."

"I'm sorry." Whatever else, Wildecent had had enough of locked doors. "Must we move everything? There's no one to help us with the heavier chests."

Lady Ygurna sighed. The young women were supposed to move out of the tower and not return so long as the Normans remained—her brother-in-law had been most firm about that. But he hadn't offered anyone's help to carry the boxes. "Very well, take what you'll need for a few days here in the hall. Alison can stay in my room with me, but you, Wildecent, you'll stay down here. Your lord father has commanded that all the cottager and bower women sleep in here so their men will be more alert.''

A shudder of outrage passed between Wildecent's shoulders; several grains of salt bounced onto the deep red cloth. She had no desire to crowd into Lady Ygurna's bed with Alison and the mute drudge, Agatha, but bedding down among the wives, mistresses, and daughters of the housecarls could only be counted an insult. It was as if her father counted Alison more precious than she, which reminded her, of course, that Lord Hafwynder wasn't her father.

Moistening her finger, she caught up the salt and savored its taste.

If that were the case, if she was supposed to spread a pallet with the gentle, but not noble, ladies, well, then she'd find someplace else.

''I'm sleeping in the storerooms,'' she told Alison, full of defiance and injured pride, once they were in the tower room and rolling their skirts and tunics into bundles.

''Do you think that's wise?'' Alison asked as her palms went clammy. She perceived the insult Wildecent felt, and knew it to be unjustified. Lord Hafwynder had made no decrees except that they weren't to remain in the tower. It had been her aunt, and herself, who had decided their purposes would be better served if there was no chance of Wildecent observing their departure. ''Wouldn't you feel better with the other women rather than alone in those storerooms?''

''No.''

A silence hung between them. Wildecent recalled that the bonds between herself and her sister had been severely tested in the last few weeks. She regretted that she had been so quick to take Alison into her confidence. ''You won't tell anyone, will you? It's not so terribly wrong. It's only that I don't want to be . . . to be with everybody else, with people I don't really know." Wildecent's shyness was legendary; she was ready to trade mercilessly upon it now.

"I won't tell anyone," Alison agreed. Lady Ygurna would be upset, but there was nothing they could do. Even if Lord Hafwynder did not immediately agree with Wildecent, which Alison suspected he would, any discussion would draw unwanted attention to the plans she and her aunt had been whispering all afternoon.

The ice ring that was so reassuring to everyone else crossed, both literally and figuratively, through their intentions.

"Will you help me sneak these things up the stairs?"

"Of course," Alison agreed quickly. Then, at least, she would know which door they would have to be wary of.

It was past sundown by the time the manor came to its rest. Two thirds of the ice rampart had been completed. The portion that would have been beyond the stream was left unfinished; the hip-deep icy water was sufficient barrier and defense should the stockade be breached along its banks. Snow was still falling, covering the ice but not defeating its purpose, as the ever-resilient Raven had proved to everyone's amusement just before sundown.

Within the manor there was no hearth hook that did not have a bubbling pot hanging from it. Lady Ygurna had already concluded that the manor's rightful, usual residents would starve before spring if the outlaws did not make their appearance by Twelfth Night. Lord Beauleyas, to his credit, had given her brother-in-law a jeweled brooch that would fetch a handsome price in Winchester—but gold was of no use when there was no food or charcoal to be had in exchange for it.

Still, with Alison helping her, it should be possible to protect the manor and feed it as well. She stood by Bethanil and sipped from each of the bubbling pots before retreating to her room. The food on her plate would be wasted and fed to the dogs. The Crab had given her a day's respite, but it called now.

She passed the girls carrying the last of their bundles from the tower and gave them leave to use the last of the heated water for their baths before supper.

It meant untying the bundles and carrying soap, oils, and clean clothes back to the kitchen alcove through the fresh snow, but both young women judged it worthwhile. They drew the drape shut and threw extra charcoal in the pit to heat the water until it stung their hands to stir the oils through it.

"I've been dreaming of this all day," Wildecent said as she unlaced her tunic and pulled it over her head. "I think I could stay under the water until morning and miss Bethanil's supper altogether."

"Don't you dare!" Alison replied with mock anger. She had plucked the short straw and would wash her hair while Wildecent sank neck-deep in the great basin.

Wildecent had removed her sodden house boots and dropped hot stones from the hearth into them for drying; Alison had both braids undone and was combing gold-blond hair that fell straight and thick to the middle of her thighs. Though far from naked, they were completely unprepared for the draperies to part and admit a man to their company.

"Your lord father told me that water would have been kept warm?" The voice was familiar—the voice they'd heard in Stephen's room calling them witches.

"We had not thought that anyone wanted to bathe," Alison spoke up, tossing her hair back over her shoulder and standing tall on the bathing platform.

Normans, Vikings, and even the Saxons long before them sprang from the same stock and though each invad-

ing or conquering wave was whispered to be the devil's spawn, there were few who believed they were ever other than men. But black-haired, ebony-eyed Ambrose, as he stood smiling at them, might well have emerged from some fairyland beyond the edge of the world.

It was more than his clothes, which fit close to his body and were dyed an intense, rich blue, that proclaimed both wealth and commerce with fabled lands and infidels. It was more than his simple appearance: a well-formed, pale face framed by long, lustrous black hair—a combination unusual in itself, as the English, who favored longer hair, also favored beards, and the Normans went short-haired and clean-shaven, lest their hair become entangled in their helmets. Nor was it his accent or manner of speech, which appeared to match perfectly with whatever language or dialect reached his ears.

Alison unraveled his mystery first, her talent rising unbidden to warn her away from this man, however charming and attractive he might seem.

Sorcerer, her mind told her and summoned up the black texture of the shield over Stephen's mind. "We have been given leave by our lady aunt, Ygurna, to use this bath. Surely, if you have waited this long, you can wait until later or tomorrow." She narrowed her eyes and imagined herself to be a fierce beast defending her home.

Ambrose flashed a gentle smile and Alison recalled her first pet, a tiny brindled cat, and its many, futile, confrontations with a world that mocked its fierceness.

"I've been in the saddle for two days running, and working for the defense of your home since dawn-light," he said, extending his hands slowly until his fingertips brushed Alison's arm. "I'm not fit to sit beside my lord at the high table."

She wanted to tell him that Jean Beauleyas wouldn't notice if he'd spent his entire life without benefit of a hot bath, but her tongue and lips refused to form the words.

"Isn't it the custom in your lands that the ladies of the house offer to rub the weariness from their guests' shoulders while they bathe?"

Still speechless, Alison managed to wrest away from his light touch. She gave ground and backed toward the draperies, letting him take her place on the bathing platform. The cloth parted behind her. They needed Lady Ygurna, but Alison knew she couldn't leave her sister in this man's company.

Wildecent surprised her, however. "It was never the custom for a man to come upon a maiden's bath," the amber-eyed girl said slowly and evenly. "And as you are a man, if you insist on your guest privileges, then you must at least wait beyond the draperies until we have composed ourselves to serve you."

He took her hand in his and raised it to his lips. "As you wish," he agreed, retreating past Alison. Wildecent's hand continued to rest in midair long after he had released it.

"He is a sorcerer!" Alison hissed across the basin. "Evil!"

Wildecent only shook her head and rubbed the back of her hand where his lips had touched it. "He is not evil," she replied, and groped blindly for her discarded house boots, her eyes never leaving the drapery folds through which Ambrose had disappeared.

"What are we going to do?" Alison muttered, flinging her talent toward Lady Ygurna, wherever she might be, and dividing her hair into three heavy tresses.

"What he has asked," her sister replied.

When her hair had been knotted into a single braid and her sleeves laced high so they would not drag in the water, Alison parted the drapery and bade their guest to enter.

She threw another plea toward her aunt, but her talent had never served to send thoughts, only to gather them, and she sensed with a deep despair that it was not going to serve her now.

Though Beauleyas called him Stephen's tutor, and even Stephen spoke as if Ambrose were in his service, the sorcerer's clothes and manners were as refined as any at the king's court. He shed his fur-lined tunic and bade them brush it carefully. Beneath that tunic was a shirt of fine black wool worked with silk embroideries in subtle patterns that numbed the eyes. Alison folded it carefully and handed it to Wildecent with a meaningful nod. Wildecent set it on a shelf and clenched her fists to keep her hands from shaking.

They had performed this ritual hundreds of times with their father, with Thorkel Longsword, with the high men of the shire, some of whom would visit Hafwynder Manor for the specific purpose of reclining in its great basin. Even Stephen had only been another body to tend. But Ambrose, flexing wiry muscles in his neck and shoulders, was more disturbing than either young woman had imagined a man could be. Alison thought of a huge wolf; Wildecent recalled the chalk dragon on the way to Winchester—and neither wished to remove the linen chemise that would uncover his skin.

"What is going on here!" Lady Ygurna demanded, swinging the drapery wide open to reveal Bethanil's bulk and cleaver beside her.

"He don't smell right," the cook explained before either sister or Ambrose could speak.

"And that, dear lady, is why I wished to avail myself of a bath." Ambrose nodded toward Bethanil, seemingly undisturbed that he was clad only in his chemise and hose.

Bethanil pushed a string of greasy hair off her forehead

and waggled her cleaver. "Don't go 'dear lady' to me," she warned.

"Enough," Lady Ygurna said, dismissing Bethanil with a flick of her fingers. "I'll take care of this now. You were right to come for me."

Smiling her satisfaction, the cook withdrew to her hearths, closing the drapes with a flourish behind her.

"By whose leave do you do this thing?" Lady Ygurna demanded. She had sensed a sorcerous presence amid the Norman presence and felt the cool surge of supernal confidence around him. Squandering her own resources, she made certain that he understood he would not have free rein in her house.

"By my lord's," Ambrose replied evenly. His feral aura flickered and then dimmed, though only he could have said whether it ebbed of his free will or Lady Ygurna's determination. A more ordinary man stood in the alcove now. He felt the drafts let in by the curtain and reached for his shirt. "I had my lord's leave earlier. If there has been an error . . ."

He capitulated too fast, Lady Ygurna thought, probing for the now-vanished aura. Her strength had never been that great, and she had been careful not to draw upon Alison's. "There has been no error," she replied as much to her own doubts as to his question. "But it is not fitting that you be served by such young women. I shall wash your back."

Ambrose hesitated, as if he might challenge her then and there. "As you wish, my lady," he said softly, lifting his chemise. "I'm sure I will be well served."

There was a flash of light that seared her eyes and left each nerve as if it had been struck by lightning. It was gone in a heartbeat, returned to the tear-shaped crystal he wore on a heavy gold chain around his neck, but Ygurna had recognized it just the same.

"Leave us," she told Alison and Wildecent.

"Did you see that?" Alison demanded when they had retreated beyond the kitchen. "Did you see that light?" She knew if her sister had not seen it, then it had indeed been magical.

Wildecent looked toward the tiny half-moon windows of the alcove. They reflected the amber glow of the candles and lamps, but nothing more. "What light?"

"The sorcerer's, Ambrose. He used his talisman, I'll wager."

"How? What talisman?"

"Sorcerers have no talent of their own. They get their strength from talismans, which are made to contain what they cannot. They're cut off from the natural strengths of God and nature, so they are always stealing power and hoarding it in their talismans." Alison raced ahead to open the door for a housecarl who was carrying a huge platter to the great hall.

The notion of stealing offended Wildecent; much as she wished to feel whatever it was that Alison and her aunt felt, she did not want to break the laws of God and man to get it. Nor had she liked the uses to which Ambrose put his power, if that was what had made them all so uncomfortable. She still did not think sorcery, or Ambrose, was evil— but there were many long steps between wrong and evil.

"Is our lady aunt in danger?" she asked, looking back to the kitchen.

"Nothing can harm Lady Ygurna in her own house," Alison replied. "Hurry up. If we aren't going to get a bath we might as well be first at the table!"

Wildecent nodded absently. She'd conduct a test, then—to measure sorcery's wrongness. If anything happened to her aunt, then Ambrose's magic was both wrong and evil, and she'd find the strength to resist its allure. But if sorcery could heal Lady Ygurna's malign disease, then she would seek its secrets.

very trestle table and bench that could be made to stand upright had been crammed into Lord Hafwynder's great hall. Jean Beauleyas and the other men from Torworden were the loudest and most noticeable of Godfrey's guests, but the homeless brethren of Saint Cuthbert's were there as well, and the cottagers he'd called in from his outlying fields and forests. So many guests, in fact, that the housecarls who normally shared his supper had, if they lived with a woman or two, retreated to their bowers to feast in private.

Battered by the noise of his own table, Godfrey Hafwynder would have been glad to join any one of them. Instead, he laughed at Lord Beauleyas's continental jokes and watched nervously for any indications that the holiday mood that kept everyone laughing rather than shouting was fading. Not that he would have been able to revitalize his hall; his own spirits were buoyed by frantic energy and an overabundance of ale rather than any true sense of confidence.

"Were I out there in those forests," he said to Jean Beauleyas, "I'd take a second thought before leaving the trees behind."

The Norman glowered back through red-rimmed eyes. "By God's will, I'd hope not! Think you that we've done all this to send them slinking off like whipped dogs? Think you that we'll chase them all over Wessex?"

"I'll be glad enough if they stay beyond my forests until the king's levy calls them to justice. I'm not for fighting them alone," Lord Godfrey replied, the ale forcing him to be honest.

"You're not alone," Lord Beauleyas shouted, a few heartbeats short of genuine anger. The tone penetrated every other conversation; the vast room fell silent. "You've got the good men of Torworden under your roof—unless you'd see them leave?"

The good men of Torworden chorused their support. Lord Godfrey felt the absence of his housecarls and berated himself that he was the one who brought discord into the room. "We'd not see you leave," he admitted loudly enough for the far tables to hear.

"Then pray that Tostig's Northumbrian dogs are fool enough to run right down to our arms for slaughter." Beauleyas stood and pointed toward Brother Alfred. "Pray for us!" he commanded.

Slashing through the sign of the Cross so quickly that his sleeves snapped, Brother Alfred led his peers in a fervent prayer that Beauleyas deemed acceptable. Actually they prayed for the soul of their departed Father Ralf who'd been a Norman himself and had understood these strangers as only their own blood could. But apparently satisfied, Jean was sitting again and blowing the top off another mug of ale.

Alison, with her hands demurely hidden by the folds of the tablecloth, shredded the fine embroidery of her belt. This was her father's hall, as it had been her grandfather's hall and Hafwynder Manor for many generations before that. She could not abide the shame the Normans hung around her father, nor his acceptance of it—though she shared his belief that fighting was best left to a general levy and not to any man or manor acting alone.

She jumped and yelped with surprise when Stephen touched her wrist.

"Are you frightened?" he asked, his hazel eyes boring into hers. "I don't think you or your sister have said a single word since you sat down."

Nonplussed, Alison stared back at him. She couldn't tell Stephen what she thought of his uncle at that moment, and she hadn't noticed Wildecent, sitting on Stephen's other side, staring at the door to the kitchens.

"You needn't be. Your home is well protected now. My uncle has made your safety his own."

The small door opened, admitting Lady Ygurna and a gust of wind-driven snow. The mistress of Hafwynder Manor slipped through the shadows to the stairwell and her room while Ambrose, still clad all in blue, closed the door quietly behind him.

"I'd rather that no one had to *make* our safety—that such protection as came from God and nature were sufficient," Alison murmured as Ambrose walked toward them.

"Wine?" Ambrose asked, resting a white-knuckled hand on Stephen's shoulder. "Or is there only ale?"

"Ale," Stephen confirmed, nudging closer to Alison so his tutor might squeeze between Wildecent and himself.

"So be it." He shouldered his way onto the bench then, placing his fingers to his lips and emitting a piercing whistle that got the attention of a towheaded servingboy. Ambrose pointed to his empty hand, then to Stephen's mug of ale. The boy nodded and Ambrose, his elbows splayed on the tablecloth, ground the heels of his palms into his eyes.

"What have you done?" Wildecent demanded. Her aunt's bent shadow against the stairwell was fresh in her mind.

"Gotten myself some ale, I hope."

He'd meant to sound lighthearted but his bath had not refreshed him in the least. His words emerged bone-weary and bitter.

"What's wrong?" Stephen asked.

"What have you done to my aunt?" Alison asked at the same time.

Ambrose pushed himself up from the table. Pale even

at the height of summer, the sorcerer now looked deathly ill. His eyes were hollow and ringed with red; his face was slack, empty of emotion. "I've done nothing to your lady aunt," he said without a trace of irony in his flat voice. "You might well ask what she has done to me."

Alison let her frayed belt drop to her lap. Surely Lady Ygurna had sensed the sorcery about this man—and, just as surely, that taint had been all but washed away. Had her aunt emerged victorious, but exhausted? She glanced at the stairway.

The servingboy brought a mug of ale, which Ambrose drained between breaths. "I think she wants her rest and privacy," he said while the boy refilled his cup.

"I can't imagine the Lady Ygurna needing rest," Stephen mused. He felt the tension but not its cause. Alison gave him a withering stare as she stood up.

"She wants privacy," Ambrose repeated.

Alison blinked and sat down with a thump. Whatever her aunt had done, it hadn't made a permanent change. Authority was returning to that cultured voice. She studied him as she had never studied a man before, gauging his strengths and weaknesses—and where she might lean to finish the task her aunt had begun. It came clear in a heartbeat; her eyes locked onto his and she gathered her resources.

The servingboy returned to the table with a hollowed trencher of Bethanil's holiday stew. Its rich aroma distracted the sorcerer; he withdrew a weaponlike two-tine fork from his belt-pouch and snared a good-sized chunk of meat.

He recognized Alison from his trance-visions; knew her impulsiveness and had seen the defiance in her eyes. Lady Ygurna had stirred frankincense and her gods only knew what else in his bathwater. She'd washed his back as if his years in Byzantium, Alexandria, and the caves of Persia were a stain that could be scrubbed away. Her oils and efforts *had* set him adrift—earth and water were the crone's elements and she'd used them freely—but his spirit went as deep as hers, and they'd been forced to reach a compromise.

Lord Hafwynder's Christmas feast was neither the time nor the place to explain this to the blue-eyed witch on the other side of Stephen. Ambrose swallowed his meat and braced for her onslaught.

"I'd rather you were friends, at least for one night," Stephen commanded, grasping both of them by the near wrist. "I am fond of you both and see no need for bickering."

Alison wrested free, realized she'd made a mistake, and let Stephen place her hand within Ambrose's. "My lady aunt is not well," she said defensively.

"Perhaps I can help her," Ambrose replied equitably, though he'd seen the malignancy in Lady Ygurna's shadow and knew, as the lady knew herself, that it could not be made to yield.

"We want no help from you."

"Alison!"

She looked at Stephen and felt her breath tighten around her heart. Time froze; each beat of her pulse lasted an eternity. Men were accustomed to obedience from women; no matter how much they loved, they wanted obedience first. She had laid herself down in his memories to secure his love but she'd forgotten obedience. Her choices seemed clear: make her apologies or lean on him again, but she could choose neither.

Stephen held her until her eyes were wide and dark with fear; then, not fully understanding why, he released her hand. "Ambrose is my friend," he whispered. "He'd never harm you."

Alison blinked and stared down at her cold hands. Time

resumed its normal pace and she prayed the confrontation could be forgotten.

Fond of her? Ambrose mused silently while Stephen's shoulders sank and he offered the Saxon heiress first ale, then sweetbreads from his own plate. Merely fond? He suspected a love charm, having already felt the powers of the herbals these women prepared, and calculated the countermeasures he would need to take if the young woman proved intractable.

Ambrose had arrived in Aquitaine full of grand philosophies and the knowledge that his own abilities lay not in the leading of men but in the manipulating of them. His sincere and loyal affection for Stephen did not conflict with his belief that here was a young man who could *do,* where he could only dream. It was essential that Stephen take a wife, and he'd always intended that his friend would find his true love freely and without interference. But he'd never bargained for a Saxon witch changing all the rules.

Still, the old crone had heard him give his word that he'd not tamper with her golden apprentice. The frankincense had given him a headache, nothing more, but his own word, freely given, would bind him to the grave and beyond. He sank deep into his private thoughts, curing the headache as he went. Perhaps it was not so bad. Perhaps Stephen would be just as happy with a wife who chose him. Perhaps there was a brighter future for his philosophies here in England than in what remained of the Frankish Empire.

"Excuse me, my lord."

The voice came to Ambrose from another world. He resisted but it came again, touching him physically this time. Gathering anger and irritation, he returned and considered the interruption.

"Excuse me, my lord, but could you help my aunt?"

It was the other one: not daughter, not sister, not

witch, and not apprentice—only a timid waif whose spirit was cloaked in shadows of her own devising. Ambrose shrank back from her emptiness and from the pinpoint glow of curiosity at its center. He concentrated his disdain and made a wall of it between them—but then, he could not remember the feral child he had been when the magi had plucked him from a Byzantine gutter for much the same qualities.

"I *need* to know, my lord," Wildecent persisted. She carried her shyness like a shield, and the light within her burned through Ambrose's wall.

"Your lady aunt is very sick," he explained patiently, still unwilling to acknowledge her demands. "There is nothing more I can do for her. She has all the medicines I could compound. I'm sorry."

"She's dying, isn't she?"

Ambrose was unprepared to discuss death with a child—for although he considered Alison a woman, he saw Wildecent as a child. She saw his hesitation and pounced on it.

"She says death is natural, that there comes a time when it can no longer be avoided or delayed. She says there comes a time when the soul must return. Do you think that's true?"

"Of course it's true," Ambrose muttered. "Everything that lives must die at the end of its appointed time."

"Is it true for sorcery as well?"

She could not have struck a more crippling blow if she'd used her delicate eating knife along his neck. "Child, I do not discuss such things."

"You called me 'Seeker' once," she reproached him. "I want to learn."

He remembered her—remembered everything about that unfortunate evening when he'd pushed himself beyond what might have been called his natural limits, and regretted it as well. His fingers were shaking as he pushed his hair back from his face. "Not here. Not now." He stifled the urge to call her "child" again, but he could not bring himself to speak her name.

"Tell me when I can come to you."

"Come to the tower later, after everyone's asleep."

She nodded, and Ambrose felt himself falling down some bleak, endless passageway. It was clear, staring into those eyes, that she was no child and that she posed a greater threat to his dreams than either her sister or her aunt.

He told himself she would not come, and clung to that hope throughout the juggling, dancing, and singing that Lord Hafwynder commanded for their entertainment. It was a false hope, though, and the honest part of him—the greater part—knew she would risk everything to come to him. He might well have asked her to meet him for a love tryst. Indeed, that might have been easier and less dangerous for them both.

He was a fine manipulator, he reflected, spinning the ale mug in his hands, then returning it, still full, to the tablecloth. He made wonderful and abstract plans, drew charts of the stars and planets, reducing love and hate to predictable conjunctions—but never for himself. Taken up by the magi as an unformed child, he'd been a blind, obedient vessel for their teachings until, after his mentor died, he'd burst from a cocoon—and found he knew little of life among men, and nothing at all about women.

The less restrained among the men, be they Norman or Saxon, were already starting to lean on their elbows and to watch the jugglers with fixed, unfocused stares. The Yulelog would continue to burn until the Twelfth Night feast, but Christmas was drawing to a ragged close. Lord Hafwynder himself made a final toast, and the drudges emerged to set about converting tables to sleeping pallets.

Ambrose bade his Lord Beauleyas and Stephen good night and slipped quietly from the hall.

Wildecent and Alison found themselves at the foot of the stairway, each politely wishing the other a good rest and hoping her secrets could not be read on her face.

The storeroom felt darker than the tunnel leading from the tower to the kitchens, and the wolf-fur blanket, which gave so much warmth and comfort within the bedstead, failed to provide either amid the sharp-cornered boxes. Wildecent heard tiny squeaks as well, and imagined, with crystalline clarity, a stream of mice rippling toward her crude pallet. It would be a long wait until the great hall was quiet and she could sneak past Stephen's room, past Lady Ygurna's room, and on to the tower.

Arranging her cloak and the blanket as best she could, she settled back against the sturdiest of the boxes and softly recited the rhymed lessons Lady Ygurna had taught her and Alison over the years. She was halfway through the litany of decoctions when sleep surprised her. It was still dark when she sat up again and struggled to remember where she was and why.

The Yulelog, which must burn the full twelve days or bring ill tidings and death to the manor, had been carefully banked with charcoal. Its ruddy glow illuminated a dozen nameless men slumped against each other, the walls, and such furniture as the drudges had not cleared away. An assortment of snores and coughs rose from the darkness, but except for the dogs fighting for scraps and the clerics praying, it seemed that everyone was asleep.

Clutching her dark cloak tightly around her shoulders, Wildecent tiptoed along the gallery. A sliver of candlelight poked through the door to her aunt's room. She paused, back flattened against the wall, and was sure she heard them whispering and moving around. She recalled the anxious look on Alison's face when she'd said good night, then continued down the stairs.

Snow was still falling as she crossed from the great hall to the tower. Its velvet darkness made it impossible to guess what hour of the night it was. The upper shutters were closed and dark. Ambrose had said to come after everyone was asleep; Wildecent's greatest fear as she slid her feet along the stone steps was that she was too late.

She knocked once, way too softly for anyone to have heard, then pressed her knuckles to her mouth, unable to cause a greater noise. Tears had begun to form behind her eyes when the bolt shot open and Ambrose pulled her through the doorway. He held the candle between them and the first tear made a broad track down her cheek.

"Go then, if you're so frightened," he said, turning his back on her. "I'm not forcing you to stay."

Wildecent tried to swallow the rock that had formed in her throat, and sniffed back the tears, but she stayed close by the door and said nothing to him.

He'd unchained their clothes chest and moved it, with help she imagined, to the center of the room. Circles and other shapes that glowed with their own light had been drawn across its lid. In the center, and looking at first like a strange collection of snow, wood chips, and stone, was a miniature of Hafwynder Manor.

"What are you making?" she asked, still not daring to take a step deeper into what had been her own bedroom.

"A symbol of your father's manor."

"Lord Hafwynder is not my father," Wildecent admitted, and found that the tremor had vanished from her voice.

Ambrose noted the difference, too. He scattered a few more pine needles beyond the snow circle and brought the candle close to her again. "I know," he said gently.

"My aunt told you?"

He felt an urge to set the candle aside, to gather her into his arms, but he fought it and contented himself with touching a strand of hair that had caught on her moist eyelashes. "The Lady Ygurna, whom we both know is not your aunt, told me only about Alison, who is not your sister. That was enough to tell me who *you* were—or were not." Another tear escaped to stream past his fingertips; he felt more brutal than any drunken oaf he'd ever discredited in his mind. "They— No, I . . . didn't mean to hurt you," he stammered.

"I understand," she replied, averting her eyes.

Ambrose hurried back to the chest where he had assembled something he could understand. "I mean to draw the outlaws here . . . to the opening of the rampart."

"Wouldn't it be better to push them away?" Wildecent asked, suddenly understanding what Alison and Lady Ygurna would do—would probably *be* doing before sunrise.

He scattered more bits of pine, then showed her the contents of a tiny sack. "Lord Beauleyas found their campsite; I gathered ashes and bits of their garbage. We can use that to draw them here, while we're ready. It's almost like an ambush."

"You would do that, then." She wiped her face on her sleeve and finally took a step into the room. "You wouldn't just hide us . . . well, *they'd* say 'within nature.' Aren't you afraid when you make magic act outright on free men?"

The young sorcerer looked up from the trail he was laying across the clothes chest. "Is it more natural to hide men like Stephen, Lord Beauleyas, and even Lord Hafwynder from their sworn enemies or to improve the chance that they'll win their battles?"

stream of white powder sifted through Alison's fingers. "Salt for purity," she chanted as the grains fell into the black stone mortar.

"Salt for purity; dragon's blood for strength," sang her aunt, adding motes of a rusty brown powder.

"Salt for purity; dragon's blood for strength; frankincense for protection from evil."

"Myrrh to guard us from death!"

With each ingredient the chant was repeated from the beginning and the mixture pounded to an even consistency. More herbs and powders, some deliciously fragrant, others noisome and foul, were lifted from the black coffer, invoked by name, and blended with their predecessors. The mortar itself had been set on a small, velvet-covered table in the center of Lady Ygurna's small room. As the chant grew longer, the two women danced a slow, stately circle around the table. Four hands guided the pestle as it rose and fell.

They had already shed their Christianity to invoke ancient and terrible aspects of the gods and goddesses who were commemorated in the neglected stone circles. Beneath the velvet was a stone the size of two clenched fists, hand-polished by generations of priestesses and incised with an endless, meandering spiral. Alison had begun the ritual by staring at that stone until the blood-dark channels flowed crimson in her mind and she heard strange, heavy voices calling her name.

Now, weaving cross-footed through the circle, Alison felt her feet begin to tingle. They moved more quickly, finding new rhythms to the chant and dragging her behind. The tingling spread to her hands, and for a moment she felt the Crab gnawing in her aunt's side, then the flow reversed. Prickling and tickling, the ancient powers rose through her like smoke and passed through her hands into Ygurna's frail body.

Her blood grew hot as they raced through the remainder of the ingredients in a frenzy until finally, the pestle rolling unnoticed from the table to the floor, they held the brimming mortar high between them. They bore it to the window ledge, where a shallow brazier of glowing charcoal rested. The powder shot sparks across the room when it struck the coals, and its pungent smoke dropped both women to the floor.

Alison awoke first, touching herself gingerly to determine if the strangeness she felt within had extended to the outer, visible part of herself. Satisfied that she remained herself, she stirred the coals of the smoldering brazier and placed a tight cover over it.

Her body belonged to someone else. Her legs were too long, her hands too fast, and her eyes inclined to see what Alison herself seldom noticed. She felt that if she had leaned in any direction she would have found the terrible goddess they had invoked and, wisely fearing such an encounter, she settled down on the bed to await her aunt's recovery.

"Was it a success?" she asked long minutes later when the old woman opened her eyes.

"Why ask me?" Lady Ygurna snapped. "You're the one who'd know." She got her hands beneath her and pushed, but her arms had no strength and she sank back to the floor. Alison offered her hands, and strength returned. "Yes, it worked."

Alison guided her aunt to sit beside her on the bed. "I feel so strange—filled with something that is not myself, and filled with myself as well. I have to think about everything: breathing, swallowing. I move myself as if I were my own puppet."

Sighing, Ygurna gathered her niece to her breast and stroked the long blond hair, so Alison would not see the thin tears slipping down her cheeks. "You are the last High Priestess of Avalon; the goddess makes herself known through you and works her magic within you. Long ago, to do what we would do this night, you would have fasted within the stones. Dozens of handmaidens would have danced in your summoning circle, and when *she* came she would have filled you utterly."

Such subjugation, even to a goddess, struck terror in that part of Alison which had always been Alison. The flames of rebellion shot up to touch that other part where they burned bright and painful before vanishing. She would not have made an acceptable High Priestess—but she was all that remained to the goddess. "Will I be enough?" Alison whispered to herself.

"You will have to be," her aunt replied, echoing the sentiments Alison heard proclaimed from the depths of her mind.

Much remained to be done, much that others should have done earlier and much that Alison, filled and made awkward by the goddess's presence, could only sit and watch.

"We should have included Wildecent," the young woman considered as they tried, for the third, unsuccessful time, to fix garlands of mistletoe and oak in their hair. "I could go and wake her. She didn't sleep downstairs, you know. She said she would sleep alone in the storerooms up here."

Lady Ygurna let the leaves fall to the floor. "No, she would be a danger to us."

"She's served us before."

"But not now—not with these Normans and their sorcerer within our walls. You know already she cannot be trusted."

Alison had made her peace with Wildecent's trustworthiness, just as she'd had to make peace with her own, but something in Lady Ygurna's comments had roused that *other* within her and Alison found herself asking questions.

"Do you really think that Lord Ambrose is a sorcerer? He didn't seem like one to me when he joined us after his bath. He didn't seem like anything but a tired man."

"He is a sorcerer," her aunt assured her, clasping a heavy, ornate belt around Alison's waist. "I had it from his own lips—bereft of God and nature. The most dangerous sort imaginable. He draws his power from himself and those he catches in his snares. His pride knows no limits, Alison, remember that. He will steal the souls of those foolish enough to love him."

"But you cut his power. He can do nothing within these walls."

"I anointed him and wrung the truth from him. He will not stand in our way, but I could not break him, my daughter. Only you have the strength for that, you and the goddess within you."

"Stephen?" That was a question from Alison's own heart, for if Ambrose truly could steal souls, then she would have to confront him to rescue Stephen's since it was clear the young man was bound more strongly to his tutor than she had bound him to herself.

Lady Ygurna held her tightly. "Tread softly, Alison my daughter. Free him, if you must—and Wildecent if she slips from the path—but resist loving him. Even free, he will hurt you because he is not one of us.

"It is the nature of men to fight—and when they lose they are purged from the land. The priests who walked beside our priestesses are long vanished, the Romans who built our bolt-hole are gone as well. Twice ten generations we have walked beside these Saxons—we have not the strength to begin again with men such as Stephen.''

"I will bind him to me," Alison replied, aware that she promised what she had already attempted to do.

Her aunt released her, holding her at arm's length. "Not now, not while he is shadowed by sorcery. He is a handle on your own heart, free for the grasping."

Guilt and fear gripped her as she lied and gave Lady Ygurna her word. She told herself that she had confronted Ambrose already, in her dreams, and driven him off, but the goddess within her was not deceived.

"You have a talent to see into men's hearts," Lady Ygurna continued. "As you grow, and it grows, do not be tempted to use it without guidance, or surely you will be cast out into the darkness."

Lady Ygurna turned away to get the covered brazier; she did not see the swift play of emotions across the new priestess's face.

Alison had felt the darkness when she challenged the sorcerer, and she felt it now beyond the goddess. Was she doomed before she had begun? Condemned by the impulsive, but not malicious, use of a talent her aunt had always said was the most tangible sign of the goddess's favor? Her frantic imagination conjured up a stern image of the goddess with her long fingers pointing toward the darkness.

She felt herself lifted like a leaf. She drew upon her talent, cast it out as an anchor, and made the goddess smile.

"I have never moved without *her* guidance," she said slowly, unaware that she spoke aloud. "Even before, when I had not seen her face smiling on me."

Lady Ygurna watched with horror as Alison's eyes glazed and rolled white. There was no mistaking the touch of the goddess—and no mistaking the lean of Alison's mind, either. A foretaste of disaster shot through her—mortal disaster for herself and something more for Alison. She knew, even as the moment passed and Alison breathed normally again, that the goddess had called her name and Alison would face the future without her lady aunt.

She gave Alison the brazier to carry and drew the laces of her cloak taut across her shoulders; Alison, filled with the goddess, would face the winter night wearing only a priestess's gown and soft suede boots. They moved cautiously down the stairway and out into the snow, but not because they feared discovery. The ashes they carried in the brazier would protect them from a chance encounter with a friend just as they would conceal the manor from the prying eyes of its enemies.

They were not, however, the only only ones abroad. Another set of footprints led away from the great hall toward the kitchens. Alison thought immediately of Wildecent. She looked up toward their room in the tower. It was hard to tell, with the snow and the darkness, but there might be light flickering behind the shutters.

"What if we aren't alone?" she asked her aunt.

Lady Ygurna followed her niece's stare to the upper level of the tower. She had not secured a promise that Ambrose would not meddle in the manor's defenses because he had demanded the same promise of her in return. Pride had kept her from lying to him. "We have the ancient powers with us," she said grimly, pulling Alison out into the yard. "He has only himself."

"Of course," Alison replied, forcing the other thoughts from her mind as she concentrated on her footing in the rough snow.

Her aunt, however, must have heard something less than complete conviction in her voice, for they halted beneath the guard-porch. Setting the brazier in the snow, then fumbling with her cloak and sleeves, Lady Ygurna finally produced a small, waxen lump that she pressed into Alison's hands.

"Chew on that awhile," she commanded.

Obediently, but unwillingly, Alison pushed the wax through her lips. It was sweet-tasting at first, but once she had swallowed it turned to fire. The sensation of being a guest in an ill-fitting body intensified. Flinging her arms wildly, Alison fell into her aunt's outstretched arms. A spasm of lightning whipped along her spine; she gulped down the rest of the wax whole.

"You must *believe*," Lady Ygurna hissed in her ear. "Feel the ancient forces rising within you. Surrender to them! You are their sword—which only your own doubt can blunt."

Alison felt the sword pass through her and cried out through black-stained lips.

"You have the strength already!" Lady Ygurna insisted, shaking Alison until the young woman's teeth knocked together, never doubting the wisdom of what she did. "Now find the belief!"

Desperate to end her agony, Alison leaped to the glow of ecstatic faith. The pain ended as suddenly as it had begun, and, regaining her dignity, she stood erect. The clear line between herself and the goddess had been destroyed by the drugged wax. The ancient deity was everywhere within, but Alison had not herself been displaced. She lifted the heavy bar from the gate and set it aside in the snow without alerting her father's guards, then she took up the brazier and led the way to the open snow beyond the ice rampart.

There was another piece of drug-laced wax tucked deep up Lady Ygurna's sleeve, for emergencies, as the first had been. But to give Alison a second taste of the ecstasy-inducing decoction might split the young woman's spirit irrevocably from her body; for Lady Ygurna to swallow the substance herself was certain, albeit painless, death. Within Lady Ygurna's darkly practical imagination there were clear circumstances when either would be an acceptable risk.

She had not dared to tell Alison how far they had wandered from the rituals and traditions she and the young woman's mother had been secretly taught. The teaching stories spoke of times when whole tribes and their herds had been concealed within a dome of magic; they also mentioned that the magic had sometimes failed—or succeeded too well—by hiding the tribe forever as fairy folk within a hollow hill. But even those failures had been guided by a small legion of priestesses and augmented by druidic sacrifice in the tribal oak grove.

Tonight's sacrifice was a single pigeon, hurriedly slaughtered and bled, and swiftly buried in the mud near the stables. The legion was only herself, fighting cold and pain and doubt. But her contagion had not spread to Alison. The golden-haired priestess *believed*, now, and could not imagine that there might have been another way. Snow melted away where she walked, and the ashen circle, while not the full three paces across, shimmered with cold, pure power.

Anything would be justified if they could preserve this last bastion of the old ways from desecration.

"Hurry up!" the gold-haired high priestess commanded. "We must be finished before the first light of dawn."

Lady Ygurna took another step through the snow. Her feet were useless blocks of wood, long past pain. Her cloak was an ice-crusted weight pulling her down into the powdery snow. She longed to call Alison back, to warm herself in the goddess's aura, but the priestess might sense her doubt and Alison herself might succumb to compassion.

She dug into her sleeve and found the second lump of wax.

The circle would be sanctified and strengthened by more than pigeon's blood.

A warming serenity lifted the older woman from her cares. She trudged through the snow with new energy and a gentle smile on her lips.

Wildecent sat on the sideboard, knees drawn up to her chest, watching Ambrose prepare his magic and trying to conceal a vague sense of disappointment. He'd completed his model of the manor, his *micros,* what seemed like hours ago, then turned his attention to the assorted garbage he'd collected at the outlaw camp. After erecting a tripod pendulum over the microcosm, he suspended bits of cloth and hair from it and set them swinging.

"What's that for?" she had asked as he painted arrows and stranger signs across the floor with his glowing paint.

"To tell me where they are tonight," he replied, drawing another knotted curve. "Homeopathic principles draw these fragments toward their whole. Living tissues—hair, nail paring, and especially blood—are best, but everything within the *micros* knows its origin and will point toward it."

"But the drafts in this room always run from that window there to the door." She spoke from experience and indicated that his shining arrow followed the usual pattern.

Ambrose set his brushes aside. "Lesson the first: the question always contains its answer; the true question contains the true answer. My *micros* was aligned by true questions. If there are drafts in this room then they are part of the true answer. The microcosm and the macrocosm always conform."

Wildecent had contained the rest of her questions, then,

and let him go back to his work. He painted with a quiet purpose most unlike the rituals she had watched her aunt and sister perform. There was no frantic singing or dancing. The sorcerer's ideal of music seemed bound up in a crystal chime he struck from time to time. Its tone was pure and echoed for long moments, but it was hardly music.

He set aside his brushes and took up a gem-tipped wand. He struck the chime twice, then started drawing his symbols in the air. Both Lady Ygurna and Alison had said there was no talent involved with sorcery and seemed to count that fact among its sacrilege. When Wildecent watched the wand whip through the air, leaving no glowing trail behind it, her disappointment burst forth.

"I can't see anything," she complained aloud to herself.

Ambrose held the wand motionless before him. "Must you see the wind to know it blows?" he demanded.

She had not meant for him to hear her, but rose to the challenge. "I see the leaves move or hear them rub together or feel my skirts swirl around me. If I do not see or hear or feel, then I do not know the wind blows."

The sorcerer nodded and pointed the wand at her. "Is your mind a prisoner of your senses? If you were shut away in a dark, draftless room the wind would still blow— and your mind would know what your feeble senses do not."

"I suppose." Wildecent shrugged and hunkered down to rest her chin atop her knees. "I wouldn't really know— couldn't really know."

He twirled the wand through his fingers, then tossed it in the air. It vanished as he spoke a single word and clapped his hands. Wildecent sat bolt upright.

"It's gone!" she murmured.

Flaring the fingers of his right hand, Ambrose spoke

another word and seemed to draw the wand from the flesh of his palm. "Your senses lie to you, Wildecent," he chided, spinning the wand some more until its gemstone tip changed from red to blue. "They can be deceived. But a mind filled with knowledge can never be deceived. Once you've learned to ask the true questions, Wildecent, your mind will never lie to you. It knows what your senses cannot imagine."

He flipped the slender rod once again and returned to drawing his invisible symbols. Wildecent pulled her knees up slowly and watched the red gem with new respect. She had just begun to believe she could see a faint crimson glow when he set the wand aside and suspended his crystal pendant from the pendulum.

"Now you must be quiet," he cautioned her, settling onto a cushion that left his eyes level with the fire-sparkling stone. "I use the *macros* to build my *micros*. Now I must reverse the process and impress the truth of the microcosm onto its parent."

An uncontrolled shiver raced down Wildecent's back. She thought nothing of it, but Ambrose demanded to know what had flashed across her mind.

Wildecent gestured helplessly; the thought had been so vague, but the image it left behind was not one she wished to share. "Suppose," she said cautiously, hoping that Ambrose could not snare the actuality from her memory, "suppose something touched the macrocosm—right now, while you were touching it, too."

Ambrose frowned. "She would not promise. The true question contains the true answer: what your aunt has done was, is, and will be part of my doing."

He struck the chime and lost himself staring at the crystal.

awn light found Alison with tears running down her face. She had completed the narrow ash circle around the manor and cast the empty brazier into the snow. The goddess's warmth still protected her from the cold and gave her both strength and sureness to leap safely across the stream where a dark shape lay across the grayish snow. Those parts of her that were one with the goddess exalted that they had done what they had set out to do, but the simpler person who was Alison Hafwyndersdattir was shamed by the price they had paid.

"There's no pain," her aunt mumbled as Alison fell to her knees in the snow. "I'm almost gone . . . There's very little left to hurt, my love. I'm not frightened; you shouldn't be either."

The words for blessing and parting formed at the back of Alison's mind but she refused to utter them. She refused to say anything at all, lest those other parts of her take control. She'd use the goddess's strength, though, without such hesitation, and gathered the stiff woman gently in her arms.

Icy fingers closed over hers; her aunt's eyes burned with an unhealthy vigor. "Leave me here," the old woman commanded. "It's my time." But Alison only shook her head and began the grim trek back to the stockade gate. Lady Ygurna whimpered deep in her throat and pressed her blue fingers against Alison's wrist. "They're coming! I feel them. They're coming up the ridge. There's blood in their eyes, on their hands and feet. They follow the blood. They only see the blood!"

Alison shook her head, but she did not jump back across the stream. She saw what her aunt saw: a small horde of ugly-spirited men following a trail that led to Hafwynder

Manor. The goddess told her the trail was sorcery, an abomination laid across the earth—and perhaps the goddess was right. It didn't really matter. The outlaws would follow the trail; they'd never look up to wonder where the manor was; they'd never notice that it had been hidden; they'd only follow the trail that led straight to the stone tower.

Great sobs shook her shoulders and a cold wind whipped around her legs. She nearly dropped her aunt as the goddess's protection vanished completely then reasserted itself, much weaker than before.

"Save yourself," Lady Ygurna counseled, letting go of the girl's wrist and struggling feebly to complete her fall to the snow. "The trees will hide you."

"The trees," Alison repeated, her eyes focused in some other world. "We'll go to the trees. The oak trees will protect us."

She did not find oak trees as she stumbled across the crusted snow, but evergreens, whose needles had kept out the snow and wind, invited her to shelter in their midst. When Lady Ygurna had been carefully laid upon the rust red carpet of fallen needles, the priestess cast aside her jewelry and rolled herself inside the ice-creased cloak to pass the last of the goddess's warmth to her aunt.

A last snowflake sifted through the branches and rested on the dark wool a moment before it melted away. A tiny ellipse of orange-gold sunlight peeped through the distant trees.

"They come! They come!" the night guard shouted, striking the scrap iron with his mallet. "Along the ridge to the north. They've broken through!"

The alarm spread swiftly through the manor. Lord Godfrey raced from the hall to the guard-porch, the laces of his tunic and breeches snapping loudly against each other.

The Norman chief was not far behind, cursing the twisted leg that slowed him to a child's pace. He grabbed the sides of the plank ladder and hauled himself up beside the Saxon lord.

"Deus aeie," he whispered. God help us—as much a command as a prayer.

There were better than two dozen mounted men visible at the top of the ridge, and perhaps twice that many footmen in their wake. Had Ranulf's huge gray horse not been in the lead, the Torworden lord would have doubted it was the same band Stephen had described so many times. Beauleyas weighed the strength of his own alliance against that of the outlaws and mentally revised his plans. A flight of well-aimed arrows forced him to begin the revision again.

"Be damned," he muttered, crouched down in the shadows beside the Saxon lord, "if he doesn't know exactly what I'd do myself!"

"We aren't lost, are we?" Lord Godfrey asked, having caught the note of grudging admiration in his companion's voice. "I'll bring up my archers," and shouted their names to the empty yard below.

"Would you give the manor away?" Lord Beauleyas demanded, scrambling to the ladder hole and waving the Saxon archers back to the shadows where they'd been ordered to wait. "From yon ridge they can see every building and every man. Call up your archers! What—and let them see we can't hurt them?"

"It was good enough yesterday."

"Aye—and yesterday I did not think to look upon outlaws mounted upon my own horses and accompanied by two score of infantry. We might take one or two, but never enough before they turned away and sought an easier prize."

"Which I still say would not be so bad a thing."

The Norman scowled, which pinched his scar and made it throb demonically. "We'll see the end of it here . . . today. Call out to him. Tell him your name and promise your loyalty. Lure his men down within the ice. What would have kept them out will keep them in just as easily."

"We'll have to let them through the gate," Lord Godfrey said as the implications of Beauleyas's plan came clear to him. "We'll have them right on top of us."

They locked stares. If Hafwynder brought himself to accept the Norman position—that squelching the outlaws and whatever alliance operated through them was worth considerable sacrifice of life and limb—then luring the hillside band into the confines of the stockade was a worthy goal. But if the lives of his men and the integrity of his lands were more important than the name and allegiances of the man who claimed his oath, then fighting was the same as suicide.

Lord Godfrey was still pondering the dilemma when the man on Ranulf's horse rode in close enough to hail the guard-porch. "Ho, the manor," the shaggy but well armed man cried in understandable English. "Open your gates, throw down your weapons and stand aside."

"In whose name?" Lord Hafwynder countered. The sour ale in his stomach churned and his fingers rippled over the hilt of his sword. Every distrusting anxiety he'd felt about his Norman allies roared between his ears and echoed in counterpoint to his long-held doubts about King Edward and the entire English aristocracy of which he was a part. Whatever oaths the outlaw claimed—and by his visible strength he had to have some greater ally— Lord Godfrey's Wessex loyalties were bound to suffer.

"In the name of Earl Tostig and the King of Norway," the wolf's-head shouted, letting the gray come a few paces closer, "and the name of the Black Wolf as well."

"He'll come," Jean Beauleyas whispered hoarsely from the shadows. "His arrogance precedes him. Do what you must, but get him through the gate so we may put an end to him once and for all."

Lord Hafwynder glowered. He would rather not fight, but the notion of outright surrender to an outlaw and, by extension, the the exiled and equally outlawed Tostig Godwinson stuck in his throat. "I'll need assurances for my men and chattels," he yelled, ignoring Lord Beauleyas.

"Ye stand loyal to the Norman dogs. There're no assurances to those who've supped with England's traitors."

It looked for a moment as if pride would get the better of Torworden's castellan, as well. The Norman's scar was throbbing and his breath came in ragged snarls. But he mastered himself and spoke calmly. "Tell him we've left for Westminster. See if he'll believe we've abandoned you."

Lord Godfrey twisted a few strands of his beard and wished Thorkel Longsword were in the guard-porch beside him. Tostig Godwinson was mean-spirited and weak-willed; the families of his earldom, Northumbria, had successfully petitioned Edward and had him stripped of his title; if he became king, England would sink into anarchy. The Normans, either Duke William or lesser men like Beauleyas, were brutally efficient administrators; they could save the land from civil war, but England would cease to be his culture and society. Longsword stood apart from them all and saw their faults and strengths more clearly, but the Viking was hidden in the great hall with the rest of the men so the outlaws could not judge the manor's true strength.

"Our loyalty's to King Edward, for so long as he may live, and to his rightful heirs thereafter," Lord Godfrey shouted to the outlaws, the Normans, and to God. "We told them so before they left for Westminster."

The outlaw conferred with his men. Lord Godfrey let the hairs fall from his fingers. Although he couldn't imagine himself as an outlaw, he also couldn't imagine himself falling for the trap his Norman allies had laid.

"He's splitting his men," he whispered to Beauleyas as the larger part of the outlaw band moved to the stockade. "He's leaving the archers on the ridge and bringing up a battering ram between his knights."

"Then open the gates and leave them that way for a while. Once the battle's begun the archers must either run or join their fellows down here; their arrows won't help them."

Once again Lord Godfrey hesitated and compromised. He summoned his archers, a mere dozen men who were better trained as hunters than soldiers, and bade them fire upon the advancing outlaws. Lord Beauleyas cursed as two of the arrows found their mark and the Black Wolf signaled his band to a halt.

But the outlaws did not turn back. Their savage assault on the home of Edmund Saex had won them three days debauchery amid the ruins, and empty bellies thereafter. If they'd any hope of surviving the harsh winter, much less of returning to their base in Northumbria, they needed what lay within Hafwynder's rampart and stockade. The Black Wolf called forth an arrow volley of his own and led the charge to the gate.

The ice rampart did its main work, forcing the attackers to run a narrow gauntlet to the well-defended gate. The mounted and armored men could only shout encouragement while the footmen ran the battering ram forward. Atop the guard-porch, the Saxon archers could pepper the footmen each time they braved the gate but they were themselves vulnerable every time they stood up to take aim. When the second defending archer took an arrow it became clear that the Black Wolf would have more footmen than Lord Godfrey had archers.

"Pull the bar!" he shouted to the men below the porch as he swung down the ladder.

The gates parted with the next thrust of the ram. The Black Wolf, needing the manor and its supplies, believed it was surrendering and led his men down the gauntlet even as the alarm clanged and his own archers shouted warnings from higher on the ridge. He was in the yard with Lord Godfrey's housecarls and a handful of Normans running toward him before he realized the extent of his mistake. Taking his war ax in an arc over his head, the Black Wolf took aim at Godfrey and spurred the gray horse across the yard.

The world narrowed for each man—Wessex Saxon, Norman, or Northumbrian outlaw. The defenders had the advantage of surprise; the outlaws, even without their archers, had superior numbers.

Godfrey Hafwynder watched the horse surge toward him. Feeling as though time had slowed to a fraction of its normal pace, he gripped his own ax with both hands and prepared to ward a blow that, well delivered, could hack a man in two. He watched the razor crescent begin its descent and pushed the haft of his own ax up to meet it. Wood struck wood and the ax heads locked together. The sense of timelessness vanished as the power of both weapons shot through his arms and the gray horse became a force of pure chaos.

It was no accident that Beauleyas had set his men to fight on foot. Though the Norman knight counted himself foremost a mounted warrior, he was most particular about the circumstances in which he brought his destrier to battle. He needed a broad field for effective use of his specially couched lance, and he needed a specially trained horse, hand-led to the battlefield and practically useless for anything but war.

Ranulf's horse, indeed all the horses in the crowded yard, had no tolerance for the jostling tumult of battle. It shied sideways as the ax shadows fell across its eyes. It plunged forward in bulge-eyed panic when its rider lost his balance and sawed wildly on its reins. It reared, pulling the ax from Lord Godfrey's hands; flailed, striking the Saxon lord with its hooves; twisted, bringing itself under the ax blade; collapsed backward, dropping the Black Wolf to the frozen ground before it bolted and escaped through the gate.

Unarmed and dazed, Godfrey staggered in a circle. The outlaw leader was on the ground to his left. The axes, still locked together, were a few steps further on. A glimmer of understanding pushed the Saxon lord toward the weapons but he made no sense of the fury raging around him nor any attempt to avoid it. A faceless man, neither friend nor enemy, defending himself from the sweeping stroke of the double-headed ax, struck Godfrey as he parried and the Saxon lord fell across the outlaw's chest.

No one in the yard saw him fall. Beauleyas, protected by his hauberk from everything except the double-ax, was slashing his way through a knot of lightly armed footmen, unaware that these were the outlaw archers who had, indeed, come down to join the fracas. Thorkel Longsword held his ground on the steps of the great hall, nearly immobilized by a gash across his thigh, but still wielding a sword that was very nearly the equal of the Saxon ax.

Protected as much by his uncle's orders as by a borrowed mail shirt, Stephen fought shoulder-to-shoulder with two of the Torworden men. They best knew the dangers of an untrained horse, and had exploited their knowledge. Every horse had been driven to a frenzy; every man who had ridden through the gate lay broken in the bloody snow at their feet.

It could have been five minutes or an eternity since Stephen had drawn his sword and come running out of the great hall. His healing shoulder burned from the effort of fighting, and the mail shirt snapped taut over his chest as he tried to get his breath. Holding the sword in guard in front of him, he stared at the blood running slowly toward its hilt. He remembered killing his first man at the start, but already he'd lost track of his dead.

"You're doing fine," the veteran on his left said just as Stephen's gasping grew ragged and he lowered the blade a fraction.

"We've got them running," his other companion told him. "Now we go looking for them."

Stephen blinked and looked past his sword. It was true; there wasn't anyone looming in front of them anymore. His uncle and a handful of the Saxon housecarls were poised in front of the now closed stockade gate. The clang of steel on steel was muted, and it took Stephen a long moment to realize that the battle had moved deeper into the manor as the outlaws, deprived of an easy exit, sought shelter amid the bowers.

Lord Godfrey's archers, who had wisely stayed in the guard-porch above the fighting, were summoned to vigilance again.

"Where's Hafwynder?" Jean shouted, leading his men to the great hall steps. "Where's the Wolf?"

Thorkel Longsword looked up from lashing a makeshift bandage over his leg wound. He scanned the standing men, much as Beauleyas had already done, shrugged, and finished tying his knots.

"Can you search for them?" the Norman asked, midway between Stephen's trio and the Viking.

"As well as you," he replied, tipping his sword at the Norman's bad leg.

Beauleyas snorted and lowered his own sword in mock salute. "We'll go together, then."

The defense of Hafwynder Manor had entered its most elusive and dangerous phase. The outlaws were trapped within the stockade, but there were still more of them than defenders. Worse, emboldened by the relative quiet, the ordinary folk of the manor had begun to poke their heads out windows and doorways where they distracted their protectors and unwittingly offered themselves up as hostages.

Stephen and his flankers made their way along the livestock pens toward the stables. He was thrusting his sword into suspicious piles of straw when shouts erupted from several directions. Sidestepping back into sunlight he saw flames shooting through the straw roof of the stables.

"Sulwyn!" he shouted as all other concerns faded from his mind.

His sword arm hung limp and he was oblivious to everything around him—including the squishing sound of ice-crusted straw breaking under a man's weight. An arm snaked in from behind, circling tight and thrusting a long knife at his throat. Long days and months of practice served him well as he overcame the instinct to immediately pull away but gave himself, instead, to his attacker's momentum for the split second of time he needed to drop his sword and get his hands under the attacker's wrist.

They fell backward into the mud, Stephen driving his mail-clad shoulder into the other man's throat. He'd hoped to stun the outlaw, break free and get his sword, but the outlaw, though he grunted hard, absorbed the punishment and added some of his own as he ground a fistful of the slimy dirt into Stephen's face.

Gasping and spitting, Stephen put his weight on his

shoulders, arched his back and lashed out with the hard leather heels of his boots. He couldn't reach the man's groin, but he did bring one foot down over his attacker's kneecap. For a brief moment the outlaw's muscles were rigid with shock; it was all the young man needed to break away and roll to his feet.

He shook the dirt from his eyes and assessed his situation. His sword was closer to the outlaw than it was to him and the outlaw was a hardened cur, easily his uncle's age, who was not about to be slowed by a little pain. Weaving and back-pedaling, Stephen reached under the mail-shirt and drew his own knife, a short, thick-bladed tool more suited to slicing the odd bit of saddle leather than killing a man. But then, the outlaw wasn't wearing mail.

The screams of panicked, burning horses reached his ears. He launched himself across the mud with a scream of his own. They were in the mud again, rolling and flailing. Stephen fought without grace or skill, driven by a mad determination to rescue his horse. The mail saved him more than once until, with a thrust that had his full body weight behind it, he drove the short knife deep into the outlaw's chest.

The outlaw struggled, Stephen bore down harder until the man gasped and blood gushed over his fingertips. He left his own knife behind and, grabbing his sword and the long knife from the outlaw's hand, raced for the stables.

mbrose stared into his crystal until the candles were puddled stubs and his eyes were wide, dark, and full of distant visions. He talked to himself, using a language Wildecent had never heard, and struck the crystal chime in no discernible pattern. Then, just before Wildecent would have concluded that sorcery was a fraud, the pendulum bob began to swing in a slow circle.

Motes of reflected light shot across the walls, the miniature manor, the sorcerer, and Wildecent herself. She considered that the walls had been dark until the crystal had begun to move and that the dancing lights were not just crystal white or the gold-amber of the candle flames but all the colors of the rainbow. Sliding silently off the bed, the young woman crept closer to the clothes chest and the *micros.*

Crouched opposite the sorcerer, Wildecent sighted past the swinging crystal and saw that Ambrose's eyes registered no movement; that he did not even seem to be breathing. She tried staring at the crystal herself and quickly found herself rocking on her knees in imitation of its motion.

There was magic, all right, in that crystal, and to her own surprise Wildecent closed her eyes and looked away.

She returned to her perch on the bed and watched the *micros,* careful not to stare too closely at the pendulum. Ambrose was chanting constantly now. Sweat formed on his brow. One stream trickled into his eye; he blinked but made no other move to rid himself of the irritant. Wildecent could imagine the stinging and shuddered at the thought of either ignoring it or being so deep in a trance that she could not consciously feel it.

He struck the chime and lifted his arms in a classical

pose of benediction or power. Wildecent sat bolt upright as the pendulum's circle flattened into an ellipse.

"Follow the path," the sorcerer chanted. He might have been speaking English, or she might have become caught in the crystal's spell—the girl was not brave enough to discover which.

The light faded from the walls; a beam of light, visible in the candle smoke, descended from the pointed tip of the bob—but it did not describe the full ellipse across the *micros*. It winked like a signal lantern, marking a curve that began in the scattered pine branches of the high-ridge forests and ended directly beneath the pendulum in the manor yard.

Wildecent held her breath until her heart ached and the winking beam had blurred into a solid cone of brilliance. "Follow the path," the sorcerer chanted, and the young woman found herself rising from the bed, headed for the light. Closing her eyes wasn't enough this time. Drawing on all the will she possessed, she threw her weight off balance and tumbled to the floor, breaking the spell's attraction.

She remained that way, curled over on herself with her head lower than the surface of the cope chest, until Ambrose clapped his hands and said a word that purged the room of the crystal's unnatural brilliance. She heard him stand up and shuffle unsteadily toward the bed where he collapsed with a single groan, but it was still several moments before she dared to stand up herself.

"I want to know what you did," Wildecent whispered to the dark shadows inside the bed curtains. "You leaned on them, I think, but without touching their minds. You can't guarantee that we'll win or they'll lose, but you've made certain they'll walk through Hell itself to get to the yard."

Ambrose's soft, regular breathing was her only answer.

The candles had guttered, but Wildecent's eyes had adjusted to the dark—or rather she realized that the room was not completely dark anymore. The shutters were leaking. She pushed one of them open, casting pale light over the *micros* and stood where the sorcerer had sat.

A sharp-edged black line followed the path the crystal had set forth. Mustering all her courage and curiosity, Wildecent bent over to touch it. She drew back a fingertip blackened with fine charcoal. Smearing the soot across her skirt, she headed for the open window. As impressive as the crystal display had been, it would be magic only if the outlaws came tromping across the ridge.

Wildecent's weak eyes betrayed her. The king's own host or a herd of late-feeding deer could have been wandering along that ridge and she would have been none the wiser. She followed the reality of the *micros* path until the landscape showed more detail and the imaginary line crossed a faint gray trail beyond the rampart.

"Dear God, no," she whispered as her eyes followed the faint arc.

She'd seen trails like that before; danced with her sister when they'd made smaller circles on the dirt floor of the bolt-hole behind their aunt. She remembered the sounds she'd heard behind Lady Ygurna's door as she'd made her way to the tower and the furtive enthusiasm with which Alison had helped her carry a blanket and candles to the storeroom. But mostly Wildecent thought about the protection such a circle promised, and the black path Ambrose had carved across it.

Grabbing her cloak, she headed down the tower stairs, noting that the kitchens seemed very quiet and hoping, incorrectly, that she'd be able to slip into the great hall unobserved.

"No one's allowed in the yard," Leofric the hostler

grumbled without looking up from his stool near the hearth.

The others in the kitchen—nearly all the drudges, churls, and slaves who worked the manor—looked up, though, and stared at Wildecent across the threshold. Their first reaction was one of normal recognition: everyone had seen Wildecent and Alison come to breakfast; their second grew from the knowledge that the tower room had been taken from the lord's daughters and given to a Norman retainer, an unmarried man.

"Have you seen my sister or my lady aunt?" Wildecent asked. They wouldn't answer her, wouldn't even look at her. Her mind embraced the worst it could imagine. "Has something happened to them? I've got to see my lady aunt and my sister." She spun around the pillar and laid a hand on the iron latch.

"It's the Lord Hafwynder's command: no one's to be in the yard lest the outlaws be drawn down," Bethanil shouted across the room. "He's promised the lash and slavery to any what breaks his word." Her tone conveyed the idea that Wildecent, herself, would not be exempt from this punishment.

Wildecent stopped short. Had her aunt and sister confronted Lord Hafwynder and his Norman guests? Had the painstakingly kept secrets been exposed? She could read nothing in the cook's impassive face but hesitated to open the door to the cloister that connected the hall and the kitchen—not when she could think of another way. Reversing herself, she put one foot on the stairs leading up the tower.

"*You can't go up there,*" Bethanil shouted.

She understood, then, what they were thinking, felt that special contempt they reserved for the sins of their betters, and hated them for their injustice. "Has my lord father commanded that too?" she demanded, forcing the cook into an uncomfortable silence. She and Alison had always obeyed the hefty woman's commands but that had been courtesy, not obligation. "I go where I please," Wildecent told them as she turned her back and ran up to the landing.

Ambrose had crawled deeper into the bed to escape the cold air coming through the open window. He had caught one of the curtains and twisted it over his shoulders, but he had not awakened, and would not awaken when Wildecent called his name.

"You're no help," she muttered as he put his hand over his ear and tugged harder on the curtain. "I'll have to do it myself," she warned. She might have awakened him with a touch of her hand—but that was more than she dared with any man, especially a sorcerer.

The pendulum stood as Ambrose had left it, with the crystal bob directly, unremarkably, above the terminus of the charred pathway. The *micros* had been shorn of its mystery as well, looking more like a child's collection of sticks and stones than a miniature of the manor. Wildecent plumped the cushion and flopped down on it.

"I want magic," she informed the objects scattered across the clothes chest. "I want to know where Alison and my lady aunt are, and if they're in any danger from the outlaws or anyone else."

Nothing happened.

Wildecent plinked her fingernails against the crystal chime and winced when it gave a flat, forgettable tone. She stared and wrinkled her forehead until her eyebrows touched together. Then, remembering what Ambrose had said about the question always containing its appropriate answer, she struck the chest hard with the flat of her hand.

"Where are they?"

She tried to concentrate on the swinging teardrop, but it did not draw her in as it had during the night while

214

Ambrose had chanted. The room was bathed in the bald light of an overcast dawn, but the crystal had lost its fire. Her hands trembled with mental demands as the circles grew smaller without flattening into a directional ellipse.

Rage, frustration, and a dozen other emotions vied for dominance in her thoughts, each bearing the same feeling of failure. She launched rapid, bargaining prayers to the Church's god, Lady Ygurna's god, and whatever demonic power that had guided Ambrose, only to abjure them moments later when light did not come blooming from the crystal.

Finally she denied magic—her aspirations to it, even her sense of failure at it—to concentrate only on the fears she'd felt for the two women and the emptiness she'd feel if anything happened to them. Everything she'd ever loved or admired about her sister and her aunt crowded between her mind's eye and the pendulum bob.

A wave of empathy welled out of her and Wildecent found herself in harmony with the glistening crystal. It described a path beyond the rampart, following the ash circle and filling Wildecent with the notion that Alison, not Lady Ygurna, had cast the protective sphere over the manor and that Alison was protecting their aunt at that very moment.

Where?

Wildecent rocked in unison with the crystal as images of the icy stream, Alison's efforts to carry Lady Ygurna back to the gate, and the evergreen windbreak in which they'd found shelter flowed into her mind. She swayed, unconsciously locked in rhythm with the pendulum bob, until the juniper was as real to her as it must be to Alison, and she could feel Lady Ygurna's cool flesh against her own.

"I'm coming," she murmured, certain she could find

216

that clump of shrubbery and satisfied that magic had, at last, worked for her.

The images cleared; she braced her palms on the floor to stop her uncontrolled rocking. Sunlight struck the motionless pendulum and drew her attention to a second black streak across the *micros*. Amazed and awed by her own accomplishment, she was jolted back to unpleasant reality by the shouts of battle raging below the tower windows.

She pushed open the southern window in time to see Thorkel stagger as an outlaw's ax bit into his thigh. Then, even as she feared he was fallen and doomed, she watched as his long sword came down across the outlaw's neck, severing sinew and bone. He slumped to the ground, head bouncing from a bloody rag of flesh, and Thorkel strode over his fallen body. Wildecent's scream was lost in the general din of battle; no hunting accident had prepared her for this.

Stomach heaving, she clung to the sideboard and tried to forget what she had seen. There was only one other image: the image of her sister huddled under the evergreens. In cold, calm hysteria, Wildecent decided to find Alison. The life-and-death struggle in the yard became distant and unimportant in her thoughts, though she did pause to take Ambrose's eating knife from the sideboard and tuck it under the tight sleeve of her undertunic.

The kitchens were empty when she reached them. The men and women had either joined the fighting, armed with cleavers, pothooks, and the like, or hidden themselves away. They'd left the door open; Wildecent closed and latched it carefully behind her.

She headed for the stockade gate, having imagined it as it usually was, open and deserted. When reality presented her with Lord Beauleyas, his hauberk smeared with gore, and three equally bloodied housecarls, she almost remem-

bered what she had seen, and almost saw how close she
was to that outlaw's gaping corpse.

Then her purpose reasserted itself. There was a gap in
the stockade where the stream escaped. A small gap, because the banks had flooded in autumn's last rain and
there'd been no time to make repairs before winter set in.
It replaced the gate, in Wildecent's mind, and became her
next destination.

Though Wildecent refused to recognize the little hor-
rors and deadly conflicts raging around her, she was not
completely blind, and set her course to avoid them. Rather
than walk through any part of the yard, she headed behind the kitchen, near the livestock pens and stables, and
followed the path past the storage and residence bowers.

Bethanil called to her from behind a rain barrel, but if
the young woman had heard her own name she would
have heard the screams as well, so she just kept going,
looking neither right nor left. She neared the stable and
saw flames leaping through its roof; that was frightening
and dangerous in a different way. She changed her course
again, walking closer to the wallow, where the stable muck
steamed and kept the ground from freezing.

Wildecent saw the man jump out at her, saw his short
sword as well and heard her mind trill *Danger!* as the hysteria crested and she found herself standing there with
Ambrose's delicate knife clenched in her fist. Her look of
total, idiotic surprise saved her—or perhaps the outlaw saw
the quality of her clothes and guessed she'd make a good
hostage. Either way, he didn't run the sword through her
belly but grabbed her by the forearm and gave her a second chance.

She shrieked, writhed, and slashed with her little knife.
The outlaw had a wildcat in his hand, and realized she
was too close for his sword to be of any use. He struck
her with the pommel, but the blow glanced off her shoul-

der. He could drop his sword or his hostage, or he could try to disable her. He tried the latter, wrenching her arm in a clear attempt to break it.

Giving in to his strength, Wildecent twisted to her knees. But she could give no further, and felt a burning stab of pain shoot up her arm. Color drained out of the world; her spine went to jelly and she tried to faint, but that hung all her weight from the arm her captor still clenched tight. She whimpered and pushed herself upright.

"Release her."

The voice came from behind her and, miraculously, it was obeyed as the outlaw thrust her rump first into the mud. Cradling her numb and lifeless arm to her breast, Wildecent stayed put while her savior crossed swords with the outlaw.

She had not seen Stephen put on the hooded mail shirt, and would not have recognized him for the mud and blood that clotted his face and hair. He might even have been another of the outlaws come to squabble for the right to hold her hostage—but she prayed for him and exalted silently when the red-slick tip of his sword protruded from her attacker's back.

"Wildecent! What are you doing out here?" Stephen demanded, extending his blood-soaked hand toward her. "God's love, woman, you'll have yourself killed."

She shook her head, then slowly placed her good hand in his. He pulled her to her feet, saw her face go gray, and caught her against his shoulder as she fell. More dragging her than carrying her, Stephen got Wildecent between two of the bowers where he'd already tethered Sulwyn.

"You're hurt," he observed lamely, knowing all the signs and having a good idea what was wrong by the way she moved, or didn't move, her left arm. "Let me help."

Cleaning a wound and setting it to healing might be woman's work, but it was men who got their comrades off the field and into the women's hands. Working fast and glancing back over his shoulder more than once, Stephen loosened her cloak and untied the long belt from her hips. It was easier with a man; he had to think a moment before positioning her forearm between her breasts. There was something hard and cold in her sleeve. He pulled it out and they both stared at Ambrose's dagger.

"Alison," Wildecent whispered, which was not at all what he expected her to say.

Tucking the dagger into the folds of his leggings, Stephen whipped the ends of the belt around her waist and shoulders and bound her arm tightly in place. Surrounded by death and chaos, he could think of no good reason why the dark-haired girl should have his tutor's knife; he could think of a few that brought a faint smile to his lips. He rearranged her cloak with more care than he'd used when he'd removed it.

"Alison," Wildecent repeated before he could ask about Ambrose. "I've got to get outside and find her."

She took an unsteady step away from him. The evergreens were no longer sharp in her mind; the *micros* was blurred, and even the way from here to the stream seemed suddenly unclear. Her sense of purpose, stripped of its hysterical strength, struggled upward through shock and pain. She'd taken only a few more steps before Stephen was in front of her, demanding explanations.

Stephen knew that Ambrose had his own way of fighting and that there were things his friend did late at night that did not square with the church. He preferred not to think about them, but he accepted the truth of Wildecent's tale as it unwound in disconnected sentences. He also accepted, reluctantly, that he could not leave her in anyone's care while he searched for Alison himself.

Not yet daring to sheathe his sword, though the manor had grown quieter and no one had screamed or shouted since they'd escaped between the bowers, Stephen put his left arm around her waist and set off toward the stream, praying he did not cross paths with his uncle.

They passed unchallenged, but for Wildecent, numbed by physical and emotional shock, the journey across the manor was an endless pilgrimage. She stared at the ice-coated stream bank and swore she could not go on, but now it was Stephen, who still found Alison's face in un-expected corners of his memory, who pushed her forward.

"I'll carry you once we're through the wall," he prom-ised as he sheathed his sword and braced to support her.

She shook her head and gripped the rough wood of the stockade with the fingers of her good hand. He lifted her over the rocks and kept a hand on her shoulder as they worked their way past the unfinished end of the rampart and around to where the stream flowed into the manor.

The signs were easy to read: the discarded brazier, the hollow in the snow where Lady Ygurna had lain while Alison completed the circle, the footprints leading to the mass of juniper. Stephen muttered that he could have found the place himself, but did not try to keep Wilde-cent from following the trail to its end behind him.

Neither Alison nor her aunt moved when Stephen lifted the mantle. The older woman was a waxen bluish gray. He was certain she was dead, and feared the same for Alison when a gentle touch against the girl's cheek failed to rouse her.

"Are they . . . ?" Wildecent asked from outside the bushes.

Unable to say what he feared, Stephen brushed the blond hair aside and pressed his fingers hard into the hollow beneath Alison's ear, determined to find a pulse. His own fingers almost numb from cold, he felt nothing and was pulling back when her eyes opened.

"She's alive!"

breeze blew along the length of Hafwynder Manor's valley. A gentle breeze, for winter, that carried off the lingering smells of burned thatch and carnage. It reached under the dark wool cloak Stephen had wrapped around the pale, unconscious Alison and flipped it up, revealing the ruined boots and the snow-stained gown of summer-white cloth.

Wildecent tried to hurry forward and straighten the cloak before they passed under the guard-porch, but quickly abandoned the effort. They were on the rampart now and, with her numb left arm still bound tightly between her breasts, it took all her skill simply to keep her balance.

The gate itself was open and the guard-porch empty, as if everyone were confident that the worst had, indeed, passed. The yard was busy, though, as Hafwynder's people sorted through the bodies and struggled to recapture the frightened animals that had broken loose in the fighting. For a fleeting moment Wildecent hoped they might slip by unnoticed. That hope vanished as one-by-one, men and women silently looked up from their tasks.

There was no disguising Alison's golden hair, her unconsciousness, nor the fact that she had been outside the walls. It took no special empathy or talent to feel the doubts swirling from one staring face to the next. A dozen or more explanations might be found for Alison's presence in Stephen's arms or Wildecent's obviously injured arm—but none of them would be optimistic.

"The Lady Ygurna?" a hoarse voice called from higher on the hill. It took Wildecent a moment to recognize Tostig the Raven beneath the bruises and dirt.

"Dead."

The men and women remained silent but it seemed to Wildecent that her word had provoked an invisible, despairing sigh and that their eyes focused on her as if she were suddenly a stranger in their midst.

"They'll be needing you inside, then," old Leofric told her.

She moved closer to Stephen, her sleeve catching on the exposed links of his chain-mail shirt and extending its protection to her. "I'm frightened," she whispered as they entered the cold shadow of the great hall, but her companion gave no sign of having heard her.

It took a few moments for their eyes to adjust to the hall's darkness—to see another group of staring faces and the jumble of pallets where the wounded were being treated. The scowl that flashed over Jean Beauleyas's face was more eloquent than all the anxiety they'd seen in the yard.

"Is she?" the grizzled Norman commander demanded in his accented English.

"I think not," Stephen reassured him. "We found her and the old woman hidden in the underbrush on the far side of the stream. I don't think they'd been taken or even seen."

"Then what were they—"

The rest of Beauleyas's question was already clear in Wildecent's mind, but the Norman never uttered it. Ambrose touched the older man's arm and a glance of understanding passed between them. Wildecent understood that Ambrose's powers were known, just as Ygurna's powers had always been known without ever being acknowledged, but she understood, as well, that however strong or long-lived the bond between him and Stephen was, Lord Beauleyas demanded his final loyalties.

"And you?" the Norman demanded, staring hard into Wildecent's eyes.

"I— I—"

Time seemed to freeze while the dark-haired girl swam through her own thoughts. Plainly, the truth could not be spoken but only the most precisely constructed lie would be acceptable to all those—Christian clergy, Norman mercenaries, and Saxon retainers—gathered in the hall. She looked away from Beauleyas, to the raised pallet on which he rested his fists, and realized that her father, Godfrey, lay like a corpse before him.

"We were trapped in the solar, trying to bring more medicines to the kitchen before it was too late. We were surprised and got separated. I made my way to the bowers where Stephen found me and saved me. Then I led him beyond the walls, where I thought they might have run if they'd been able to get away."

It was not a good tale. Bethanil, standing by the hearth, saw through it in a heartbeat but the Saxon woman wasn't going to say anything—not with her lord on a pallet, her lady dead under a tree, and the lord's daughter draped in the arms of a foreigner. The others who might suspect the truth were equally reticent to challenge her. Ambrose smiled and nodded his head ever so slightly as Jean shoved himself away from the pallet.

"They say Saxon women set great store by their herb-craft: you've got your work set out for you." He gestured at the pallet where Godfrey lay unmoving.

A glancing blow from a heavy object—perhaps a double-ax, perhaps a horse's flailing hoof—had crushed the left side of Godfrey Hafwynder's skull above the temple. He should have been dead. It was no small miracle that he lived, but it would take a far greater one for him to recover. And there were no miracles to be had that afternoon in Hafwynder Hall.

Ambrose became Wildecent's hands, obeying her commands as if he were well accustomed to the role of apprentice. He asked questions as he worked but never gainsayed her decisions. The throbbing in her own injured arm and the strain of tending her father's wounds without Lady Ygurna there to correct her had narrowed Wildecent's world to a corridor bounded by fear and despair, but once or twice she heard the sorcerer grunt with new-found understanding and that gave her the courage to go on.

There was little enough she could do for Godfrey before setting Brother Alfred to watch and pray over him. Then they guided her attention to the other pallets, where those who had suffered in the defense of the manor waited for her. The afternoon wore on, exhausting the supply of medicines Lady Ygurna had brought from the bolt-hole many hours before she had made her final journey through the snow. With no thought for the consequences, Wildecent instructed Ambrose where he could find more and sent him across the yard to the solar.

Finally, there was only Alison who slept by the hearth, opposite her father, on another raised pallet. Alison whose flesh was cool and dry, whose breath came easily and whose flesh was unmarked.

"There's nothing wrong with her—except that I can't wake her up," Wildecent admitted, the first words that were not instructions to pass between her and Ambrose since she had brushed her father's light hair away from that awful wound.

"You know what she's done," he replied. It was a statement, an exchange of information between equals—not a question. "She may choose not to come back."

"Then all we can do is wait, isn't it?"

Ambrose nodded. The steel sense of purpose that had driven Wildecent past her own pain and grief slipped away from her. The room spun around her, then faded, and she found herself caught in the sorcerer's arms as the tears flooded down her face.

Every table had already been converted into a sickman's pallet; Ambrose carried her to the stairwell and braced her against the wall while he tended to the one wound she had forgotten. She whimpered as his fingers probed for the fracture and fainted when he found it, but she was too exhausted to resist and the bones snapped easily back into alignment. He had it splinted and bound back between her breasts before she recovered.

"Move your fingers," he commanded.

She did, one by one, and knew what he had done for her. "You didn't need me telling you what to do," she accused weakly.

"I was honored to learn the ways of the *wicca*."

"I am not *wicca*," Wildecent replied, remembering how she had sent him, a sorcerer, into the bolt-hole.

He put an arm around her shoulder and helped her to her feet. "You're wise enough."

They brought her broth from the kitchens, where Bethanil was preparing a sober feast from those beasts who did not survive the fires. She sipped at it, knowing she needed nourishment, then let it grow cold. They brought her father's chair from the shadows and put it by the hearth for her to sit where she could watch both Godfrey and Alison and listen to Brother Alfred's Latin prayers.

Time passed in a slow, gray dance. The upper windows were lost to darkness; more logs were placed within the hearth; another brother took up Alfred's chanting. Wildecent closed her eyes and drifted toward sleep until the shadow fell across her face.

Thorkel Longsword stood between Godfrey and her. A bloody rag was knotted across his thighs. She thought perhaps he'd come late to have his wounds stitched shut but he'd come to see Lord Hafwynder and brushed her concerns aside with thinly disguised annoyance.

"What do you want, then?"

He laid his hands on Godfrey's slowly moving chest. "Let him die, Wildecent," he whispered. "Your aunt would have understood. If I'd been the one to find him it would never have gotten this far. He brought down the Black Wolf—let him die a hero."

"It's in God's hands," she told him, though she understood his request.

"Your hands are God's hands."

"I'm doing nothing—what else can I do? How can there be a Hafwynder Manor without a Hafwynder to give it a name?"

Thorkel's hard face softened a bit in the firelight. He took a step closer to her and spoke even more softly. "We did not win today, Wildecent. Perhaps if he had not fallen or if she had not run beyond the stockade— But no, even then we would have lost sooner or later. It was not the Black Wolf we were fighting but the Normans—and we let them through the gates ourselves.

"Your father knew, I think, from the beginning. He did not want to see what happens next. Let him die, Wildecent—or surely I shall kill him. And your sister too. The Saxons—even the Vikings—have exhausted themselves; the world is flowing toward new blood. Your eyes are open, child; you and I, we'll see the future and survive, but let these die in peace."

Wildecent picked at the fleece packed around her broken arm. She made a tight little wad and let it drop into her lap. "God's will," she repeated—because she would not accept responsibility for the truth she heard in his voice—and would not meet his eyes again.

He left as quietly as he'd come. When she thought she was alone, she allowed the tears to escape again and sank into the darkness of her own despair. Lady Ygurna was gone and Thorkel Longsword was right about her father and sister.

"Are you in much pain?"

The voice startled her. She stared at the silhouette in panic before remembering Stephen's voice and the outline of his youthful strength. She shook her head and hoped that if she refused to talk to him, he might go away. But Stephen was rarely that perceptive—or considerate.

"Why were you crying, then?"

"Why?" Wildecent repeated, losing control over an ugly, ironic laugh. "Everyone I've ever cared about is dead or dying. Wouldn't you cry?"

"No. I'd pray to God for their souls, then I'd get my sword."

If Wildecent had had any doubts about the truth of Thorkel's advice, they vanished in the face of Stephen's simple and violent sincerity. "I can hardly take up a sword, can I? And whom would I fight? Your uncle? You?"

"No, we'll protect you. We'll take you with us—Alison too when she gets better. We'll take you back to Tor-worden and then maybe even back to Normandy."

There was nothing to be gained by arguing with him. However much Wildecent feared the idea of Beauleyas's sort of protection she could not deny how much she and the other survivors of Hafwynder Manor would need it. So she listened while he related the plans his uncle was already making for their future and reminded herself that she had already used the *micros* and would use it again if she had to.

When he left, Wildecent's cheeks remained dry and her mind swirled with thoughts of survival. She did not notice that her sister's eyes were open and watching.

"Wili?"

229

"Alison!"

Scrambling awkwardly, Wildecent stumbled to her sister's pallet. She clasped Alison's outstretched hand in her own, then trembled and gasped as she tried to find words to describe all that had already happened.

"I know," Alison assured her. Her grip was firm and there was no trace of illness in her eyes.

"Our lord father—"

"I know; I *saw*—it was Lady Ygurna's parting gift. She showed me the victory and the warning just before she died."

Alison's eyes went bright and Wildecent saw pools of unshed tears welling up. She remembered that Thorkel said both Hafwynders would be better off not knowing what had happened. Her sister wasn't going to die; was not, in fact, as weak and exhausted as Wildecent herself. Yet the long afternoon of washing, stitching and bandaging had changed Wildecent and she could no longer crawl timidly under Alison's shadow.

"Nothing will be the way you remember it," she told the blond young woman who had slept through the most important day of their lives. "Everything's already changed. We are to go with the Normans, enjoying their protection at Torworden, as soon as you've got your strength back."

A grimace, which Wildecent mistook for grief, hardened Alison's face. Wildecent closed her eyes and wondered where she'd find the strength to sustain them both in the times ahead.

"Don't worry, Wili," Alison assured her. "We're more than a match for them."

CONQUEST

UNICORN & DRAGON™

VOLUME II

usk had settled over the secluded valley. Mist rose from the rain-moist ground, but the sky overhead was clear with the promise of pleasant weather. A solitary rider broke away from the muddy track and guided his horse uphill to a patch of forest overlooking Hafwynder Manor.

The woods were quiet except for the patter of droplets blown down from the branches. It was too early in the season for birds and insects. The land had not yet felt its last wintry frost, and though the shrubs and trees were showing new growth, most animals still heeded nature's warning to take shelter through the night. No eyes took note of the black-haired man unbridling and hobbling his horse before he entered a dense juniper copse.

Ambrose did not think of nature as he set his lantern on a sarsen boulder and withdrew a middling-sized leather sack from beneath his cloak. Insofar as he or his teachers understood the words, Ambrose was a rational man: a man who understood that humanity stood at the apex of creation, far above the constraints of primitive nature.

He would prove that before this evening was over.

Stakes, lime chalk, and silken twine, withdrawn from the sack, were used to create a perfect circle on the freshly sodded ground in front of the boulder. Then, through the aid of knots tied in the cord, an equilateral pentagram was marked off along the faintly glowing circumference. Finally, using the first stake-hole he had made, Ambrose set a small silken packet into the earth.

It had become dark. The ground mist had grown palpably thicker. Ambrose's black hair glistened in the lantern-light where the mist touched it. His hands grew chafed and stiff. A part of him cried out for a fire—preferably in a proper hearth in a proper room; but Ambrose was as accustomed to denying his physical wants as he was to ignoring the discomforts of nature. He closed his mind to the aching,

I

pressed a teardrop-shaped crystal between his palms, and sat, stiff-backed, on the boulder.

A crescent rose above the trees on the opposite side of the valley. The young sorcerer felt the mist become silvery in the moonlight. He shut his eyes and concentrated entirely on the contents of the little packet at the center of the pentagram. Discipline was the key to the esoteric mysteries he'd studied in Byzantium—not sensitivity, and certainly not moon-induced ecstasy. Ambrose's will, channeled through tongue-twisting mnemonics and the clear quartz crystal, would make his sorcery.

Ambrose had known before they'd buried Lady Ygurna that he'd need to meet with her again. He'd taken tiny amounts of hair, skin, and blood from her corpse, infused the motes in myrrh, dried them, then wrapped them in silk and carried them against his flesh throughout the winter—all in preparation for this moment.

Ygurna, a priestess of the old Cymric gods as well as chatelaine of the manor in the valley below, would answer his summons. There was arcane art between them— rival arts. The microcosmic bit of her earthly body merely made her return easier, and might make her more amenable to his suggestions.

The moon rose above the mists and trees. It shone onto the grave at the center of the juniper. The mist became opaque and viscous. The copse became still: beyond naturally quiet as if time itself had been stopped.

Ambrose lowered the crystal and opened his eyes.

"So, you have wrought your will against nature, have you?"

There was no mistaking Lady Ygurna. Tall, steely, and slender, for all that her form was greenish silver mist. The voice was hers too, although Ambrose could not have said if she spoke or if he simply felt her thoughts within his mind.

"Mankind always stands opposed to nature. It is not fitting that we be ruled like sheep; we are rational as nature is not."

2

The mist-figure smiled. "Rational, are we? More's the pity of it. You're sitting out here in the damp talking to a woman long dead. Only a man . . ."

"You're not long dead, Ygurna. It is scarcely three months since the Black Wolf threatened and you walked your circle across the snow. You are still very much bound to this earth, very much in the thoughts of the living."

Ygurna wavered as if thought or doubt cost a measure of her substance. She tilted her head like a cat or dog listening to a far-off sound. "No. No, it is over. Long over. We have peace now." She retreated to the rim of the lime-drawn circle.

"It's about Alison, Ygurna," Ambrose whispered before she tested the limit of his power to hold her here.

She had devolved into a column of swirling mist, but her niece's name brought her back. Her eyes took form again once the mist touched the silk at the center of the pentagram.

"Alison? What about my sister's daughter?" Her voice was still an empty breeze through the branches.

"She has not undone what she did."

"And you want me to do what she will not?" Ygurna's personality had waxed strong again; her voice was a cackle full of knowledge and spite.

"You could." Ambrose forced himself to stare into the mist as she grew more cronelike. He was only a mortal man despite his discipline; his flesh had an instinctive fear of death. He channeled his remaining faith into the geometria he had scraped into the turf. He *wanted* to be fearful, but a Zoroastrian magus did not *need* to be fearful.

The mist caressed itself, sounding like twigs scraping against each other—or bones. "What was done will be done, and cannot be undone. My sister's daughter has become a player in her own game. The best sacrifice is made by the holy or the innocent."

The sorcerer's concentration faltered as he realized that the ghost he had conjured was not alone in the mist.

Ambrose's human curiosity asked who, or what, might have accompanied Ygurna into his circle; he stifled it and strengthened his will against nature, death, and evil.

The mist recondensed into the woman he had known.

"Stephen does not belong here," he explained patiently, as if to a child.

"What was done is still done," Ygurna explained, twisting uncomfortably. "Alison has been accepted, and she has accepted him. They have become a part of something much larger. She will not be allowed to undo it."

"But you could."

Ygurna looked away, seething with some unexplained turmoil.

"Surely Stephen is not the one *you* would have chosen for her . . ."

The ghost snapped upright, moving more solidly than Ambrose had anticipated. And the other presence, the one that had spoken through the sound of scraping bones, was with her again.

"He is, after all, not one of your kind, not of your blood," Ambrose added quickly as his own fears finally freed themselves.

The mist spoke in a voice that came from every corner of the copse. "It has happened before; it will happen again. There is no native blood in Britain—only what blood has conquered. First there were the Celts who pushed the Picts to the edge of the land. Then the legions who conquered the Celts and lived among them until they were both abandoned by Rome. The world grew small again, but the Cymry—the Romans and Celts intermingled—remembered. The English came: Saxon, Angle, Jute, and Friesian. They conquered in blood again, but the Cymry still remembered their promises and survived. We were hidden, but not forgotten. We made the sacrifices still. The English were accepted; the land stayed green.

"Then the Vikings came—who cared only for the sea and glory. We could not accept them, and our bond with the land has grown weak. The promises are forgotten; the sacrifices are forgotten. Our land is naked—ripe, again, for conquest. But the Cymry remember. We will try one last time. A new hero will be chosen; blood will make the land fertile again.''

Ambrose was afraid of the mist, but not its prophecies. Sorcery and magic weren't necessary to know that England would soon be enveloped in catastrophic war. The island's native dynasties had all failed, and her riches caught the eyes of other ambitious rulers. Harold Godwinson, who held the throne since Christmastide, might have been born on English soil, but he was no more an *English* king than Harald Hardrada of Norway or Duke William the Bastard of Normandy.

"I will have Stephen back," the sorcerer warned the evanescent pillar.

But the mist did not hear him. It grew brighter, and Ambrose, on his rock outside the circle, could feel the gathering power.

"He comes," Ygurna cried, seeking to free herself from the pentagram. "He comes. The green king comes. The land shall be reborn in blood!"

Power swept through the juniper. It rasped through the trees and sucked up the mist. It obliterated the circle and pentagram beneath a shower of winter-killed twigs. Then it was gone, and the moon was behind the treetops, sinking toward morning.

Ambrose tried to stand, but he might as well have been part of the boulder beneath him. He was numb from the buttocks down, and no amount of discipline could restore him. He pushed and fell to his knees where the pentagram had been. Ambrose could no longer deny the pain and fear. He was shivering and sweating as he dug the knotted square of silk out of the wet grass. He placed it inside his tunic and moaned as the cold thing slid across his chest.

Knowing he would not stand until he had been warmed

by the sun, he crawled to the back of the rock where his cloak lay as he had left it. He forced his legs straight, then rolled himself into the thick, fur-lined wool.

Dawn could not be that many hours away.

tephen found Ambrose's horse nibbling grass. He recognized the trees and the junipers within them. He called his friend's name several times before dismounting and leaving his own horse ground-tied. There were a hundred places he'd rather be, a thousand things he'd rather do; but he forged past the damp evergreens and stared at Ambrose sleeping beside Ygurna's grave.

"Look alive, now," Stephen commanded, giving Ambrose's shoulder a shake.

The sorcerer groaned, opened his eyes, and did not recognize the face staring down at him. Stephen snatched his hand back and, standing up, turned away.

"For the love of God Almighty, Ambrose, why this place?" There was weariness and despair in his voice, but not enough to endanger their friendship.

"God Almighty, I think, had very little to do with it. Here, give me a shove or I'll never unwind myself from this thing."

Stephen helped him out of the cloak and then to a seat on the boulder. "Did my lord uncle know, or was this his idea in the first place?" Stephen asked as he gave Ambrose's cloak a vicious snap to remove the dew.

With a loud sigh, Ambrose wrapped the cloak around his shoulders and declined to answer the question. There had been a time—several years ago in France, while Stephen was still a child—when sorcery had not stood as a wall between them. Then Stephen had found his tutor's mysterious behavior to be a fine source of adventure in an otherwise constrained, predictable world. But now that his education as a feudal warrior was complete, Stephen was an unwilling party to his friend's secrets.

"Shall we say Lord Beauleyas did suggest I might scout ahead before we arrived at the manor."

"And did you find anything?"

CONQUEST

"Hafwynder Manor is much as we left it: preoccupied with its own problems and unaware that a stranger was riding on the hill above it. Their ewes are dropping early, and the men have been dispersed to the high fields. The rest would not interest a man of the world like you or your uncle."

Stephen stared at the shapes scratched across the turf and the debris that littered this copse but nowhere else. He knew why and how the Lady Ygurna had died; he had been the one to find her lying dead in this very spot. He knew as well not to ask questions for which he did not truly desire answers.

"If I bring your horse, will you be able to ride from here? I left the men before dawn, and surely they are not far behind me."

"I guess I shall have to, won't I? I think I'll be fine once we get moving."

"You need someone to take care of you, you know," the younger man remarked once they had cleared the copse and his friend was walking on his own. He was smiling as he glanced at Ambrose; then the smile vanished.

Everything had been simpler before Stephen had made his way to his mother's half brother, Jean Beauleyas, and Ambrose had accepted service to the same man. Friendship overcame the inequalities of their ages, experience, and inclinations. They had been encouraged to rely upon each other. Stephen was the sole heir to his father's many manors. He'd need a strong arm to keep the peace among them and a trustworthy steward to manage them. Then Stephen's father had been slain in a pointless skirmish and his mother had been forced to marry a neighboring lord with no use for a raw lad who was none of his blood. Not when he had three sons of his own—each older than Stephen—and not enough land to keep them from each other's throats.

Now his mother was dead as well—poisoned—and he had gone skulking to her remaining relatives, hoping for

9

some change in fortune that would lead him and Ambrose back to France.

Or Ambrose hoped. Stephen hadn't mentioned his lost patrimony since Christmas. He was at an age when young men are apt to be smitten, and Alison—with her deep blue eyes; long, golden hair; and innocent manner—was just the sort of woman to produce a powerful smile. Magic need not have been involved at all—but it had been, though Stephen refused to believe that.

The sorcerer, who took great pride that he had never tampered with a freeman's thoughts, despite the ability to do so, considered Alison an affront to all magical arts. He clung to her act of immortality, keeping it always as the focus of his outrage lest he slip into a sort of professional jealousy; for, try as he might, he could neither undo nor mitigate the changes she had wrought. He had not, however, the faintest notion that Alison had changed him, without recourse to her magic, far more than she had changed Stephen by using it.

"Are they well?" Stephen asked when they reached the horses and Hafwynder Manor could be seen below in the valley.

"Well enough," Ambrose replied quickly, knowing there was no *they* in Stephen's mind, only Alison. Because of Alison, and Alison alone, Stephen had risked his uncle's wrath to lead this return to Hafwynder Manor. Ambrose hoisted himself into the saddle without assistance and was of that much grimmer countenance when he faced Stephen again.

They rode just within the trees, following deer trails, until the curve of the land put them beyond the sight of the manor's lookouts. Not that either man expected the English to be alert for strangers. The English were unaccustomed to the suspicious habits of the French. Neighbors here were generally friendly, and a man might reasonably expect to die in his bed, as King Edward had done the past Christmas. Such tranquillity and trust would serve these people poorly in the months to come, and gave the few land-poor Normans already on the island a sublime sense of superiority.

Stephen touched his spurs to his horse's flanks, broke from cover, and led Ambrose on a fair ride across the downs to the narrow track where they rejoined the other men from his uncle's stronghold, Torworden. If these five oath-bound men had questions about the comings and goings of the one they called the Greek—and they did—they kept them to themselves. It was not for them to question the decisions of Lord Beauleyas, not when the lord's word was law, and law was the edge of his sword. Especially when opinion was still divided about Stephen's prospects at Torworden. The smarter men, veterans like Hugh de Lessay and Alan FitzAlan, who rode with Stephen now, appraised the young man's style beneath his inexperience. They wagered the old man would make Stephen his heir once William took the island in hand, and placed their bets accordingly.

The escort fell in silently behind Ambrose and stayed that way until the track wound its way to the foot of the hill where Ambrose had passed the night.

"Break out the pennants," Stephen commanded.

Two of the five tied strips of embroidered cloth to their spears; then they moved forward to provide more tempting targets than either Stephen or Ambrose. They were much relieved when the assembly gong was struck and the gates swung open to greet them.

The early spring rains had not erased the marks of the battle that had been fought within Hafwynder Manor's yard. Charred timbers still outlined the byres that had been set afire. The whitewashed sides of the hall and the nearby stone tower were scarred by those same fires; the manor lacked the manpower to bleach them anew. Raw mounds of earth marked new household graves on the slope behind the hall itself. There was a similar but larger mound farther downstream, outside the manor stockade, where the Black Wolf and his outlaws shared a common grave. The most noticeable scars, though, remained on Hafwynder's people and on Godfrey Hafwynder himself.

The lord of the manor stood in the doorway of his hall, flanked by his two daughters. His hair and beard were freshly combed, his braes hung loosely around his legs, and his embroidered tunic was brilliant in the morning light. But his movements were flaccid, and there was no glimmer of recognition in his eyes when Stephen led his horse up the path to the hall. Alison took her father's hand.

"Stephen, Lord Beauleyas's nephew, is here, Father."

Obediently the blue eyes focused where Stephen stood. The youth smiled awkwardly and extended his hand, which the lord of Hafwynder Manor ignored. Disappointment showed clearly in both young women's faces. Alison gripped her father's hand more tightly, and Wildecent, the petite, dark-haired sister, hid a tear behind her sleeve. Stephen pulled his hand back and trapped it in his belt as if it, and not Godfrey, was the source of their discomfort.

"He has not recovered at all since your last message?" Ambrose asked in a detached but not unkind way as he came up the path after leaving his horse with one of the manor's servants. His English was good, as were his French, Latin, and Greek. He learned everything quickly and completely. Most feared his sorcery, but his mind was his sharpest weapon.

"Some days we think he knows us," Alison answered quickly, looking up into eyes that did not know her today.

"And the other times . . . he is like this?" Ambrose took Godfrey's hand into his own and squeezed hard. There was no reaction in Hafwynder's face.

Alison hesitated, then shrugged a tentative agreement. "We have done all that could be done," she said with a trace of defiance in her voice.

The blond heiress had cause to be defensive. She had spent the night before the Christmastide battle practicing the earth magic of her maternal ancestors. The ancient powers had noticed both her and her aunt, but they had not protected the manor. Wildecent and Stephen had found her in an exhausted stupor beside Lady Ygurna's corpse. Stephen had carried her back to the manor. For the better part of a day and a night, Alison had lain beside her father before the hearth in the great hall. The family that had protected the valley for generations had seemingly abandoned it.

With Ygurna newly dead and Alison reckoned among the dying, the wounded turned to Wildecent, the other sister—a timid child of unspoken birth. Wildecent herself had been injured; a broken arm was bound against her breasts. She'd turned to the foreign sorcerer, Ambrose, and used him as her hands. They'd worked with quiet skill throughout that very long afternoon, but with every wound they stitched, every bone they splinted, the manorfolk looked to the raised pallets where the Hafwynders lay, and their sense of hopelessness grew.

When Alison had recovered she blamed herself for all that had happened and tended her crippled father with obsessive concern.

"To do more would be to call upon black arts," she warned, staring hard into Ambrose's black eyes.

"Assuredly," Ambrose agreed.

He would have said more but their five Norman companions, still clad in heavy hauberks and conical helms, came up to the doorway asking if the horses should be set in the English stables or in a separate line. They did their asking in Norman French, and the alien words pierced the shield surrounding Godfrey's mind.

"Outlaws! Traitors! Murderers!" the blond man shouted as he shed his daughters and shouldered his way to the enemy.

Godfrey had been a strong man before his injury; his daughters' care had kept him from becoming a weak invalid. Whatever he saw standing behind Stephen, he had the strength to kill it with his bare hands. The surprised soldier fell backward and saw his death upon him.

Wildecent screamed, Alison raced for the stables, and Stephen struggled to pry Godfrey loose without further injury to anyone. The manorfolk gathered, shaking their heads in worried silence, unwilling to lay hands on their lord, however mad he might be. Not so the Normans, who struggled to separate the combatants. Stephen ordered two of his men, Hugh and Alan, to restrain the English lord. He felt the manorfolk's distrust focus on him and was supremely relieved when Thorkel Longsword, the manor's steward, charged up the path from the byres.

The Viking's face was grim; his hands and tunic were smeared with blood. Stephen took a long step backward before a single word was said, and signaled his men to release their prisoner.

"My Lord Hafwynder!" Longsword shouted, taking Godfrey's hands between his own. *"Friends,* Lord Hafwynder. These men are our *friends!"*

The fire faded from Godfrey's face. His arms fell back to his sides and he stood empty of thought or reason. The Norman escort relaxed. There was no insult in a madman's assault; there was no honor to be gained in reprisals against the befuddled gentleman who now sat meekly on the bench where Thorkel put him.

The man Godfrey had attacked was bleeding. Hugh de Lessay offered him a cloth, and after a nod from Stephen, led the Torworden men away.

"This has happened before?" Ambrose asked, suspecting he knew the answer.

Alison spoke first, a single shrill no!, but a glance from Longsword, whom Jean Beauleyas had left in charge here, made her quiet.

"He knows us, all right, after his own lights—but strangers set him raving. See to your lord father now," Thorkel added with a curt nod to the young women.

The sisters hurried to straighten his tunic and wipe the traces of blood and spittle from his sandy hair.

"The good brothers at the chapel think he's still fighting the Black Wolf and seeing those men come through his gates. Myself . . ." The tall man paused, thought better of his comments, and only shook his head. "There's problems with the ewes in the byre," he said after a moment. "You can follow me down there."

An adult lifetime spent on the English island hadn't touched the Viking core of the man who had stood at Godfrey's right side these last five years. His thoughts could be guessed by any man who knew the Viking ethic: Godfrey Hafwynder should have died in his final battle. At the very least someone should have prevented his soft-hearted daughters from bringing him back to this unmanly madness.

No one knew where Thorkel Longsword had been before he appeared in Godfrey Hafwynder's service. He was a mercenary, but he had no use for gold. And Stephen, now following him down to the sheep-byre, was keenly aware that there was no aspect of life in which he felt he could match the Viking strength for strength. No area save one: Longsword had no affinity for leadership. He dominated the crippled manor, but Stephen—who had been taught to command men as he was taught to ride or hold a sword—could see that it languished without direction.

The thought put steel in Stephen's stride. He stood before the sheep-byre and looked straight into Longsword's eyes. "I've come on Lord Beauleyas's orders to bring Hafwynder's treasure to Torworden," he began.

"That—and to fetch your fine stallion back?"

Stephen grinned and inwardly admired the man who had guessed the argument with which he had won his uncle's permission. Sulwyn's injuries—and his own—had been the first strands in the ties that now bound the English manor to the Norman stronghold of Torworden in the North. The seven-year-old chestnut was Stephen's most valued possession. Beauleyas might know in his heart that his nephew was dangerously smitten with the English heiress, but he could not deny the young man the opportunity to retrieve his prized horse.

"I'm looking forward to riding him home."

"Today would be soon enough for me, but I suppose you'll be wanting to wait a few days to see everything's counted properly." Friendship faded from Longsword's voice.

Stephen knew something was not as it should be or as his uncle had said it would be. "What's wrong? You've told my Lady Alison and her sister, haven't you?"

Thorkel made a dismissing gesture with his hand, then swooped down to grab the ewe that was trying to escape. "They won't like it. They'll make a man's life a misery with their whining and pleading; he won't get a decent meal for weeks. So why tell them? They'll go anyway." His hands probed through the unshorn fleece and then, satisfied that there was no bleeding, let the mother join her snow white lamb in the far corner.

"It's not the women," he began again as he stood straight. "There's been a muster called. Godfrey held this land from the Godwinsons. Harold Godwinson's lord and king both; he asks for men and supplies. We've sent enough of each and we'll have to send more when planting's over. You should be grateful the herald had no eye for horseflesh or your beast'd be gone to carry the king."

Buried in the speech—an exceptionally long one for the Viking—was the notion that the English king was putting a claim on Hafwynder's treasure. Longsword would not have been able to deny Harold's messenger the men and gold that had been demanded. And Jean Beauleyas would find that he could deliver that much less to his own lord, Harold's enemy: William the Bastard, Duke of Normandy.

"Aye, it will need counting, then," Stephen agreed, already wondering how he would explain the loss to his uncle. "Is that the worst of it?"

Something very like rage passed over Thorkel's face; Stephen stiffened, fearing he had awakened the dread *ber-serkerang* that lay in the heart of every Viking.

"The worst is watching a good man cry for death. His body knows, and what's left of his mind. That's why he sees traitors and outlaws in every face. The ladies, though, they'll see none of it. It's just as well to a woman to have a man with his head in her lap. Just as well until the reavers come to the gate and there's none to protect her or her pretty things—"

"Are there reavers about, then? My lord uncle will want to know."

"Reavers of the worst sort: good men intent on ward-ship. It's a lot of land to leave this way. The girls take care of their father: whoever takes care of the girls has all this valley at his beck and call."

"We'll take care of Alison and her sister: myself and my uncle. We'll have them gone from these parts soon enough; then all you must do is defend the land—which oughtn't be difficult if the king's summoned the *fyrd* for the summer season."

Thorkel snorted a veteran's derision, completely un-impressed that the Frenchman knew the native term for the king's summoned army. "You leave the worrying and planning to Lord Beauleyas 'til you've some meat under your belt, lad."

Stephen fought a blush of discomfort. "I'd like to see my horse," he mumbled.

The Viking pointed to another byre. Stephen heard Longsword's peal of laughter as he hurried away. Twin fires of shame and anger burned in his cheeks. He was grateful that the English had kept Sulwyn apart from their own beasts and that no one saw him bury his face in the stallion's mane.

"I should have known better than to tell him what to do or how to do it."

His fingers locked in the coarse hair and pulled hard

against it. Sulwyn rumbled with surprise and swung his head, teeth bared, around to investigate.

"He missed you. I have an apple for him. He likes them."

The voice, unmistakably Alison's, was right behind him. A slender arm came between him and Sulwyn. The stallion relaxed and took the fruit delicately from her steady palm. Stephen lost his tongue between the excitement of having her close by and the outraged betrayal of watching Sulwyn eat from her hand.

"He'll bite," he managed after an awkward moment.

"Not anymore. We've had enough time to become friends," Alison assured him.

"He's *supposed* to bite! I trained him not to trust strangers."

Stephen glowered at Sulwyn, who stared benignly with bits of russet stuck to his lips. A plowhorse—a cud-chewing cow—could not have looked so harmless. Stephen had a good mind to put his fist into a solidly muscled, coppery shoulder, but Alison was watching, so he confined himself to a friendly pat.

"Oh, he tried a few times, but I guess I remind him of you," Alison said, letting the stallion rub his face against her.

Stephen saw no point in telling her that he never took such liberties with the animal, which had bitten him many, many times. Now that she was standing beside him, he had no desire to talk about Sulwyn at all.

"I am glad to see you well recovered. We were sore worried for you when we returned to Torworden," he mumbled, wishing he were glib enough to sound friendly and well-mannered at the same time.

"I've missed you," she replied in her forthright way. "Nothing is as it was before you arrived, and if it must be different, then it is better to have you here. I'm certain the manor will seem happier now that you've returned."

He shrugged. "I'm honored that you held me in your thoughts, my lady, but in truth it is my lord uncle's thought that Hafwynder Manor is no safe place with England's throne usurped and challenged. He has sent us—me—here to fetch you north to Torworden, where you'll be better protected—"

Alison's artless friendship vanished. "Just me?" she asked.

"Nay, we would bring your sister, Wildecent, as well. And a serving woman, perhaps, for Torworden is not yet so civilized as your English manors. And such treasure as is moveable and can be loaded into carts for the journey—"

"And my father? You mean to bring my father to safety as well?"

Stephen's mouth hung open. His uncle's orders had been blunt and specific: the sisters, the treasure, and such folk as the women would need to attend to them; Godfrey Hafwynder was to remain on his manor. With Alison tucked out of sight behind Torworden's walls, the Norman claim to Hafwynder Manor was secure no matter what happened to her father.

"I will not leave my father," Alison insisted, correctly interpreting Stephen's lengthy silence. "He will die without me. The wolves will tear him limb from limb. You must know that, Stephen. You *must!* You must help me!"

Her voice went shrill and her eyes burned so bright with blue fire that Stephen wished to look away; his thoughts seemed disconnected from his body. It came to him that she was probably right and his uncle terribly wrong. Godfrey Hafwynder should not be abandoned to his fate, even if that meant defying Torworden. There might even be—the notion came to him the longer he stared into Alison's beautiful eyes—wisdom in challenging his uncle. He would be his own man then and, having defended Alison, her manor, and her father, he would be welcomed by Harold when the English king gave comeuppance to the Bastard Duke of Normandy.

An image grew in his mind, an image of sitting in Hafwynder Hall and ordering his Norman uncle back to France. His muscles thrilled with a sense of power, then shuddered. Beauleyas would strike off his head in a moment. He was succumbing to some forlorn English dream and shook himself free of it—but not of Alison. Convincing the young heiress that her future lay with him alone, to the exclusion of her past and family, would not be easy. But, as the woman who haunted his every dream, she was definitely worth his efforts.

"Of course I'll help you," Stephen replied, daring to take her cold, trembling hands in his own. "But I can best help you at Torworden, and *you* must learn to trust my judgment on your behalf."

"I won't lose my land. I won't leave my father!'

"Your father hardly knows you," Stephen explained, doing his best to sound compassionate, "and leaving your land to stay at Torworden is hardly losing it."

Alison shrank away from him. Her face mirrored a stunned surprise. Stephen thought he heard her whisper, "You're supposed to do what *I* want!" but she had fled from the byre before he could demand clarification.

ildecent was in the buttery choosing cheeses for their supper when her sister raced into the kitchen. She didn't see Alison's face, but the sound of both the outer and inner door slamming against the wall told Wildecent everything she needed to know about Alison's mood and destination. The former was stormy and the latter was their bedroom in the tower above the pantry.

"It's that Frenchman," Bethanil, the cook, shouted when the door at the top of the tower stairs slammed shut.

Wildecent bit short a barbed reply. In the months since their aunt's death, she and Alison had been responsible for the daily life of the manor. Lady Ygurna had seen to it that they were capable of doing all that needed to be done—but there was, they had discovered, a great difference between knowing how something should be done and seeing that it *was* done.

The manorfolk did not resent the sisters, but for generations the folk of Hafwynder Manor—be they free, slave, or somewhere in between—had done what they were told to do. They waited to be told even now when they each knew more about their tasks than their mistresses did. It was the time-honored way; and the folk of Hafwynder Manor were honorable.

Lady Ygurna had treated the young women as equals when she taught them the responsibilities of the manor, and so it was as equals that they attempted to replace their aunt. Solemnly they had divided their aunt's keys and sworn to accept each other's word where it applied. Then they had discovered that manor life did not lend itself to neat divisions. Meals got served, and the pantries were maintained, but the manorfolk were choosing sides—and the side they most often chose was nostalgia.

Before their aunt's death Bethanil would never have

dared express her opinions, much less shout them across the kitchen. Then again, before Lady Ygurna's death Alison never would have excused herself from her chores and gone trysting in the byres. And although Wildecent had become much more certain of her abilities since Lady Ygurna's death, she was in no way ready to tell Alison what the latter should or should not do. Though their aunt had never shirked her responsibility for their behavior, her death had not shown the sisters their responsibility for each other.

Alison was throwing things. The sound echoed down the stairway into the suspiciously quiet kitchen.

Taking one of the yellow wheels from its shelf, Wildecent laid it on its side and attacked it with the cleaver. Her back was to the kitchen. No one could see the flush burning across her cheeks. All her frustration, even the frustration she would not acknowledge, was transferred to the knife as she whacked it through the hard crust.

Just like them, Wildecent thought as she delivered another stroke to the cheese. *All smiling to themselves. Laughing at her. Laughing at me because I don't know what to do about it.* Something hit the upper door and fell to the floor in pieces. *Our bowl! She's gone and broken our washing bowl!*

The cleaver wavered in her hand. She had half a mind to storm up the stairs herself, but the other half—the half that envisioned the smirks and chuckles that would follow her exit—won out. She separated the sloppily cut wedge and returned to the kitchen, doing her best to imitate her aunt.

"What about bread?" she inquired slowly and evenly. "They'll expect more than a loaf for each man. Do we have enough?"

"Only black bread, with husks, my lady," Bethanil replied, looking properly attentive. "It's the end of winter, you know."

Of course she knew. The manor was lucky to have any flour left after sharing their stores with the cottars who'd

22

been burned out by the Black Wolf at Christmastide. "It's better than they'll have seen for many a day—"

Alison descended from the tower, blond plaits and forest green cloak streaming behind her. She didn't notice them staring, but they, from Wildecent to the lowliest half-wit drudge, saw the high color in her cheeks. She flung the outer door open and did not bother to close it behind her.

"She's going to the weaving solar," Wildecent whispered, unaware she'd spoken aloud.

"Likely enough."

Wildecent whirled around, gesturing at Bethanil with the point of the cheese. "You worry about the bread," she commanded. "What my sister does is none of your concern!"

Momentarily cowed and contrite, the stout woman took the cheese into her own ample hands and held her tongue as Wildecent sped out the door. "Close that door," she barked at the drudges.

Alison had been more careful with the solar door; it was both closed and relocked. But it was one of the few locks for which both young women possessed keys, though Wildecent, shaking with nervousness, made several false starts before she got it unlocked. Her sister had heard the fumbling and was unsurprised when Wildecent finally pushed through the door.

"It's about time."

"You weren't acting like you wanted, or needed, my companionship," Wildecent replied. "You were doing quite a good job of destroying our bedroom without any help."

Alison had no time for the gibes which had become a regular part of their conversations. "He's taking us to Torworden," she shouted, knowing it would explain almost everything.

And it did. Thorkel Longsword mentioned the Norman lord's proposal each and every night. The men were

23

virtually unanimous: with Godfrey Hafwynder crippled, his manor was no place for his unmarried heiresses. A woman could own her own property but a man believed he owned the woman. Two attractive heiresses in a lordless manor were a dangerous temptation to any man.

Wildecent sank onto a spinning-bench with a sigh. "All of us?" she asked. "When?"

"No, not all of us. That's the worst of it. Just us; our lord father's to remain here—"

"God's will be done," Wildecent muttered reflexively.

"No it isn't. It's those shave-necked Normans up at Torworden. It'd serve their purposes right well to have me under their thumbs."

Wildecent's timidity masked a quick mind; behind her shyness she was an astute observer—especially of Alison. She wagered silently that there was something more to her sister's anger, and that something was, as Bethanil had suspected, Stephen. Throughout the long weeks since their aunt's death, Alison had assumed that Stephen would do as she wished.

She had also noticed that Alison said *me,* not *us*—and that was cause for concern. Wildecent had nothing of her own; she and Alison were not blood sisters. Wildecent's only claim to the privileges she enjoyed had come from Godfrey Hafwynder's generosity. What little might be known of her true heritage, if she had any worth mentioning, was locked in her lord's addled mind. No matter how bad Alison's position might become, Wildecent's could become much worse. Rather than dwell on how much she stood to lose, Wildecent decided that Alison, in her self-centered frustration, had simply misspoken and forced the thought from her mind.

"What did Stephen say?"

"Nothing."

"Then it was Longsword who told you?"

Thorkel Longsword had sworn an oath to Torworden's Norman lord while Godfrey yet lived. It might have been expedient, even wise under the circumstances, but it could have the Viking declared an outlaw if the new king, Harold, heard about it. King Harold could make both young women his wards, if he chose, and then Wildecent would suffer nothing worse than an honorable marriage to a man she might never love or like.

"No," Alison admitted, visibly reluctant. "Lord Stephen told me. He's come himself to see that everything valuable, including us, is loaded into carts and hauled to Torworden."

"And our lord father's not valuable enough?"

Strength was important in the higher strata of English society—as it was everywhere. An older man, even a physically crippled man, might get by on the strength of his personality, but a man without his mind, as Godfrey Hafwynder had become, was a lamb among the wolves. The love the young women felt for him was irrelevant, and a danger to all it touched.

"They don't know what they're doing," Alison murmured, her voice full of hidden meanings. "If they knew what's good for them, they'd leave me alone."

Then—while Wildecent was torn between a desire to console her foster sister and an equal desire to know her secrets—a hardness came to those sky blue eyes. An ugly grin stole across Alison's face, and Wildecent no longer wished to share the mysteries that Ygurna had revealed to one girl but not the other.

"They *do* know," Alison swore. "Why else send Stephen and the sorcerer? They know, and mean to do it anyway."

"Do what, Alison?"

"Ambrose knows that I am the last priestess. He seeks to control me and my choice!"

Wildecent rolled her lower lip inward. At times she wondered if Lord Godfrey were the only one whose wits were addled. "Don't talk like that," she said, gripping her sister's upper arms gently. "Our lady aunt said the time was past and forgotten when the land was made fertile with a hero's blood. No matter what happens, there's not going to be a blood sacrifice . . ."

Alison wrested free. "Lady Ygurna didn't know *everything.*"

Alison had been with the Cymric gods. They spoke to her in her dreams and, although she couldn't remember their words when she was awake, she knew she'd promised to do something important: something wondrous and terrible. But a *geas* had been laid over the promise and she could neither discuss it with anyone nor remember it herself.

"What are you going to do?" the dark-haired girl asked fearfully as Alison lifted a section of the mosaic floor.

"If we're leaving, this has to go."

Wildecent blinked. The threatening fire was gone as if it had never existed. Alison was herself again and speaking sanely. Of course their pharmacopoeia would have to be included among the valuables of Hafwynder Manor—included or destroyed.

But because this was Alison and Alison had a wild magical talent, which she was apt to use whenever it suited her, Wildecent hesitated before descending into the earth-walled bolt-hole. She checked her most recent memories: what she had said, what Alison had said, and how they had stood while they spoke. Alison could alter a person's memories; she could add a notion or take one away. Wildecent was the only one who understood the extent of her sister's power, and the only one with conscious defenses against it. There were no gaps—this time.

"While you're about it, we should make something up for our lord father," Wildecent said as she descended the wooden ladder into the bolt-hole.

A questioning look came into Alison's face then vanished. There was no way they could serve dinner to their guests and have their father at the table with them. "I feel guilty somehow, whenever I do this," she admitted, reaching for a glazed jug. "He drinks it readily enough, even knowing that he's going to fall asleep and wake up in a little locked byre . . . but I wouldn't want it done to me."

"You begin to sound like Thorkel Longsword," Wildecent said recklessly. "It's a sleeping draught or some of Ygurna's black poison, you know that."

Alison's hands trembled a moment, then were still. "They'll not have our lord father," she said. "His mind will be restored when this is over. I will see to it." She filled a small vial and put the jug back on the shelf. "Here, take this over to Bethanil. We've a lot to do."

"It will take us 'til summer," Wildecent remarked, looking at the cluttered shelves and boxes.

"He wants to leave as quickly as possible," Alison said flatly.

"Alison!" It was just another kind of madness to think the effects of a prosperous and ancient manor could be made transportable in so short a time. "Why, we haven't nearly enough chests and boxes, and our carts are scattered all over the manor—"

"I'd guess it's different in their precious Normandy."

"Surely Stephen—"

"Lord Stephen's mind will not be changed."

Wildecent was curious—achingly, silently curious—to know what had passed between them in the stables. Alison must have used her talent on him as well as more ordinary female wiles; and it must have failed spectacularly. "I guess we'd best get started, then, and hope that when the Frenchmen see what a big task it is, they'll think better of the whole thing," she said with false cheerfulness.

"We can always hope and pray," Alison agreed, though her tone implied that she expected little success. She looked at the heavily laden shelves and appeared defeated by them. "Maybe you'll have more luck than I have."

Alison waited until Wildecent was off the top of the ladder, then climbed it herself. Had she ever been able to confide all the successes and failures of her talent, she would have been able to do much to reassure Wildecent.

She might even have been able to lance the festering sores of doubt that had grown within her, for the *geas* was not always comforting and it did not always make her strong.

That December night, when her aunt had pushed her deeper into magic than she'd ever gone before, Alison had welcomed the embrace of the Cymric gods. After surrendering herself to them she'd wrought a protective sphere over the manor—a sphere that failed only because the Greek sorcerer had confounded it. But the failure of her magic hadn't undone the promise that lay beneath the *geas*.

When Alison had awakened in the great hall of Hafwynder Manor, her father lying mindless on the next pallet and her aunt with the other corpses in the sheep-byre, she had not known herself. There was no smooth bridge of memory across that bitter-cold night. Her childhood had been severed and her magic was tainted by something she could not understand.

Not vanished, Alison admitted to herself, but changed and unreliable. Strange thoughts lingered from her dream-wracked nights—lustful, unmaidenly thoughts; bloody thoughts. She sensed she had the power to send a man to his death, but she could not alter Stephen's simplest desires.

Alison pressed her knuckles against her eyes and convinced herself it was the raw weather that made them water so. Each night she slipped a little further into the *geas* world.

Some night, any night now, she would overcome the *geas* and confront the promise she had made. Alison feared that night because some echo of her childhood said she would go mad when she set foot on that path. Not the generally benign madness that blanketed her father, but something terrible and beyond absolution.

"You coming or not?" Wildecent called from the kitchen door.

Alison turned the key and hurried across the yard before her sister called again. There was suspicion in Wildecent's face, but she said nothing and Alison was grateful for that small blessing.

Pleasant aromas had spread from the kitchen to the nearby hall, luring visitors and residents alike. Since Twelfth Night at the end of Christmastide and their muted celebration of Harold Godwinson's coronation, Hafwynder Manor had been a solemn place, but the Normans expected a welcoming feast.

The trestles were set in a formal U with a high table set between two longer rows. The high table, which was, in fact, no higher than the others, was covered with linen and graced with chairs rather than simple benches. The nobility could come and go at their individual pleasure and did not have to sit thigh-against-thigh with their companions.

All too soon it was time for Alison, as her father's legitimate daughter and recognized heiress, to sit in the most ornate of the chairs and signal the beginning of the meal. She perched on the edge of the hard wooden seat, looking as uncomfortable as she felt—or as uncomfortable as Wildecent in the chair beside her. Stephen sat on her other side and she spoke politely with him, as a chatelaine was expected to do.

"You seem to have recovered well enough from your wounds. Do you still have any pain?"

Stephen looked away from his bread, giving her his full attention. "None at all—hardly. I shall be able to begin work with my sword once we return to Torworden. My uncle's men are well impressed with your English herbals. You'll be much appreciated—you need not worry on that account."

Inwardly Alison wilted, though she made a brave show of graciousness. The last thing she wanted to do was practice herb-magic at Torworden, but she dared not say that. Instead she asked simple questions about France and watched him eat.

His manners were as good as any Englishman's, certainly better than the other Frenchmen—though he claimed that practically no one at Torworden was French. He was from the south, while his uncle was a Norman. The French were those unfortunates who had a Capetian king as an overlord. Alison paid scant attention to his catechism; all she noticed was that he was different, and not because of his continental habits. He watched her with a measure of distraction, of obsession. She had not meant for him to love her like this when she first laid her image over his fantasies. But now, as it had turned out, she needed him, and she meant to control him.

"I've spoken with my sister," she said after the meat was served. "She says that, even without Father, if we are to transport our valuables it will take considerable time to prepare them. And the tracks, of course, are treacherous at this time of year. I cannot see us coming to Torworden before summer." She smiled artlessly.

It didn't work. Stephen took a sip of cyder and said, "Then you'll come without your dower goods. I'll have you out of here in two days. You're more important than your father's gold."

Alison wanted to shout that her father's wealth was more than gold; that marriage had never been in her thoughts when she tampered with his fantasies. She didn't. Everything she said, no matter how she said it, with or without her talent, was only making matters worse.

She did not look forward to telling her sister that their situation had gotten more precarious, and she dreaded the dreams that would come this night.

"You needn't look so glum," Stephen chided, to no avail.

It was not much better on Alison's right, where Wildecent found herself sitting next to Ambrose. Wildecent had tried not to think about the sorcerer during his absence. Now that he was beside her, she lost the battle completely. Ambrose was a door to what Lady Ygurna had denied: a key to the arcane arts that depended on dedication, not wild talent. Ambrose was also Ambrose: dark, mysterious, and sensually attractive.

He was the personification of everything that could tempt and ruin her. Wildecent had the sense to fear him, but she no longer had the strength to put him out of her thoughts. She was glad he did not seem to mind that she was so obviously ignoring him. The dinner passed in awkward silence.

"I wish it were over," she whispered finally to Alison.

"You too? We can take care of *that*, at least."

Alison proclaimed it was time for the bard to take up his instrument and begin the night's entertainment. In the next breath she ordered another round of the manor's potent cyder, and with the third she demurred that her guests and her own men would enjoy themselves more if they did not have to worry about their manners in the presence of ladies. Then she and Wildecent, the only two in the hall who could possibly claim that distinction, retreated.

'm sorry," Alison snapped impatiently once she and Wildecent were in the bolt-hole. "You know I didn't mean to do it."

"I know you didn't mean for it to fail."

Wildecent could spare little compassion for Alison. She had been unhappy to learn that they could not wait for their baggage to be loaded onto carts before going to the unknown world of Torworden. Skillful mismanagement would have kept those carts unfilled for months. "You never think," she complained. "You just go ahead and *do*. Well, how long do you think we have? A week, a fortnight?"

"We leave the day after tomorrow, I think."

"Lord God Almighty have mercy on you, Alison. We'll barely be able to get our clothes loaded in a day. What about all this—" She gestured at the shelves. "We'll have to destroy the whole lot of it. Lady Ygurna will rise out of her grave if we leave her legacy where some fool can stumble onto it."

If she hasn't risen already, Alison thought, after failing utterly to calm Wildecent with her magic. "I'd almost rather leave our clothes chests behind. I don't even know what kinds of plants grow near Torworden and . . ."

"And what? Come on, Alison. What else went wrong? What else did you do?"

The blond girl could endure only so much guilt before pride got the better of her. "I didn't do anything. We all had a hand in healing Stephen, didn't we? I guess our plants don't grow in Normandy, or if they do the women there don't know what to do with them, because I got the sense that we're going to have our hands full of bandages once we get to Torworden." She saw Wildecent's brow rise higher and preempted whatever her sister might be thinking. "*Egede,* Wili, it's hardly my fault that we saved his life."

Whether it was the truth of Alison's words or the

crackle of anger in her voice as she spoke them, Wildecent swallowed her own indignation. In the days to come they would only have each other to rely upon. Truly, her sister had never precipitated more disaster with her talent, but just as truly she had never admitted her defeats so readily.

"This is of our own making, then," she agreed sadly, convincing herself that it was no longer relevant who had done what in the past with the uncertain future looming before them. "We'd best be getting on with the sorting and packing if this is the only full night we'll have."

Alison set the first of many containers on the work-table. "We'll take what's needed for healing; Stephen won't balk at that. And what we know can't be replaced in England. The rest we'll destroy or hide."

Wildecent was already gathering the most basic medicines and laying them carefully in a deep basket. From time to time she or Alison would trudge up the wooden ladder with a heavy basket or fetch bits of carded wool to pack between the delicate vials. Travel by oxcart was not a gentle experience. They'd consider themselves fortunate if half the bottles survived. Leaves and powders were less fragile, but it seemed that those herbs that would travel best were also those that would likely grow within easy distance of Torworden.

At last, long after midnight, when the hall had grown quiet and they'd replenished their lamps many times, they faced half-empty shelves and the hardest of the night's tasks.

"I can't bear it," Wildecent complained, struggling to pick her way toward the stables with an overflowing arm-ful of fragrant herbs. These were the exotics, the ingredients of magic. They opened no doors for Wildecent, merely gave her a headache. But they were the heritage of ancient England and everything a Norman presence threatened.

"Then don't think about it," Alison snapped as she heaved her burden onto the manure and thrashed it with a nearby pitchfork.

As if either of them could *not* think about it. Laying Lady Ygurna in the earth beside the junipers had not been nearly so hard or so final. Yet they weren't finished. Not everything in the bolt-hole pertained to healing or the Old Ways; some of the earthen jars held poisons, which they poured into the frigid waters below the fish weir—believing that the swift-running water would render the fatal liquids harmless. They vowed that they would take none of the noxious drugs with them, save those that were diluted to produce purgatives, pain-killers and sleeping draughts, yet each hid a tarry lump in her sleeve. One never knew what the future—especially a Torworden future—might hold.

The bolt-hole was nearly barren then, its bare earth walls exposed and stripped of its scents and mysteries. Alison picked up a necklace made from apple seeds, blew away a cloud of dust, and sank down to the floor. There should have been two of them, she remembered. When they had been very young, not long after Wildecent had first come to Hafwynder Manor, Lady Ygurna had treated them with complete equality. They'd both worn seed necklaces one early spring night when she'd led them to the forest to watch the rebirth of the greenwood.

A night almost exactly like this. Wildecent had been cold and miserable, and more than ready to believe she saw green giants moving through the mists. Lady Ygurna had smiled and embraced her but, of course, it had been a mistake. The world never came to life for the dark-haired orphan.

"It's so hard to imagine leaving here," Wildecent said. "I can barely remember any home but Hafwynder Manor, and I can't imagine Torworden at all."

"Stephen says it's on a high hill," Alison answered absently, not looking away from the necklace. "He says that when the sky is clear, you can see a horse a half-day's ride away."

"I won't like it then."

Wildecent didn't like heights, didn't like the squat

stone tower Lord Godfrey had built to contain their bedroom and the food pantries, and she was nearsighted. She had trouble seeing from one end of the great hall to the other, much less seeing a horse a half-day's ride away.

"You'll come back here," Alison continued in the same dreamy voice. "We'll both come back here someday."

Wildecent brightened, unaccountably relieved, though her sister's gift for prophecy was a chancy thing at best, observed most often in the breach. "Then we don't have to destroy all this! We can just leave it here."

"Huh?" Alison shook herself free of mental cobwebs and remembered what she had just said. She tucked the necklace into her sleeve as she got to her feet. "It's not that simple."

"You said we'd be back, Alison. I was looking at you. I saw it in your eyes. You *said* we'd be back."

Alison didn't deny her prophecy but could not explain the complex web of gods and sacrifices that lurked beneath the *geas*.

"Alison . . ."

The bolt-hole had never been that important to Wildecent. She'd learned the herbcraft, all right, better perhaps than Alison, for she relied on hard memory, not intuition. It had been different for Alison, marked by her aunt to be a hidden priestess of an almost-forgotten tradition. Herbcraft was the least of the skills Alison had learned in this subterranean room.

For ten years their status had been clearly defined: equal sisters in ordinary tasks, incomparable in all others. That balance had been subtly altered in the months since their aunt's death. Wildecent had proved herself stronger and more capable than Alison had imagined a head-blind woman could ever be.

Alison had not felt threatened by her foster sister for many years. Wildecent had been called her *half* sister when she'd first arrived. For several years Alison endured the suspicion that her beloved father kept a mistress somewhere. She also believed it was her father's Saxon blood that endowed her magical powers. She wasn't told the truth until Wildecent proved resolutely head-blind.

The orphan was no kin to anyone on the manor, and magic was the Cymric heritage of Alison's mother and aunt. There'd been Cymry in France, Lady Ygurna had explained, justifying her own behavior. There'd been a wild hope that the dark little girl had been *sent,* but she had only been found.

Alison's love for her father was no longer compromised. Wildecent could be loved but need never be feared. And wild magic was Alison's alone.

You and you alone will become the priestess, Ygurna had said many times, *a guardian of the Cymric ways, and because of that you must learn compassion as well as strength.* Alison knew she had more mastery of strength than of compassion. But she tried, when she remembered; and this time she remembered. "Well, we can't just leave everything sitting on the shelves. Without someone to watch them, sooner or later they'll collapse. We must set what's left on the floor and conceal it." She watched a smile of relief soften Wildecent's face. Compassion had its own rewards.

They worked together emptying the shelves. Their exhaustion abated as ancient objects revealed themselves, objects Alison herself had never seen.

"Who are they?" Wildecent asked when they had three ferocious-looking plaques on the ground between them.

Each was a wood carving, though each was a different wood: that in itself gave Alison a clue. Traces of paint still clung to them; their faces had been green, their eyes had been crimson. Their expressions were fierce, almost grotesque. They might have been the faces of imaginary animals, but they weren't.

"The tree kings," Alison explained. "The Oak King—see, he has acorns in his hair. The Holly King, the one with thorns. And the Ivy King, with those little curly things."

Wildecent let her fingers run lightly over the age-dark

wood. They were masks, she realized, with holes above their ears for thongs that had long since disappeared. No one had worn them in her lifetime, she was certain, nor for a good many lifetimes before that.

"Shouldn't there be four of them?" she asked after another moment's thought. Numbers had power in the Cymry myths. Everything had its appropriate number, and four was the number for green, living things.

Head propped against the heels of her hands, Alison seemed to give the matter thought, though actually she was only determining what she could say. She had never seen the masks before; she recognized them from her nightmares. "The fourth king has no face," she answered in carefully measured words. "He takes his head from the hero."

"You're talking about blood sacrifices again . . ."

Alison sighed. "It happened."

She expected more questions, but mercifully, Wildecent seemed satisfied—or sufficiently disquieted—with what she had already learned. Alison's heart had almost returned to its normal rhythms when Wildecent reached for a rickety basket they'd rejected earlier in the evening.

"I think we should bring them with us—"

She's head-blind! Alison screamed to herself. She had decided to leave the horrific things behind and now her sister—her *head-blind* sister—was doing the *geas*'s work. She said nothing as Wildecent buried the leering, toothy faces beneath loose coils of rough-spun wool.

Wildecent had experienced no supernal revelations. No voice had told her to bring the kings to Torworden, except they set her fingers tingling when she touched them. They were like Ambrose's crystal: talismans for storing power, though it was certainly odd to find such things here. Natural magic resided only in living things: it could be enriched, but not increased; shared, but never taken. This was the dichotomy that made all sorcery repugnant to Alison and Lady Ygurna.

The masks possessed power no piece of wood should

37

rightfully possess. They emanated sorcery, yet they were here, in the bolt-hole. Wildecent hefted the basket, then set it down again. "Maybe we should burn them instead."

Their eyes locked across the lantern-light.

"Why would you say that?" Alison asked cautiously.

"Because of what they are," her sister replied with equal caution.

"What *are* they, then?"

"Magical."

"The seed necklaces are magical." Alison held the necklace out. "You wouldn't think of burning this, would you?"

"No."

"Then why these?"

Wildecent swallowed hard. It was one thing to know that Alison had replaced Lady Ygurna, but quite another to be interrogated by her. And yet, as her thoughts and reflections expanded, it was not so bad after all; Alison had, as usual, led the way earlier when she'd admitted how she failed with Stephen.

"It is sorcerous," Wildecent said calmly.

"How would you know?"

"I'd know."

Alison sat back on her heels not quite surprised, not quite shocked, and not at all certain where she was going from here. She knew instantly how her lady aunt would have reacted; she knew how she should react. It took a little longer to discover her own reaction.

Across the pool of light, Wildecent also waited. With a simple statement she'd declared herself anathema to all that the Cymric heritage represented. She, too, knew how Lady Ygurna would have reacted—and would never have volunteered the information. Alison, though, was her sister in everything but blood. They weren't as close, perhaps, as they'd once been, but love, trust, and a common past had to count for something.

"When? How often? With that foreigner Ambrose, right?"

Wildecent breathed more easily. That wasn't hostility in Alison's voice, but something more like the conspiratorial curiosity of their childhood.

"Only once, the night before—well, you know before what. I knew from the way you were acting that you and our lady aunt were up to something, but I was afraid for you, for both of you. I didn't know what you could do. I think, I honestly believe that all I wanted to do was help.

"Ambrose had already said he could teach me sorcery. I went to him, meaning to ask him to help, or to show me how to help. But he was already working his own rituals." Her hazel eyes misted. Even in front of Alison, she couldn't escape a thrill of excitement. Ambrose had drawn power through his talisman; an ordinary man with extraordinary power: the memory was tinged with guilt but no less delicious for that.

"Oh, Alison, he'd made a miniature of the manor and set his crystal above it, then he concentrated his thoughts through the crystal, into the miniature and into the world. He drew the Black Wolf to the manor—because he wanted victory, not protection, I guess. But I could feel it, Alison—like I never felt anything that you or Lady Ygurna could do.

"And then, later, when I understood what had happened, when I saw your circle beyond the stockade, I used the miniature myself to learn what had happened to you."

Alison found her hands were shaking. Compassion. Where had her compassion been, or her aunt's, when they'd given Wildecent a glimpse behind magic's curtain, then condemned her to wait forever on the outside? How much temptation could love withstand? Alison lowered her eyes, knowing she would succumb to temptation more completely than her sister if her gifts ever vanished.

When Alison looked away, Wildecent's doubts overwhelmed her. "I've thought about so much since then. I still don't know if sorcery itself is evil, but I keep thinking: what if I'd gone to that room for him instead of his sorcery? What if he hadn't crossed your circle? I feel myself being weighed for what I did that night. I felt my judgment when I sat beside him at the high table tonight—and I wanted to run away."

"I don't think you did anything wrong," Alison began, speaking to her own distress as much as her sister's. "Our lady aunt knew what she was doing. She knew what Ambrose was and what he could do. She took the poison with her; I saw her take it. And I don't know—I just don't know—if anything could have made any difference.

"We can't burn the masks," Alison said after a long pause. "We can't even leave them behind. If we hadn't seen them— No, there are many paths, but home is always home . . ."

Wildecent smiled weakly, remembering how many times Ygurna had muttered that proverb under her breath. Then she carried the broken basket up the ladder and put it with the others. The rest of the night, what little of it remained, went by quickly. Alison unveiled another of their aunt's secrets when she pulled another panel from the ceramic tunnels of the old Roman hypocaust and fitted it into place beneath the mosaic. Then she scattered broken bits of tile and loose dirt across the panel until, if the uninformed or unsuspicious had by chance lifted the mosaic, it looked like the nearly ruined foundation of any other structure that had endured since the Roman Empire had abandoned the British Isles. It was not necessary to conceal the bolt-hole; merely to make it seem uninteresting.

Pale pink streaked the eastern horizon when they emerged from the weaving solar for the last time. Cocks had already crowed, and it would not be long before the manorfolk woke up, if they were not already awake and assembling in the kitchen. The nobility, warriors and landowners, could drink cyder, ale, or mead until mid-

night and sleep until well past dawn. Not so those who supported them.

Unfortunately for Wildecent and Alison, the only path to their tower bedroom lay through the sure-to-be-rousing kitchen. Taking care to keep her keys from jingling, Alison reopened the door and searched through the baskets. She found a handful of fresh mistletoe and gave half to her sister. They smeared the sap on their hands and tucked the broken leaves in the soles of their boots.

Thus invisible, or at least unnoticed, they tiptoed across the courtyard, eased the kitchen door open, and crept stealthily to their rooms.

"I'll sleep until noon," Alison proclaimed once the door was bolted behind them. "I don't care what anyone thinks."

luxurious morning of sleep was not, however, what fate held for them. It seemed they had only just fallen across the bed when something heavy pounded on the door. Alison stumbled across the wooden planks, suddenly mindful of light streaming through the shutters, and the mounds of clothing they'd left strewn across the floor.

"What?" she grumbled, unwilling to open the door.

"It's time you two were awake. There's work to be seen to, and that Frenchman wants to speak with you. And your father's poorly for waking up without seeing you!"

Only the last persuaded Alison to face the obviously irate Bethanil, but she braced the door against her shoulder. "Tell everyone we'll be right there."

"As you wish, my lady."

There was nothing particularly servile about Bethanil's manner as she trod heavily back down the stairs. The cook knew that they were to be taken north to Torworden, and she might well guess why neither of them was up and about for breakfast.

She'll run the manor once we're gone, Alison mused, and run it better, no doubt. "Come on, Wili. I know you're awake!" She took her frustration out on the blankets Wildecent clutched tight around her. "No rest for the weary. You know that."

"Wha'd she want?" Wildecent asked through a body-shaking yawn.

"The day of eternal judgment."

Wildecent had already caught the mood of the day, and shared it to the extent that she didn't want to talk or move either. Still, it wasn't fair to blame Bethanil for their problems. On any manor there was always one person—usually a freewoman, often the cook—who stood between the chatelaine and the manorfolk, just as the noble lord always selected one man to be the chief of his housecarls. Bethanil depended on the sisters; she did not dare, or want, to usurp their authority, but her anger was justified when they failed to perform their duties.

"You heard what she said about father?" Alison asked as she laced a single layer of hose beneath her linen undertunic.

"I'm hurrying, Alison." Wildecent shoved her foot into the nearest boot—it didn't matter which—and craned her neck to catch her reflection in the polished bronze mirror. There were dust smudges on her cheek; she wiped them as best she could on her sleeve. Alison had, after all, broken their washbasin. Her hair, she knew, should be rebraided, but there was no time for that.

"Do you want me to go to our lord father or deal with Stephen?"

"Talk to Bethanil first." Alison thrust an arm down the sleeve of her tunic. A broken fingernail caught on the hemstitching. Both the nail and the embroidery ripped loose. "Oh, bother it, do what you want. Talk to Stephen first; he seems to be making all the decisions around here anyway."

"You take care of our lord father, then."

Wildecent was still fumbling with her sleeve laces when she reached the kitchen where Bethanil, fists on hips, was waiting for her.

"We've got to know how many's for dinner and if they're wanting meat. I'll not have Godeshalt wringing necks for no good reason. Leeks 'n' eels is good enough unless they complain."

The thought made Wildecent's stomach turn. "I'm going to talk to them now—"

"And what shall I do until you're back?"

Was this truly what their aunt had endured every day? Dozens of people unable to move until someone made their decisions for them? "Lord God Almighty and all the holy saints, Bethanil, it's *your* kitchen. You know what's needed here better than I do. Count the fish in the salt-house for all I care. I'll be back as soon as I can."

She blinked as she entered the bright morning sun, then noticed how it highlighted all the tracks they'd made the night before in the soft mud. Groaning inwardly, she hurried across the line of paving stones to the hall.

Thorkel Longsword, Stephen, Ambrose, and the rest of the Torworden visitors were seated on benches and stools contemplating a still-cold hearth. Her groan became a low growl as she realized none of them would ask to have the fire rekindled, much less get down on their knees to do it themselves. Piercing their circle, Wildecent approached the hearth.

Men spent half the year campaigning, traveling, or hunting. Surely every one of them was more adept at prodding the embers to life than she was, but no—men ruled in the great hall and those who ruled had no need to work. Folding her skirt so only the underside touched the ashes, Wildecent took up the fire tools.

"Nay, we're comfortable as it is," Ambrose interrupted.

He was lying—a social lie, a civilized lie that was supposed to soothe everyone's feelings. But then, perhaps they hadn't noticed—men were notoriously indifferent to comfort. Wildecent got to her feet and slapped the gray dust from her hands, noticing as she did that there were two empty stools at the bottom of the circle. Ambrose gestured toward them with his eyes, but Wildecent continued to stand.

"We had expected both of you," Stephen began, gesturing more broadly for her to be seated. "But perhaps it's just as well that you've come alone. Last night Lady Alison said you made the decisions"—which was a great surprise to Wildecent—"and so surely you would be the one she'd listen to—if you were convinced of our good intentions."

Time had come to do as she was told. Wildecent took her perch and stared back at them. Stephen was clearly as uncomfortable as she was, but that was apt to be a small satisfaction in the end.

"We English count sensibility as a virtue in women," she replied, smiling as she imagined Alison might.

Stephen muttered something under his breath and passed the initiative to Ambrose, who spoke dispassionately. "When first we spoke of Torworden and the need for you and Lady Alison to be brought there you seemed understanding enough—"

"It is not the leaving that upsets either of us," Wildecent replied, stretching the truth a bit. "Merely that Lord Beauleyas has not extended his hand to our lord father; nor will his nephew extend it on his behalf. Surely a daughter's devotion to her father is not another isolated English virtue?"

"*Deus aie*," Stephen swore. "Hafwynder nearly went berserk when he heard three words of Norman French. Even if I wanted to overrule my uncle, how could I possibly bring your lord father to Torworden?"

"Then leave us alone. We're safe enough here. We'll care for our father and see that the crops are put in—"

"I warned you," Thorkel cut in. "There's no talking to an Englishwoman when her mind's made up. Just put them in a cart and take them away—if you think your French fortress is ready."

Stephen gave the Viking a dark look. "Wildecent, please, you're only making matters worse for all of us. No one wants to take you away from Hafwynder Manor against your will—"

"You just want us to change our minds, to set aside everything to become Norman hostages?"

"No one mentioned hostages," Ambrose said mildly.

"No one needed to," Thorkel said.

A faint ruddiness stained Stephen's cheeks, and Wildecent wondered if Thorkel Longsword had the truth of it. But Longsword was a risky ally. He followed his own path and let no one walk beside him, not even those to whom he'd given his oath. Regardless of Alison's dire dreams, there was no small risk in leaving the crippled nobleman in Longsword's care.

Stephen caught her staring at him; she lowered her eyes and waited for one of the others to speak. If her few childhood memories were right, she was already a hostage of sorts sent to England by people who were long forgotten for purposes no one here had ever known.

Stephen cleared his throat and turned to his companions. They spoke in rapid French, shutting out the Viking and Wildecent. Longsword did not seem to care, but Wildecent, hearing her name spoken several times, resolved to learn Norman French as quickly as possible.

Finally Stephen addressed her in the competent English he'd acquired courtesy of Alison's intrusions into his private thoughts. "I have decided to leave Alan FitzAlan, Serlo, and Gauche-Robert here. Alan will guard your father; Serlo and Gauche-Robert will ride with the baggage train. You and your sister, though, will leave with us tomorrow after breakfast—I trust that gives you enough time?"

Wildecent blanched. "Your offer is most generous, but there is so much to do. I just do not see how we can be ready in less than a fortnight," she began, and watched Stephen's face shift from hopeful to angry. "Three generations of Hafwynders have lived here," she explained. "And a dozen families dwell in our cottages and use our oxen. Even if we could sort through everything here in a single day—which we cannot do—there's much of value beyond the hall . . ."

Stephen glanced at FitzAlan. The taciturn man shrugged, then nodded. "I do not think my uncle meant to strip the manor bare. He needs to protect at Tworden only those things likely to tempt an honest man. It does not matter if the baggage is delayed until the oxcarts can be brought here. If you will show Alan FitzAlan that property which should be loaded, he will see to the details."

Wearily, Wildecent conceded defeat. These men would

not lose sight of their goal. She and Alison were going to leave their home in less than one day; there was nothing to be done about it. "I will show your man through the storerooms—"

"Don't forget the cook," Ambrose interjected.

"Yes, and we're to bring your cook. There's no cook at Torworden to compare with yours. My uncle would have her prepare our food for your pleasure and his."

Wildecent nearly lost her balance from surprise. Beth-anil was a freewoman, not a chattel to be bartered back and forth between manors. "I cannot command Bethanil to go to Torworden. Her family is here. She has every right to remain here whether we stay or not. She's a free-born woman with property of her own."

"I'm sure Lord Beauleyas will pay her a good wage, enough to house her family in the village," Ambrose suggested. "Explain to her how much he liked the food she prepared and the order of her kitchen. Perhaps she'll be flattered and agree to come of her own accord."

Wildecent envisioned how Bethanil would react to the proposal that she trek halfway across England to cook for a foreigner. She was so caught up imagining Bethanil's indignation that she paid no attention to Stephen's final words and found herself standing alone with FitzAlan be-fore she had properly collected her thoughts.

"We must go to the kitchen first," she informed him, and led the way from the hall.

She paused at the door. Bethanil was scolding an un-fortunate drudge who'd dropped an egg.

"Perhaps if I waited in the hall?" FitzAlan suggested.

"Perhaps you should," Wildecent agreed. She watched him go, but then, instead of confronting the angry cook, she headed for the back of the manor yard where byres sprang haphazardly between the great hall and the stock-ade.

Alison had Godfrey sitting in the sun and was carefully combing sleep-tangles from his hair.

"Did they relent?" Alison asked without looking up from her tasks.

"Did you expect them to?"

"I . . . I had hoped Stephen might see things differently this morning."

An honest hope, or had her sister been, despite her previous disasters, trying to influence the young man's thoughts again?

"He did, a bit. He did say we could ride rather than travel in the carts. So that's something. But, other side of the coin, he insists there's no need to wait until the carts are back. He's leaving three men behind; they'll oversee the loading of the baggage and protect our lord father until we can make our appeal to Lord Beauleyas. And we're to bring Bethanil, if she'll come. They said Jean Beauleyas will offer her enough wages for her family to have a house in the village."

But Alison, for once, was thinking more deeply than her sister. "A house in the village? What sort of place are we going to, where the cook's family lives someplace else?"

She smoothed her father's cornsilk hair until it concealed all traces of the still-ragged scar above his ear. There was some truth in Thorkel's accusations. In health, Godfrey had never been overfastidious about his appearance. His comfort had mattered more than his cleanliness, though he seemed not to mind the constant attention his daughters now focused on him. If he even knew they were his daughters. He smiled when Alison called him Father, but he didn't say her name; he hadn't said anyone's name since his injury.

The little boy who sat in the dirt at Godfrey's feet, caring for his body's needs and such minimal wants as he still had, took up his post. Godfrey smiled again and patted the lad on his tawny head.

"Do you have treasures?"

The boy dug deep into the pouch slung inside his braes and produced the crushed remnants of a bird's egg.

"Oh, treasures indeed!"

Alison spun around. "He won't even know when we're gone," she said in a tight, husky voice.

Wildecent laid her arm around her sister's waist, but Alison stepped free, shaking her head as her shoulders hunched forward.

"I'll be in the gallery with FitzAlan, the man Stephen's left as overseer," Wildecent said softly. "When you're ready."

She felt the pain of Godfrey Hafwynder's decline differently than Alison did. Indeed, though she would not admit it aloud, Wildecent thought Longsword might be right. Almighty God had simply forgotten to gather Lord Godfrey Hafwynder into his arms. The arcane arts—Ambrose's sorcery and Ygurna's magic—had made the divine oversight possible. No wonder the Church stood against the arcane in every form, decreeing there was no difference between sorcery and the magic so carefully preserved beneath the manor's weaving room.

The Church was many things in eleventh-century England—and none of them all-powerful. Some clerics said that Joseph of Arimathaea had fled to Britain with the Holy Grail in the first century; certainly the Irish had brought Christianity to the Saxons not long after they'd conquered the Cymry. There were Frenchmen who preached that the English church, having fallen away from Rome and into the influence of the Irish, was scarcely better than no church at all. At Hafwynder Manor they kept a chapel a half-day's journey to the north and kept the rest of religion further away than that.

Wildecent pulled her thoughts back to the problem at hand and headed to the hall, where FitzAlan was mending his boots. He bit off the thread and followed her up the stairs. The first of the storerooms she unlocked was filled with bolts of cloth, boots, and other articles of clothing. A lord had a responsibility to keep his men fed, housed, and clothed. Most of the housecarls had already been summoned by King Harold but, in Wildecent's mind at least, so long as there was a Hafwynder Manor this particular room should remain untouched.

"These remain as they are," she said slowly and clearly.

FitzAlan shrugged. "It's gold and the like we're interested in, my lady, not your house goods."

No wonder the Normans expected the women could pack their valuables in an afternoon. Hafwynder Manor was comfortable and secure but hardly one of England's great estates. Many of its treasures were sentimental rather than valuable. So she led him to the one room where such treasures as had been given to Godfrey and his ancestors by *their* lords and masters were stored.

The door had just swung open when Alison ran up the stairs to join them. "You'll take him into our treasure room?" she demanded.

Wildecent was stung by her sister's accusatory tone. "I don't think I have a choice. It's our gold they want—"

Alison stood between FitzAlan and the door. "You'll have what remains of our king's gift. And you'll trust us to prepare it for you."

The Norman was accustomed to taking orders. He gave one of his many shrugs. "As you wish, my lady. Set the coffers before the door." He turned and disappeared down the stairs.

"He'll be in here the moment we're gone," Wildecent objected once they were alone.

"I'm not leaving them with the keys."

The women had the keys to every casket and coffer, but neither of them had had the time to learn what each box contained. There were some secrets their aunt had never shared. They knew what was in the coin chest—or, more properly, what wasn't in it since Harold's men had extorted an extra levy—but there were another half-dozen chests piled beside it.

"I'd like to take it all and bury it in the forest," Alison complained. "If this doesn't belong to us, then it should belong to our English king, not to some French bastard.

But we owe Torworden for Christmastide, and it will go hard for our people if anything comes away missing."

It was barely midday when they arranged a stack of heavy boxes outside the storeroom door. Alison removed a key from her ring and handed it to FitzAlan. "You may place the treasure in the weaving room."

FitzAlan's eyes never left the keys she did not give to him, but he said nothing. The locks could be broken once the women were gone. "As you wish, my lady," he told Alison as he strung the key on a thong of his belt-pouch.

Then it was time to face Bethanil, who reacted to the Norman proposal much as Wildecent had imagined she would.

"Wages," she sputtered. "Wages as if I were some forsaken day laborer with nothing to call my own? See Godeshalt groveling for work in some muddy dunghill village? See my children run off with ne'er-do-wells and Frenchmen?" Her cleaver slammed through a half-dozen leeks, then swept the pieces into the stewpot. "I'll ride with the baggage carts," she told them as she lined up another handful of leeks. "I'll do that for Lady Ygurna, for her soul's rest, and I'll talk to your French lord, and maybe I'll take up his kitchen for him. But my family stays here on Hafwynder land—you tell him that for me."

"I can't wait to see the look on his face when we do," Alison whispered as they left.

y late afternoon the sisters had done all that could not be entrusted to lesser hands. There was nothing left to do but wait. They watched as journey-bread was baked, and took careful note of the way the setting sun lit the great hall's thatched roof. Their melancholy became contagious, infecting all who gathered for the meal. There was neither singing nor boasting from either the English or the French. The eels were consumed in gloomy silence.

Only the kitchens and the byres, where the manorfolk dwelt with their families, produced laughter that night. But, then, lives were not changing dramatically in those places. The valley was fertile; it would always attract a protector, and a protector always needed common men to do common work. Benign master or harsh, their lives changed little so long as the land grew green each spring.

"We leave at sunrise," Stephen said in a low voice that nonetheless carried through the hall. "Everyone should get some sleep."

Benches and stools scraped through the rushes as men rose with the same lethargy that had marked the entire meal. Englishmen shuffled forward to say their flat goodbyes to Alison and her sister. They had endured enough already, and saw too much more on the horizon, to let emotion creep into their farewells. Alison mumbled the right responses, but she, too, was numb—wishing that it were over, that it was next spring and all this a fading memory.

The young women left the hall and carried a torch across the garden to the door that led to their bedroom tower and the kitchens. Wildecent held it open, but Alison shook her head.

"I want to be alone, I think," she said. "I'm too tired to sleep. I'll just go sit someplace."

Wildecent nodded and watched as her sister headed toward the stream. She felt tired enough to sleep forever. But her drowsiness vanished once the upper door was closed and the candlelight flickered over the compact bundles they had made of their belongings.

The bed was unchanged, the aroma of sweet grass and their perfumes still hung in the air, but the room was no longer theirs. Wildecent draped her riding cloak over her shoulders and closed the door. Her first thought was to join Alison. But Alison wanted to be alone, and she herself had nothing in particular to say. The dark-haired woman wandered among the byres instead.

Standing outside Lord Godfrey's quiet byre, Wildecent thought she could hear him snoring. Alison had cried when they brought a dinner tray to him. She'd gotten down on her knees and begged him to say her name—all to no avail. Wildecent had hung back then, as she did now. She remembered no father but Godfrey Hafwynder, yet she felt very little pain on leaving him.

Her memories of a life before Hafwynder Manor were dreamlike paintings without life or movement. The strangers, her true mother and father, who wandered though her past meant less to her than the heroes of the sagas they sang in the great hall. Her parents had abandoned her, anyway; she owed them nothing. Yet the knowledge that she had been cast adrift once before worked to cut her free again. She felt nothing for her lost past; she would not let herself feel anything for the present.

Wildecent was appalled by her own coldness. She summoned despair, hoping to turned the emptiness into grief. She summoned pleasant memories and ruthlessly reminded herself of what she was losing, of the unknown she faced.

You won't find any place better than this. You've had love here, and comfort. Without Lord Hafwynder, you're nothing. A bastard, an orphan; no fortune, no name. And manorfolk won't take you in. You're not one of them: your hands are clean. They'll cast you out, and you'll die along the road some-

place and go to an unhallowed grave. Wildecent's stomach finally tightened. The sadness of every bleak moment hardened into an iron knot. She'd created her own nightmare, and suddenly she no longer wanted to be alone.

Moonlight guided her to the soft banks of the stream. It ran swift with snow-melt. An unsuspecting person could be swept away; a despairing young woman could disappear forever. Alison's footprints descended to the water's edge—and then moved on. Wildecent followed the trail until it vanished in the straw-covered dirt by the animal byres. She searched each one, convinced that only by sharing her sister's grief could she bear the internal pain she had so foolishly called into being.

The weaving solar was empty, the bolt-hole just as they'd left it the night before. Nor had Alison returned to their bedroom. The great hall leaked the sounds of men sleeping or talking in low, uncatchable voices. Holding her breath until it hurt, Wildecent stole along the back wall and up the stairs into the gallery. But the storerooms were locked and silent, as they should be. She went back to Godfrey's byre and opened the door far enough to see that Alison was not there; then she went to the pens where the weakest lambs and ewes were kept.

Wildecent was on her way out of the manor, to Lady Ygurna's grave—the only remaining place she could imagine Alison visiting on her last night at Hafwynder Manor—when she saw a flash of light from the ruins of the old hall.

The old hall had burned down in Godfrey's youth—a not uncommon fate for wooden buildings that sheltered large, unvented hearths. Most everything salvageable had been removed long ago. Only the mews were there now, far from the distractions of the manor. It was just possible that Alison had gone to see her hawk.

And while Wildecent was ready to go beyond the stockade in search of her sister, she was grateful to have somewhere else to look inside the walls. She was rewarded and stunned in the same heartbeat. Alison was in the mews, but not alone and certainly not grieving.

"There is more to this world than one manor," Stephen was staying. "I want to show it to you. I want you to be with me, at my side, just the two of us, forever."

Wildecent leaned against the old, flaking timbers, unable to approach them or to leave.

"I love you." He took her hand between his own and brought it to his lips. "You're everywhere—in my dreams and memories. It's as if I've always known you—or wanted to know you."

Alison shivered, and he held her tighter. She could no more undo what she had done than return a plant to its seed. She was sure of his love, but she would never know if it had been given freely.

Stephen was hardly the man her father would have chosen for her—or one she would have accepted just a few short months before. He was aggressive; he sang love ballads that made her ears turn red, and he kept close friendship with a sorcerer. At the same time, Stephen had fire and strength. He made her feel alive and her skin tingled when he touched her. Alison did not intend to set him free. She would not risk losing him—or angering the gods she and her aunt had awakened at midwinter. But she was not ready to surrender to him, either.

"It's too soon," she hedged. "I could love you, maybe I do love you, but now everything is turned upside down. I do not want to make a promise I might regret." She was honest, at least, and keeping an unusually short rein on her need to *make* him understand.

"That will be soon enough for me." He brought her hand to his lips again, then dared to clutch her tighter. "I can wait to show you the world," he said after he'd kissed her.

"I do not want to see the world," Alison insisted. His ardor unnerved her. "I've never wanted anything more

than this manor. I . . . I'm my father's only living child.
I'm his heiress. He raised me to love this valley."

"My father's lands were in a valley, too. The hills were
golden, the flowers sweet, and the summer never ended."

Alison shook her head.. She had seen those landscapes
when she'd invaded his mind and rashly scattered her
image across his fantasies. His pulse throbbed against her
fingers; she wondered if she could ride its rhythm back
into his thoughts. She had replaced his other women, she
could replace those golden hills with England's misty
greens. It would be very easy to do.

She realized that she touched his mind in just such a
way while she dreamed. The *geas* lifted for a moment and
she saw Stephen lying in a spring green field. Dead. Then
the *geas* closed. Alison could still feel his pulse and,
though her talents ached to be set free, she pulled her
hand away.

"You can't understand, Stephen. I have obligations
you cannot begin to imagine." She shivered. *Obligations
I do not want to imagine.*

Alison thought she saw her aunt's ghost hovering in
nearby moonlight. She begged for forgiveness, strength,
and understanding, never guessing that she sent her appeal to Wildecent's shadow.

"I understand more than you imagine," Stephen protested. "I have been Ambrose's friend for many years.
I've seen the sacrifices that sorcery can demand." He felt
her shudder in his arms and, misunderstanding her reasons, pulled her tightly against his chest. "I know him
to be a good man," he reassured her, "for all that he
willingly travels a path where weaker men might be
damned. Surely you are no less than he is."

Wildecent watched her sister slowly relax in Stephen's
arms. When they kissed, the dark-haired girl felt a tear
slip down her cheek. She rejoiced that Alison had found,
by whatever means, that most precious of all things: a
man who would cherish her. At the same time the core

of despair she had brought to the ruins throbbed larger with each beat of her heart.

She knew she should turn away—each moment she remained made the agony worse—yet she could not leave. Every gesture Stephen made was burned into her memory. Only when he released Alison and they began to speak too softly for her to overhear was she able to wrench herself away. Wildecent leaned against the charred doorway, clutching her stomach, reliving what she had seen.

"Were you truly surprised?"

Wildecent jumped upright. Her hand went to her sleeve, where her knife rested in an embroidered sheath. It sounded like the sorcerer, but she could not locate him in the darkness.

"Lovebirds among the hawks; appropriate, don't you think?"

"Ambrose?" She peered into the deep shadows, cursing the darkness. "Ambrose, is that you?"

"It seems we were both wondering where our friends had gone." A hand wrapped over her arm, urging her further from the doorway. She followed her arm and marveled that he moved so quietly.

"Do you understand what your sister has done?"

Her body moved through indecision: nodding, shaking, and shrugging, all of which he felt rather than saw. "It's her life," she whispered. They had stopped. She could see his silhouette against the moonlight but no detail of his face.

"Then you don't understand. You don't know what is going to happen. Stephen is not free."

That, somehow, brought Wildecent back to one mind and one place. She snapped her arm downward; he wasn't expecting a move and she broke free. "If he's not, then she was right to interfere. Alison might act before she thinks, but she didn't act with malice."

"Well put—but not what I had in mind. Stephen isn't free to marry her; that's all. He cannot make Hafwynder Manor secure for either of you. He hasn't told you about

Eudo; he hasn't told you much about Torworden at all, has he?''

"He doesn't talk to *me,* anyway."

Ambrose overlooked the irritation in her voice. "My young friend has lost his patrimony in France. He came to his uncle with no more than the clothes on his back, his weapons, his horse, and me . . . and now I serve Jean Beauleyas and not Stephen. He needs his uncle's support if he's to try to regain his lands; in turn he must support William the Bastard's designs here, because that's one of the conditions Beauleyas put before him. The other is more subtle. Beauleyas never got children from his wives—he got a bastard, though, Eudo, and Eudo's none too pleased to have distant kin throwing a shadow over his dubious rights.

"Beauleyas's a canny old wolf. He's never made his will known. He won't split what he's got to give; he'll wait to see who survives to claim it."

"He can't mean that," Wildecent protested. The memory of the Norman's scarred grin played in her mind and she knew the old warrior could do that, and more, if it pleased him.

"Eudo thinks he does—and that's really all that matters. Whatever other little games you, your sister, and your aunt might have played, whatever you think of me—and I have never compromised Stephen as your sister has—you should know that Eudo's cunning, and I'd not wager against him. And tell your sister as well that we may yet have to run for France with our tails dragging—and no room for a woman."

Wildecent swallowed hard. The more she heard of Torworden the less she looked forward to being there. "We'd be better off here," she muttered. "You'd be better off here."

"Stephen won't hide behind a woman—and woe betide the woman if he did."

"Why are you telling me this?"

"Because you're sensible and I hope you can talk your

sister into releasing Stephen before it's too late for both of them.''

A nervous laugh made its way through Wildecent's clenched teeth. "There's much *you* don't understand. I've told you we're not sisters, and I can only convince Alison to do something she already wants to do. Besides, she couldn't release Stephen now if she wanted to."

She heard him shift his weight from one foot to the other and imagined chagrin settling on his face. Still, she expected him to say something, if only because she believed his willful sorcery to be the equal of Alison's wild magic. When the silence lengthened she grew uncomfortable.

"Is it that bad? I know Alison, and I know that it's gotten beyond her somehow. She hasn't been herself since . . . that day. I don't think she can control her magic anymore. Can't you do something? It never really was Alison's fault. She'd never put someone in danger like that."

"Especially herself, you mean? And yes, it's that bad. I'd been trying to convince him to return to France before he took that accursed message for Pevensey." The confidence had faded from Ambrose's voice, replaced by a frustration Wildecent could well understand. "We should have taken our chances in Sicily."

"Does he know you care this much for him?"

"Does he know—yes. Does it matter—no, or worse than no. He thinks he can beat Eudo in a fair fight—or an unfair one, if it comes to that—and he does not think it at all strange to find his every dream absorbed by the woman he loves. He knows how I feel, and dismisses my fears out of hand."

His last words could have been her own and so, when Wildecent answered, she spoke as much to herself as to Ambrose. "Eventually you have to decide—choose—whether you follow them wherever they go or whether you run."

The moon had risen further, casting faint light into their cul-de-sac. Wildecent watched him plunge into his own thoughts, staring and measuring. But he was no more surprised by her words than she had been.

She was like Thorkel Longsword, with no sense of place in the world, no roots. Only a sister's friendship with Alison. Would she stay beside Alison, quiet and patient, now that she was no longer needed, hoping that someday her situation might improve? Did she cut loose and look for another English noble to befriend her? Or was that impossible as well? Was it the convent or life in Alison's shadow?

"It's late. I'm going back to the tower," she said.

"Let me escort you through the dark."

It was brighter now than it had been when she'd picked her way across the manor yard to the ruins. And she had half a mind to tell him that—or just less than half a mind, for she allowed his hand to slide under her arm. In fact, everything seemed divided into equal or nearly equal parts, so that her own decisions were random and surprising, even to her.

"What will you do?" Ambrose asked midway to the tower.

The choices hovered in her mind, none better than the other. But they were all influenced by the feel of sinewy strength beneath her sleeve. "I don't know," she replied, and heard an unwelcome plaintive note in her voice.

"You could learn to take care of yourself."

Sorcery. She could take care of herself with sorcery—if she dared to ask. Wildecent clamped her mouth shut, determined to keep her turmoil strictly to herself. Ambrose sensed something, maybe the sudden tensing of the arm he supported or maybe something else, and brought them to a stop, face to face.

"I could teach you what you'd need to know."

"Why?"

"Do I need a reason?"

A thrill of danger shot down Wildecent's spine. "I will," she whispered, and ran from him across the yard to the safety of the tower.

ildecent was asleep when Alison finally returned. She closed the door quietly and envied her sister's peaceful breathing, confident that she herself would lie awake until dawn, remembering what had—and what had not—happened in the mews. But sleep came quickly to Alison as well, and she was untroubled by nightmares. They were both resting easily when Thorkel Longsword put his fist against their door.

"Be time you were awake and eating!" the Viking shouted.

Alison rubbed her eyes and gave Wildecent a poke in the ribs. The tower room was dark as night, without the least hint of dawn in the shutter cracks. She stubbed her toe getting out of the bed, then barked her shin against the clothes chest while groping for the lamp. All in all, not the best way to start off what she firmly believed would be one of the worst days of her life.

"It's not even morning yet," her sister complained, eyes watering in the dim light from the oil-lamp.

"You'll get no sympathy from me," Alison replied in a voice that invited none in return.

Wildecent rubbed her eyes and walked slowly into the garderobe. She stared at the heavy wool of her hose as if she'd never seen it before, and needed several tries to get one cloth bound smoothly against her leg. The thought of dealing with the other strip overwhelmed her, and she sat with it draped over her calf.

By then Alison was washed and nearly dressed.

"They aren't going to leave without us," the wide-awake sister snapped. "You'll just annoy them—so hurry up!"

"I'm doing the best I can."

"Will you want anything for breakfast?"

"Anything warm."

Alison was gone, and Wildecent tackled the remainder

63

of her clothes. She was still yawning when she reached the bottom of the kitchen stairs.

"She's gone to see the horses," Bethanil informed her. "There's gruel on the sideboard."

Wildecent gripped the wooden mug with both hands and took a noisy sip of the steaming liquid.

"You're welcome, my lady," Bethanil grumbled.

"I'm not awake."

"You're lucky to be going off with the Normans and not to a convent!"

Wildecent shrugged and, cup in hand, left the warm kitchen for the stables. Daylight was a pale gray band along the eastern horizon; the hens and roosters were still sleeping. The stables, however, were busy, as riding horses were saddled and pack animals loaded. She scratched the forehead of her own little brown mare and gazed into eyes nearly as befuddled as her own.

"Didn't you bring our bundles down?" Alison asked as she led her mare down the aisle.

"I don't remember you asking me to."

"I didn't think I'd have to *ask*."

Muttering to herself, Wildecent trudged back to their bedroom. She shouldered as many of the waterproof sacks as she could and went back to the stable.

Wildecent was almost alert when the traveling party gathered in the yard. Five tall Norman horses, including Sulwyn, who hadn't been ridden for months and who fought Stephen's every command, overshadowed an equal number of English ponies. Two squires, one a Norman lad, the other a towheaded English boy, would ride atop pack animals while Eodred, the hawkmaster, rode a mule and carried two hooded birds on a roost that fitted against his saddle.

Eodred's presence was a surprise to Wildecent, though remembering where Alison and Stephen had spent the evening, she guessed she knew what had happened. At least they were bringing her bird as well.

Most of the manor turned out to say good-bye, save,

of course, Lord Godfrey himself, who had not yet shrugged off his sleeping draught. The Norman party had been split apart as Stephen promised, with three men remaining behind. Those three—Alan FitzAlan, Serlo, and Gauche-Robert—embraced their departing comrades with a fervor more often found in the final hours of a hopeless siege.

Both women put on brave faces as they departed the manor—which was expected of them. The facades crumbled the moment the familiar stockade was lost to sight. To his credit, Stephen tried—without notable success—to cheer his charges. He sang verses from the sunny lands of Aquitania, but their meaning was lost to everyone but Ambrose, who seemed immune to their humor this morning. Stephen's efforts were further hampered by the need to control his froth-flecked horse.

"You should have left him behind," Ambrose shouted after he had pulled his own horse beyond the reach of the chestnut's teeth.

"He'll settle down," Stephen insisted as he shortened the reins.

Ambrose muttered something about stallions, mares, and springtime, then dropped back to leave Stephen and his fractious horse in isolation at the head of their party. Stephen considered the entire situation with a stream of curses in a half-dozen dialects. He had recovered from the arrow wound, but his shoulder ached from the task of keeping Sulwyn on the muddy track. Had it been possible he would have preferred the placid gelding he'd ridden from Torworden to the manor, but he had secured Beauleyas's permission to lead the group because of his horse, not the heiresses, and he did not dare return without them all firmly under control.

He braced the reins between his left hand and the pommel, and rubbed his sore shoulder. Sulwyn felt the change in pressure and balance. The stallion clamped down on the bit and bolted away from the track. All eyes turned toward Ambrose.

"Leave him go," the sorcerer said. "He won't go too far—I hope."

Hugh and Guy, both veterans in Beauleyas's service, were as skittish as Sulwyn when it came to taking Ambrose's orders, but in this case they stood down. The group drew closer together without Sulwyn's disrupting presence and moved more quickly to the junction of Hafwynder's track with the ancient Icknield Way.

Stephen returned after midday while they rested the horses and ate from the provisions Bethanil had prepared. His tunic was muddied from shoulder to hip, and Sulwyn's bright coat was dull with sweat, but man and beast seemed to have reached a truce. They were winded, though, and Sulwyn needed to cool down before he could eat any of the grain they carried. It was well into the afternoon before they were remounted and continued west.

Foreigners were not generally welcome in England, and the Normans were the least welcome of all. The men of Torworden lived off the land when they traveled, making camp in the abundant ruins that dotted the countryside or taking refuge with those few of their countrymen who had survived a general purging of French influence some twenty years earlier.

They could hardly expect the young women to share their primitive camps. More civilized accommodations needed to be found on this journey. Alison suggested several of their neighboring peers but the Torwordeners, to a man, rejected guesting with the native aristocracy. The choice was narrowed to those freeholdings and inns that might, for a price, provide a night's rest for strangers.

"There should be a path to a freehold not far beyond the bridge," Alison assured them as the late afternoon sun shone into their eyes. "Our lord father stayed there."

Wildecent glanced sideways at her sister. "Not when he could help it, he didn't," she hissed.

Alison shrugged, and guided her mare behind the others as they headed down the spur.

The freehold might have been a pleasant manor a long time ago. Now it was a sullen place whose pointed-timber palisade was its most noteworthy feature. The yard within was a sea of mud—complete with pig wallows—and the hall itself was dilapidated, with a dozen or more alcoves sprouting out beneath its eaves.

Except for the animals, the place seemed deserted; no one responded to a shouted summons. The two squires were dispatched to rouse the innkeeper. The boys sank into the foul-smelling muck. No one came forth to open the doors, and for a moment Wildecent thought they might be reprieved. Sleeping in her cloak could only be better than venturing inside this place.

Then the doors were pushed open and a balding, filthy villein stepped out. He gave them a looking-over and was less than enthusiastic about having Frenchmen and their women under his roof. But, he explained, it was early in the traveling season, so he reckoned they could settle in two of his alcoves.

"If you've got coin enough," he added.

"We'll give you your coin," one of the Norman men-at-arms snarled, rattling the chain fittings of his scabbard. "Right down—"

"We'll give you your coins," Stephen interrupted. Among his uncle's army orders was an admonition to keep the peace and give the natives no cause to hate the Normans more than they already did.

It was just as well Stephen had a full coin purse riding next to his thigh. The night's lodgings and food were expensive—doubly so because the owner accepted coins only and nothing in trade. Or nothing in trade from Frenchmen.

The squires were directed to the stables, a line of open stalls whose timbers had withstood at least one sizeable fire. Alison and her sister were helped from their horses and escorted into the hall. There was no threshold, so the mud continued some three paces into the dark and fetid room. Wildecent fought a surge of panic as the doors swung shut behind them.

"We'll die here," she whispered to her sister.

"Well, we won't eat anything—that's for certain."

Once he had his coins—and perhaps because he'd seen how many more there were—the villein insisted they sit at the table nearest the pit-hearth and sang the praises of his goodwife's cooking and beer. And though the English would have preferred a simple request of bread and cheese, the Normans, who were paying for the feast, called forth the best the kitchen could provide.

While Alison searched her trencher for bits of un-spoiled meat, Wildecent contented herself with chunks of bread soaked in the flat, bitter beer. Even at the end of winter the lowliest drudges and slaves ate better at Hafwynder Manor—or at least they knew what they were eating. It was this uncertainty that kept the Hafwynder folk cautious when another bowl of the greasy brown stew was placed on their table. None of them had ever eaten at a table that did not belong to Lord Godfrey or one of his peers in the shire. Not so the Normans.

"Stephen did say they wanted us to bring Bethanil," Alison mused as she and Wildecent watched him grab a gristly wad of meat from the common bowl. It was not his table manners that distressed her—they all brought their own knives to the table and got their food from the common dishes to their own trenchers as best they could—but his gusto eating a meal that turned her stomach.

"And if they don't have their own cook, perhaps they're not used to better," Wildecent added without much conviction.

Only Ambrose displayed any reluctance to take a third helping of the stew the slovenly drudge brought from the unseen kitchen. Alison was grateful when he called for cheese and received a creamy wedge that surely had been cured somewhere else.

"Here, take as much as you want," he offered when

he noticed how little they'd eaten. "I thought you said you'd traveled this way with your lord father?"

"We traveled from one manor to the next, never on the tracks and never staying in freeholds," Alison admitted.

He pushed the rest of the cheese between them. "Eat it all. It's apt to get worse before it gets better."

Which it did, and sooner rather than later. Once the meal was over they were shown to the alcoves where they were expected to sleep. The mud shifted beneath the rush-covered planks when they entered the cramped chamber. Alison's hair brushed against the steep roof, and the beds were little more than straw heaped in a corner. The doors had no locks and there were, of course, no windows. The men generously agreed that the sisters would have one alcove to themselves and that two of them would sleep on stools propped against the closed door. They seemed quite satisfied by the arrangement, which kept two of them away from the filthy straw. Neither Alison nor Wildecent could say the same.

"I can see it moving," Wildecent murmured after the door was shut.

Alison took the tallow-lamp from her sister's trembling hand and held it closer to the straw. "Not quite."

"I can't sleep there. Oh, Lord God Almighty, the angels and the saints—why is this happening to us?"

"Lady Ygurna would know what to do."

"Our lady aunt would never *be* in this position, Alison. No one would have dared to move her off the manor."

"That's not what I meant. She'd know what to do about the fleas and whatever else is in that straw."

"She'd burn it—and this whole place around it," Wildecent said with a faint, bitter laugh.

Alison paused and chuckled herself. "She might," she agreed. "She'd get that kitchen into shape, she or Bethanil herself. But what I was thinking of is—"

"Left behind at Hafwynder Manor waiting for the ox-carts, Alison. There's nothing we can do."

"I could try, Wili."

"The last time you *tried* something, as I recall, we found ourselves in a worse way than we'd been before."

Alison made a grim face and set the sputtering lamp on a crude shelf. "I don't deny it, but I've been feeling, well, different—better—since we left the valley." She held up a hand to cut off Wildecent's rejoinder. "No, even you know what it's been like—as if there were something in the air, something more than our lady aunt's death or our lord father. I've seen it in your face."

Grudgingly, Wildecent agreed that leaving Hafwynder Manor had not been as hard as she'd expected it would be. She was homesick and heartsick, but those emotions were directed toward a home that had ceased to exist after Christmastide. The gray depression of the last three months was already fading.

"I don't feel a heaviness inside me anymore," Alison continued. "It's as if—well, you wouldn't understand, but I think I could make those bugs *want* to go someplace else."

But Wildecent did understand, though she was not reassured. "I'd still rather you didn't try," she said after a long sigh. "Not with everything packed away. I don't want to think of what would happen if something went wrong . . ."

"No, Wili, it'd be just like leaning on anyone else, just a little push. There's no danger," Alison replied in her firmest voice, though she was well aware that what she had in mind was like nothing she'd ever tried before. There was no sense of mind, or even identity—as there would be in a horse, cat, or cow—swarming through the straw. Instead the bed radiated a more primitive sense of life. Alison imagined a wall the vermin would not care to breach and was eager to create it.

Lady Ygurna would have done it differently: through pungent herbs and incense. She and Wildecent would have been as irritated by the aroma as the fleas and lice. This would be so much more effective, easier, and quicker. She rubbed her hands together then extended them, palms downward, over the straw. She closed her eyes and erected the first course of her wall.

Her flesh began to tingle as the mental energies were channeled out of her body. There was warmth at her fingertips, then nothing, as her wrists were forced apart and down to her sides. Alison opened her eyes and glared at her sister.

"No," Wildecent commanded. "It's not right for you, Alison. It's not *natural.*"

Alison's indignation emerged slowly from her magic-tinged relaxation. "What do you mean: not natural? Everything I do is *natural.*" She saw the questions in her sister's troubled eyes. "Just because our lady aunt couldn't do something doesn't mean that it's sorcery, Wili. I can do things she couldn't do, but it's just what's inside me—nothing more or less."

Wildecent felt her sister pushing at her mind, emphasizing with her very unnatural abilities just how natural and ordinary she truly was—and, especially, how her power was untainted by sorcery. For a moment Wildecent grasped the opposite—the naturalness of sorcery shone against the wildness of Alison's emotional power. Then that notion became absurd; the insight vanished.

Her sister was innocent—a unicorn who savored peace, harmony, and purity for all that it was also the invincible champion of the forest.

"I only thought . . ." Wildecent mumbled, releasing her sister's wrists and shaking her head in an effort to remember just what she had been thinking.

"You meant well," Alison assured her. "From the outside it's easy to get confused. Trust me."

While Wildecent held the lamp and silently watched, Alison held her hands over the straw again. Nothing changed. There was no aura of light or rustling as the bugs abandoned the straw, only Alison's soft assurances that all had gone well.

And it had. Alison was satisfied that her magic was once again under her control. Wildecent had forgotten, for the moment, that there was any reason to suspect her sister's powers. They slept peacefully, spine against spine.

he sisters were more refreshed than their companions, none of whom had slept well. Each man, including Ambrose, displayed welts where he'd entertained the freehold wildlife. They slapped and complained their way through a cold breakfast. The young women began to hope that the living conditions at Torworden might be better than the food.

After breakfast they bought a wedge of cheese and some sausage that, like the cheese, had not been made at the freehold. Their horses were waiting in the yard, as eager to be gone from the place as their riders.

"We've enough food to ride straight north from here," Stephen said as he mounted and led the way through the gate. "Unless someone wants to try another inn?"

"Be needing to soak my head after this one," Hugh de Lessay said, agreeing with him.

"Your inns are better in France?" Alison asked.

"Better in Normandy."

Alison was disinclined to believe him, but not at all sorry they would be traveling cross-country. Compelling the vermin had given her new insight into the workings of her own talent. Among the English she understood the unspoken words connecting one thought image to the next. Most often she worked her private magic through subtle rearrangement of those silent words. She understood only a few words of French and was unable to manipulate the foreigner's thoughts unless, as she had done with Stephen, she actually descended within their memories. With the vermin, however, she'd simply forced her desires upon the outer world. She believed she could push Ambrose and Stephen apart in a similar way—but to do so she wanted the informality of an open-air camp. She looked back over her shoulder, smiling as she appraised Ambrose, and he, not knowing the source of her satisfaction, smiled back.

They continued along the Icknield Way. The track followed a natural ridge across the landscape and provided an easier course than any other they'd find until they cleared the Uffington Down. Men had been walking or riding along it since there had been men in England. Centuries of use, rather than Roman engineering, had determined its course through the forest.

Stephen had good cause to remember this portion of the Icknield. In December, wolves had attacked him not far from here, drawn by the blood frozen to his shoulder. It crossed his mind that it was too far between the Uffington chalk carving and Hafwynder Manor for an injured man to have traveled on a bitterly cold night; that he and Sulwyn should be nothing more than a jumble of mouldering bones. He remembered praying that night for sanctuary. He'd reached a sanctuary—and not the infested barn where he'd just passed an uncomfortable night—but he couldn't convince himself that God had heard his prayers. Ambrose and now Alison insisted they watched over and protected him. Stephen had always dismissed such words as utter nonsense; now he was less certain.

Anything arcane, even magic that might have saved his life, made Stephen uncomfortable. He forced himself to concentrate on the track instead. Trees grew thick beside the path; the upland downs, when he saw them, were still a wilted brown. Caught from the corner of his eyes, however, a green aura hovered above the grass, and the nearby trees shimmered red with swelling leafbuds. The promise of spring was a force that could be tasted and smelled.

It was a bit early for the itinerant tradesmen, pilgrims, and crafters to begin their seasonal journeys, yet they were not alone on the Icknield. Twice during the long morning they exchanged greetings with other travelers.

"Where'd they be going?" Guy asked after a man leading a string of heavily laden donkeys disappeared behind them.

"To London," Alison replied, "and beyond to where King Harold's called out the *fyrd* to defend the land."

The Normans grunted and spoke quickly among themselves, reminding their English companions that William the Bastard, their liege-lord, considered himself the rightful king here. A collective chill fell over the party. Harold Godwinson was a popular man in these parts and had done the king's work after Edward had retreated into an admirable but impractical asceticism. Harold was the only Englishman with the strength to rule. The commonfolk and the nobility alike trusted him; they certainly perferred him to any foreigner.

Springtime's gentle beauty was deceptive. By the time the hillsides were green and dotted by sheep, the campaigning season would be upon them. The Normans, who had the most to gain, radiated satisfaction; the English were silent.

The track curved southward and the forest thinned. Finally it descended from the ridge crest and brought them out of the forest for their first view of the great white chalk carving above the village of Uffington.

"Know you who set it there?" the Norman squire asked his English companions.

"It's always been there," Alison replied.

"The old gods left it," Wildecent corrected, "like they left so many other things."

The foreigners mumbled among themselves. Normandy, like England, was cluttered with mysterious derelicts from another time, but ancient monuments seemed more plentiful here, and more powerful as well, as if whatever had erected them still claimed the land. Ambrose made a thoughtful study of the enigmatic figure as they left the track and set out across the downs.

On a clear day the graceful abstract carving could be seen at the far end of the downs, almost a day's journey away. Close by, it dominated the landscape, a presence that was felt even when it was deliberately, carefully, not observed.

"What's it supposed to be?" the Norman squire asked.

"A warning."

"The bones of one of them old gods."

"A sign to the gods and all else that this land *belonged* to those who sacrificed for it," Alison explained.

There were no end of notions among the party, English and Norman alike, but Eodred got their attention when he made his charges bate and rattle their bell-crusted jesses.

" 'Tis where Saint George fought the dragon," the hawkmaster claimed. "He rode his horse into the sky and struck his spear in the devil's one vulnerable place. 'Twas a mortal wound and brought them all to the ground, with only the saint said to survive. 'Tis clear for all to see. Yonder's the mount where the dragon's blood first fell." He pointed to the bald crest of a nearby drumlin. "There'll be nothing growing there 'til Doomsday."

He said he'd grown up in sight of the carving and that he'd learned the truth from the parish priest, who'd read it from a book. Everyone knew that truth resided in the chained books of church and monastery libraries, but the carving did not seem to mark a saint's victory over evil. No one disputed Eodred, and no one believed him, either.

Ambrose guided his horse between the sisters' ponies. "So do you think we see the bones of a dragon or a horse?" he asked lightheartedly, though neither woman was deceived by his tone.

"The dragon," said Wildecent.

"No, his horse, a unicorn horse," Alison averred. "It protects this place, even in death."

Ambrose made a show of studying the creature. It might easily be a dragon, since no one alive had ever seen a dragon and it did not at all resemble a horse. Yet if it were a diabolic dragon, then men should be wary, for there was beauty, grace, and power in it.

"Perhaps a bit of each—if they died together," he suggested.

Both young women gave him a sidelong glance.

"You'd like that," Alison accused after a moment's consideration. "Everything all jumbled together so you couldn't tell one part from the other. Good from evil or right from wrong. That would suit you, wouldn't it?"

Ambrose replied with a smile that was no less enigmatic than the carving. "I shouldn't think I desire anything that you would not yourself desire."

Alison was spared from responding when Stephen shouted and slapped his heels against Sulwyn's flanks. "Let's see it up close," he called over his shoulder as the chestnut thundered toward the lower slopes of the down. Alison turned away from the sorcerer and followed Stephen, leaving Wildecent alone beside him.

All attention focused on her, as if she could do something about the pair's impulsiveness. Wildecent glanced around, and found herself looking into Ambrose's black eyes. He was smiling as if to ask, *Well, young lady, will you follow the lovebirds or remain here with me?*

Wildecent concentrated on the meandering of the reins through her fingers, and felt her stomach contract. Alison and Stephen didn't need her—wouldn't want her now that Stephen had reined Sulwyn to a walk beside Alison's nut brown pony. They wouldn't likely send her away, but she'd be intruding, and red embarrassment spread from her back up her neck. The question became, was it worse to be the third in a pair or to bask in the discomfort of Ambrose's smile? If Ambrose were simply a sorcerer the decision would have been easier to make or justify. But there was more than sorcery in his smile.

"Join your friends, if you wish," he said as she made up her mind to do just that. He kept his mount at a steady pace a half stride in front of hers.

"I shall," she replied, looking once again at her hands.

Godfrey Hafwynder had loved his pleasure. He loved to hunt and had never let his lack of sons deprive him of companionship when he did. His girls were accomplished riders, and though their mounts were small by continental standards they were as good as Wessex grass had ever produced. Wildecent took the reins in both hands, urged the pony into a pivoting rear, and escaped behind Ambrose's larger horse before anyone saw the scarlet blush on her cheeks.

The smile faded from Ambrose's face as she set out after the others. Her sable plaits flew free of her cloak, and her skirts blew back to reveal more of her legs than a man was accustomed to seeing by daylight.

"I expect we'll be going no farther today," he told the rest of them, annoyed by the tightness in his throat. "We'll set our line over there, in the lee of the dragon's blood, where that finger of trees comes down from the forest."

"Rather be well out of sight of that thing," Hugh muttered.

Ambrose turned around in his saddle. "A God-fearing man like you, Hugh, afraid of a relic of Saint George?" he asked drily, and all objections ceased.

Magic of considerable power lingered in the area, and Ambrose was of a mind to explore it. He left them to set the camp as they wished—and to mutter what they wished—while he set off up the bald knob where the dragon's blood had fallen. Yet the bare patch of ground, once he reached it, held no fascination. Instead he stared at Stephen and the women playing a game of blind-man's bluff around the white beast's head.

Ambrose had never truly belonged anywhere or to anyone—not to the magi who had rescued him in Byzantium, nor to Stephen, nor certainly to Stephen's ruthless and uncouth uncle, Jean Beauleyas. He was nearly Guy's age but he looked younger. His education had been of the mind; he'd never developed the deep chest and broad shoulders of a warrior. And he'd never spent a season or six campaigning, gathering the scars and fractures that made a warrior old before his time. He was seven years older than Stephen, and those years had given him an armor of cynicism that, along with his sorcery, served him well enough against a world that found endless reasons to distrust him.

If there was a place for Ambrose, it was within the Church. Saint George was a magus and warrior before he'd become a saint. A churchman's career didn't begin until he was thirty—when a militant nobleman was beginning to think of passing the burden along to his sons, if he had them. Some of the magi in Byzantium had been European churchmen making their way eastward in search of a more perfect wisdom than could be found in the remains of the Western Empire. On their advice Ambrose had taken a deacon's vows before entering France—he had credentials as a scribe or tutor, but no binding commitment to the Church.

He had ambition, and pursued it carefully throughout Stephen's adolescence. The south of France, the ancient province of Aquitania, was rich enough to spark many men's ambition. Too many men. It languished in anarchy while upstart northerners, calling themselves kings of France and dukes of Normandy, stumbled into undeserved ascendance.

"We belong in Poitou," Ambrose whispered to the unheeding figures in the distance. "In Anjou, Cahors—anywhere but here."

This last year, since they'd taken service with Stephen's uncle, had been a disaster for the sorcerer. Beauleyas had no lands of his own in the south. He had been eager to lend his late sister's offspring a hand—but once he'd gotten Stephen in his grip he was loath to release him. And Ambrose found his own ambitions were nebulous beside the endemic Norman lust for land, wealth, and prestige.

But worst of all was England itself. Someday Ambrose would return to Byzantium, he promised himself. He'd alert the magi to the uncharted power and mystery of this island. The first thing he'd say would be *Beware the women*. The men here were like men everywhere, but the women who held the island's magic used it in a way a man could neither understand nor defend against.

He wanted to get Stephen back to France, back to the time when their goals had been the same: the recovery of Stephen's patrimony and the judicious expansion of it.

But mostly I want to get myself away from here before it's too late.

And he was not watching Alison or Stephen as the prayerful thought rolled through his mind.

The sun still stood some distance above the downs when everyone returned to the camp. A fire had been started, a lean-to erected for the sisters, the horses hobbled and set to grazing on the brown grass. Everything seemed settled until one of the hawks bated and screamed on her perch, drawing everyone's attention.

Alison had pulled on a heavy leather gauntlet and coaxed the hooded bird onto her wrist. She carefully stroked its breast with her free hand. "Hooded all day with the fresh air in your nostrils," she murmured, and it calmed. She carried it back to the campfire. "Can we fly them before dark?" she asked Eodred.

The old Saxon shook his head, a bit dismayed that she would even ask to release the valuable bird in a strange place without fresh bloody meat to lure it back.

Stephen saw the old man's disappointment. "Well, we can at least scare up some game. We'll fly them in the morning."

He took a bow down from the crook of one of the trees and headed into the low brush. Though the bow was a secondary weapon for a nobleman, who expected to confront his enemies face to face, it was not one which he ignored. When he wasn't fighting or training to fight, a wellborn man hunted for food and pleasure. The grimaces spreading from man to man around the fire had nothing to do with the young man's ability, but reflected that this was the second time in a single day he'd gone off on his own.

"Like as not there's nothing in range," Ambrose called without effect to his friend's back.

CONQUEST

No one was surprised when Alison took her hawk back to its perch, then scampered after Stephen.

"That one'll be the doom of us," Hugh protested, and for once Ambrose was in complete agreement with him.

he travelers gathered around the fire were quiet and minus two of their party. Stephen hadn't returned; neither had Alison. The men, who had settled on rocks, saddles, and fallen logs, watching the stewpot as the sun set, doubted they were lost. Stephen hadn't been blind to the beautiful heiress pursuing him.

"It be the best way," Hugh affirmed to no one in particular. " 'Specially when they're willing."

"An' when they're not, as well," the Gascon replied with a sly laugh.

Wildecent shrank under the lean-to. The afternoon's blue skies were gone, replaced by low, menacing storm clouds. She wanted to insist that the men go out to search for her sister, but they would only laugh lewdly if she did, and she couldn't face that. Not when they had the truth of the situation.

Courtship, here and everywhere, was chiefly concerned with land or dynasty rather than any notion of affection. It was conducted, especially among the wellborn, by the eldest and most powerful men of the family; the least of those consulted was the intended bride.

In better times Alison might have looked forward to all the proper rituals and a goodly measure of influence over Lord Godfrey's final choice. Now, with her father incapacitated, no brothers to stand for her rights, and a king whose reign was apt to plummet into war, she faced a future with no confidence that her wishes would count for anything at all.

Yet in all this bargaining for power and status there was one simple escape. The Holy Roman Church, always eager to extend its influence, held that marriage was a sacrament not lightly set aside—binding in this life and the next. As a sacrament it was subject to God's law, not the petty rules of men. The Church was pragmatic about this; there were enough uncertainties about God's law to keep

Rome's canon lawyers busy and rich. But the sum of the matter was that a promise of marriage, even in the absence of mortal witnesses, was a sufficient demonstration of the sacrament for an almighty, omnipresent God.

It was undoubtedly true that making off with the woman, willing or not, and keeping her in a place of some seclusion until an heir arrived was the clearest way for a pair to declare its marital intentions. But a promise in a woody grove as a chill rain began to fall was equally valid, albeit somewhat more difficult to prove.

Plight-troth, the Church called it, and it filled many a calculating dynast's heart with ice-cold dread. It could emerge from a man's youthful past: a moment's folly casting a pall of illegitimacy over an innocent generation. Invoked by rebellious sons or daughters, it could wreak havoc with a family's carefully nurtured alliances. Falsely sworn by a hot-blooded young knight, it was many a maiden's undoing. And yet, for all its weaknesses, it offered Stephen and Alison a slim chance to command their own destinies.

The men who pulled their cloaks around their faces to keep out the fine rain, and hunkered silently by the sputtering fire, saw an heiress such as Alison as the embodiment of land and legitimate children. They had little doubt that Stephen was bright enough to discern his best interests in the situation; it was a measure of their respect for his future power that they did not challenge his claim to her. Wildecent felt differently, of course, but of all those huddled in their cloaks, she was the most confident that the pair had shared just such a promise.

It was well past nightfall when the rain stopped. The camp was redolent with the smells of moisture on fresh, fertile earth. The horses whuffled as they dreamed of sweet grass; the men simply snored, and Wildecent rolled herself tighter in her cloak, ignoring the steady drips that fell from the crude roof of the lean-to.

Across the camp, hidden in the absence of firelight, Ambrose heard her turn away. He waited a while longer.

When she had remained silent for several moments he stretched himself upright. The clouds had thinned a bit, not to full moonlight but enough that a man might see his hand before his face or a tree in his path. Enough that a sorcerer might draw upon the power residing in his talisman and seek after his friend.

Stephen was with Alison, of course, and for that reason Ambrose was not unduly disturbed by the difficulty he had locating their path. Little as he liked the notion, he knew Alison had won. His hope now was to persuade them both to leave England quickly for the continent. Jean Beauleyas would not approve of their arrangement.

There was a special urgency to Ambrose's search. Lovers were notoriously unobservant, and there was something brewing in the dripping forest. He'd felt it rise as the rain ended. It was part of this magic-ridden land and none of Alison's making. He had studied it from the camp, but his careful, logical training could not penetrate its mysteries. It reminded him of the wind that blew around Ygurna's ghost and left him with a feeling that insects were marching relentlessly along his spine.

His cloak caught on unseen twigs; his passage was neither silent nor peaceful, but he had their trail now. The mark he'd placed on Stephen's thoughts so many years before clung to the bushes the younger man had pushed aside. Ambrose traced his friend no differently than a dog trailed its quarry, though the sorcerer followed a scent that was perceptible only in his arcanely trained mind.

Twice he found places where they'd sought shelter from the rain. The forest, though, was leafless, and the protection of its bare web of branches was not enough to satisfy the pair. They'd kept moving.

At least they moved away from the nexus. He wondered if Alison felt the power rising from the moist ground and had the sense to leave it alone.

She must, he thought, wiping the moisture from his face and pulling his cloak from the clutches of the nearby shrubs. *Surely she knows she's won now; she wouldn't risk what she's gained. She may even suspect it's my doing. As if I could. The magus who controlled this forest could control the world, and the gods as well.*

A humorless grin tightened Ambrose's face. His Byzantine mentors had enough trouble transmuting base metal into gold; they rarely attempted actual creation, and he was many years short of their skill.

The sky revealed the waning crescent moon and the brightest of the stars. There was more light, but it did him no good. The forest trapped the rain-mist beneath its branches. The air became translucent, and Ambrose was forced to move more cautiously.

It was only mist, he reminded himself. There were mists everywhere. Fogs rolled in off Byzantium's harbor, across the peninsulas of Normandy, and even in the pleasant lands of Aquitania. Mists of this English island should be no different from mists anywhere else, but they were, and the prickling irritation along Ambrose's spine became a subtle agony.

Because he was determined to avoid the branches around him, they became more numerous and tenacious. A cold, black twig lashed out of nowhere, striking him across the eyes. For a moment he was blind. He put his hand to his face, convinced that the moisture he felt was not rainwater but blood.

Let her *protect Stephen,* he swore, wiping his hand uselessly on his damp cloak. He could see, but his resolve had been shattered. *It's* her *damned forest.*

Ambrose thought again of the power manifest in these trees. There had always been rumors of barbaric fringelands where gods still moved among their worshippers and the arcane obeyed no laws, only a shaman's whim; but none of the Zoroastrians he'd known gave credence to them. The magi, his mentors, would want to know about this place. Ambrose could almost hear them counseling him to abandon Stephen and seek the source of the forest's power.

Friends can be found anywhere. The face of Masianos, first of the magi, swam before his mind's eye. *But true power's source is a rare thing.*

So they followed him, then—well, he'd always suspected they did. Why take an orphan from the gutters, educate him, mold him, provide him with life's advantages, if you didn't plan to collect the debt somewhere down the road? But they didn't compel him—not unless they already controlled the power of this forest. Ambrose did not choose to turn away from Stephen's trail until he felt the power tremble and begin to flow toward the center of the woods.

He moved toward the nexus, flowing with its summoned power and no longer plagued by brambles. He moved faster now, in rhythm with the pounding pulse of magic. The mist compacted, like wisps of carded fleece; it gave way as he pushed deeper, and upward to the crest of a drumlin invisible from the edge of the wood where they'd made camp.

Caught in the magical stream, buoyed by its energy and excitement, Ambrose shed his fears and cautions. He saw the luminescence hovering over the knob and hurried toward it. He inhaled deeply and felt its raw vitality sting through his lungs, then, as the mists parted for the final time, he collapsed to his knees.

There was an oak here at the top of the drumlin. A gnarled tree as old as the earth itself, shrouded with luminous mist. But it wasn't the oak that held the Byzantine sorcerer transfixed—or not only the oak. The mist had form—if one dared look into it. A face as big as the tree itself, fierce-eyed, grimacing, and with endless green-growing vines streaming from the corners of its mouth. It made no sound when it heard Ambrose's stifled scream, nor gave any indication it noticed him at all.

Ambrose clutched last year's grass and braced himself against the magic stream that flowed over him toward the leering giant. He closed his eyes and sought peace within himself and his crystal talisman, but the lifemaker was stronger. He was driven to open his eyes and glance again at its awesomeness.

The clearing was not silent. The oak groaned as the vines whirled through its branches and spread back into the mist. Everything the vines touched sighed and heaved as life was restored to it. Even the grass in Ambrose's hands quivered. He released it, but not before he felt it grow supple and green against his palms.

There was no mastering this power, no sequence of geometry or mnemonic that could circumscribe it. Not since his childhood in the gutters of the Imperial City had Ambrose known such abject helplessness and terror. He would have fled, if his body were not transfixed and beyond his mind's command.

So he stared and knew, in time, that he was not alone in the mist.

It was difficult to break the spell and look from the vine-spewing face to another part of the misty ring where a dark-cloaked figure stood. *Stood,* while he groveled like a whipped dog. Ambrose acknowledged only the barest abstraction of god, yet he offered up an impassioned prayer that his shame remain invisible when silver blond Alison came before the oak.

Alison had recognized the power throbbing atop the drumlin without knowing its name. She had not come to it until Stephen was asleep. Nothing in the rituals Lady Ygurna had taught her dealt explicitly with the green giant who breathed life and springtime back into the land, yet old knowledge rose within her and she approached him without fear.

He was the fourth king, of course: the nameless one, the most powerful one, the one who claimed the head of the strongest hero of the land. She'd seen the tree-high face much as Ambrose saw it while she stood in the mist, but within the clearing, she saw the king himself, the green man-shape of him, amid his court. She recognized the goddesses she'd met at Yuletide and made obeisance to them.

They gave her fairy-gentle smiles and welcomed her.

"We must dance," they said in one rich voice.

Leafy garlands materialized and twined through their arms, gathering Alison into their circle. She knew there had to be some risk in cavorting with immortals, but the growth pulse pushed fear from her, and she lifted her feet freely to its rhythm.

They sang, and she added her voice to theirs. They spun at a dizzying speed until the clearing, the mists, and the tree kings blurred together. Alison was aware of the untamed energy of springtime, and then, before she had an instant to become fearful, the earth opened and the dancers sank into a hollow hill.

Panicked, Alison released her hold on the garland—and felt the raw, moist earth surrounding her. She tried to breathe and found her nostrils filled with dirt; she tried to scream and found her jaw constricted by the real substance of the hill. Black terror engulfed her until the goddesses grasped her arms.

"Do not break the chain," they commanded, laying the garland again in her hands. "Only through its abundance of life are you here safely."

Alison gave a jerky nod, as if she still doubted her freedom to move. "Where am I?" she asked.

The goddesses laughed and the laughter changed them, allowing Alison to see them as individuals. One resembled her aunt, Ygurna; a second seemed to be a reflection of herself; the third was familiar in an aching way and might have been her mother. Three aspects: crone, maiden, and mother; then they stopped laughing and the individuality vanished.

"You were named to serve us, and your service has been chosen," they said sternly, drawing the garland tight and pulling her into their midst.

"I . . . I know that," Alison stammered, not quite frightened but suddenly cautious.

"You will choose the hero."

Alison nodded. This was the promise hidden in the *geas;* the task that was inescapable. "I will do what must be done."

They were harsh for a moment. Alison swallowed hard. She had indeed made a promise to these powers, and whatever tragedies she could imagine, she knew they could conjure circumstances far worse if she challenged them. They studied her and she wondered if they knew how reluctant her obedience might be. Then their features softened and the wild pulse of life penetrated the mystic hollow once more.

"Dance, little sister," they sang, relaxing their hold on the garland so they might all move more freely.

She danced with them, swirling and singing while the hollow shrank. They danced to the surface of the world and along the great green tracks through the trees and meadows in promise of what summer would be. She danced far longer than she'd thought possible, and clenched the garland in crabbed fingers, knowing that her body was still flesh, and exhausted.

As time wore on she wondered if she had already chosen and sacrificed. Perhaps this endless spiraling and chanting was her eternal doom for sins she had not known she had committed. Perhaps time itself was a circle and this was torment for sins she had not yet committed. Alison cried for help or pity, but her voice was caught in the song and her words blended seamlessly with those of the goddesses. She thought there could be nothing worse, and tried to pry her fingers free of the garland.

Only a faint glow along the horizon, which she took for dawn, dissuaded her. She held on and sang, though tears were flowing down her cheeks, but she did not pray. She was already with those who might have listened.

The mists lost their power as dawnlight touched them. Alison scarcely remembered sinking into the dewy grass, nor the last echoes of the spring-making song as it vanished for another year. She was dazed, drunk with exhaustion, as she heaved upright and stared without comprehension at ragged vines cluttered in her bloodless hands.

Alison willed her fists to open. The garland fell free, or vanished, she couldn't tell which. And she no longer cared. She took an unsteady step toward the scrub at the edge of the clearing made by the ancient oak's shade. There was something in the high grass . . . not a rock or a log . . . a cloak . . . a man . . . a creature of flesh and blood like herself.

She took another step, but the third was beyond her strength. She fell gently onto her side, arms outstretched, her fingers barely touching the thick, ordinary wool. Then she fell asleep.

They were still like that—Ambrose curled beneath his cloak and Alison reaching out to touch him—when, as the sun crested, Stephen pushed through the underbrush and found them.

tephen stopped outside the clearing. He recognized Ambrose's black cloak and Alison's deep green one. For a moment he thought they been set upon and slain, but he dismissed that thought quickly; no brigand would leave those heavy, valuable cloaks on a corpse. Yet it might have been easier if they had been killed. Then he could let his imagination concoct a benign explanation. As it was, he'd have to discover what had led Ambrose into the forest and taken Alison from his side. He'd learn what had brought them together under this huge and forbidding tree.

He did not want to know why Alison, to whom he'd promised his eternal life, was reaching out for his best and only friend as if her soul had depended upon it.

His palm wiped over the wrapped-leather pommel of his sword, an unconscious gesture that said much about his state of mind as he stepped out of the high grass. He knelt beside Alison, almost touching her shoulder, then reconsidered and went to lean against the tree.

Ambrose and his lady had made no secret of their dislike for each other; Alison hadn't, at any rate. They stood on opposite sides of everything, especially their precious notions of magic and sorcery. He was the only thing that held them together, and he felt them fighting over him like hounds over a bone.

Stephen caught himself rubbing the sword pommel again. Alison hadn't wanted to pledge her love. He'd had to plead and finally threaten before she consented— and even then she refused to consummate their love. She was quick enough to say she needed him, but Stephen was sadly certain her mind was not clouded with his image as his was with hers. All Alison's fire showed in her dislike—no, her hatred—for Ambrose. What was lacking in her declarations of love was altogether present when she denounced his friend.

He stared at them, convincing himself that only the arcane—not their professed affection for him or their often-voiced dislike for each other—could have brought them together like this. Common sense, if not concern for his immortal soul, advised Stephen to leave them to their just fate—but he was of an age where neither of those wise forces could sway him. He continued staring and was unsurprised when Alison rolled over and looked at him. He was not, however, prepared for the look of terror that passed over her face before she composed herself and greeted him with a shy smile.

"What a relief to see you standing there . . ."

Stephen let that lie pass, as Ambrose was stirring now and he was coolly eager to observe what passed between them. But Ambrose, paler than usual and shaking like he'd drunk the island dry, gave nothing away as he raked his fingers through his disheveled hair.

"Perhaps I shouldn't ask—" Stephen began.

"You shouldn't," Ambrose replied evenly as Alison muttered a heartfelt "Please, don't."

Stephen pounded his fist against the oak and let the effort push him upright. "Then let me guess. You heard some ancient music playing. You heard fairies dancing. You saw angels and a golden ladder to Heaven itself!" He'd spat out his hurt and his anger. His palm brushed the sword pommel again. He pulled his hand away from the weapon, but the agony remained. From early childhood he had been taught to be a knight, a noble man whose every emotion—every pain or twinge of anger—was channeled into his sword arm. He needed something in his hands: something to swing, something to break. He tore a low-hanging branch from the oak.

"Stephen," Ambrose said in a deliberately calm voice. He'd seen the cold rages that made these knights the most efficient warriors the world had seen in a thousand years—and made them damnably unpredictable friends as well. "Stephen," he repeated as the younger man swung the branch.

Alison took a tentative step forward and opened her mouth; Ambrose shot her a harsh, silencing glance, and for once she obeyed.

"Enough, Stephen!" He caught the branch when it next swung by and braced himself against his friend's greater strength. The wood bowed as Stephen trembled with uncontrolled emotion. Then, as suddenly as it had begun, the rage vanished. Stephen threw the branch down as if it, and not he, had been the cause of the outburst.

"You take too many risks," Stephen said to both of them, his voice still ragged.

The young knight watched as Alison glanced warily in Ambrose's direction. He'd frightened her—and the shame of that, the confusion and the pain, cut deeper than his anger. He lashed out, kicking the branch into the high grass, completely heedless that he'd done nothing to reassure her.

"Shouldn't we be joining the others?" Alison finally asked.

"Assuredly—once we figure out exactly where we might be." The words were out of his mouth before he'd considered their tone or impact. Even Ambrose seemed uneasy, and Ambrose was usually unperturbed by his moods. "No matter," Stephen said into their silence. "They can't be far, and that damned white beast won't be hard to find."

He sprang upward. His arms caught around a sturdy branch, and he wrestled himself higher until he could see over the tops of the nearby trees. The chalk carving dominated the horizon and a bit to its right was a thin plume of smoke that might well be his own men getting their breakfast. He was about to leap back to the ground when he caught Alison's voice and paused to listen.

"It's all your fault," she accused.

"*My* fault. However could it be my fault? They were *your* gods, *your* rituals; I assure you I had no power—"

"If you hadn't been here he wouldn't have gotten angry like that."

There was a pause; Stephen forced his fists to relax lest he break something before Ambrose had a chance to speak.

"Then you don't know his kind very well, do you? Or do you think you can train him to eat from your hand as you trained his horse?"

Stephen slumped back against the bole. He revolted against complexity; a warrior's life demanded a simple world—clear cases of right and wrong where battles were fought and the noblest knight emerged victorious. He loved Alison, that was simple enough, and in a different way he loved Ambrose as well, but they confounded everything. They compelled him to understand their arcane world, even if he would not embrace it, and they reduced the code of chivalry to swirling, angry confusion.

He let go of the branches and dropped free, savoring the shock as his feet slammed into the ground. Pain—real pain, the pain of muscles and bones—was something he could understand. Alison was at his side before he got to his feet.

"You fell! Are you hurt? Here, let me help you up."

Misunderstood again, Stephen got up without her help. He started to explain how he felt, but stopped when he saw the wounded, frightened look in her eyes. So he put his arms around her, feeling how much smaller she was, and weaker, and in need of his strength, not his anger. He found the taut muscles at the back of her neck and massaged them until they began to relax.

He thought she might be crying and held her closer against his tunic so he would not have to know for sure. There was a strange expression on Ambrose's face when their eyes met—not quite defiance, but a wariness. Perhaps it wasn't so complicated, perhaps it had nothing to do with the arcane, perhaps—despite his protestations—Ambrose had a simple hunger for Alison after all.

Stephen tensed. It would be a foolish friend who attempted to step between him and his chosen lady. It would be a man who was no longer his friend . . . Then the tension vanished, pushed aside by Alison's smiling image in his mind. He was reminded that she'd already pledged her love and her loyalty. There was no need to doubt her. Whatever was wrong was undoubtedly, and purely, the sorcerer's fault.

At the back of his mind Stephen recalled that he seldom thought of Ambrose as "the sorcerer." And although they'd argued over many things, they'd never once been attracted to the same woman. He could settle it with a few simple questions, but the urge passed and he buried his face in Alison's sun-touched hair.

He lost himself in her scent and presence, savoring the image of her running through a flower-strewn meadow. There was a pressure to remain in the reverie, but no amount of loveliness could completely seduce Stephen, or erase his uncle's stern visage from other portions of his mind.

"We'd best be going," he conceded, pushing her away.

Collecting his bow and quiver from the high grass, Stephen struck off in the general direction of the smoke plume he'd spotted from the oak's branches. He thrashed swiftly through the damp tangle, satisfied that his companions were pressed too hard for idle conversation.

Stephen's trailbreaking cut across a deer track, and he could no longer justify crashing violently through the brush, even though the track afforded everyone a chance to catch his breath. By then the tense silence was too well established for either Alison or Ambrose to consider breaking it until Stephen did himself.

He was grinding through the events of the last few hours, fitting them into his own memory and smoothing them into a tale that would satisfy not only the men waiting at the edge of the woods but his uncle, should word of this adventure reach those ears. The simple truth left too many gaps; he was tinkering with additional motivations when the track suddenly widened. Had he not been looking for excuses, Stephen would not have given the clearing a second thought, but as it was he paused.

Men had camped here sometime since the last leaves had fallen from the trees. Piles of decaying manure and broken twigs testified that a horse-line had been set between two trees. A fire pit had been dug against a rock. Two cheap earthenware jugs, cracked by frosts and half-buried in the leaves, lay at the edge of the clearing. Nothing extraordinary, but it bothered him, and he spread his arms to keep Ambrose and Alison from brushing past until he'd deciphered the rest.

Stephen considered the various types of travelers who might have stopped here during winter. Torworden men made such camps; so did pilgrims, outlaws, and other wanderers. There was no sign that the place had been occupied for long, yet some care had been taken in selecting it. It wasn't far from the Icknield, but hidden and inconvenient—unlike his own camp, which could be seen from the ridgeway. No wagon would have reached it; the heavy jugs had been brought here by donkey or on a man's own back. He could hardly guess its purpose until he spied a flash of blue amid the earth tones of the forest floor.

A feather, dyed and trimmed as fletching for an arrow, then apparently broken and discarded. Stephen sank down on the fire stone and studied the clearing again. He had a pattern now—a pattern that made his shoulder ache. All through winter the lands around here had been menaced by an outlaw band led by one who called himself the Black Wolf and who appropriated the blue-fletched arrows of Harold Godwinson's men for his own. It was such an arrow that had speared into his shoulder and still lay among his possessions at Torworden.

He twirled the broken feather against his lips.

"Any ideas?" Ambrose inquired, having recognized the feather, if not the other signs in the clearing.

Stephen paused before answering, prodding through the forest debris with his toe until he'd exposed a discolored length of wood: an arrow withy. He imagined himself sitting here on a cold winter day, replenishing his supplies from the well-hidden cache, warming himself by the fire and taking a few moments to sort through his arrows. He'd never believed that the outlaws who killed his companions and wounded him lived by their marauding alone. They received help from someone, and this was the clearest proof he'd yet seen. He shared it with Alison and Ambrose.

Alison had questions, but Stephen was moving again, plunging down the track at a slow run, putting greater distance between himself and his companions, who were less impervious to turned ankles and burdened with heavy cloaks.

"You'll leave us behind!" Ambrose shouted, and Stephen slowed without turning.

"Thank you," Alison murmured to him, though the discomfort at being grateful to the sorcerer almost stifled the good manners Lady Ygurna had labored long to teach her. "My boots aren't meant for these paths—"

"Why didn't you just *wish* him slower, then?"

The young woman came to attention, flicking her braids over her shoulders with a smooth toss of her head and glaring at the sorcerer with undisguised outrage. "I don't play games, sorcerer," she warned as she pushed past him. "And I won't have you standing between us."

Ambrose hesitated a moment, then followed her. There was no small folly in provoking her, not now that he'd witnessed the power that stood behind her, yet more than ever Ambrose was determined to break the English girl's hold over his friend, whatever the cost.

Stephen heard them talking, and resisted the temptation to turn around. He loved Alison best when she was alone in his arms or alone in his thoughts. There was peace at those times, which was far more than could be said when she was near Ambrose.

He expected better from his friend. Ambrose had read all the philosophers and knew that there was no rational way to deal with women. Stephen, who had never been in love before, considered it perfectly expectable that his thoughts were disordered because of her. There was nothing magical about it—or nothing but the magic that God, in his wisdom, had given to women anyway.

Ambrose never agreed. He claimed Alison didn't offer love but a twisted witch-talent that invaded a man's thoughts and left him without a will of his own. A weighty accusation, and one that Stephen was always determined to examine for himself the next time he and Alison were alone. But he never did; he never even thought about it until he saw Ambrose's disapproving face again.

More than once Stephen hoped that Ambrose would fall in love himself—perhaps with Alison's sister, which would be pleasantly convenient, or, failing that, with any available woman. Listening to them stomp along behind him, he considered that it might be time for action to replace idle thought. The bawdy songs of Aquitania were filled with helpful examples. He smiled as the choruses came back to him, and his mood lightened.

He felt more cheerful than he had since leaving Hafwynder Manor, and his mood survived the wary glances he got from the men and from Wildecent, who had become the keystone in his plans for dealing with Ambrose.

He fed the men the same tale he'd unravel for his uncle, focusing their attention on the camp he'd discovered rather than the absence that had led to its discovery. While his men talked of outlaws and Alison and Ambrose wolfed down their breakfasts, Stephen studied Wildecent, who sat alone and lonely by the lean-to.

It should be easy. Viewed by herself, Wildecent was pretty enough; her quiet reserve would suit Ambrose. The girl had to be aware that she'd lost Hafwynder's protection, and Stephen was certain he'd observed some hesitant attraction between the two already. Most importantly, his wit and manners rarely failed him with Wildecent as they so often did with Alison.

He had his tactics prepared and was about to approach the dark-haired girl when Alison slipped her arm beneath his.

"It would seem so lovely, wouldn't it—if my sister and your friend could find the love that we have," she said wistfully. "Too bad it can't be."

Once again everything that had seemed so simple was shaken. "Can't be . . ." Stephen repeated as his thoughts shifted and stretched and finally balked. "I think they'd be perfect for each other."

Alison slid around so she was looking straight into his eyes and there was no mistaking the unhappiness in hers. "Well," she explained, "I guess I can't speak for Ambrose, but I have spoken to my sister and she is much discomforted by your friend's foreign ways. She'd be too shy to say anything herself, but I'd take it very amiss if circumstances—any circumstances—forced them together."

Stephen blinked and let go of his love's wrists. It was unthinkable that he should deliberately make her unhappy, but, just this once, he simply couldn't agree with her. "We'll see," he said gently. "Perhaps once we get to Torworden, Ambrose will seem less strange to her . . . and to you." He tried to gather her into his arms, but she resisted and confronted him with undisguised anger.

"Never, Stephen. You'll have to learn to listen."

In a heartbeat Stephen's world was desolated by her scorn. He blinked back tears and let her go. Every thought and memory urged him to fall to his knees, but he knelt only to God and his lord. When he did not move, Alison turned and walked away from him. His anguish faded slowly.

hough the rain stopped, the blue skies that had brightened the first days of their journey did not return. The travelers rode northward for five days under bald clouds. There was a soft beauty in the pale colors of the new leaves and flowers against the colorless sky, but it could not compensate for the dampness that penetrated every layer of clothing on every back.

The journey had become sheer torment for the women. They were unaccustomed to riding day after day and they had never been schooled to ignore pain. Their muscles ached; their legs were chafed raw. Eodred flew the hawks alone, and if Stephen had wandered away from the campfire one of these later nights, Alison would not have followed him. She and Wildecent were content to move as little as possible once evening rest was called. They both longed for the deep wooden bathtub in the kitchen alcove back at Hafwynder Manor, but neither was so cruel as to mention it out loud.

Indeed, since that morning when Alison, Stephen, and Ambrose had returned from the forest together, the sisters had been estranged from each other. In such a small group it was impossible to be far apart or to avoid conversation altogether, but they spoke little. Alison began the estrangement by rebuffing Wildecent's innocent curiosity about the night she and Stephen had spent in the forest. But Wildecent had been easily and quickly dissuaded. The dark-haired woman passed her time with Eodred, helping with the hawks, or with Hugh de Lessay, who reluctantly helped her learn his language.

Just what, exactly, *had* happened that rainy night was not a complete mystery to Wildecent. There were no more powerful moments than those when the seasons changed; the burst of red buds and green leaves that had occurred the morning after Alison's disappearance was hardly coincidental. Nor was it coincidental that her sister's talents were more in evidence than ever. When they were together Wildecent felt an almost constant pressure against her thoughts and memories. The leanings that warned her away from Stephen were understandable, but the maelstrom that followed every time Ambrose's name was mentioned had a dangerous tenor, and Wildecent willingly kept her distance from all three of them.

She ate her lunch beside Eodred, trying not to listen too carefully to the old man's ramblings. He, like everyone else, had noticed the changes in Alison. He said she looked *serene* with Stephen sitting beside her, but many of his comments seemed to have second meanings. Wildecent would have preferred to eat with Hugh, if that hadn't meant standing on her aching legs.

Everyone at Hafwynder Manor had known what Lady Ygurna was and what Alison would become. Eodred's wife's family had dwelt on Hafwynder holdings as long as living memory could attest; he himself had taken care of the hawks since Lord Godfrey was a child. There was much genuine affection for the Hafwynders in the hearts of those who lived on their lands, but when Eodred stared at Alison, Wildecent wondered if affection would be enough.

The skies, which had darkened throughout their meal, opened. Not a driving rain that might be expected to run its course in an hour or less, but a gentler one that could easily last the rest of the day and into the night. Wildecent pushed herself to her feet, shook the crumbs from her clothes, and steeled herself for the afternoon's agony. She was startled when Alison approached her.

"Stephen says we could reach Torworden tonight if we ride hard and fast."

Wildecent rubbed her hand across her forehead—a reflexive gesture now that Alison could not ask a question or make a statement without putting some measure of magic behind it. As a matter of course Wildecent began to reject the notion, just to demonstrate her independence, then reconsidered. It would be better to ride a few additional hours than to sleep in the rain.

"Whatever it takes," she agreed wearily. "A roof over my head, a warm meal, and a dry bed—sounds like heaven to me."

Alison was no less bedraggled than her sister. Her hair had frizzed and surrounded her face like a mist. The rosy glow in her cheeks looked hectic, a reminder of how ill she had been at Christmastide. She was not the robust pillar of strength she had been before her aunt's death. A freezing night beneath the juniper—not to mention all that had happened since then—had left her a nervous shadow of her former self.

On impulse—her own impulse—Wildecent pulled her sister into a heartfelt embrace. "We'll be there soon, then we can rest . . ."

Alison returned the affectionate gesture. "I knew you'd agree," she whispered in her sister's ear.

The moment broke as quickly as it had arisen. Wildecent turned away lest she snarl that she had agreed of her own free will and not because of magic.

"You're so moody these days, Wili," Alison complained as she went to rejoin Stephen.

"Just like you, Alison," Wildecent muttered as she took her pony's reins from the English squire. *Just like you to think that I'm the moody one when it's you making everything unpredictable.* She accepted the boy's help in mounting and settled into the saddle with a groan that covered her emotional pain under a physical one.

All that had been merely damp became thoroughly soaked. Clouds settled in the rolling valleys. They couldn't see the thick forests of the Wychwood until the trees closed in around them. It was hard riding, but not especially swift as the horses made their way along the uneven, muddy track. There was no conversation, only a string of grim-faced riders pushing homeward.

The final barrier was the river Windraes itself. Swollen

from snow-melt and spring rains, it was a dirty torrent. Stephen circled them within the trees.

"The only bridge is 'round on the other side of Torworden itself," he explained. "I know our horses can swim it, but what about your ponies . . . and you?"

"We were born here," Alison averred, not looking back to see if Wildecent agreed or even troubling to lean on her magically if she didn't. "Let's just get to the other side."

Stephen directed Sulwyn toward the bank. "I'll try it first, to test the footing—"

But Hugh would have none of that. The Windraes was treacherous, and neither he nor any of the other Torwordeners had any desire to tell Jean Beauleyas that his nephew had been swept away a few miles from the keep. They'd sooner drown themselves. So Hugh made the crossing first and pronounced the footing no worse than was to be expected. He tied his horse and stood on the bank ready to help the next half-drowned man up the steep, slippery slope.

Stephen and his companions needn't have worried. The sturdy English ponies had kept pace with their larger brethren from the start of the journey and weren't about to be bested by three lengths of churning water. Even burdened by swirling skirts, the ponies plunged in without complaint and scrambled to the high ground without any assistance. Their riders did no less. The one animal who balked was Sulwyn, who had had enough of rain and wanted nothing to do with water in a more concentrated form. His flanks were bloody from Stephen's spurs before he leaped to the middle of the stream and started swimming.

"Damned fool beast!" Stephen shouted, springing down from the saddle and threatening the stallion with his fist.

They were both showing white around the eyes when first Sulwyn, then Stephen, relaxed. For once Wildecent approved of the uses to which Alison could put her talents, and even shot a sly grin to her sister.

Water still streaming from their boots, the party made its way to the Torworden track. The dismal afternoon became a gloomy evening. There was no way they'd reach Torworden until well after dark, and no way they'd stop before they reached it.

Wildecent had passed the upper threshold of discomfort. Numb from neck to toes, she fell asleep until the track became steeper and the men congratulated themselves on a safe, if soggy, homecoming. Once she was awake, the fetid reek of the settlement ensured that she would remain that way. Only Stephen, at the front of their line, carried a torch. He could see a few feet of track; they followed him blindly. All the English knew was that Hafwynder Manor never smelled this bad.

At length torches wove down the hillside to join them at a leveled place partway up the slope. The greetings were all in Norman French, but some of the men carrying the torches were English and recognized Alison as one of their own.

"So you're the heiress from the southern manor?" came the overly familiar greeting from a man who put a firm grip on the pony's reins.

"I've come to Lord Beauleyas for protection in these troubled times. King Harold himself has given permission." That was a lie, of course, but Alison counted on the power of the king's name to protect her from Beauleyas and his men.

She was mistaken. No one who dwelt at Torworden would openly dispute Duke William's claim to the throne. The English king's name brought a snort of laughter that froze Alison's heart.

"Take your hands off my horse!" she commanded, pressing sore calves into the mare's sides and backing her away. The man let go, but the look he gave her was amused, not respectful. Alison was outraged and she reacted as she always reacted: impulsively and magically.

Her willfulness swirled out—and washed away without effect.

No one had been aware of her efforts. The renewed sense of power she had during the journey was gone. When the Normans had visited her father's manor and filled the hall with their foreign chatter she'd been indignant, and refused to learn any scraps of French conversation. She'd learned little more during the journey, though Stephen offered to practice with her. She didn't need to speak French with Stephen; her meddling with his fantasies had given him a superb command of English. Now, surrounded by voices she could not understand, she was frightened, and guided her pony to Wildecent's side.

"What are they talking about?" she whispered urgently.

Wildecent shrugged and shook the water from the edge of her hood. "It's so fast . . . I understand maybe two words in four, I think. Something's wrong, maybe. There's no place for us or—"

"Who's *that?*"

More torches had criss-crossed down the hill. They hissed and smoked in the rain but gradually they were turning the faceless mass of the Torworden garrison into individuals. One such individual, a latecomer who did not carry his own torch, caught Alison's eye. He was a heavyset man some few years older than Stephen. His features weren't unpleasant in themselves; it was the way his lips twisted back when he smiled, the way his eyes disappeared when he talked, and the scorn in his voice as he addressed the returning men that made him unattractive.

Neither young woman knew who he was, but he had to be someone of some importance, for the other Torworden men deferred to him, and Stephen gave him his full attention. Wildecent recalled her conversation with Ambrose and judged that this was Eudo, Jean Beauleyas's bastard and the one most directly diminished by Stephen's accomplishments. She was about to share her observation with Alison when the conversation became particularly strident. With a shout that could only be a challenge, Stephen threw Sulwyn's reins to another man and sprang to the ground, the sputtering torch before him as a weapon.

The Torwordeners moved swiftly between the enraged men, surrounding and separating them from each other. Before the Englishwomen could sort through the ill-lit faces, Stephen appeared at Alison's side.

"Go with Hugh," he ordered.

Alison reached out to touch his shoulder, then pulled her hand back. She used her talents impulsively, and on those rare occasions when she gave a situation any thought, she knew when to stay out. This was such a time, and she meekly consented as Hugh took her pony's reins, leading her and Wildecent away from the excitement.

"It's nothing to worry about," Hugh said unconvincingly.

Torchlight fell on a series of wattle-and-daub huts that were as slick and shiny as the churned-up mud beneath their horses' feet. Alison regretted her meekness when the Norman came to a halt beside one of them and wrestled the door open.

"You'll be more comfortable here."

He saw them across the threshold and shoved his torch into a wall notch, where it seemed certain to ignite the thatched roof. Then—before either woman protested—he vanished into the rainy night with their ponies.

"More comfortable than what?" Alison complained. "The pigs? The sheep? The goats?"

Wildecent removed her cloak and looked around for a place to put it. She spun like a forlorn top. The hut's furniture—if it could be dignified by the word—consisted of a square box bed, a rickety stool, which might actually be a rickety table, and, of course, the torch Hugh had left stuck in the wall. At length she spied a chopped-off crook in one of the upright timbers and hung the cloak on that.

"I'm glad our lord father didn't come with us," Alison murmured as water plinked into the straw covering the floor.

"It's a mistake. It's got to be a mistake."

Alison hung up her cloak on another crook and clutched her arms across her breast as she gave the hut another examination. These *were* Torworden's guesting rooms, and this wasn't likely to be a mistake. She tried the door. It refused to open and so, fearing they might be locked into these miserable quarters, she gave it a tremendous tug. It popped open and brought a gust of wet wind between them.

She thrust her head into the night and shouted, "Aren't we even going to get our supper?" No one answered, and after a moment, at Wildecent's insistence, she shoved the door closed again.

"I simply don't believe it," she continued, thumping down into the straw of the box bed. "I simply don't. It's all a horrible dream. I'll wake up and I'll be back at Hafwynder Manor where I belong."

Wildecent said nothing, but sat down, and they put their arms around each other for comfort and warmth. The torch fizzled out. Neither was close to sleep when the door thumped open.

"Stephen!" Alison called in hope more than belief.

"Sorry to disappoint . . ."

Ambrose stepped down into the straw, removed the spent torch from its notch, and shoved his own into its place. He stepped aside, shook the water from his hair, and allowed two men to enter the hut behind them. They deposited their burdens, then departed on the sorcerer's command.

"Stephen is with his uncle," Ambrose explained as he sorted through the parcels. "And the rest—well, the less said about that the better, I suppose."

He produced a thong from his sleeve and a lamp from

the parcels, and in short order light was flickering down from a crossbeam. His second feat of civilization was a trio of mugs and a flask of warm, spiced wine, which he shared before revealing his true marvels: a hearty supper; thick, dry blankets; and the leather sacks of clean linen each woman had left on the pack animals. It was almost too good to be true, and halfway through her wine Alison said so.

"Why you?" she began, emboldened by the wine and too tired to care how he might react. "Why're you being so generous? We're hardly friends, you know."

A faint smile formed on Ambrose's face as he carefully swept water from the cloak he'd hung beside the others. "I'd scarcely presume to argue with you, my lady," he said with exaggerated politeness. "But I do have my own sense of honor. I was part of your escort, and this hill is, for the moment, my home. I do not see guests sent to their beds with empty stomachs or dripping linen—"

"Strange—I'd always thought you English set great store by hospitality."

Since Alison and Ambrose could not speak without sparring, it fell to Wildecent to effect a truce. "I don't think I've ever eaten a better stew," she interjected.

"If that were the case, Lord Beauleyas wouldn't want Hafwynder's cook almost as much as he wants its land and its daughters."

Alison nested her dishes in the straw beside her. "I won't stay here," she warned. "I won't live in a byre unfit for a whipped slave. I won't be held against my will . . . and so long as I or my father lives, no one will take Hafwynder Manor from us." Fire and determination ran through her words as she stood and glared at the man she considered her enemy.

But Ambrose did not respond directly to her challenge. He kept his voice soft and sincere. "My Lady Alison, if you have any hope at all of keeping your precious manor, you'll *do as you're told*. You might just as well be in an-other world—in Normandy itself—right now, and if you're half as clever as you think you are, you'll start thinking first and acting later.''

"I have my rights. Stephen—"

"Leave Stephen out of this!'' His voice rose into an uncharacteristic shout; he paused, swallowed hard, and continued in a more normal tone. ''Very well—we are *not* friends. But we share a friend, and if you love him as he loves you, don't tie yourself like a stone around his neck: you'll both drown.''

Wildecent tried again. ''Was that Eudo out there, the one you told me about? The one who was scornful and whom Stephen was about to fight?''

''You recognized him, then, the Beau-Bastard? You might take note: he doesn't think his rival should have the credit for bringing Hafwynder Manor and its treasure into the Beauleyas fold . . .''

Alison restrained the indignation she felt at the discovery that Wildecent knew something about Stephen she did not, and sought to correct the situation. ''This Eudo, he's Jean Beauleyas's natural son, and he fears that Stephen threatens whatever inheritance he might receive?''

Ambrose nodded. ''Not without reason.''

''Well, he shall see he has nothing to fear . . .''

It became Ambrose's turn to issue a warning. ''Don't even think about it. These are not the sort of men you can twist to your will—"

''Not my will alone,'' Alison shot back. ''You know what I could call upon.''

Wildecent shrank back; one didn't need to know the particulars to follow the general flow of this conversation. But Ambrose shook his head in mirthless laughter.

''Do that. These Normans will be impressed. They'll go to the top of your hill, cut down your oak tree, and put up a church with walls three feet thick. The world hasn't seen men like these for a long time, dear lady. Northmen with a taste for civilization; Vikings for the Church of Rome. Their own land isn't big enough for them. They fight, and feud, and murder endlessly; the only time they unite is to ravage someone else's lands. They have no art, no learning, no religion—but they usurp ruthlessly. And, by the mystic two, they rule as well as they conquer.

"Everybody wants a Norman or three in his pay—and fighting somewhere else. They'd crusade for the devil himself, if Satan had made them half as good an offer as the pope. They don't need your magic; they've got their own! You'll have no influence over them."

"Speak for yourself. Stephen's no Norman."

"Hah! Let me tell you about Rollo the Red—Bloody Rollo. Once, he boiled an abbot in holy water. He made war on all his neighbors, and when he finally died, poisoned by his children, they carved his flesh from his bones and fed it to the ravens. He had a child at every hearth in his domain, but the two you'd be most interested in are Jean Beauleyas and Mabelle . . . Stephen's mother. Shall I tell you *why* she feared to return to Normandy after her first husband's death?"

Alison shook her head. The violence in all of France, not just Normandy, was legendary. Murder was commonplace; if a man or woman happened to die unmarked by violence, poison was always suspected. Stephen could not have grown up ignorant or untainted, but Alison had no desire to know the extent of his education.

"Leave us," she said, with her back to Ambrose and a cautioning eye at her sister lest Wildecent object.

Ambrose threw his cloak over his shoulder and opened the door. "Be careful," he said as he vanished into the night.

III

here were no windows in the hut—no warning that dawn had come and long since gone when the young women finally opened their eyes and stumbled about the dark room.

"You must be wary of Ambrose," Alison admonished. "He has the power to tempt you."

"Umm . . .?"

"No, I'm serious. Aside from Stephen, he's the only civil soul here. It will seem natural for you, my sister, to be paired with him, Stephen's friend. Even Stephen has almost succumbed to the idea. And the sorcerer's already shown how he intends to seduce us with kindness. You will have to be wary."

"Umm . . ."

"Wili! You're not listening to me!"

Wildecent paused in the braiding of her hair. "I *am* listening to you. What I'm *not* doing is arguing with you at this unholy hour of the morning. Alison, I simply don't agree with you."

"He's poison, don't you understand that? Think what he's done to Stephen! What he's done to the men of Torworden to make them brutes and animals!"

"What he's done *for* Stephen is spare him from becoming another Eudo. I'd think you owe him a debt of gratitude. Eudo made my skin crawl. Ambrose wasn't bragging about what he'd done here, you goose, he was saying what he couldn't do—and what you shouldn't try to do."

Alison had nothing left to offer but a dramatic sigh. She stomped through the straw and wrestled the door open, blinding them both with sunlight. *"Egede,* it must be midday," she groaned with her arm up to protect her eyes.

"We're off to an outstanding start," Wildecent agreed. Nothing about Torworden was familiar or inviting. Already the disagreement they'd had in the hut seemed insignificant. In this strange place, they needed each other too much to argue over men or magic.

Torworden had sprung into existence two years before, when Jean Beauleyas secured permission from King Edward to dwell in English lands until such time as Duke William of Normandy claimed the English throne. Notwithstanding his agreements with Edward, Harold's sacred oath, and the betrothal between Harold and the duke's daughter Adele, William expected trouble gaining the English throne. He could scarcely expect otherwise: he had been fighting all his life. Wanting and fighting were inseparable in William's mind. He wanted England; he expected to fight for it.

His directions to Jean Beauleyas had been precise: find a defensible place away from English eyes, secure it, hold it, and wait. Beauleyas had followed the instructions scrupulously.

Torworden commanded a sweeping view of a clear route from the North into the English heartland. Duke William had expected to fight Scots and the various Scandinavian kings. He'd hoped Harold Godwinson, his prospective son-in-law, would be foremost among his English commanders. The earl's betrayal had hurt the duke deeply and personally, and made a shambles of his plans. Torworden would be nowhere near William's fighting when it came.

The motte was a huge earth mound constructed atop an already substantial hill. A bailey for the men and their horses had been created at the base of the motte following the lines of the original crest. Here were the lines of partially enclosed stalls that the women had smelled in the rain; here, too, were the long barracks where the men lived; and the sunken huts where guests spent the night. Other structures, smaller than the sunken huts, were filled with supplies.

Torworden had been preparing for a siege since its foundation. There was no life here, not in the same sense that there had been daily life at Hafwynder Manor. No common people dwelt behind the stout earthworks and their crowning stockades—only knights. There was a day-village at the foot of the hill, more squalid than anything the women had seen before, where Englishmen provided services to these foreigners who paid with money—when they paid at all—because they did not produce anything themselves.

"Where are the fields? The byres?" Alison asked an Englishman who'd just come through the stockade gate leading a donkey.

The man pointed at the arc of forest behind the crude buildings at the foot of the hill. "Yonder, my lady. At Lachebroc, the old village beyond the Windraes."

Alison was pleased to learn that there was at least a village nearby. Although villages were not closed, familial communities like Hafwynder Manor, they were respectable places. Tradesmen and artisans might congregate in a village and its men might work the land of several manors. "Is your village prosperous now that Torworden is nearby?"

"Prosperous?" The man repeated the question as if the notion had never occurred to him before. "Before we tilled fields for the Bishop of Winchester, what lived far away and cared nothing for us. Now our lord and his men're on the other side of our hill. We feel his eyes on our back and his foot on our neck every day."

Neither woman was so naive as to believe life everywhere was as pleasant as it was at Hafwynder Manor. There were slaves at Hafwynder Manor, and cottars, whose lot in life was little better. A woman like Bethanil might be a freewoman, but she was dependent on the goodwill of the Hafwynder lord, who could turn her out in the cold as he could not do with his slaves or cottars. And there were men of the local hundred who lived little better than their animals and were never more than few morsels ahead of starvation.

But the young women had never encountered the bleak spirit that marked the man before them.

"Your wives and children?" Wildecent asked hesitantly. "Do they suffer, too?"

"Those of us as could sent them away long ago. Begging your pardon, my lady, this is not a place for an honorable woman."

He tugged at his donkey's bridle. They plodded past, leaving the sisters with the unsettling notion that he either considered they were not honorable women or that their honor would not last for long.

"No wonder they need a woman to supervise their kitchen . . ." Wildecent murmured when he was gone.

"Bethanil won't stay. I wouldn't have her living here. It's bad enough we must be here. Our blood defends us."

Wildecent said nothing, though Alison's confidence hardly reassured her. Bethanil could trace her lineage in Wessex almost as far back as the Hafwynders could, while Wildecent knew the names or stations of neither of her own parents. She was suddenly—uncomfortably—aware that the rain had made her gown shrink. The cloth pulled tight across her breasts and hips. She tugged at it and wished she hadn't left her heavy cloak in the hut.

The Englishman and his donkey had come to the inner stockade that surrounded the base of the motte. He unloaded the baskets and jars from the beast's back. The track that led from the day-village to the bailey-yard where the women stood stopped at the inner gate. The only way up the steep motte was a spiral of split logs shoved into the mud. The Englishman balanced a heavy jar across his shoulders and became his own beast of burden. There were other men about, some Englishmen by their clothes, but no one offered to help.

"I don't think I'm going to like it here," Wildecent said.

They continued their explorations. There was little open space within the bailey. It was unlikely that domestic gardens had ever been planted here. Men as sullen as the one they had already met worked the stables, loading manure into waiting oxcarts.

The bailey wasn't a quiet place. A farrier was working among the horses, and some of the workmen sang or shouted as they went about their labors. Still, the greatest furor came from the other side of the motte, and it was toward those shouts that the women headed. What they found was not surprising. They'd already learned that Torworden was preeminently a stronghold; a lodging for knights. It was only natural that these men would need a place to practice their peculiar craft.

Not that a young Englishman didn't learn his martial arts, but there were no sons or fosterlings at Hafwynder Manor, and such seasonal practice as the grown men needed they got casually in the grass beyond the stockade. Here at Torworden the practice arena was the focus of daily life. The entrance of the donjon overlooked it; yet another wooden fence separated it from the rest of the yard. There were easily forty men, armored as suited their personal tastes, brandishing blunted weapons. They flailed away at each other, shouting encouragement or learning some refined method for separating an enemy from his life.

A row of tall shields rested along the fence, each in perfect condition. The looped guiges, which allowed the knight to sling the shield around his neck while he rode, were new leather. The enarmes had been freshly padded to ensure a firm grip in combat. The hides had been bleached then painted with a variety of bright designs. Neither Alison nor Wildecent could doubt that the owners of these shields were not merely ready for battle; they welcomed it.

Stephen was not there, nor were any of the men who had traveled from Hafwynder Manor, but Eudo was. The powerful young man had laid claim to the center of the arena and was calling for challengers. Despite the cool breeze he was naked to the waist, and swinging his sword slowly through arcs and feints. He proved to all who watched that he knew his craft, but he did not impress the women.

"Whatever else may be true of these Normans," Alison said after a moment watching him. "I think they're among the ugliest men on earth."

Wildecent nodded, though the allegation was not entirely true. Eudo's bearing made him distasteful, not his features. Still, there were aesthetic differences. English warriors marked their skins with scars and tattoos, like the Scandinavians; smooth, pale flesh was a telling sign of inexperience. The English found beauty in their hair; they cultivated it among both men and women. Unmarried women displayed their hip-length plaits proudly. Boys weren't men until their beards were full.

The Norman host was not immune to the allure of a woman's hair, but they considered their own a dangerous vanity. Their beards were cropped short lest they become tangled in their hauberks or offer a fatal handhold to an enemy. The ideal knight was clean-shaven, but even a Norman chin could not withstand daily rasping with pumice or the edge of his knife. Torworden faces were most often shawdowed with stubble. The same smooth-skin ideals applied to a Norman knight's neck, where hair could interfere with the fit of his conical helmet. His bare nape was as distinctive as a priest's tonsure.

Thus Eudo, who prided his martial prowess above all else, had a welter of cuts on his face and nape, and his reddish hair resembled a small wig sliding forward across a bald skull. A skilled observer might have guessed that, whatever the success of the English king, the English hairstyles would triumph over the Norman ones. Already about a third of the men were content to trim their beards and napes rather than submit to the rigors of shaving. Such compromise only accentuated Eudo's brutishness.

"He's like a rutting bull," Alison decided. "Come, let's see if we can find where they've sent Eodred and our hawks."

They headed back toward the stables and huts, wandering without success until their hunger overshadowed their curiosity.

"Do you think anyone would mind if we went down to the day-village below the gate?" Wildecent asked.

"No one's said we couldn't."

Alison led the way back to the gate which was, at this hour, standing open and unguarded. Skirts gathered up, they were picking their way through the mud when a hand fell heavily on Alison's shoulder.

"I go with you," Eudo announced, pushing between them without lifting his hand from Alison's shoulder. His English was slurred, but he did not need many words to make his meaning clear.

"Take your hand off me," Alison commanded, to no effect.

The mood become dangerous. Wildecent took a step backward and was caught from behind. Terror rose above all other feelings as she remembered how she had been similarly captured at Hafwynder Manor during the Black Wolf's attack. Her body went weak with the memory of the outlaw twisting her arm until it snapped. Whoever held her was not yet hurting her, but she had no will to resist him, and watched in bleak silence as the confrontation continued. Alison attempted to slap Eudo's hand away.

"You amuse me," Eudo said as he parried with a rock-hard forearm.

Alison was a head taller than her sister and strong for a woman, but she was no match for a knight. She winced as her arm struck his. Her eyes widened. Wildecent was certain her sister put all her will into a burst of magical thought—and equally certain that it had absolutely failed to affect the laughing Eudo.

"Lord Stephen—"

Eudo cut her off. "You are, I think, too much woman for my little cousin . . ."

Alison recalled that she had seen no other women at

Torworden since their arrival. She had compared Eudo to a rutting bull without realizing what truths the allusion might hide. In her mind she cursed Stephen for bringing her here, then she remembered the plight-troth. "We are plighted to each other," she announced, and saw she'd made a serious mistake.

Something akin to blind hatred narrowed Eudo's eyes and tightened his grip on her shoulder until it took all her strength not to shout with pain. He was brutal, but not stupid. He thought while he held her, and his face slowly relaxed into a satisfied grin.

"Stephen makes promises he cannot keep," he said, flinging her backward into the arms of another crony. Then he barked a command in French and the men all laughed. Wildecent was dragged farther away and Alison was given a shove toward the open gate. The women had a helpless heartbeat with which to look at each other before another man caught Alison and threw her over his shoulder. She screamed and hammered at his back with her fists, but he was running and almost through the gate when an arrow dropped one of the men and everyone froze.

Alison heard Jean Beauleyas's voice booming from the donjon just before she was dumped to the muddy ground. Eudo's men stood motionless, under the watchful eyes of Beauleyas's personal archers, as the lord left the tower roof. They stayed that way as he led a procession into the bailey-yard.

She was still sitting in the mud when Beauleyas ordered them to stand aside. Her unceremonious fall had addled her thoughts. She saw Stephen standing beside his uncle but she could not understand why he looked so grim.

Beauleyas had injured one leg many years before. Already bowlegged from a lifetime in the saddle, he habitually balanced on his good leg and did not, at first, seem a figure to command respect from his powerful son. But Eudo looked nervous when he was called forward.

The Beau-Bastard hesitated under rapid questioning,

and was rewarded with a blow that staggered him back two steps. He was a man, but Beauleyas was his lord and father, so he bore the insult in sullen silence. The question was repea.ed.

"She claims they promised to each other before God," he answered in English. "She was not to be promised. I had your word. Stephen disobeyed you."

The lord of Torworden was not pleased. He studied Alison with casual contempt and turned to glower at Stephen. "Is this true?" Beauleyas demanded of his nephew.

Conscious of the attention focused upon him, Stephen came forward. He gave no indication he was even aware of Alison, but he spoke clearly and in English for her benefit. "Yes, my lord, it is." Beauleyas struck him as he'd struck his son: a closed-fist blow that resounded through the yard. Stephen held his ground and did not stagger back. Blood streamed from his nose; he ignored it and faced his uncle with quiet dignity.

The simmering conflict between the two prospective heirs lay naked in the bailey. Eudo, who had embraced all the explosive virtues appropriate to his station, against Stephen, whose irregular education had taught him something of restraint and strategy. Jean Beauleyas did not know what to make of his sister's disenfranchised son, so he turned away and considered the cause of the outburst.

"You have been the death of a good man, lady of Hafwynder. What do you say for yourself?"

The blood had drained from Alison's face. Her whole body trembled as she picked herself up from the mud and shook her skirts straight. Then she steeled herself and faced him as a daughter of English nobility with a longer heritage than his own.

"His blood is not on me," she averred, speaking slowly to keep her voice from rising into a woman's hysteria.

"You behaved wantonly. You made a rash and foolish promise. You betray your freedom. I may punish those you led astray. How shall I punish you?"

The world had constricted until it contained nothing but her pounding heart and the cold, calculating eyes of the Norman lord. "You have no right to punish me," she said, though she understood perfectly that the discussion was not about rights but power.

"I must know you will obey me. I must see this futile vow repudiated. You are not some base-born wench who may give her body as she pleases."

Alison blushed a violent crimson. "You have not the right!" she shouted. "Only my lord father may give my hand in marriage. I shall not be made to marry without my consent nor place Hafwynder lands in the custody of a man I do not chose!"

"Your lord father no longer knows your name."

She looked quickly through the crowd and saw that no one, not even Stephen, would intercede for her. They reminded her of wolves cowed by their leader—a man who had brought all his commanding energies to bear against her. Wisdom counseled to accept her defeat and acknowledge his power. But Alison Hafwynder had never been known for her admiration of wisdom.

"I appeal to my lord's lord—to Harold Godwinson, Earl of Wessex and rightful king of England," she proclaimed in a voice that was once again even and controlled.

Beauleyas was unperturbed; he even gave her a little smile. "Ah, yes—the rightful king of England, for the moment. I thought of him after I left Hafwynder Manor. He is a busy man, harried on every front, scarcely able to consider the fate of one heiress while his country prepares for war.

"I sent my messenger to Westminster offering myself as lord and guardian for all that belonged to your father. You need not doubt that my petition was swiftly granted."

Alison's head slumped forward. She stared at the ground, unable to say anything more.

But Jean Beauleyas was not quite finished. "I would

have you all remember," he proclaimed, "that I am myself without a wife. I'll have the life"—he paused to stare equally at his natural son and his nephew—"of any man who interferes with my ward."

Alison looked up. Despite her efforts, there were tears running down her cheeks, but they had no effect on Beauleyas, and she did not turn to look at Stephen.

"Take her up to the donjon," Beauleyas told the man standing nearest to him, and Hugh stepped forward to take Alison's arm and lead her limply to the gate. The men began to disperse. Wildecent was left alone. She stared blankly at Beauleyas. "That one, too. No sense having one of them locked up and the other running loose."

He spoke in French, but Wildecent understood him well enough and walked meekly toward the gate without assistance.

he full power of Torworden could only be appreciated from the motte. The donjon resembled the tower at Hafwynder Manor in style, but far exceeded it in size. Windowless stone foundations descended deep into the natural hillside. Each side of the square they created was the width of Hafwynder Hall. The upper stories of the donjon were wooden—the motte was too young to support a donjon built entirely of stone—and were reached by an external wooden stairway.

If it was difficult to imagine an enemy charging up the natural hill to the bailey, it was impossible to imagine a successful assault on the motte and its donjon. Siege was the only way to bring down a donjon, except for arson, which accounted for the dressed stone heaped at the base of the motte awaiting the conversion of another wooden wall to unburnable stone.

The heroic scale of the donjon was not translated to its interior. A timber wall divided the entrance level. The larger portion served as Torworden's great hall. Its floor was made of wooden planks that echoed when the heavy-footed knights trod across it, and its hearth was carved into the outer walls. Tables were nowhere to be seen, and the most sophisticated piece of furniture was a low-backed chair draped with animal hides. Neither frescoes nor tapestries relieved the blank walls. This part of donjon was, after all, only temporary. Nonetheless, it had a depressing effect on the two Englishwomen.

Unembroidered hangings, little more than blankets hung on hooks, concealed two passages through the interior wall. The sisters were escorted into the rear room, which took up no more than a third of the entrance level.

"I thought it couldn't get worse," Alison said when they were alone.

The room was shuttered and dim. Though nothing more substantial than the drapery separated them from

the outer room, the aura of a prison clung to the place. Alison no longer contained her sobs, and sank to the floor.

Wildecent said nothing, but unlatched the shutters for light and air. While Alison cried, her sister studied the room.

"Well, brace yourself," she said after a few moments. "I don't doubt that it's going to get worse."

Alison looked up slowly. The lord's bed dominated the far end of the room. It stood on a platform and was hung with heavy velvet and dressed with fine linen. No one had bothered to straighten the linen; Beauleyas's night shift trailed to the floor on one side. The remainder of the room was dominated by locked chests and boxes: Torworden's treasury kept safe by its lord.

"At least he considers us valuable," Wildecent said after a moment.

"How can this be happening? Where's Stephen? Eodred? Anyone who could take us from here? I'd rather run and hide in a convent than spend a night in this room!"

Wildecent laughed. Whorehouses had better reputations than England's convents. Then she looked closely at Alison's face and realized she was sweating feverishly.

"Why don't you curl up and get some sleep," she suggested, knowing Alison would never take more specific advice from someone who healed by memory rather than magic. "We'll survive this somehow."

"We must do more than survive," Alison replied, her voice turning shrill. She went to the foot of the huge bed and stared at the rumpled linen as if she could read her future in its folds. "There must be a purpose to this. A grand design that will point us to triumph; an unveiling of the Old Ways—"

Wildecent said nothing. She'd burned through a lifetime of outrage when she'd watched Jean Beauleyas assault his heirs and humiliate her sister. She'd looked inward and found neither the stoic courage that fueled

Alison and Stephen nor the sullen hatred that strengthened Eudo. She'd bend her knee if that was what it took to maintain a facade of dignity. Wildecent admired her sister, but could not imagine imitating her. She had no interest in grand designs, and nothing but fear for the bloody old gods of Britain.

"I'm not you. I've lost everything before," Wildecent explained in a rare allusion to her shadowed infancy in France. "I don't remember names or faces. Maybe in time I can forget Hafwynder Manor . . ."

Of course not, Alison thought, more absorbed in her own thoughts than Wildecent's confession. *I'm the one they've called upon. The one they've chosen. The inheritance of land from my father; the power from my mother . . .* Her vision blurred as her thoughts plunged back to the moments she had spent with the ancient gods. *The hero must be chosen. I must choose the hero.*

The *geas* was weaker now. Alison could see the masks of the tree kings waiting for her to choose. Except there were four masks now. The last hung upside down and was drenched in blood.

Blood flowed across Alison's inner eye, staining the disarrayed linen. She turned away from the horror and began to gasp for breath. The sky beyond the open windows turned green, and she collapsed headlong across the bed.

Wildecent could not reach her before she fell. There could not be a worse time for Alison's mysterious maladies to return, and Wildecent cursed the ancient gods Alison and Lady Ygurna venerated who had not prevented it. Alison's hands were icy, her eyes had rolled back in her head, and all their herbs were in sacks at Hafwynder Manor. She tugged and pushed until Alison was swaddled in blankets.

The sense of outrage Wildecent had thought extinguished flickered back to life. It had no focus, as if she could not choose among the many sources of her bleak anger: Alison, whose magic would be their downfall? The ancient gods, who inspired Alison's most reckless actions?

Lord Beauleyas, who had power in this world? For that matter, why not focus on Stephen, whose mishaps had begun the changes in their lives? Or Ambrose? Or Lady Ygurna?

There were so many targets, Wildecent had not selected one above the others before faint color had returned to Alison's cheeks and her skin felt normally warm to the touch. Wildecent freed the bed hangings so the light would not fall across her sister's eyes, then went to the window.

A slow-moving entourage made its way past the long stables. She could distinguish Beauleyas's distinctive walk at its center and the black-clad presence of Ambrose a step or two behind, but she saw no one who might be Stephen . . . or Eudo. Eudo! The Beau-Bastard might come bursting in and find Alison helpless in his father's bed! There'd be hell to pay afterward—but afterward would be too late for Alison.

Wildecent shut and bolted the door beneath the blanket draperies before she thought better of her independence. If Jean Beauleyas wanted the door locked, he'd have commanded it. And having seen the Norman lord's rage, Wildecent was not about to do what he had not commanded. *What will be, will be,* she decided and reopened the door.

She paced the length of the room, rubbing her palms against her thighs. Of all the things she had dreaded about Torworden, she had never imagined its most insidious torture: boredom. At Hafwynder Manor there had been no time for idleness. A year's spinning and weaving was scarcely complete before the next year's began. Wildecent felt as naked without her spindle and sleeveful of carded fleece as she would have felt without her linen. A whirling spindle was soothing in its own way and required just enough attention to keep a mind from wandering where it ought not go. It was hopeless to expect that Beauleyas counted a spindle among his treasures, but Wildecent looked.

Alison had rolled onto her side and was sleeping peacefully. Jean Beauleyas had gone to the other side of the motte, where his men could be heard practicing. Wildecent realized she had a headache from hunger and remembered the leftovers back in the hut. She braved the outer hall in search of food and found nothing the dogs had not already investigated. Disgusted and still hungry, she returned to the bedroom and settled herself amid the boxes of Torworden's treasure. Many a slave had a less comfortable bed; she willed herself to sleep.

She awoke with the floor shaking and the walls echoing with the sounds of men's shouting in the outer hall. The shadows had moved to the other side of the room. Wildecent judged she'd slept until the late afternoon and, despite lingering hunger pangs, felt better for her rest.

"They'll be the death of me," Jean Beauleyas could be heard shouting.

Wildecent crept closer to the drapery to catch the flow of his conversation, grateful for the hours she'd spent listening to Hugh de Lessay talk about himself. Crouched on the floor, she could see Beauleyas striding around his chair, a piece of cold chicken in his hand. Her mouth began to water; it took a conscious effort to examine the other faces.

Ambrose leaned casually against the far wall, looking out the window past his goblet as if his thoughts had returned to whatever place he called home. Wildecent knew him well enough, though, to know his distraction was a sham and that he alone was following the debate carefully.

"So young Stephen found more blue fletching. What does that prove?" a man as grizzled as Beauleyas himself demanded. "What does that tell us we didn't already know—except that he was a damned lucky fool when he ran off with the English bitch."

Hugh rose to Stephen's defense. "It reminds us, if we'd forgotten, that we are not alone in coveting England. Tostig Godwinson plays his own games. He's made allies in the North. We do not know if that fletching lay on the leaves a night or a month. The peasants here look to us for protection. For William's sake—for our honor's sake we owe them our duty and our swords."

Beauleyas rasped his fingers along the scar on his cheek. "Indeed," he agreed cautiously.

"Tostig's not in the North—and he's not with Hardrada in Norway," the original doubter asserted. "Tostig's gone to his cousin in Flanders. If he invades this spring it will likely be from the south—just as Duke William will."

Hugh was distressed but not dissuaded. "His alliance with Hardrada holds. There is still danger in the North. They've made oaths to each other—"

"A Godwinson oath is worthless," Beauleyas interjected, using a lordly tone that brooked no disagreement. "Tostig's a kinslayer. No one trusts him."

Which was true enough. Tostig Godwinson's failings had precipitated the anarchy creeping across England. When the men of Northumbria had sought to have another man as their overlord—any man but the rapacious, unpredictable, and immature Tostig Godwinson—Tostig reacted with rage beyond the bounds of reason. He had attempted the murder of his own brother, Harold, and of his brother-in-law, King Edward. There were those who said it was Tostig's revolt that broke the king's health and sanity.

There was a new earl in Northumbria. Tostig had spent the fall and winter visiting his wife's kin and powerful men who, for their own reasons, encouraged his imagined grievance. What better way for Hardrada of Norway to sneak onto England's throne than to give Tostig an army and let the Godwinson brothers destroy each other? William of Normandy was among the few whom Tostig had not courted—but William did not need a madman to better *his* claim to the English throne.

"We ought to investigate," Hugh said, determined to save face.

"Shall I send a messenger to Hardrada?" Beauleyas snapped, his patience clearly at an end.

Ambrose pushed away from his wall. "Send out some of the men. They're restless. It's not a fool's errand if it keeps the peace. They may turn something up, they may not. It won't hurt to let the folk know we're the enemies of their enemies."

Beauleyas grinned. He kept his Greek around to have the benefit of his deviousness. He cared not a whit for the state of the sorcerer's soul, only that he provide clever advice—and, on occasion, invoke those powers an orthodox Christian might not. "I like that," he told his other men. "A hunting party."

The men fell into a heated discussion of who among the Torworden garrison should have the honor of plunging through the countryside. Wildecent took the opportunity to retreat from the curtained doorway. She itched in four places and dared not move while she was near the drapery. Hopefully she owed her discomfort to nothing worse than the aftereffects of holding still too long; if not, only a herbal bath would get rid of the fleas, and the saints alone knew where she'd find a bathtub at Torworden.

She was scratching her right calf when she realized Alison was awake and standing at the foot of Beauleyas's bed.

"What's going on?" Alison asked, stretching her arms over her head and giving a great yawn as she did.

"Our lord is meeting with his men. They've been talking politics—"

Alison wrinkled her nose. "He's not our lord, not yet he's not. I don't believe he's sent a messenger to our king. That was just talk for his men's benefit. Beauleyas hasn't won yet. Threats won't be enough."

Wildecent studied her sister in the fading light. Since Christmastide Alison's illness, if it were an illness, had evolved a particular pattern. She fainted in a thoroughly terrifying manner, then she fell asleep, and then she woke up unaware of either her collapse or the reasons for it. Wildecent watched another moment and reconsidered her judgment: Alison's behavior went beyond a simple loss of memory. It was as if she'd spent her dreams someplace where her strength was restored.

"I do not think we should do anything rash. We need more time to learn their ways. To learn what is possible and what is not—as Ambrose suggested," Wildecent said firmly.

A baleful look passed across Alison's face when the sorcerer's name was mentioned, but Wildecent had already crept back to the drapery and missed it.

"What are they saying?" Alison demanded in a loud whisper, unable to understand the conversation herself.

Wildecent countered with a slashing gesture for silence. "They're sending men out of the castle to search for outlaws," she whispered. "Keep quiet or they'll know we're listening!"

"Sending who? When? What outlaws?"

Wildecent's hand cut through the air again, this time with enough force to make her sleeve snap. Alison resigned herself to watching over her sister's shoulder.

"Twenty men-at-arms?" one of the older advisors asked with some dismay. "Who will lead that many? Will you travel with them yourself?"

There was only one chair in the hall that had both arms and a back: the lord's chair. Jean Beauleyas made good use of its superiority as he sprawled, raising his good leg up until it rested on the carved griffin of the armpiece. "Too early in the season for me," he averred. "But you're right, it's a goodly number of men. It will, I think, take both Eudo and young Stephen to keep things in hand."

That brought Ambrose back from his wall. His expression was dark and worried, but he was not the first among Beauleyas's men to speak.

"It will take more than twenty men to keep those two from killing each other this summer," Hugh said.

Beauleyas grinned again.

"What's going on?" Alison hissed; she'd heard the names and seen Ambrose's reaction. She and the sorcerer were enemies because they shared the same concerns; she knew to be worried.

"You don't want to know."

The Norman lord had swung his leg down and was sitting upright in his chair again. "I'll not have the one defying me and the other lying to me—"

"My lord, it is not in Stephen's nature to either defy or lie to you." That from Ambrose, who had joined the informal circle.

Now another side of Beauleyas's lordship asserted itself—the side that feared the cleverness in the sorcerer's eyes, and feared the way both he and Stephen could stand calmly before his rages. "He would concoct this tale of outlaws in the woods to cover the fact he meant to have the heiress for his own! For all I know he may have lain her down in the forest and taken her there and then—but it won't do him any good, I'm telling you that. It's not her purity I'm interested in. It's her land and her loins: I'll have a son yet!"

Ambrose appeared to back down. Only a slight stiffness in his movements indicated he was not content to have his problems with Alison resolved in his lord's bedroom. Wildecent took note of his reticence and admired him. Her admiration was interrupted; Alison could no longer contain her curiosity.

"What's going on? They're angry. Is Stephen in some sort of trouble? Is he in danger?"

Jean Beauleyas glanced over his shoulder. Wildecent bit back a harsh reply and whispered, instead, "I don't know."

"Her father is not dead yet." That from one of the younger men of the council.

"Her father is an idiot! A man without a brain—why else did I tell my nephew to leave him behind? I've got what matters now, and if the damned wench will use her head she'll realize she's got the best of it. She'll be better off than the rest of her English sisters!"

Ambrose ventured a soft question. "And what about her sister, my lord?"

"Hafwynder told me himself the dark-haired one was his ward. An orphan he'd taken in for charity with no family or fortune. She doesn't figure in my plans at all. She can join a convent for all I care."

"I had wondered if, perhaps, since you see fit to marry Alison yourself—"

"Waters run deep, eh?" The scar on Beauleyas's face twisted his broad grin into a sneer. Wildecent was trembling and clutched Alison's hand without thinking. "You want her for yourself?"

The merest trace of redness marred Ambrose's pale complexion. "No, my lord, for Stephen . . . or Eudo, whichever of them survives—"

"She's an orphan, man! A common whore for a mother and God Almighty knows who for a father—Hafwynder swore she wasn't his get."

"She's French—"

"So much the worse."

"My lord, I think—"

"I don't care what you think, man. She's no different from a wench from the village. I don't care who wants her. God's blood, if you decide you *want* her—she's no part of my honor. But even my bastard's blood is too good for her to marry!"

There was nothing more for anyone to say. Ambrose retreated and Wildecent hid her face behind her free hand. Alison pulled her sister away from the curtain, into the dusk-lit room.

"What did they say? What's wrong? I heard them mention my name. What did he say? Is he going to keep Stephen and me apart? Does he think he can force me to his bed?"

For a moment Wildecent was frozen between rage and

horror. She opened her mouth, but no sound came out—
no angry words for Alison's insensitivity or pleas for compassion. Then she ran sobbing to the treasure boxes, and
did not care who in the outer hall heard her cries.

f Wildecent had hoped for comfort while she cried, she was doubly hurt. Alison had recognized no name but her own, and worried for no fate but her own or Stephen's. She left her sister huddled amid the treasure boxes and went to the outer hall, determined to wring some explanation from the man who claimed to be her lord.

A small troop of day-laborers had come up to the donjon from the bailey and were erecting tables for the lord's supper. There was a well in the bailey, and a bread oven, but all other food was prepared at the foot of the hill and carried each evening to the griffin chair where Jean Beauleyas chose to eat.

Alison was noticed, but no one spoke with her—not even Stephen, whose face was swollen and bruised from the blow he'd taken on her behalf. She caught his eye, but his expression was unreadable. She took a step toward him, but an Englishman was at her side, telling her it was time to go to the stool beside Lord Jean Beauleyas. She cast another glance in Stephen's direction, but he had already taken a place near Hugh de Lessay.

The food was cooling—as it could not help but be, considering its journey—but it had a pleasant aroma. Wildecent inhaled the last of her tears. She was hungry enough to face Jean Beauleyas and the rest of his men. Shaking her plaits behind her shoulders, smoothing the folds of her skirt, and withdrawing her hands demurely in her sleeves, she pushed through the drapery.

And came to a stunned halt.

Alison was already at the high table, sitting on Lord Beauleyas's left side. No stool was set to Alison's left, nor was there any other empty place at the linen-covered table. Wildecent dug her fingernails into her palms and tried to swallow the lump in her throat. Did they expect her to serve her sister? No, they expected her to serve the lord's intended wife.

A common woman of no particular parentage might be grateful for the opportunity to pour a noble lady's wine, to fetch her dainties from a distant platter and offer her own sleeves as a napkin. But Wildecent was not a common woman, regardless of her parentage. Had she been naked she could not have felt more shame; had the Church not forbidden it, she would have plunged her dagger into her heart.

"My lady?"

She turned. Ambrose. *Ambrose,* her mind's voice repeated but her tongue could not recognize him.

"You were listening earlier, weren't you?"

Numbly, willing muscles to move but not feeling when they did, Wildecent nodded. There was concern in his face, but precious little compassion. Still, when he extended his hand, she unknotted her own and placed her fingers across his.

"Will you share my plate?"

Again she nodded. The lump fell from her throat to her stomach; she wished she and it could fall through the floor. He led her to the far right end of the high table and, in a voice every bit as commanding as the Norman lord's, demanded another stool be brought to his side.

It was a subtle thing to share a person's plate—not the same as sitting to one side or the other, sharing only common platters and a water bowl. She and Alison often shared a single, bread-covered plate. Sharing was a mark of closeness. It was an honor between equals . . . or lovers, though some fed their dogs in just such a manner. Wildecent did not know if sharing Ambrose's plate was an honor for her.

Of course, they had to sit close together. She could smell the scent of him—rather spicy, as if he masked himself behind musky perfumes. Certainly he was fastidious at the table—using a little gilt fork while everyone else, including herself, was quite comfortable using the left hand to fish food from the common platters and the right to bring it from the shared plate to the mouth. English society was considered quite civilized, even overcivilized, but Wildecent felt coarse beside him.

They shared the same wine cup. Wildecent was careful to reach for it only while he was chewing, lest he reached for it as well and the wine cup become a love cup. She was careful where she looked as well—never to her left, where she might meet Ambrose's eyes; nor further left, where Alison could be heard engaging Lord Beauleyas in artless conversation; nor out to the center of the hall, where she was certain she'd meet a dozen pairs of condescending eyes.

Then she was careless and reached for the wine cup when she might better have reached for her bread. His fingers closed over hers and she had no choice but to look at him.

"I thought you, of all people, knew not to be afraid of me."

Her hand went limp beneath the mild accusation. "I . . . I'm not afraid . . . of you. But I have no *place* here. I can be cast aside without a moment's hesitation. In his eyes I'm no different than anyone who warms his bed at night."

"You could be raised up just as easily."

She shook her head. "Alison perhaps, but not me. I'm no fool, *Lord* Ambrose." She put her bitterness in the honorary title. "It does not take land or noble blood to give me wisdom."

He had the courtesy to release the wine cup. "I have never thought you a fool. But you would be a fool if you surrendered easily. Someone went to considerable trouble to see you safely into England. Surely it would have been easier to put you in a convent someplace in France—"

The wine burned in her mouth and throat. "I do not think of such things," she insisted weakly.

"You should. Jean Beauleyas will."

"You'll put ideas in his mind?"

Ambrose managed a laugh. "Like your foster sister, Alison? Let us agree that neither of us is a fool, nor is the lord of this donjon. What you heard notwithstanding, Lord Beauleyas gives nothing away but that he gets its value back. It won't take sorcery to get him thinking about you."

"He may take too long, then. I learned today it will be no easy thing to live at Torworden."

The sorcerer took the cup from her hand. It was empty; he called for an English boy to refill it. "I have," he assured Wildecent, "defended myself in the most ordinary of ways. I do not encumber myself with a sword because I do not need to—not because I cannot use one to good effect. My shadow is long enough to protect you—and Stephen."

The boy came back with the wine. Wildecent stared past Ambrose and for a moment found herself looking straight into Alison's eyes.

"It was one thing," Ambrose whispered in her ear, "to plunge into Stephen's private thoughts while he lay injured. But it is something else that she does now. She has bound him so close that I cannot see between them. I think even she knows it is beyond her control. You may tell her I will help break this binding if she cannot. All she need do is ask."

"She will never do that," Wildecent whispered as Alison glowered. "She would sooner die, and take Stephen with her, than turn to your sorcery. Besides, they love each other. How it began doesn't matter now."

Ambrose frowned. "Stephen loves her because he has no choice. I cannot be certain about Alison. Your sister is not the woman she was. Her mind is no more her own than her father's is."

"Alison has been ill. She is weak, and tires easily; the journey exhausted her more than she will admit. She feels the changes in our life, and grows melancholy. She thinks of Stephen because he is the sun of her life." Wildecent tried to sway the sorcerer with her eloquence, but his frown deepened.

"She has nightmares, does she not? And fainting spells? No—don't deny it. I can read the truth on your face."

Wildecent shredded the embroidered hem of her sleeve. "Alison would never hurt anyone. She loves Stephen. She's promised herself to him. You heard her—"

"Lying does not become you, Wildecent."

She flushed scarlet and gulped the wine.

For her part, Alison saw Wildecent's whispered conversation with the sorcerer, and her final radiant blush, as nothing short of betrayal. She had not forgotten her foster sister, or abandoned her. Indeed, Alison had never been more aware of her obligation to the girl her father had brought to Hafwynder Manor. She would see Wildecent well-settled—once she had her own situation in order.

Beauleyas was courting her; she'd been courted often enough in the past to recognize the signs. But the Norman's politeness was facile. It would be so much more convenient if she agreed to marriage. His pleasantries—phrased in English, of course—served only to make his true goal easier to see. Why else ask how many men had sworn to her father and how many of those could bear arms? She replied politely, and truthfully, for he might have sources of his own, but she kept her emotions close about her.

From time to time Alison cast a discreet glance at Stephen. Discreet because Eudo was watching, and she knew that Eudo would move swiftly against Stephen where he did not dare to move against his father. It was a dangerous game she played: dissembling with Beauleyas to keep his son at a distance, while seeking a clear avenue to Stephen. Even with her magic, Alison's ingenuity would have been taxed, but she faced these Frenchmen with nothing more than the ordinary feminine wiles any head-blind woman possessed.

And, in light of that, Alison had short temper for Wildecent's blundering. She was preparing an oration calculated to reduce her sister to obedience, when Lord

Beauleyas pounded his fist on the table. The hall quieted. He got up and shoved his chair aside.

Jean Beauleyas held the oaths of a half-dozen Englishmen. Even among the men who had followed him from Normandy, there were a handful of dialects and regional loyalties. When he addressed his entire company, he spoke slowly and in a mercenary argot Alison could comprehend. Thus she learned that twenty men would leave Torworden in search of outlaws and minions of the Norse king, Harald Hardrada.

She approved, in a cautious way, until Beauleyas proclaimed that two men would lead the party: his nephew and his son. Then Alison, like everyone else, gasped inwardly. She threw caution to the winds and confronted the cat-smiling nobleman as soon as he settled in his chair again.

"Murderer!"

His smile never wavered. "You must share the blame, my lady. I controlled their rivalry until you set yourself between them."

"Set myself between them! I never laid eyes on your bastard until this morning!"

"You see what you cause by meddling in men's affairs?" His voice grew harsh and his eyes flinty. "It is not a mistake you will make again—now that you are *my* ward and will become *my* wife."

Alison's acid curse was lost as Eudo, drunk on wine and his father's favor, shoved platters, plates, and cups to the floor. He bestrode the table and bellowed his father's war cry. Men who had no love for the Beau-Bastard took up the cheer. A sense of fellowship spread through the hall. Perhaps it infected Eudo; perhaps he was simply smarter than most believed. He opened his arms to his cousin.

"Let us be brothers," he invited.

All eyes turned toward Stephen; the hall was quiet again, but none was quieter than Alison and Ambrose. Alison felt her thoughts twist into a plea for Stephen to reject those outflung arms. Everyone blinked as thunder crashed against Torworden's donjon; when their eyes opened again, Stephen had vaulted atop his own table. He assayed the distance separating him from his cousin: too far for a standing leap, so he took a falling step to the floor and bounded up to accept his cousin's embrace.

Close beside each other—Stephen a bit taller, Eudo somewhat broader in the shoulders—the family resemblance was strong. A warlord would be proud to make either his heir. Yet it was equally clear, despite the fraternal support they proclaimed, that they could not stand for long on the same mountain. In some eyes, Stephen was the superior leader: subtler, deeper, polished with a fine charisma.

Yet others detected the softness of the Mediterranean: an indolence, an appetite for unmanly loves of women, cleanliness, and luxury. These preferred Eudo, whose appetites matched their own.

The young men shrugged off each other's arms. While the hall still echoed with unwon praises, they exchanged looks that promised their next embrace would not be empty-handed.

"Wine and ale for our men!" Stephen proclaimed, lest anyone dwell too long on the falseness of his affection for his cousin.

Alison pulled her lips into a thin, pale line as the English servants assembled at the outer door. Another peal of thunder had rocked the donjon; the open shutters showed dark stains where the first raindrops had struck them. Yet the English, solid freemen who had, perhaps, farmed this land before Beauleyas made it his own, were sent back into the night to haul casks and skins for their patrons' pleasure.

She sent another thought winging across the hall to Stephen, chastising him for mistreating her people, but—like her earlier pleas and commands—it did not touch his conscious soul. When Stephen was among his peers he was as impervious to her magic as Beauleyas himself. And Beauleyas, though he kept a sorcerer near his right hand, was utterly untouched by anything arcane.

The English heiress made a show of turning her wine cup upside down and realized, belatedly, that only Beauleyas had watched her.

"Do you refuse to wish them godspeed?" he challenged.

Alison shook her head but refused to right the cup. "I would not be served by men who labor like beasts."

"Torworden is served by freemen; did *I* object when you sent *slaves* to serve me at Hafwynder? I do not ask them to like me, and they do not need to ask me to protect them. How well did you protect your people? Can you protect them from Harald Hardrada, much less Duke William?"

He did not talk down to her—she was grateful for that—but his confidence was unassailable. So long as he and his kind dwelt in England, neither she nor her father nor all the Hafwynder Manors with their full larders and tidy stock pens could promise protection to anyone.

"King Harold will drive you back across the Channel," she replied with more hope than conviction.

Beauleyas ran his finger along his scar as another man might absently scratch behind his ear while he sought the best answer to an annoying question.

"It was over long ago," he began, speaking as softly as the raucous bragging in the hall would allow. "Before you were born; before *I* was born. Our Normandy was held by the first Duke Richard. We still spoke like Danes, and our rivalries were not with the French but our Viking grandparents. Your England had a king—Ethelred . . ."

Alison grimaced: Aethelred Unraed, Ethelred Bad Counsel, whose mismanagement had plunged England into civil war a half century before.

"Everyone had an enemy in the Danish kings Svein Forkbeard and Cnut. Duke Richard had a daughter, Emma. When Ethelred married Emma, alliance was made between the English kings and the Norman dukes. The Danes got nervous and the damned Capetians in Paris got greedy; there was war. But the English king had no stomach and the Norman dukes could not win alone. Ethelred was killed; Emma sent his children to Normandy, then married Cnut. Both Normandy and England fought for their lives.''

The saga was sung differently in Hafwynder Hall, but Beauleyas's version was not wrong.

''Kings are annointed by the Church; so is a Norman duke. He carries the souls of his people on his shoulders like a priest. Between her two husbands Emma of Normandy got a handful of children. The English dynasty should have been strong for generations—but it wasn't. Twenty years, my lady, for twenty years your English nobles tried to make grist of your Norman-Danish meal, as we Normans made grist of our French neighbors.

''We came through the fire as tempered steel. You—your greatest families were dust by the time King Edward reached the throne. For English advisors Edward turned to Godwin of Mercia—who revealed his lineage to no man, not even his king! Duke William may not have the blood of Alfred or Cerdic in his veins, but, *Deus aie,* who IS this man you call your king?''

Alison bit off the reply that William was a bastard. It was irrelevant. William knew his parents; he honored his common-blood mother and ennobled his half brothers, but no one, not even King Harold himself, knew the names of Godwin's parents. Bastardy was an inconvenience easily overcome by a man of strength, but unknown ancestry—hidden, concealed ancestry—implied a shameful ancestry, and that was a fatal flaw.

''He was a good earl to my father. A strong warlord for Edward.''

Beauleyas closed in for the kill. ''These things and more he would have been had he kept his oath to William and not taken the throne for himself. Together, England and Normandy would push Hardrada back to Norway and then deal with the Capetian fools in Paris! He broke a sacred oath, Alison Hafwynder; by your own laws he should have been executed, but you crowned him king!''

To Alison's surprise there were tears in his eyes. She

had no interest in politics, yet she felt a poignant empathy with Harold.

"What was he to do?" she asked, not caring that her voice strained and broke. "Where was William of Normandy? Where is he now? England must have a king, and Edward had no sons. Harold Godwinson did what was best for England. What more can a *king* do?"

Beauleyas traced his scar again in silent agreement. "The tragedy must be played out," he conceded. "Sacrifices must be made."

Alison swallowed her tears in a hard lump. Haloes grew around the torch flames, and her stomach churned in rhythm with the thunder.

Sacrifice!

For a moment the Norman lord's face blurred. It became the face she'd seen in her dreams and in the forest, his scar mimicking the tendrils of life flowing from the Green King's mouth. It became her father's face and the face of King Edward—whom she'd glimpsed just once in her life. Then it became King Harold's face—or perhaps just an Englishman's face, for she'd never seen an image of their new king. Alison closed her eyes hard.

"Are you unwell?" Beauleyas inquired.

She opened them again and stared into the Norman's eyes. The light had lost its radiance, but she felt as if she'd fallen from a great height. "I am . . . tired. I would retire, if I could."

"I shall have a chamber prepared for you."

He called two men and pointed to a frayed tapestry beside the outer door. Numbly Alison realized the donjon contained more than the two rooms she and her sister had seen, but she was still too stunned by her visions to feel at all grateful or relieved.

f you please, Lady Alison . . ." Hugh held the tapestry back with his left arm—and opened the door to the outer stairway with his right.

Alison looked up at him, aware that, as he and Guy stood, no one in the hall would realize she had not climbed the interior stairs but had descended the exterior ones.

"If you please . . . ?" Hugh repeated.

She had a satisfying image of Jean Beauleyas's rage when he discovered she was missing, and gathered her skirts under her arm.

"Why?" she asked when Guy threw his cloak around her for protection from the weather.

The men held their peace. Though they laid only the gentlest of guiding and supporting hands on her as they negotiated the slick, muddy log path from the donjon to the bailey, it was apparent they were following orders, and explanations had not been included.

Lightning struck so close Alison could smell it. The thunder was so loud she felt it. Despite herself, she cowered in Guy's arms. He held her steady. She could feel his body trembling—though he did not seem the sort to fear the elements.

"Quickly now," Hugh called, as if either of them needed any urging.

Then they were in the bailey-yard, splashing through the puddles past the stable lines. Alison moved too cautiously for Hugh, so he swooped her up and carried her to the sunken hut where she'd spent the previous night. Guy pulled the door open, and Hugh thrust her across the threshold before swiftly shutting the door.

If this was Lord Beauleyas's idea . . .

"Alison?"

Stephen's voice. Alison cast back her borrowed cloak as he stepped into the lamplight. They embraced, kissed until he winced, and she pulled back to study the dark shadow that spread beside his nose. Feather-light, she drew her fingertips across his injuries, appraising them as any healer might, until he caught her wrist and pulled her hand away.

"I hate him," she proclaimed. "I'll run away. I'll jump from the roof of the donjon—"

"It won't come to that," Stephen assured her.

"He's sending you to your death!"

He caught her other hand and gathered them both between his own: the symbol of fealty and protection from lord to vassal. "He's sending my cousin and me out to do what must be done. I am not blind to Eudo, but we will not take our quarrels beyond Torworden's gate. That would be both dangerous and dishonorable—"

"Don't be foolish, Stephen. He told me he did not expect you both to return—and he did not seem to care which of you killed the other."

Stephen's face grew hard with thoughts that led away from this moment, but he had taken some risk to be alone with his beloved and did not intend to waste precious time arguing about Eudo. Releasing her hands, he pulled her close and rested his unswollen cheek against her damp hair.

"I'm sure if I were going to die beneath Eudo's hand, Ambrose would take great pains to warn me. I'll hear no more of it tonight."

His fingers moved beneath her braids, loosening the laces at the neck of her tunic. His lips followed the curve of her cheekbone and chin until they rested against hers. When Alison was relaxed and no longer protesting he carried her through the straw to the box-bed and lay down beside her.

As bastardy was a Churchly sin of no great import to folk of either high or low birth, so virginity was a Churchly virtue and already nullified by the plight-troth they had sworn in the forest. Yet Alison could not give herself to any man—not even Stephen, who loved her.

Plight-troth or no, she captured his roving hand and let hot tears fall onto his neck.

With a sigh that shook his whole body, Stephen levered himself onto one elbow. "There is nothing to fear. No one shall come between us, I have sworn that," he said, smoothing her plaits against her ears. "I doubt, sometimes, that I am as firmly fixed in your heart as you are in mine."

Alison's tears turned to shame. She could be sure of Stephen; she had—as he said—fixed herself in his heart. Before Stephen had stumbled into Hafwynder Manor, all injured and mysterious, Alison had given few thoughts to love. She had trusted her father to sort through the shire swains who paid court in the great hall. She would say yea or nay, of course, but a man was the best judge of other men.

Since the plight-troth, Alison had seen that there was more to the bond between herself and Stephen than either her own meddling or love. She didn't love Stephen; she needed his love. The thought of him lying dead somewhere filled her with horror and sent cold tremors down her back.

The Cymric gods had accepted Stephen as her lover. They appeared in her dreams to praise him—then, invariably, the dreams became black nightmares. He was her hero, and she built a wall around her heart. Alison held Stephen's love—the love she had brought into being—at arm's length, knowing she must surrender it.

Stephen knew nothing of old gods or dreams. He only knew that he had hurt her with his words. Women were, after all, not like men. He caught her tears on his sleeve and directed dire thoughts toward the Englishmen who were so callous with their daughters that they were not taught to trust the men who cared for them. All of England would be better off when William got the island in hand. If he could make a good show of himself in the coming campaign, Stephen was certain the duke would overrule his uncle in the matter of Alison Hafwynder and her land.

They rested side by side, lost in their own thoughts, while the storm passed beyond Torworden. There was still thunder. They did not hear Hugh's knocking, and he had to push the door open.

"It's time."

Stephen grumbled something unpleasant in Greek he had learned from Ambrose, and pushed himself free of the straw.

"Do not worry about me," he commanded, giving her one last kiss before sending her to the donjon and his uncle.

"I must. Nothing must happen to you," Alison insisted, wresting herself free of his grasp.

He had not really expected her to say anything else. "I am no soft English lord to sit quiet on my lands counting my sheep," he warned her as he searched within his tunic for a pouch. "Still, if you must worry, hold this as a token of my love."

He put a small object in her hand. An earring—only one; the other had been sold during the journey to Torworden—that had long been in his father's family. The stone was not large, but it glowed with a rich, emerald fire in Alison's palm.

Green, she thought, unwilling to wrap her fingers around it as he expected her to do. "Dear God, Stephen—by all that you hold holy—"

Folding her fingers over the gemstone, Stephen tried unsuccessfully to hide his disappointment. Most men of his station, especially at his age, were not wealthy in possessions. A good sword, good armor, and a strong horse were more important than gold. He had not yet begun the campaigning that would lead to land and treasure. Yet the emerald was beautiful, and Alison had stared at it as if it might sprout legs like an insect.

He resented the way she spurned his gift, hooking it casually into her linen undertunic before taking up a sack of her clothes that lay in the straw. He remembered the warnings he'd had from Ambrose and thought to turn Alison out of his heart. Then she looked up at him, and he realized the pain of loving her was far less than the pain of losing her.

Hugh came into the hut and picked up another of the bundles. "We'll see her safely to the upper room," he said quickly.

Stephen said nothing as his men escorted his ladylove away. The thunderstorm had left a gentler rain in its waked. Gentle, but still winter-cold. He pulled his tunic high around his ears and scrambled toward the long barracks. It had been less than a week since he had pledged his love to Alison, barely a season since he had first met her, and though he would admit it to no one—not even admit it fully to himself—he welcomed the chance to leave Torworden.

Alison held her head high through the rain as they climbed the log path to the tower. She knew what the men with her must be thinking. They'd think less of her if they knew how the emerald burned against her skin.

The hall still echoed with raucous shouts and slurred proclamations. They ascended the interior stairs without attracting attention. Pleasant incense hung in the air; light outlined a wooden door at the top of the stairs. Alison clutched her sack tight as Hugh rapped on the door.

It swung open, revealing the first comfortable room Alison had seen since leaving Hafwynder Manor. Wool tapestries shrouded the walls; a hot brazier sat in a stout, sand-filled box; a washbasin sat on the sideboard, with steam rising from its depths.

"Saints and angels be praised," she whispered, taking a long stride into the room and letting her sack fall to the floor beside her.

"Good evening, Lady Alison."

She spun around to the feared and hated voice. Ambrose knelt amid an assortment of scrolls and manuscripts, some of which had already been placed in the chest at his side. Wildecent, looking guilty, sat on a stool beyond the chest. The finer details of the room—the images woven into the tapestry, the strange objects beside the washbasin—now caught Alison's attention.

"Lord Beauleyas suggested you might be more comfortable here," Ambrose said, rising to his feet.

"I . . . I don't want . . ." Alison remembered Hugh and Guy standing behind her. She didn't discuss magic in front of the head-blind, not at Hafwynder Manor and certainly not in a sorcerer's chamber.

Wildecent stood up and took the bundle Guy had carried from the hut. "Thank you for remembering my clothes," she interjected gracefully. "I'm sure, Alison, there is no better place in all Torworden for us to stay."

None of the men missed the duel between the sisters. Ambrose gathered his papers and shoved them into the chest, letting its lid slam shut as he joined the other two men beside the door. "I'm sure you'll rest comfortably here," he said, leading the masculine retreat.

"How could you!" Alison swore once the stairway was quiet.

"How could I what?"

"How could you agree to spend the night in *this* room?"

The smile on Wildecent's face was not a pleasant one. She scattered the contents of her sack across the bed with one violent shake, then turned to face her sister.

"Would you like the truth, dear sister? Shall I remind you that no one is fighting for *my* inheritance? No one makes rash promises to *me* in the greenwood. Shall I be my common, coarse, bastard self and remind you that I cannot choose much of anything, but must grab what passes my way like a drowning man? Or perhaps I should ask you how you came to be with Hugh and Guy. Why is your tunic so wet? Why is there straw sticking in your hair?"

Mortified, Alison reached for her plaits and removed

an offending bit of yellow grass. Then, satisfied that she had humbled her sister sufficiently, Wildecent purged the anger from her voice.

"Actually, it was much as Ambrose said, though he did not mention the village girls who joined us in the hall after you left. I think Lord Beauleyas finally realized he could not seat wenches beside us if he was to keep control over his men. Most of the men he has here have neither family nor fortune—and they are all a long way from home. I don't think he regrets bringing us here, but I suspect we'll see a lot of this room."

"It reeks of sorcery!"

"It reeks of sandalwood—I put the incense in the brazier myself."

"You know what I mean. It grieves me, Wili, to see you enrapt with a sorcerer. The Cymric gods do not abandon you merely because you cannot speak with them. They'll protect you—"

"They'll have their hands full protecting you from your three men, Alison. They won't have time for me. I've seen how we're watched. If I'm to be thrown to the wolves, I'm grateful to be caught by a wolf with clean hands."

Alison considered her sister's words, then knelt down to warm her hands over the brazier. "I am stretched and bent until I feel as though I will break. I wish you truly were my sister, Wili. I wish we truly shared everything. I feel so terribly alone."

"It would be different, but no better," Wildecent said coldly. "And I wonder, now, if any of our dreams could ever come true. I do not think even Lord Godfrey knew who my parents were or why they sent me away. Sooner or later it would have come to this, I think. I'm glad you have Stephen—but I must find my own course."

Wildecent meant to be firm, but not to show her bitterness. She meant to break the false bond of sisterhood between them but leave the threads of friendship intact. She couldn't begin to guess how Alison would feel, but she certainly hadn't expected her to burst into tears.

"I'd gladly give you Stephen," Alison sobbed, producing the emerald earring and holding it above the brazier.

Wildecent hid her hands in the folds of her skirt. "Stephen loves you, and you love him. Between the two of you, I expect you'll have your way in the end."

That brought more and louder tears. "He can't love anyone but me. And I don't want to love him—not anymore. I'll be the death of him."

Head-blind she might be, but Wildecent could tell when something was said for effect and when it contained a grain of unnatural truth. "Alison, what have you seen? Since Christmastide you've talked of blood and sacrifice. Until a week ago it was our lord fa— Lord Godfrey's death, now you're talking about Stephen the same way. What do you see when the madness comes over you?"

Childlike and guilty, Alison shuffled her feet and twisted her shoulders. She wanted to confess, but the images grew misty. The *geas* clamped down on her thoughts. Her eyes and limbs grew heavy. The emerald winked with seductive warmth; she clasped it onto her tunic again and went to the bed as if Wildecent had vanished from her world.

The dark-haired woman watched her go. If this were magic, she'd choose sorcery. Ambrose's eyes were never so unfocused. She pulled the muddy boots from Alison's feet and tucked the bedclothes around her. Her sister began to speak in a sleeper's voice, but Wildecent did not try to understand. She lowered the bedcurtains and left Alison to her strange, dreaming world.

Alone beside the brazier, Wildecent was drawn to the chest Ambrose had left unlocked. She had gotten a glimpse of the scrolls and manuscripts as they were tucked away. Most were in languages she did not recognize, much less understand; a few were in Latin, with which she had a halting familiarity, but none had been in English. Still, she lifted the lid and stirred through the scraps of parchment.

But while kneeling beside it she felt a draft and then, seeking its source, discovered a low passage behind the tapestry. She lit an oil-lamp from the brazier and crawled into Ambrose's inner sanctum; he had not, after all, forbidden them to explore his quarters. The sanctum was about the size of the bedroom, but austere and cold. A spider's-web dome of shining wire was suspended from the beams; a pattern of mind-addling complexity was drawn on the floor beneath it. Scattered along the walls were sacks of dirt, stones, scraps of cloth, miniatures of buildings, and machines whose purposes Wildecent could not guess. She remembered the *micros* Ambrose had constructed in the tower room at Hafwynder Manor and knew this was where he worked his major sorceries.

The wire web was elongated, dropping toward the floor at the northern limit of the circle. A cushion rested outside the complex pattern, showing where Ambrose knelt during his sorcery.

This is how Alison got into trouble, Wildecent reminded herself as she approached the cushion. *Tampering with Ambrose's sorcery. Leave it alone. If anything could be done, Ambrose should do it. I could ask him—he said he'd teach me . . .*

Her wisdom vanished in the drafts that pervaded the room and kept the wire basket in constant, shimmering motion. Wildecent touched an exposed wire, and got a lightninglike spark for her effrontery.

Get out of here, she told herself as she knelt down on the cushion. *You'll get hurt. But I didn't get hurt before. I saved Alison's life.* She recalled Alison's listless body lying in Ambrose's bed. *I should just ask him. He won't turn his back on Alison. He said he'd help her . . . if she wanted to set Stephen free. I think she wants to set him free now, but she can't.*

He'll know how to stop the Cymric gods. He could set them both free.

Wildecent stared at the floor. Her eyes followed the maze of lines, pausing at the symbols inscribed at some of its junctions. Alison and Lady Ygurna used herbs to achieve an ecstatic union with nature; Ambrose followed the paths he'd drawn with colored chalks and the shadows from the wires that hung over them. He also used a talisman and, remembering that she had no such object, Wildecent relaxed. Without a talisman she could work no sorcery.

The sanctum was peaceful in a way that churches or the bolt-hole at Hafwynder Manor were not. There was an emptiness here that allowed Wildecent to spread her worries and concerns over a larger area. She used the pattern on the floor to guide her. She imagined the bolt-hole at one juncture, with Alison and her aunt beside it. Those three intersections in the south—were they the three wood kings . . . or were they Stephen, Eudo, and Lord Beauleyas . . . or Lord Godfrey, Stephen, and . . . who? In the center, where the powder was thick, and glinted in the lamplight, was that Ambrose . . . or was that she?

Wildecent shook her head. She didn't want to think about Ambrose, at least not while she was thinking of Alison and blood sacrifices. A powerful gust of wind drove rain against the outside walls and set the wire trembling. The shadows moved, and Wildecent rocked back on her heels.

But it was too late. The hypnotic movements of the wire-cast shadows had her. Even her prayers and curses fell into its rhythms. She looked past the patterns, past the donjon into a dark, cramped hut where someone slept restlessly.

"Ambrose? Ambrose? Ambrose, I've made a terrible mistake. I didn't think anything could happen—"

Light came. Wildecent was not surprised to see the sorcerer sprawled on his back, his bare shoulders visible above the blankets.

"I'm sorry, Ambrose. I'll get this undone . . . somehow."

His lips parted. He seemed about to wake up when—
to Wildecent's utter horror and amazement—a ghostly
Ambrose separated from the sleeping figure. He held his
arms before him and made slow passes through the air.
He seemed to be reaching for her—and it seemed he could
not reach her.

"Ambrose, it's me—Wildecent. I'm sorry—"

"Wildecent?"

His eyes opened—very much his eyes, just as it was very
much his naked body. Wildecent averted her eyes, and
noticed as she did that she was also ghostly: faintly glowing, definitely naked. The glow turned pink.

"What haunts me?" Ambrose's eyes grew wider. He
made warding gestures with both hands. "Alison?
Ygurna? The green power of the forests?"

"No, me—*me*, Wildecent," she protested before realizing that he could not see and hear her. There was some
small comfort in that. "I'll leave. I'm trying to leave."

She thought it might actually be possible. She had tried
and found she could move, then she hit something—his
wardings—and now when Ambrose looked at her, Wildecent knew she was visible. She expected anger but what
was in his eyes was hardly anger.

"How did you come here?"

Suddenly he was no longer naked but clothed in rich
garments of black and silver. Wildecent felt her naked
image glow crimson. She did not have the power to clothe
herself, and Ambrose did not look away. She tried to
explain the tangle of thoughts that had brought the web
to life. At last he turned away from her.

"I should have known from the first," he said, more
to himself than to her. "You are too much like me. I
found the magi in much the same way." He shook his
head, remembering some private joke. "They had to take
me in . . . make me part of their brotherhood. I was too
much of a nuisance to leave outside. In that you are not
enough like me—I dare not bring you close."

CONQUEST

Wildecent reached out for him. She felt, rather than heard, his scream.

"Gods! Dear lady—have you no mercy?"

But Wildecent had felt it—a spark that shot through her insubstantial body: a sense of life, of ecstasy. She knew what he meant. Men and women could be sorcerers; they could live in the outer world—have lovers as they wished. But they were advised not to look to each other for such pleasures, for when sorcery wove through passion, the lovers might well lose their separate souls.

Ambrose threw up a barrier between them. The last thing Wildecent felt before a wind swept her back to her own body was his anguished denial: the triumph of the mind over the heart.

t was still raining the next morning. A ca-
pricious wind drove cold needles of moisture against Ambrose's face. He hurried
up the log steps of the motte.

The great hall was deserted except for a
hound, feasting on the dregs of dinner, and two ragged
Englishmen scrounging in advance of the hound. None
of the three noticed the fluttering drapery that marked
Ambrose's passing. He paused outside his room to remove his cloak and boots before pulling the latch-string.

Putting the women in the upper chamber of the donjon had not been Ambrose's idea—no matter what Alison chose to believe. When he had sworn his services to
Beauleyas, the Norman lord had, in turn, promised Ambrose privacy. The sorcerer wouldn't complain—not
aloud, anyway—but he meant to secure his possessions,
if it was not already way too late.

He expected the sisters would sleep late. His bed was
as comfortable as anything Hafwynder Manor had to offer, the tapestries kept the room quiet, and his sandalwood incense was not without its soporific qualities. He
put a lock on his manuscript chest, then raised the tapestry Wildecent had discovered the previous night. Once
inside his sanctum, Ambrose lowered behind him a panel
Wildecent had not discovered. Then he opened a high
clerestory shutter and checked the room for damage.

A pool of oil stained the floor where Wildecent had
dropped the lamp in her escape after their midnight encounter, but otherwise the room was undisturbed. Ambrose sighed; he had hoped for chaos. He studied his
basket of light: the wire and silk web suspended from the
ceiling. It had not even swung out of alignment with the
geometria inscribed on the floor. All was as he'd feared,
and he marveled that he had not suspected anything before.

The girl had used his talisman at Christmastide without

destroying either it or herself. His master in Byzantium might have been capable of such a feat; or his twin, if he'd had one—or the woman who fit snugly into all the hidden places of his heart.

He unknotted a length of red silk, removed a silver wire from the basket of light, and twisted the wire around his finger. The dome wouldn't work for him until he replaced it—and shouldn't work for Wildecent. Then he closed the shutter. Unless they were very observant they'd never know he'd come back to his chamber—and if they did notice, he hoped they'd take it as a warning.

The practice arena was deserted. Not even the most dedicated Norman chose to improve his skill in such miserable weather. A few men congregated in the stableyard tending their horses, a few more could be heard laughing and swearing in the long barracks. Most of them, including Beauleyas and all those who would ride out with Stephen and Eudo, had gone down to the village to be shriven.

The Normans and their companions gave only passing thought to their souls. The wealthier among them bought salvation when they endowed a church, but the rest attended to their sins only at the start of the campaigning season or other holy days. The men of Torworden had caroused until dawn, then staggered off in search of a priest.

Ambrose had never confessed his sins. It did not seem likely that a man who raised the spirits of the dead could only be absolved by a superstitious parish priest. If he needed to be absolved at all.

He headed for the jumble of huts and stalls outside the bailey gate. Torworden was an enigma on the English landscape. Jean Beauleyas had wrought changes all along this stretch of the Windraes, but he had not induced the families of the nearby village of Lachebroc to settle within sight of his walls.

Artisans, farmers, and tradesmen had been drawn by the needs of forty-odd men. They came each day to the gate to offer their services and vanished each night to live with their own kind. The Torworden men had to go outside for everything they could not, or would not, do for themselves. Ambrose got his bread at a ramshackle hut and would have stopped at a fuller's stall to have the dirt brushed from his cloak if it had not been raining.

Pondering the twists of fate that had brought him from the magi of Byzantium to the rain-slick cartways of England, Ambrose left the nameless day-village behind. Asia Minor was not immune to bad weather, but it was not a place where rainy, overcast skies were the norm. Good weather was God's weather here in England. Nothing grew in the Mediterranean world that could compare to the greens of England's forests and fields, but by Ambrose's careful calculations there were four miserable days for every clear one.

With the world constricted to a circular patch seen through his cloak's hood, Ambrose wondered—and not for the first time—why his masters had pointed him westward to complete his education. A stone turned under his heel, and he skidded to one knee before regaining his balance. He stopped dreaming of sunshine and watched his footing more carefully.

Ambrose left the cartway for a steep footpath a bit before the river-straddling village of Lachebroc. A staff would have been useful, this final leg of his journey, but he reached the ruins of a hermit's rectangular cell without falling. He and Stephen had discovered the stone cell shortly after their arrival at Torworden the past August. They each had other retreats now, but the hermitage was still their favorite whenever life at Torworden became unbearable.

Huddled into a corner, Ambrose let his mind escape into contemplation of alchemic transformations—specifically the one producing dry heat. Stephen would find him eventually.

"You look absolutely miserable, my friend," Stephen

began sometime later when, fresh from the Lachebroc church, he stumbled into the hermitage.

Ambrose hadn't expected to be discovered until much later in the day; he suspected his friend had been looking to get away by himself also. As always, Stephen disdained a cloak's protection. His hair was plastered against his face; his cheeks were red and his words made wispy clouds between them. Ambrose, by contrast, had managed to dry the inner layers of his clothing and was almost comfortable. "Not so miserable as you," he retorted.

"Ah, you should have seen me earlier this morning. The wine had flowed freely since sunset—"

"Spare me."

"Make room on the bench?"

Ambrose shifted around so they both could sit in the shelter, though his legs were once again exposed to the cold rain.

"Don't suppose you could start a fire for us?"

The sorcerer cast a withering look. "If I could start a fire, you don't think I'd need you to suggest it, do you?"

"You said you never stop learning."

"For a man who's been on his knees baring his sins and soul to his God, you're in extraordinarily good spirits. I don't suppose you could be persuaded to take them elsewhere?"

Stephen shrugged, but his smile faded. "I'd been shriven before I left for Pevensey at Christmastide. I haven't had much opportunity for sinning since then."

"Opportunity or desire?"

The young knight sighed, a steamy exhalation that left him hunched over and morose. "God knows what's happened to me since then," he conceded, "but not any priest. She loves me, Ambrose, I swear it. She's given me her troth—" The sorcerer raised his eyebrows and Stephen looked down at his feet before continuing. "But not as I love her," he admitted.

"You don't really love her." Ambrose paused. "Not freely."

Stephen hid his face in his left hand and parried Ambrose's words with his right. "You don't understand. You're right—but you don't understand. It is because I *do* love her. What's done is done. I realized that last night. She's run rampant through my memories; I see her in places she's never been, doing things she will not do—does it please you to hear me admit that?—but I can't bear the thought of losing her."

"We should leave this place, Stephen; leave England altogether. There're other places to win a name and fortune. We could go to Sicily. Surely there's a place there for two sell-swords . . ."

"Two?" Stephen asked, lowering his hand.

Ambrose nodded.

"You'd set aside your sorcery?"

Ambrose nodded again, wondering if Stephen would ask why; wondering how he would answer if Stephen did. But there was only silence, and silence made him uneasy. "I can," he said defensively.

"Set aside sorcery or take up a sword?"

"Both—if necessary."

Stephen leaned back. "Hmm, you're fast enough with your damned Greek sword, and you ride well enough. You're as good an archer as I am—we've proved that often enough—but you can't ride and fight at the same time—and you don't know the first thing about a lance—"

"I'll learn!"

Stephen shook his head. "Too late. I learned to fight; you learned to read—"

"And you could learn to read if you wanted to."

"You're serious, aren't you?" the younger man said, as much to himself as to his friend. "You want out of here that bad, and you want to be done with sorcery?" He looked into the rain, piecing things together before he looked back at Ambrose's face. "What's happened to *you?*"

Ambrose recalled what Wildecent had awakened within him. He sought words to describe it, but there were none in any of his languages. When he finally spoke he touched only the very edges of his turmoil. "If I do not leave soon, I fear I may never leave. I have no defense against the magic of this land."

"Of the land or of the woman? I *did* notice Wildecent last night."

"They are not sisters, you know. At first I felt sorry for her—"

"At first?"

"She grew up with Allison . . . and Ygurna. They told her of magic but denied her the practice. Of course there is some attraction—"

Stephen laughed and shoved Ambrose's shoulder. *"Deus aie!* I grew up around you and I never felt the least attraction! So, you've finally found yourself a woman. It's about time." Then, more confidentially, "You're not breaking any vows, are you?"

The sorcerer could not suppress a grim smile. "No, no vows. But a man like myself must be very careful. And I was not careful at all."

"No one's going to stop you from marrying her, like you said—they aren't sisters. You aren't going to have to fight your kin for her."

"I could become obsessed by her. There would be nothing else in my world except her. I could starve and not care so long as she was with me."

Stephen understood that feeling; it gnawed in his gut even as they talked. "Do you think leaving England would solve our problems?" he asked.

"I cannot see how leaving would make them worse."

For several moments Stephen stared at the trees. He felt the grief of leaving Alison—the empty places in his memories—and knew in time the grieving and mourning would fade, as it always did when the living kept on living. Then he shook his head. "Not now," he whispered. "It's more than Alison, Ambrose. It's my honor, my name. I'd be leaving her to Eudo or my lord uncle himself. I can't leave until I know I won't be abandoning her."

"She is what they call *witegestre,* Stephen, a priestess of these forests—a witch. You might abandon her, but I do not think she will be abandoned."

Now Ambrose had pushed the matter too hard. Stubbornness and pride hardened Stephen's face. "You can go; I give you leave to go back to France, or Sicily, or Byzantium if that's what you want, but I will stay until Alison and her lands are safe."

"You have forgotten your homeland."

"Haven't you?"

They sat listening to the rain. Ambrose was wet to the skin, cold to the bone; he had not forgotten Byzantium, but he could conjure none of its warmth in his mind. He willed himself to ignore the coldness in his hands and feet. His will broke, and a shiver ran along his spine. "I gave my word to your father that I would help you so long as we both lived—"

"Cheer up, then," Stephen said, punching Ambrose's shoulder again. "If my cousin has his way, you'll be on a ship for France before the trees are full green." It had been a jest; men always laughed when they could not feel heroic, but the humor was lost on the sorcerer. Stephen stared at Ambrose's sodden hood, unable to see his friend's face. "I'm not going to die, am I, Ambrose?" he asked in a tight, boyish voice. "You'd know if I were going to die, wouldn't you?"

Ambrose shook his head. The hood fell back and they looked into each other's eyes. "So long as I remain here I will not look into the future, Stephen—not even to see tonight's supper. But I will know if you are ever in danger, and I will do what I can to help you."

"*Deus aie,* how did it come to this?" Stephen asked, not expecting an answer, and not getting one either. He waited until a frigid trickle of water slid past his collar before jumping to his feet. "If there are no answers, my friend, then there's no use in sitting out here in the rain . . ."

Ambrose managed a weak smile as he got to his feet and pulled his hood around his face again.

"And, if you're not peeking at the future, then you don't know which of us will get to Lachebroc first. But I say the one who gets to the millrace last buys ale enough for both of us!"

Stephen was off, whooping and shouting as he crashed through the trees. Ambrose hesitated; the gap between them felt far wider than seven years. He grabbed a winter-killed sapling, thinking he'd best have a staff to negotiate the steep path. He felt weary, exhausted . . . *old*. And suddenly he could not let Stephen beat him to the millrace. Sweeping the heavy cloak under one arm, he plunged recklessly down the slope after his friend.

"He's been here," Wildecent said. It was almost midday and the sisters were just getting dressed.

"How do you know?" Alison looked around the chamber, unable to see that anything had changed until Wildecent pointed out the lock on the manuscript chest and the tapestry, which, when she turned it up, revealed a solid panel rather than the crawlway she remembered. "Why should he care about a piece of cloth?" Alison asked.

"I don't know," Wildecent lied.

"Well, it must mean something. He came seeking in here while we were still sleeping. We'll have to check if he's set some sort of trap for us—"

"He wouldn't do that, Alison," the dark-haired girl insisted. "He's not petty."

Alison let the laces drop from her fingers. "Don't get involved with him, Wildecent. No matter what good you think might come from it, don't meddle with sorcery," she said in a voice that was more pleading than angry. "It may be that we can no longer be as sisters but, please, don't meddle with him. The price is way too high . . ."

Wildecent turned away. *Little do you know, dear sister. Little do you know.*

he weather had cleared by the next morning. Alison and Wildecent stood at Ambrose's window and watched the men ride north from Torworden. It did not promise to be a dangerous journey; they wore mail hauberks, but they laughed and rode easy in their saddles. They'd be gone about a fortnight, following the Windraes until it met the Roman road they called the Foss Way, then northeast into the old Danelaw where Hardrada and Tostig would have spies if they had spies at all.

Alison remained at the window, fumbling with the neck edge of her linen tunic, after Wildecent had gone back to mending a tear in her sleeve.

The garrison had been reduced by half. Torworden was rarely quiet but it became more relaxed as the fair weather held. Men tended their horses and lazed in the sun, enjoying their rest at the start of what promised to be a long campaigning season. A message had arrived from William of Normandy; Lord Beauleyas had Ambrose read it aloud in the hall. The duke was gathering men, hiring ships, and buying supplies, but he would not land in England before he had secured the pope's blessing. The men rolled their eyes—few things were as slow as the Papal Curia.

They took more care with their armor and their swords after that. Harald Hardrada wouldn't wait for the pope. And if Harald swept down from the North, Torworden would muster with the English. Harold Godwinson might have two enemies in William of Normandy and Harald Hardrada of Denmark—but that didn't make Harald and William allies. But if Beauleyas led his men with Godwinson against Hardrada, what would he do when William finally set sail for England?

The dilemma made Torworden's lord irritable and he shared his ire with everyone. Norman honor would best be served by heroic death in a battle vanquishing Harald of Denmark and critically weakening Harold of England—but no man wanted to die.

Alison felt the ambient nervousness. Her command of Norman French improved each night as she sat on her stool beside Jean Beauleyas. He explained his dilemma, but she had no thought for honor, only for the peaceful life at Hafwynder Manor that seemed inexorably doomed. She fretted about everything: her father, Stephen, the manorfolk, her own fate, and the nightmares that were becoming worse, until everything was one thing and it gave her no peace.

She did not confide in Wildecent. Her foster sister was firmly in the sorcerer's shadow, though Alison watched them closely and noted they derived no pleasure from each other's company. They ate little from their shared plates and looked past each other when they conversed. In other times she might have sought her sister and comforted her—even though she loved a sorcerer—but in these times Alison had no strength for anyone but herself.

The two women were together constantly, however. Jean Beauleyas wanted it that way. They did their sewing under watchful, masculine eyes and were confined to the donjon and bailey. For nine interminable days the young women dwelt in their separate, anguished worlds. At dawn of the tenth day the walls between them shattered.

Alison burst from her nightmare. The *geas* had weakened; images lingered after her eyes were open. In her right hand she held a sickle, in her left, a man's head. There was warm blood running down her arms, and nothing within the dark confines of the bed could convince her otherwise. With a guttural wail, Alison thrashed through the curtains and shook the nonexistent blood onto the floor.

Wildecent looked up from the far side of the brazier.

Each was disheveled and vulnerable in the ruddy light. Each retreated behind defensive, empty masks that revealed nothing. Then slowly each realized she had not been caught by the other.

"I had a dream," Alison admitted.

"I couldn't sleep."

"I keep having the same nightmare over and over again. Each time it lasts a little longer; I get a little closer to the end."

Wildecent pulled a stool closer to the brazier so Alison might sit, if she chose. "I'd guessed as much," she said slowly.

"I make the hero's sacrifice to fertilize the land."

"I'd guessed that, too."

"With my own hands. I can feel the blood, but I can't see his face . . . yet."

"Maybe once you do, you'll know how to stop it."

"Maybe." Alison came closer to the brazier, then wearily sat down on the manuscript box. "Why couldn't you sleep?" she asked, more to fill the silence between them than from any curiosity.

"I guess I don't want to dream either."

"The hero's sacrifice?" the blond woman asked, feeling her heart start to pound, but Wildecent shook her head. "Ambrose? I—I have noticed you together. I should have . . . I didn't."

Wildecent looked up from the brazier. "Oh, Alison, can't you put that out of your mind?" But her voice was flat and her eyes were empty. "Ambrose isn't stealing my soul any more than he ever stole Stephen's."

"But—I *felt* sorcery. I did, Wili. There was something dark and heavy . . ."

"Stephen was seven years old—and he had a habit of running away from his tutor. Who got in trouble when *we* weren't where we were supposed to be, Alison? How often did Edwina get a beating instead of us? Ambrose marked Stephen so he could find him when he went hiding. Tell me you wouldn't do the same."

Alison plucked at the loose stitching of her sleeve and chewed her lip before answering. "You believe him?"

Wildecent nodded. "And you? Has he marked you so you won't get lost?"

"No, he hasn't. He couldn't—even if he wanted to."

"Our magic—the pure, wild magic of the forests and of the moon protects you?" Alison asked almost eagerly, unable to surrender her distrust of sorcery.

Wildecent got to her feet and strode to the other side of the brazier's pool of light. "I don't know why I even talk to you, Alison. You never listen. You're the one who goes around leaning on a person's thoughts; twisting their memories around. Ambrose can't do things with a *thought* the way you do. He has to plan; he has to have a reason. There's almost nothing wild about sorcery."

"Almost?"

Almost—but that *almost* lay like a sword between Wildecent and Ambrose. It kept Wildecent awake at night with the ache of knowing he, too, couldn't sleep. "We, Ambrose and I, are too much alike," Wildecent explained, choosing her words carefully. "We cannot be near the unrevealed world together. There would be too much . . . passion. We would lose ourselves in each other and"—she brought her hands together with a loud clap—"it would be over. I would not care for myself, I think, but he has so much to lose. We dare not even touch each other, for fear of what the spark might ignite. Sorcerers, it seems, may not love."

Alison recognized in Wildecent's voice the same morbid certainty she heard in her own thoughts. For the first time, she also heard the absurdity. "Don't be such a goose," she spat quickly. "Love and passion are the heart of magic—"

"Not magic, sorcery. Sorcery is order and reason. It stands opposed to nature."

"Then sorcery is a blind fool!"

Alison marveled at her own conclusion. With the *geas* exposed, it no longer mattered whether sorcery and magic were fundamentally opposed or fundamentally the same. All that mattered was that sorcery might free her from the obligations of her promise to the gods. Not that she would ever use sorcery, of course—there were still some thoughts that were simply unthinkable—but Wildecent might be induced to help.

"I believe I have been wrong," Alison began, catching Wildecent's attention immediately. "Magic and sorcery are different, but they do not need to be opposed to each other."

Wildecent considered Alison's sudden change of heart with evident distrust—but she considered it all the same.

"Now we know you have no aptitude for magic," Alison continued. "Yet you cannot learn sorcery because magic's passion stands between you and Ambrose. And because I did not understand the cold nature of sorcery, I overreacted to its presence in Stephen's thoughts."

Wildecent was not lulled by Alison's facile logic, and told her so with a dark glance.

Alison abandoned subtlety. "I can help you, Wili. I can give you a charm that will hold you and him safe from passion, but I'll need something in return."

"What?" Wildecent replied suspiciously.

"I need your help to protect Stephen from my dreams." Alison removed the emerald earring from her sleeve.

"Why turn to me? If you want to protect Stephen, talk to Ambrose."

Alison shook her head; she could not tell the sorcerer that this had all begun as a moment's jealousy. Her motives had been pure enough when she'd begun her quest through Stephen's memories, determined to free him from sorcerous domination—pure, even if incorrect. But Alison had been piqued to see that the women of the young knight's fantasies all looked more like Wildecent than her . . . and so she'd changed them. Not for love of Stephen, or for his love, but because he fancied small-boned, dark-haired women.

And if Ambrose would get angry because of her original motives, Alison knew he'd be justly furious when he learned that even now she wanted to set him free not to spare him—she did not, in her heart of hearts, believe he could escape her *geas*—but because she did not want his blood on *her* hands.

"You're the one I trust, Wili," she said finally.

"I'm no sorcerer, Alison. Ambrose and I—we've talked about sorcery, but he hasn't taught me anything."

Alison surged to her feet. "I trust you; I know you can do it. We're helping each other, just like we always used to." She put her heart into her words, but she followed them with a twist of her magic. *I'm sorry, Wili, I truly am—but I need your help.*

Magic rushed around Wildecent like a flooding stream. She could have fought it, but this time it was easier to move with it. "And, in turn, you'll give me what I need?"

Alison nodded.

They were sisters again. Laughter radiated from Ambrose's chamber, but it was shrill and born of a need to trust rather than any recapturing of trust. Ambrose had told Wildecent many of his secrets and, though he had not shown her how to work the panel to his sanctum, she knew where the lever was. She poked, prodded, pinched, and wriggled until the panel slid back, and she led Alison through the low door.

"What is that?" Alison asked as Wildecent cranked the ceiling open and light fell onto the web of wire.

"He calls it a 'basket of light'; it concentrates the power of sorcery."

Some similarity existed between magic and sorcery, Alison realized. She also cast a circle to concentrate magic's power, marking its perimeter with salt, water, and ashes before inviting the Cymric gods to share it with her. She had no need of wires, chalk, or silk, but she understood why Wildecent would take a position at the northern edge and instruct her to take the emerald to the center.

"I don't think this will work—" Wildecent settled under the point of the web but did not complete her thought.

"I have power within me," Alison reminded her. "Surely that is better than any cold crystal."

Wildecent gave a tentative nod. "To begin: concentrate on the image." Her hands began to shake and sweat. "Bring Stephen's face into the emerald . . . No. No, Alison. I cannot; I don't know what words to use. Something's missing. I don't want to go on." She began to rise.

"It's all right, Wili," Alison commanded. "You are the anchor; I will be the seeker."

"No. No, Alison—" But Wildecent did not have the strength to resist her sister's suggestions.

Alison knelt beneath the high arc of the basket of light. Her eyes were closed and the emerald caught the dawning sun in her cupped hands. Wildecent felt something shimmer through the wire tracery above and between them. Sparks and streaks of lambent green shot from the earring to the wire matrix. First Alison, then Wildecent, were swallowed in an emerald aura that sang against the basket of light.

Stephen rode on Eudo's left. A lance was balanced in his right stirrup although the surrounding forest was quiet. Too quiet. He was not alone in his unease as he rolled his gloved fingers across the rough haft of the lance. They all felt it, even Eudo, whose face glistened with sweat beneath his helm and coif.

"I feel eyes on our back," Eudo muttered, glancing away from the road.

"If there are, I wish they'd show themselves."

"I wish we could see more than a man's length into those damned trees."

Stephen bit his lip. It went against his grain to agree with Eudo, but he did agree. The English forests were forbidding in ways he could not describe. They were darker and wilder than they should be; they dominated the deteriorating Roman road. *Hwiccawudu* this forest was called; in English, Wychwood, the Wise Forest or the Witch's Forest.

He thought of Alison, and told himself there was no need for worry. They'd be at Torworden the day after tomorrow. They'd found no spies in the Danelaw. The worst of the journey was over.

They crested a hill and were confronted by a fallen tree blocking the road. They guided their horses into the stump-side of the forest.

Stephen heard a war cry and turned around to see a heavy net descend over the middle men of their column. He had a moment to wonder who had ambushed them; then he was surrounded and fighting for his life. Reflexes that had been hammered into his limbs took command. His shoulder dropped as he lifted the lance. His shield swung forward on its guige and his left hand grasped its enarmes before the lance was couched beneath his right arm. He took note of the weapons he faced: axes, single and double; the armor: inferior to his own; and his first target: a footman about to put his double-bit ax in a man still trapped by the net.

He came in from the side, ramming a man-width of iron-sheathed wood between the enemy's ribs; he let the falling corpse twist the lance free, and, with a shout of encouragement to his comrades, spurred Sulwyn about to face another assault. He couldn't count the men they faced or realize that there were, perhaps, too many for them to overcome, but his heart was pounding and he was praying as he lowered the bloody lance.

This one wore a hauberk similar in style to his own but constructed of leather scales and metal rings rather than dense chain links. He fairly ran onto the lance, but his scaled hauberk fouled the barbs, and the lance-head could not be withdrawn. Stephen thrust the useless weapon away, drew his sword, and kept Sulwyn pivoting.

The English battle-ax was a formidable weapon against the sword—even if the swordsman was mounted and the axman was on foot. Stephen gasped for breath and waited for someone to close with him.

He heard Eudo cry out, and the scream of his horse as it went down. He tried to get closer to his cousin, and they closed on him with a rush.

The sword's advantage was its mobility, its thrust, and its long, deadly edges; its disadvantage—against the ax—was a lack of power. A solid cut from an ax could do more damage than a similar cut from a sword, though a single sword-stroke in the right place would kill a man. Stephen kept his sword arm moving, deterring the axmen from committing their heavy weapons, waiting for the right moment.

It came. He brought the sword down and felt the shock as it bit deep into the enemy's unprotected neck. The bearded man dropped, and Stephen wrenched his sword free.

Eudo was swinging his sword double-handed and using the death throes of his horse to keep his back clear. Three men lay in the dirt around him; one writhed in agony; the other two were motionless.

The Normans acquitted themselves with the cold ferocity for which they were justly feared. All but three of the trapped men had cut their way loose. More than a dozen of the ambushers were dead or dying. It wasn't enough; the ambushers had archers with them as well. Arrows skidded off the chain mail or snagged in the felted padding beneath it.

The men of Torworden kept their vulnerable faces down and were slowly, individually pushed deeper into the forest. Here branches grabbed at the swirling swords; hidden roots tripped the war-horses. Stephen's style grew desperate; he and Sulwyn bled from a half-dozen minor wounds.

He backhanded the sword across an enemy's face and was, for a heartbeat, revolted by his own brutality. He lost awareness for an instant—when he regained it, he was looking at death. He couldn't parry the downward arc of the ax; it was going to hit something.

Stephen was not aware of driving his spurs into Sulwyn's flanks.

The horse reared. The ax came down in its shoulder and rose out of the axman's hands. Stephen dropped his feet from the stirrups and kicked free of the collapsing horse.

Reflex. Reflex and training. He couldn't hear himself screaming or feel the tears streaming down his cheeks. He charged the disarmed enemy, impaling him. That was a mistake: in the moments it took him to pull the sword free, pain shot across his back.

His shield was useless. He tried to shake it loose but his arm was slow. When his enemy grabbed it, it came free. The inside was brilliant with blood.

It's over, Stephen thought as he scrabbled backward, as pain gave way to a numbness no amount of discipline or will could overcome. *I'm dead.*

The green aura within the basket of light flashed crimson and began to churn malevolently. The women were caught in the sorcerous and magical wind. Wildecent tucked her head to her knees and Alison cried out.

Stephen!

Deep in the Wychwood, Stephen heard his name; heard Alison's voice. The sword was heavy in his hands, its point wobbled as he drew himself up for a final defense. The enemy was careless, already gloating. The young man had the satisfaction of knowing he would not die alone as the ax crashed through the ribs.

Stephen!

Alison fell to her knees beside him. Blood flowed from the corners of his mouth; his breath came in horrible gasps that rattled through the gaping wound. Alison's healer's reflexes were as deeply ingrained as any warrior's. She would watch him die. It wouldn't take long. She pushed his helmet back; there was no recognition in his eyes. He was already past any awareness of pain. He'd be dead before she'd begun to cry.

"What are you waiting for?"

Alison looked up into her sister's merciless eyes.

"Shall England survive? Shall we have a new king?"

It wasn't Wildecent, though Morrigan with her tangled black hair and her bloodstained robes resembled Wildecent. The only bright aspect of the goddess was the delicate silver sickle, which she placed in Alison's hand.

"What you have nurtured in love must be reaped in blood!"

Morrigan's fingers wove through air; Alison's fingers moved in harmony, reaching beneath Stephen's coif. Another figure joined them, a man as green as Morrigan was crimson. He had no head, but his gaping neck did not bleed.

"Give the king life!"

Alison pulled Stephen's head across her thigh, exposing the pale flesh of his neck. He was already dying—nothing worse could be done to him, and something of the England she loved would survive. She brought the edge of the sickle against his neck. Beads of blood seeped up where the supernaturally sharp silver touched his flesh. The necessary stroke would be gentle, like cutting water, and clean.

A shudder wracked his body. Dark blood flowed from his lips.

"Now!"

"No!"

She flung the sickle at the goddess and shoved Stephen's mangled corpse to the ground. The headless green man flailed the air before him. He dropped to his knees; his hands smeared across Stephen's face. But the sacrifice had not been made, and an ominous wailing filled the forest.

Alison crawled past Sulwyn and began to run.

he forest sounds pursued Alison. They changed as she ran, becoming the clang of an assembly gong. She embraced the noise, expecting it to pull her back to Hafwynder Manor. Instead she found herself in an unfamiliar room.

When she saw Wildecent, curled up at the edge of a sorcerer's circle, she recalled Torworden, and then everything came back. She had succumbed to sorcery. Images of Stephen's death in her arms, of crimson-streaked Morrigan, and the headless Green King hovered in her mind's eye. At least Alison hoped they were merely images placed there by the Cymric gods to chasten a rebellious priestess. She prayed they were not real memories of real events—but she did not know where to direct her prayers.

Alison reached out. There were crimson smears on her hands and tunic. Fresh blood. Stephen's blood. She stared at the marks, willing them to vanish, but they were very real.

"Wili!" she croaked. "Wildecent!"

Dark braids brushed over the chalk; hazel eyes looked up. Wildecent's hands and clothes were unstained, but she remembered everything. They groped toward each other; a sprig of holly fell to the planking between them.

"It was a dream," Wildecent whispered, stroking Alison's blond hair. "A nightmare. It didn't happen."

"Stephen's dead!"

"No. No he's not. It wasn't real. It didn't happen."

"Look at me, Wili. *Look at me!*" Alison pushed away from her sister and spread her arms. The blood had not, would not, disappear.

The gong still clanged. Men were running up the stairway to assemble on the guard-porch that surrounded Ambrose's chambers. It did not seem possible to either horror-struck woman that their misadventure could endanger Torworden itself. But then, it did not seem possible that it had happened at all.

"We've got to get out of here," Wildecent hissed.

Alison obeyed silently, crawling back to the bedroom. Wildecent cast a glance around the room. Nothing was amiss or out of place except the holly. She refused to speculate where it had come from, but she snatched it up before she blew out the lamp. By the time Wildecent returned to the bedroom, Alison had stripped to her linen shift, and was rasping at the bloodstains on her hands.

"I killed him," she repeated in rhythm with her rubbing. "I killed him."

"You didn't kill Stephen," Wildecent assured her, taking the coarse wool away.

The ruckus outside grew louder, but nothing intelligible penetrated the walls. Whatever was going on had everyone's attention. Wildecent allowed herself the hope that it was Stephen himself returning to give the lie to all she and Alison had witnessed.

"Get dressed," she urged Alison, thrusting a clean tunic into her hands.

Alison opened her mouth to argue just as someone put a fist to their door. She wasn't hysterical enough to greet someone in her linen, and hastily wriggled into the tunic. It slid down past her shoulders as Ambrose pushed the door open.

"Alison, Wildecent—you'd best . . ."

Wildecent pulled her sister's laces tight, but the sorcerer wasn't looking at them. The tapestry concealing the door to his sanctum had been left askew, but even that didn't hold his attention for long. Alison's clothes lay where she'd left them; the red stains were plainly visible.

"What have you done?" he demanded. Both women stood mute, and he repeated the question as he grabbed Alison's discarded tunic and touched the stain. He put his finger to his lips, then threw the cloth to the floor.

"You damned, abominable fools!"

His rage was more controlled than most men's, and all

the more frightening because he did not shout. He glared at Wildecent; she felt her heart sink. Alison looked away but he grasped her jaw and forced her to look at him.

Alison had never met anyone who was stronger than she was—not in an arcane sense. Until the coming of the Normans she'd never met anyone whose mind she couldn't manipulate. She never gave a thought to mental defenses because she'd never needed them. Ambrose's cold fingers, and the willpower marshaled behind his eyes, revealed a new dimension of fear to her.

"Tell me!" he commanded.

The whole misadventure, from the very beginning to the disaster in the grove, poured out of Alison's memory. He released her, but she had relived it all in a few heartbeats and leaned against the bed.

"Priestess? Do not flatter yourself. You're a spoiled child, a conniving pawn. You don't know yet that you've been used. A common murderer has more conscience than you!"

Alison slumped forward, and Wildecent rushed to catch her. "She didn't kill him, Ambrose. It was a dream," the dark-haired girl insisted despite her sister's stained tunic.

He was unmoved. "I'll deal with both of you later. For now I'm to escort you to the bailey-yard, where you'll welcome the caravan from Hafwynder Manor. And you'll act as if none of this has happened—do you understand?"

It was an impossible request, but both women nodded obediently.

"And let me assure you"—Ambrose took Alison's face between his hands again—"dear lady, it is not finished. Your blundering witcheries will not succeed. I will fight your damned bloody gods and your headless green kings if I must. But know this right now: your sacrifice failed; your king has no face and Stephen is *not* dead!"

His tone was as cruel as he could make it—and that was cruel indeed. It brought a flood of tears from Alison's eyes, and wracking sobs from her throat. She tried to get her arms around him, but he eluded her.

"The bailey-yard!" he commanded, giving them both a shove toward the door.

Wildecent stayed at her sister's side, still supporting her. They made their way down the steep stairs with the outraged sorcerer at their heels.

"He's alive!" Alison gasped, relying entirely on Wildecent to guide her. She missed a step, and both women lurched against the inner wall. "It can be undone."

Alison was pale and came down the log pathway slowly, but knowing that Stephen's death was not irrevocable was a powerful tonic. Bright sunlight and fresh air restored her strength. She was smiling when they reached the bailey.

There were only three carts, each pulled slowly by a team of oxen. Bethanil sat in the first, her pots and pans piled high behind her and her drudges walking stolidly beside the oxen. The second cart was covered and held the manor's treasure. The third carried personal possessions, including the baskets from the bolt-hole. Each cart was driven by a Hafwynder man. Greetings had been exchanged and the carts had passed under the stockade lintel before either sister realized something was terribly wrong.

All three Torworden men—Alan FitzAlan, Serlo, and Gauche-Robert—rode behind the carts. FitzAlan had the reins of a fourth horse tied to his saddle. The man on the fourth horse was not Godfrey Hafwynder but Thorkel Longsword, and he rode backward with his legs tied together beneath the horse's belly. Alison surged forward to demand an explanation, but FitzAlan would speak only with his lord.

"I bear witness to a crime," FitzAlan proclaimed once Beauleyas approached.

"He murdered our lord!" Bethanil shouted in plainer language that was echoed among the other English.

"Had you a reason?" Beauleyas demanded, while Alison struggled to get closer to the conversation.

"Not I, my lord, but the Viking. He struck Lord Godfrey's head from his shoulders not three days after his daughters had left." FitzAlan spoke clearly so all in the yard could hear him.

"Cut the Viking free and bring him forward," Beauleyas commanded.

A pathway was cleared and Alison was able to push her way to the edge of the crowd. She looked into Thorkel's face and knew the accusation was true. Hissing like a cat, fingers hooked and teeth showing, Alison launched herself at the murderer, but Ambrose caught her before anyone else was aware of her attack. His fingers probed the hollows beneath her ears and Alison found herself unable to move.

"There'll be no more bloodshed from you, my lady, not for any reason." He relaxed his grip somewhat—she could breathe and swallow normally—but a light pressure remained, and she dared not move against his wishes.

"Do you admit your crime?" Jean Beauleyas inquired in English. "Do you admit the murder of Godfrey Hafwynder, lord of Hafwynder Manor?"

The tall, blond Viking had suffered during the journey. His clothes were torn. A purple contusion swelled the right side of his face. He must have lost a few teeth as well, for he spoke with difficulty. But he spoke defiantly.

"I served my lord as he would be served. He was felled when Edward died, and should have accompanied his king into the next world. The gods cried out for the blood they had been denied, and I gave it to them."

Pagan practices persisted everywhere, but they were never mentioned aloud. The gathering in the bailey at Torworden drew its collective breath. For Alison the shock struck more slowly. Thorkel Longsword might cast his prayers to Thor, Odin, and that ilk, but his prayers had been *heard* by the ancient Cymric gods.

Alison kicked Ambrose in the shin and broke free, only

to find Wildecent holding her back. "They took my lord father," she cried, her words lost in the general tumult as Jean Beauleyas pondered justice in the matter. "It's my fault. I would not give them Stephen so they took my lord father instead!"

"Thorkel Longsword murdered our lord father," Wildecent insisted. "Murdered!"

"Because I refused to give them Stephen!"

"Didn't you understand FitzAlan? Our lord father was slain weeks ago. It has nothing to do with us or with Stephen. It's not our fault."

Alison quivered and stared coldly at her foster sister. Head-blind; even though she had witnessed all that had happened in the grove, Wildecent was still head-blind. The gods were not constrained by mortal notions of time. They could make a heartbeat last forever or age a man in a single night. They could fold time back on itself so all days were endlessly alike. Or they could rip time apart until no one could say what truly had happened or when.

Taking Godfrey Hafwynder instead of Stephen was a simple trick for the gods—but head-blind Wildecent would never understand that. The only one who would understand would be Ambrose—and he was worse than no one at all. So Alison surrendered to Wildecent, as much a prisoner as the Viking.

Jean Beauleyas had scratched the scruffy beard around his scar, he'd hitched the leather belt of his tunic, and he was ready to pronounce judgment.

"By English law—" he began.

"*Riste blodorn paa rygen!*" Longsword's voice rang out, and he straightened his beaten limbs to tower over the Norman lord. "No coward's English law! I claim the Blood Eagle!"

Beauleyas's brows knit together; he consulted with his men, none of whom knew what dignity the condemned man claimed. The Normans had been Vikings themselves not five generations ago, but they'd kept only the vigor of the North, none of the rituals. It remained for the

English, who'd been surrounded by Scandinavian customs since King Alfred's day, to explain Longsword's demand.

Eodred stood between Beauleyas and the criminal. "He claims his crime is against man's law only. He wants a hero's death: the Blood Eagle. He wants his ribs hacked through on either side of his spine and his living lungs lifted onto his shoulders. He would fly to Valhalla with his dying breath."

Jean Beauleyas paled. "Is this his right by law?" he asked quietly.

"I'll send him to his gods," Bethanil proclaimed, standing up in the oxcart and brandishing her cleaver for all to see. "For my lord and my ladies."

FitzAlan and Serlo wrestled the cook to the ground.

The Norman lord was astounded by the events in his bailey—and next to rage, astonishment was his most dangerous emotion. "Enough!" he shouted. "He is not a hero, and a cook does not dispense justice. All of you—stop gaping and go back to your tasks. A Viking's execution is none of your concern!" Then he told Serlo and Gauche-Robert to lock Longsword beneath the great hall.

Alison pushed past Wildecent, scarcely aware that she'd drawn her knife. "He has taken my father's life. His own is forfeit and mine to claim!"

The look in Beauleyas's eyes was more deadly than the look in her own. Torworden and Hafwynder men reached out to restrain her. Eodred himself pried the blade from her hand. She struggled until Beauleyas struck her; then she went limp.

"Take her up to the donjon. I'll have peace in my bailey!"

The little crowd dispersed as men carried Alison up the log path. Only Beauleyas, FitzAlan, Wildecent, and Ambrose remained by the gate. Wildecent came forward to reclaim the keys they had left with FitzAlan. The knight unhooked his belt and allowed them to slide toward her hand. The iron scarcely touched Wildecent's fingers before Jean Beauleyas took her wrist in a grip that made her cry out in pain.

"What do you think you're doing?" he demanded, squeezing until the keys fell to the dirt between them.

"Since our lady aunt's death we have held Hafwynder's keys—"

"Do you learn nothing from what I tell you? You are a nameless bastard and you have nothing whatsoever!"

FitzAlan looked away. He knew how the lord's temper always found a target every time he was discomfited. He knew what it was like to be that target—but that was no comfort to Wildecent, who staggered backward. Her mouth opened but no sound came out.

"Take her to my chamber. She'll learn this time! I'll put the proper look in her eyes."

Ambrose came from nowhere to pick up the keys and hand them to his lord. "As you wish, Lord Beauleyas." He put an arm around Wildecent's shoulders and guided her away. "He'll forget by tonight. I'll see to that."

Events had moved too swiftly for Wildecent. She tried to understand what had happened, tried to shake free of his arm. The layers of memory parted slowly. "You're touching me. You said we couldn't touch each other . . . mustn't touch—"

"I said I loved you. I was wrong."

"But, tonight . . . Why help me?"

"Because I'll need you and your damned sister tonight. After that I don't care who takes an interest in you—or for what."

They were on the far side of the motte, out of Jean Beauleyas's sight. Thorkel Longsword had already been taken into the donjon; the man carrying Alison had paused to get a better grip on her before climbing the stairs to Ambrose's chamber. Wildecent surprised even herself with the vigor she put into the slap that resounded on Ambrose's cheek. His hand went to his face and Wildecent backed slowly away.

He raised his fist at her, then caught himself. "She was

covered in his blood, Wildecent. Perhaps she didn't sacrifice him before, but now she'll do anything to get her father back. Do you dare deny it?

"And you helped her. Dear God, Wildecent, you helped her do it! Is this the magic, the sorcery you freely choose? Is this what love, and loyalty, and honor mean to you?"

Wildecent preferred his anger to the anguish she now heard in Ambrose's voice. "Is Stephen truly alive?" she asked softly.

The sorcerer turned away and put his hand over his eyes. "I don't know. I always thought I'd know . . . I touch the place where he is in my mind, and he's still there, still safe. I touch his blood . . ." Ambrose's chest heaved and it was some moments before he could continue. "I think—no, I *believe* Stephen is alive, but I don't know where . . . and I don't know when." His arm dropped to his side.

Wildecent took his hand. There was none of the ecstasy they had feared these last two weeks. Only an ordinary hand, moistened with tears. He would not look at her.

"I'll do whatever I can do to get Stephen back. Alison, too. Whatever must be done, I promise it, my lord."

He still would not look at her as they started climbing again, but neither did he pull his hand away.

lison heard a bar drop into place outside the door. She was locked in, confined as she had never been confined—and she didn't care. For four months, since she and her aunt had tried to protect Haf-wynder Manor from its fate, her nerves had been rasped by the conflict between the magical and the mundane. Now that, too, was over. Every sense had been reduced to numbness; every emotion had burned itself to a cold cinder.

The man who dropped her on Ambrose's bed had not even realized she was conscious. Alison could summon no anger toward him. Even the grief she summoned for her father was a distant thing. She was aware of no spe-cific feeling, only a weariness that seduced her into sleep. She retreated within herself.

The bed rippled like a pond in a gentle summer breeze. She imagined drifting beneath warm sunlight—and slipped between the threads of reality. The sun disappeared be-hind wispy black clouds, and the wind carried a discor-dant chorus. Alison arose from a silk-draped barge, and stepped onto dry land.

This was a strange twilight world with no shadows or brilliance. It was autumn here, with flame-colored leaves and crisp grass beneath her feet. The wailing drew closer. Alison climbed the riverbank and scanned the dull gray horizon. A flock of black birds circled in the distance, moving slowly toward her. Hitching her skirts through her belt, she ran toward them.

A procession approached. Women, several dozen of them, rode mares the color of dried blood, and carried ravens on their outstretched arms. Hundreds more of the black birds wheeled overhead. The women wore stern, identical expressions. They hid their hair beneath black veils and their hands in leather gloves. They wore robes of deepest crimson, embroidered in gold and adorned with garnets that flashed blood-red in the strange light.

None looked toward the blond woman standing before them.

The first rider reined her mare to a halt. "Who are you to block our path?" she demanded.

"I am Alison Hafwynder, of England." She paused, and saw that neither her name nor her homeland brought a glimmer of recognition. "From the land of the living."

The woman turned to one of her companions and exchanged an enigmatic glance. "This too is the land of the living," she said with a touch of irony, a touch of malice. "But I do not think it is your land."

The procession split in half and flowed around her. As they rode by, Alison noticed that each of them had a silver sickle suspended from her belt, a sickle such as she had cast at Morrigan in the grove. She called out to them, demanding explanations, but they ignored her.

"You have used me!" Alison shouted. "You have tricked me. You have seduced me into betraying those who love me and you have made me an instrument of sacrifice. You owe me answers!"

They were unmoved by her protests; not even the horses or birds looked her way. Alison stared into each face, bringing her talent to bear in the hope that she could wring words from one of them. Most of the procession had passed by when one rider looked down.

"Ygurna! My lady aunt!" Alison exalted, weaving through the blood-bay mares to walk beside her aunt's stirrup. She tried to embrace her aunt, but the raven opened its beak and drove her back. "Lady Ygurna, help me—please . . ."

"You have failed us," Ygurna said, her jaw tight and her lips scarcely moving.

"It was not supposed to be like this. You knew what I had done. I did not mean for anything to go this far. He was never supposed to die! I couldn't take his life. I couldn't. It's not fair! How can anything be made whole with blood?"

Lady Ygurna's hands trembled; the raven bated with a grating cry. In the front of the procession the first rider turned around. Then they all turned and their eyes made Alison's skin crawl.

"You opened doors, created possibilities. Perhaps you did not intend anything, but you are dedicated to the gods. All that you do is done in their name. All that you have is theirs as well. The best sacrifice is made by the innocent and the holy. Nothing excuses you."

Alison took a step backward, dazed by her aunt's coldness. She had to run to catch up again. "Where are you going? What are you doing?"

"We go to complete the winnowing of the land. We have winnowed one battlefield; we ride to the last. All will be decided there."

"I must do something. I must make it right again."

"Join us."

Alison saw a riderless mare beyond Ygurna—where she would have sworn there was nothing at all a heartbeat before. She approached it. A vision engulfed her when she touched the mare's flank.

These women rode invisibly among the men during battle. They sought the mortally wounded men, and with their sickles made ritual incisions across their chests. The dying men's lifeblood was squeezed onto the land. It was the final vision beneath the *geas.*

Once she mounted she would be one of them. With all the rest of the long-dead Cymric priestesses, she'd reap the battlefields, renewing the land with warm, dripping blood. Alison could see the final battle toward which they rode. Normans would be there, and the English. She recognized Eudo's face and reached for her sickle—but it wasn't in its place at her waist.

The tableau shattered. The ravens surrounded her in violent chorus. Alison realized the procession had circled back, and the first rider stood before her. The sharp edge of a silver sickle glinted in Alison's face; she dropped the mare's reins and backed away.

"You have no gathering knife," the woman said in a beautiful voice that belied the harshness of her expression. "You cannot become one of us without your gathering knife. And if you cannot ride with us, then you must be sacrificed."

The other women began an antiphon: Not one of us, *sacrifice!* Not one of us, *sacrifice!* Alison looked for her aunt, but Ygurna had submerged into the chant. All the women had their sickles raised. The ravens were diving toward her, reaching for her eyes. She batted one of the birds away, then turned and ran.

She saved herself only because the women were unaccustomed to the unexpected. They were startled by a sacrifice who shouted and waved like a lunatic. The two women toward whom Alison ran lost control of their mares, and she was able to break out of the circle. The ravens pursued her to the river, where she found her barge had been replaced by a cup-shaped white hide coracle. The birds whirled around her head but they did not prevent her from leaping onto it.

"Take me home!" Alison shouted, as the round-bottomed craft bobbled into the current. "Take me home!"

The hide boat was steadied and began to move downstream.

It was late afternoon before Jean Beauleyas returned to his bedroom. He led a procession of knights and peasants, Normans and English carrying the Hafwynder treasure. He seemed genuinely surprised, and more than slightly displeased, to find Wildecent sitting by his hearth.

"My lord," she said, pushing the cat she held onto the floor.

"Get me some wine!"

She started for the door but halted when Ambrose called her. Another man ducked out.

"I hardly think Lady Wildecent knows where to find wine in the day-village," Ambrose explained.

"It's time the *lady* learned to do something useful!"

Wildecent took another step toward the door and again the sorcerer caught her eyes. "There'll be time enough for that later, my lord. She might be useful to us now."

Beauleyas spoke in French. "Why should I believe what any damned Englishwoman tells me? They're all devious. Devious witches." He walked to where Wildecent stood and grabbed her by the shoulder. He twisted her around until she faced him. "You and your sister, witches—both of you. Why should I take a witch into my bed where you'll work your curses on me?" He shook her as a cat shakes a mouse. "I should burn that damned manor to the ground!"

He thrust her aside. The English from Hafwynder Manor were gaping at him in horror and disbelief. When Beauleyas spoke again it was in a dialect they could understand.

"You're all peasants—and I'm your lord. Alison Hafwynder is my ward—not your mistress. And that one." He gestured where Wildecent cowered. "That one is simply mine."

Ambrose frowned, but before he could attempt to mollify his lord, Bethanil shoved her way to the forefront.

"You'll not be eating from my pots," she began, disdaining all honors and formalities. "I'm a freewoman and I'm not beholden to the likes of you."

"Then you, goodwife, may take the wench with you when you leave—but do not go back to Hafwynder Manor, for that is mine and I do not tolerate your insolence."

Bethanil propped her beefy hands on her hips. "Lady Wildecent is no kitchen drudge," she said with ringing finality, but she did not say she'd risk leaving.

"What is she then? Your dead lord's bastard? An orphan he found in the city and took in for Christian charity? She'd be dead but for him, and she'll be grateful to me if she knows what's best for her—''

The cook hesitated, then retrieved a velvet-wrapped treasure box from another of the Hafwynder men before advancing closer to the red-faced Norman. "My lord," she began in a more respectful tone. "It's true we don't know who her mother was, and that our lord was willing that she be considered his bastard. But Lady Wildecent's neither foundling nor orphan." Beauleyas opened his mouth to object, but she kept talking. "This box came to the manor when she did." She offered Beauleyas the box.

"FitzAlan!" Beauleyas raged in French, "what's the meaning of this? Do these peasants think to offer me what is already mine?"

The soldier shrugged and looked away from his lord's wrath. Beauleyas tore the velvet loose, but his anger evaporated when he considered the object the cloth had concealed. The ivory box glowed with age. The gilding on the carved stags that covered the top and sides was still intact. It was too delicate for a metal lock; three ivory pegs held it shut. And it had no place in the treasure of a rural English nobleman—or a rural Norman nobleman for that matter.

Beauleyas set it on the table and carefully removed the pegs. A silk scarf was folded within it. He unfolded it and stared at six huge coins sewn carefully onto the cloth. The coins were of a style he had never seen before, but were most obviously solid gold. They so captured his attention that he almost missed the pieces of vellum that remained in the box. These were covered with writing, and he thrust them at Ambrose.

"Here, read them to me!"

Ambrose stared at the largest of the three pieces. "It's in Hebrew, my lord."

"*Deus aie!* What have the Jews got to do with her? What does it say?"

"I don't know, my lord, there're some languages I can recognize but cannot read. Perhaps in Leicester—"

"Don't tell me I'm harboring a Jewess! Never mind Leicester. What about the other pieces?" he shouted.

Ambrose studied the other two scraps. "My lord, I think we should be alone."

The bedroom was cleared of everyone except Ambrose and Jean Beauleyas. Even Wildecent was sent into the hall, and FitzAlan was told to keep everyone—including himself—from the drapery.

"So, what are they?"

"They're receipts my lord, written in two columns, then torn apart. Lord Godfrey kept one half, the other remained with a Nathan of Winchester—"

"More Jews!"

"Yes, my lord. But Wildecent is no Jewess. Listen: 'By this I swear, before God and my kind, that the child Melisande, daughter of Count Arnulf and his wife, Phillipa—' "

"*Count* Arnulf? Who by the holy saints is *Count* Arnulf?"

" '—is alive and thriving in my care. I attest this with a lock of her hair and a drop of her blood to be sent back to her mother. In return I accept these two gold *mancuses* for her upkeep until Easter next, when I shall come again and her family may reclaim her.' It's sworn and sealed. The other is much the same except . . ." Ambrose paused to recheck his Latin. "It mentions returning milk-teeth and the name Saint Suzanne."

"*Deus aie,*" God help me, Beauleyas swore in a more respectful tone. "I know Arnulfs and Phillipas by the handful; even a Melisande or two—but one family, and a count?"

"It is not impossible, my lord. And these coins. Hafwynder could have run his whole manor for a year on two of these coins—"

"Not if he were trying to keep the child hidden," the ever-pragmatic Beauleyas averred. "They'd have to be melted down. By all the relics, man, look at them—look at the profiles. Have you ever seen people dressed like that?

"By their marks they commemorate the baptism of King Clothar—"

"Clothar? There hasn't been a King Clothar in three hundred years. And six of them; the family still had six of them . . . at least six of them after three hundred years. Rich bastards . . . Saint Suzanne—I know a town of that name, and a dozen churches . . . a priory . . . Bring the girl and the cook back in. Maybe they remember something."

Wildecent stared in awe at the gold discs. She admitted what little she could remember of her childhood. Yes, she thought she might have lived in a stonework donjon once before and, yes, she remembered men with mail and swords, but she remembered no names. Beauleyas turned to Bethanil.

"You were there, weren't you? You folk see everything. What did you see?"

Bethanil knew little that was not already revealed in the scraps of parchment. The little girl was about six when Lord Godfrey brought her to the manor. She spoke nothing but French then, easily frightened and wary of everyone, though Alison eventually won her friendship. They called her Wildecent because she recognized it as her name beneath their accents.

When she had been with them a year, the Lady Ygurna had pricked the child's finger onto a white cloth and clipped a lock of her sable hair for Lord Godfrey to take with him to Winchester. The ritual was repeated the next year and the year after that, but when Hafwynder returned from Winchester the third time he still had the cloth and the tiny braid. The Jew was gone, and Wildecent's family was known to Almighty God alone.

Beauleyas grumbled his thanks and sent Bethanil away so only he, Ambrose, and Wildecent remained. It was beginning to get dark, and men could be heard erecting tables in the great hall.

"You're saved," Jean Beauleyas admitted, holding the gold-crusted velvet in his hands. "Someone tried very hard to protect you; someone had powerful enemies and something that was worth protecting. I don't know your people, but the south is riddled with counts—and feuds. The gold stopped. You may be as out of luck as my nephew, Stephen, but you might be worth more than your foster sister. And, just like her, you're my ward; your gold is mine and your future is mine."

Wildecent nodded, not that she equated herself with Alison, but that she understood she had become a valued pawn rather than a common one.

"Go now, make yourself ready for dinner. You shall continue to sit with us at the high table."

She nodded again and headed for the door. Ambrose was there first to open it for her. "Do we still have an agreement?" he asked softly, since it wasn't through his efforts that she had been reprieved.

She glanced up at him and nodded with her eyes alone before running through the doorway.

here had not been enough time for Bethanil to unload her pots, pans, and knives. Supper at Torworden that night was no different than it had ever been—at least as regarded the food. The men knew their lord was a richer man now and that a murderer languished in the locked storerooms beneath the hall. Jean Beauleyas had made no proclamation regarding his second ward, the dark-haired woman, who continued to share a plate with his sorcerer.

Still, there were few secrets in a donjon, and most of the men showed Wildecent some greater courtesy than they'd showed her on other nights. Likewise, they made no mention of the empty stool beside Lord Beauleyas. Alison had not come down for the evening meal, nor had a plate been taken upstairs to her. Wildecent explained that Alison remained in seclusion out of respect for their father. No one argued, but no one completely believed her. There were no secrets in a donjon.

"Has Alison agreed?" Ambrose asked Wildecent casually while they sat beside each other.

Wildecent swirled the wine in her cup then set it down without drinking. "She is lost in her own world. I had to bind her with sheets lest she harm herself while I ate supper with you. There will be no talking with her tonight."

"We do not have time, Wildecent. She left Stephen someplace where only she can reach him. You and she knotted the fabric of time itself. It was an act against reason *and* an act against nature. One of you must untangle it."

Wildecent shook her head. "I don't know. I don't know how to get there. I have no magic of my own. I know nothing of sorcery. Both of you seem to expect me to help, when I have no power of my own."

Ambrose lifted the teardrop crystal from around his neck and placed it in her unwilling hand. "What do you feel?" he demanded, closing his fist over hers. She cringed and wriggled her fingers beneath his. "Try! Don't give up so easily!"

The sharp edges of the stone cut into her skin. She squirmed; he squeezed tighter. Then warmth spread from Ambrose's hands and the crystal no longer hurt. Wildecent had never held the talisman before, never felt the sorcerous beacon that connected Ambrose to his younger friend, yet even without that experience, she could tell something was not right. Stephen was there—whatever, wherever "there" was—but he was trapped like a fly in amber. Barring the arcane, the magical, or the sorcerous, his only way out was death.

Wildecent looked up into Ambrose's eyes. "There's nothing I can do."

"You were there, weren't you? You were beneath my basket of light. Perhaps if you sat at the center and I along the circumference?"

She wrested her hand free as her whole being recoiled against that idea. "I can't," she insisted. "I won't try. I won't go there again."

Ambrose's eyes cursed her silently and he left the table. Wildecent stared at the plate without eating. In one day she had learned more about her ancestry than she had ever imagined. The stigma of bastardy had been removed. She had a new name, but she felt more at the mercy of those around her than ever. The dinner was endless; so was the climb from the great hall to the upper room she shared with Alison.

Wildecent sat on the edge of the bed and offered her sister slices of apple soaked in wine. To her surprise, Alison ate them eagerly. The wine brought color to her cheeks, and she gained enough strength to sit up.

"They have not finished with me," Alison explained as she took another slice of apple from the dish. "I have escaped them once, but they are not satisfied. It is not enough that they've taken our lord father; they would have both my heroes."

Wildecent shuddered, spilling wine across her skirts. "Our lord father is dead. Stephen is going to die," she said, hoping to convince herself if not Alison. "There is nothing that can be done except make matters worse!"

Alison gripped her sister's hand with a wild strength. The little plate went flying across the room. "I will make fools of them all. Every last one of them. They tried to use me, but I am more than they are. I have danced with the goddesses, while they have only gathered blood from the dead—"

Wildecent shoved Alison back onto the pillows. She wanted to believe that Alison was maddened by grief and fever, but there was no madness in her sister's eyes. Alison spoke of goddesses, and Wildecent began to suspect devils. She wanted to run down to the bailey-yard and search for Ambrose. But Alison had enthralled her and she could not move.

"All I need is the silver sickle," Alison whispered. "The silver sickle, and they shall have sacrifice and blood enough for the end of time."

With great difficulty Wildecent shook her head and took a step backward. "It's wrong. You must not shed a man's blood, Alison—no man's blood." She had not expected her words to affect Alison, but they did, and the blond woman slumped forward, her face hidden by her tangled braids.

Wildecent put her hands on her sister's shoulders. "What will be, will be, Alison. There will be life without our lord father; he was dying anyway, Alison, we both knew that. And there will be life without Stephen; you, yourself, said you never really loved him. But we can't make time flow backward, and we mustn't shed more blood."

Alison looked up. The wineglow was gone from her cheeks; her eyes were red-rimmed and hollow. "They tricked me, you know—used me—even our lady aunt. When they saw what I'd done, they came to me in my dreams. They said if Stephen died loving me, if he died by my hand, England would be safe and the Normans would never come." She leaned her head against her sister's breast. "It is so hard. I'm sworn to the land, Wili. My mother, my grandmother, all of us—all sworn to the land. I was born to do this. I can be the hero. If I can find the sickle, I can go back to the grove. Everything will be all right . . ."

She tugged at the binding sheet Wildecent had twisted around her waist, but her strength was fading and she couldn't pull the linen free from the bedframe. She said something more about the grove and the sickle, then fell back onto the pillows.

Wildecent tucked the blankets under Alison's chin and lowered the curtains. She was appalled by the idea of blood sacrifices, but even more determined that Alison would no longer be used by anyone or anything. She stared, not seeing anything until her sight fell upon the holly.

Two of the deep green leaves had fallen to the floor; several more were bruised. Wildecent lifted the branch carefully, afraid it might crumble—or slice through her fingers. She went to the wall, grabbed a corner of the tapestry, and whipped the branch across it. She'd hoped the cloth would come apart, proving that the holly was the silver sickle that Alison had cast at Morrigan's breast. But the tapestry remained intact. She opened the panel and took the holly into the sanctum.

She intended to demand the transformation of the holly into the sickle, as she had once demanded knowledge of where Alison lay beneath the junipers. She hadn't understood the *micros* when she'd made that construct work; she was not concerned that she did not understand the basket of light or its underlying *geometria*. She knelt on the northern pillow and concentrated her thoughts until the veins of her forehead throbbed and sweat ran down her back.

The branch remained resolutely holly beneath the center of the inverted wire and silk basket.

She crept to the center of the geometria, clutching her skirts tightly under her arm and careful not to disturb any of Ambrose's marks. With the branch pressed between her palms she tried again. Her heart pounded; her breath grew ragged and her palms became sticky.

The holly thorns pierced her skin, but the branch had not become a sickle.

Frustrated and overwrought from her exertions, Wildecent crept back to the bedroom. Those bundles from the oxcarts that had not been taken to Beauleyas's treasury or kept with Bethanil had been brought upstairs. After checking that Alison still slept, Wildecent ransacked the baskets until she found the masks of the three kings—one of whom was the Holly King—and carried them into the sanctum.

The outer circumference of the geometria was quartered. Wildecent arranged the kings at the outer quarters, sat in the north, and tried again. Five more times she tried, changing the positions of the kings before each trial. Finally she set them as they had been when she'd first laid them out—Lady Ygurna had said that chance held the greatest measure of truth—and crawled back to the center where the holly lay.

She spared nothing. Waves of heat flowed down her arms into the branch. The branch grew warm between her hands, but it would not change.

"You're going about it wrong."

Wildecent shrieked and flung the branch across the room. Her eyes recognized Ambrose long before her mind or heart. He was dressed in black and midnight blue, as was his custom, but these were not the austere clothes he wore in the sunlight. His velvets were as dark as winter, his silks shone like moonlit summer sky, and across both fabrics metal threads glinted in the lamplight, elaborating the patterns of the geometria. Wildecent was still panting and unable to speak when he gathered up the holly and laid it on the pillow.

His hands were elegant, moving with mystifying competence to bend a wire here, straighten one there, and unwind a fine one from the index finger of his right hand.

"Come here," he requested, extending a hand toward her. His voice was honey coating her fears. She reached for him and he grabbed her wrist. He pressed the sharp tip of the wire against a vein; her blood spiraled along the metal. "Now, where do you want to go?"

The bloodletting was more shocking than painful. Wildecent was transfixed by the dark beads clinging to the wire as Ambrose wove it into the basket of light. Then he took his talisman and suspended it from the same bit of wire. Wildecent's blood flowed downward, coating the crystal.

"Please don't tell me you don't know where you're going." There was pure and human pleading in his voice as he knelt down to stare at her.

"I wished to change the holly into a sickle," Wildecent said, snatching the branch from the pillow and retreating back to the center of the geometria. She felt the wires changing above her. Her heart trusted the sorcerer, although her mind did not.

"What would you do with the sickle?"

"I don't know—" She watched his face fall. "I don't . . . I can't put it into words, Ambrose. I'll know once I have the sickle."

He gave a weary smile and extended his arms crosswise from his shoulders. The wires of the basket of light began to glow, and the talisman shuddered and slipped to the first nexus of silk and copper.

"It must be a silver sickle," Wildecent added quickly.

His eyes opened once, then closed, and he began to chant. Wildecent tried to listen to his words—if they were words—but sorcery flowed beneath the chant, not within it. The talisman moved from joining to joining, sometimes rising against the curve of the basket, sometimes skittering along the circumference, making the entire web sway in the lamplight.

Wildecent felt nothing at first—less than she'd felt when

she'd struggled to focus her thoughts beneath the incomplete basket. Then the holly grew heavy in her hands and began to pull her downward. She was startled.

Don't drop it! Ambrose's exasperated voice boomed directly into her mind.

Wildecent clutched the silver sickle as it bore her downward through the donjon tower to the storerooms where Thorkel Longsword awaited the Blood Eagle. The air shimmered. Wildecent was in the condemned Viking's cell but they were not alone.

The three green kings stood vigil at the quarter marks—grim, disembodied faces. Wildecent remained at the center, standing rather than kneeling, and facing the pallet where Thorkel slept.

Get on with it.

She looked around, but Ambrose had not made the descent in any physical sense. Wildecent's courage balked. She stared from the sickle to the sleeping man and knew, beyond any doubt, that she could not hack apart his ribs or lift his fluttering lungs onto his shoulders. She couldn't even take a step forward.

By whatever you deem holy, woman—do something! I cannot hold this forever!

Wildecent whimpered and took a step forward. Thorkel opened his eyes. He saw something—but not Wildecent, for the names he whispered were strange to her. He was shackled; heavy chains grated across the stone as he ripped his shirt open. His bruised and beaten back was exposed to her, awaiting the ritual that would transport him to the gods of his people.

"I cannot. Forgive me." Wildecent whispered apologetically as she came around to stand at his head. "It must be our hero's sacrifice. For the land. As you gave our lord father—"

Her fingers obeyed her thoughts without feeling. She yanked his four braids upward and slashed across his naked neck. She held a goddess's sickle in her right hand;

it cut easily through bone and sinew. And—more miraculously—it seared the wound. There was very little blood.

If there had been blood, Wildecent would have fainted, sorcery or no sorcery. Without blood, she clung to consciousness—a tight grip on the sickle, a tighter grip on Longsword's grinning head—trying to breathe and vomit at the same time.

Get back to the center!

Wildecent heard Ambrose. She felt the apprehension in his voice and understood it. The green kings were beginning to move. She was more aware of her danger than was the sorcerer beside the geometria above her, but she made no move toward the center.

I can't hold you!

She hoped, as the green men surrounded her and bore her off, that Ambrose understood that whatever happened would not be his fault—any more than it was going to be hers. Then, as the world became a black maelstrom, Wildecent didn't think of anything at all.

She was back in the grove. Stephen was dead. His corpse lay at her feet. Blood still oozed from his wounds and his flesh was still warm to the touch, but the timeless moment had ended. Stephen was dead.

Alison should have been there but was not, and Wildecent began to fear everything had been for naught, for the green kings were gone as well. She felt a thinning of the magic and sorcery that insulated her from the passage of time. She could become stranded *here* and left outside the flow of events as Stephen had been. It was unlikely Ambrose would be able to find her if he had not been able to find Stephen.

Wildecent's only hope was that Alison would eventually arrive—though eventually and eternity might well mean the same thing. Gingerly, she set her burdens on the ground and shoved her wind-blown plaits behind her ears. Then she picked up the sickle and the head, and settled down to wait beside Stephen.

CONQUEST

Time had little meaning in the grove. The shadows didn't move; Stephen's wounds didn't harden, and it was only with the greatest of difficulty that she could feel her heart beating. Perhaps her emotions were frozen as well, since she grew no more apprehensive as she waited.

"They'll come—eventually," she told herself, and Stephen, and Longsword's head.

And eventually they did.

Alison came first, in a white coracle sailing a stream that shimmered in some other world. They could see each other but they could not hear.

"I've got the hero's sacrifice," Wildecent shouted, raising the head. She made each word clear and distinct, hoping Alison would see their meaning.

Alison was startled by Wildecent's gesture. Her hide boat bobbed and rocked as she fell back against its rail.

"Take Stephen away. I've promised that you'll set him *free.*" Wildecent enunciated the last words as broadly as possible, but there enwas no gesture she could make with a severed head in one hand and a sickle in the other that would make meaning clear.

Alison said something in reply. Wildecent tried to shape her lips in imitation, hoping to learn the words by their physical shapes, but she had no knack for it. There was a breeze across the treetops now, blowing counter to the stream. She set the head down again and placed the sickle beside it; then she reached into the stream and grabbed the rail of Alison's boat.

The physical force of the wind roaring between their worlds deafened her. "You must take Stephen away!" she shouted, but mostly she braced herself and slowly tugged Alison, the boat, the stream, and the other world across the grove.

She needed another hand, or six, but Alison was fully occupied bailing water out of the hide boat, so Wildecent took the sickle, stabbed through the hide, and anchored the two worlds one to the other. Alison roared a curse that cowed the wind; then she noticed Stephen. She dared not leave her boat any more than Wildecent dared leave the grove, but together, as gently as possible, they moved Stephen's body past the sickle.

"Set him free," Wildecent admonished, touching Alison's arm. "Whatever the cost—set him free. I'll see to this place."

Alison nodded and pushed free of the grove—taking the sickle with her.

Wildecent did not have time to be angry with her foster sister. The sun had moved across the open sky above the grove with gut-wrenching speed. It was night, and the winds descended to the forest floor. Shadowy figures emerged from the dark trees: gods and goddesses, some of whom she knew from before. She recognized Ygurna among a group of dark-robed women, but there was no affection in her foster aunt's face. Wildecent had a moment to marvel at her own audacity before a green man strode into the grove wearing Godfrey Hafwynder's head. She lifted Thorkel Longsword's head and greeted him.

"I have your sacrifice," she said in a voice that did not reveal her terror.

"It is too late," the giant said with her foster father's voice.

Wildecent swallowed hard. Her arm shook and Longsword's teeth clashed together with a sound that set her stomach reeling. "This is the man we give you," she said uncertainly. "We didn't give you the other ones. You can't have them. Not Stephen, and not my lord father."

"Who are you who says what the gods themselves may or may not possess?" A stately woman, looking very much like Wildecent herself, separated from the darkness and came to stand between the green man and Wildecent.

Before Wildecent could answer, a goddess who looked like Alison as Morrigan resembled Wildecent entered the argument. "We needed a conqueror, a hero who loved the land of the Cymry. We marked the one from over the water, but the living priestess betrayed us. So we took this one, whose conquering blood is many generations weak though his love was strong. This I understand, but what is *that?*" She pointed at Thorkel Longsword's grinning head.

Wildecent saw her chance. "He is also a man from across the waters; a man from a conquering race." So far she'd told the truth and gotten their attention, but Thorkel Longsword had never loved anyone but himself. "I do not know if he loved the Cymry," she hedged, "but he asked for a hero's death. He is the one who killed my foster father."

The sister goddesses looked to the green king. Communication passed among them without words and made Wildecent nervous. She gripped Longsword's hair tighter. Time was passing quickly now, or at least her heart was pounding. Then the man, the fourth green king, who had no image of his own, placed his hands against Godfrey Hafwynder's temples and lifted the head from his shoulders. The Alison-goddess took the now-white head lovingly in her arms, and the headless king reached out to Wildecent.

Her hands trembled; she feared the touch of his miscolored flesh, but his fingers were strong and warm when they brushed against hers. She released her burden and began to breathe easily again.

Longsword's face was green now, as were his braids and eyes. "It is good," the king said with Thorkel's voice. He began to smile before he left the grove. Wildecent said nothing as first the goddesses, then the others slowly left the grove. Finally only Ygurna remained.

"You," the old woman said, shaking her head slowly. "I would never have believed it would be you."

"I did what I could, Aunt."

"You have not done enough, you know. It's no good to give him Thorkel Longsword's head; Vikings are almost as useless as Saxons. Our king needed new vitality— and you didn't give him that. Oh, England may not be destroyed, but it will bleed, and it won't bleed any less because of what you've done in this grove."

"You're just bitter because Alison didn't do what you wanted her to do."

Ygurna lowered her eyes in defeat. "Maybe so, maybe so. I never had the gift of vision. But then again, neither have you—or you'd never have come to a grove set apart from all other places and all other times. I do not believe you'll find your way home so easily."

With that she was gone, and Wildecent, who now felt time moving around her, considered the truth in the dead woman's words. For the first time she realized that she was not the only living thing in the grove. Sulwyn was cropping tender grass at the edge of the trees.

She approached the stallion warily, but he seemed undisturbed by her presence. The Torworden men claimed no woman could ride one of their horses but, in the circumstances, Wildecent thought it was worth a try. She gathered the reins in one hand and heaved herself up into the high saddle. He felt her weight land on his back, and reared. Wildecent pressed in with her knees, clutched the reins and the pommel in a death grip, and closed her eyes.

Sulwyn plunged and kicked, then stood still. Wildecent opened her eyes and found herself seated on a milk white horse. By then, after everything else that had happened, very little could surprise or unsettle her.

"I don't suppose you know the way home?" she inquired.

"Of course I do," replied the horse goddess, Epona, and she began moving down the path.

he white hide coracle spun back into the current. It drifted low in the water under the weight of both Stephen's armored body and Alison. She bailed continuously. There was no time to think about the fast-running stream or the corpse braced against her legs.

Alison had escaped the coracle once before; she'd dived into the stream and returned to Torworden. She'd come back hoping to find Stephen's grove, and to steal him away from the Cymric gods. She tried not to think about Wildecent and scooped another handful of water over the side.

The coracle tipped precariously as the stream descended into another stretch of rock-strewn white water. Alison shrieked, clung to the rail like a half-drowned animal, and prayed Stephen's weight wouldn't drag them under. Then it spun out into water that was calm by comparison. She cupped her hands and began, once again, to bail.

The water wasn't cold, but Alison's arms were like lead. She slid down until her neck rested against the rail, and closed her eyes. The stream flowed out of twilight and into moonlit darkness.

Most streams flow eventually to the sea, but this one, Alison suspected, would dive beneath the earth. She could ride until it descended, or she could let the coracle sink in the next rapids. Either way she'd have taken Stephen to the world beneath the hills; the summer land where he would await rebirth.

She'd have set him free, as everyone asked her to do, and she could return to her own life. If she was lucky she'd never have to deal with gods or magic again. Then it began to rain—and the rain was cold.

"It's not fair!" she yelled at the clouds.

Faint luminescence rose from the stream itself. The

banks were not more than a dozen feet away. Alison tore strips from her linen, knotted them together, and attached the makeshift rope to the sickle. It was pitch dark beyond the banks, with nothing to recommend one side over the other. She cast the sickle to the right. On the third try it caught, and she was able to pull her ungainly craft toward land.

She was luckier than she'd dared hope. Though she rattled her teeth bouncing over several boulders, those same boulders created a calm pool beside the steep bank. She clambered safely onto land.

Alison's legs ached when she tried to stand up straight after being hunched over for so long. The weight of her water-logged clothing was more noticeable on land and, after a few moments, she began shivering as well. She wanted nothing more than to crawl under the nearest tree. Instead she lay down at the stream's edge and reached into the hide boat.

Moving Stephen's body into the coracle had taken all the strength and desperation she and Wildecent could muster. Lifting it straight up was more than Alison alone could manage. She gave up and began to cough. As a healer she knew to fear the sounds rasping from her chest more than anything else the gods chose to heap on her shoulders.

"I tried," she croaked to the darkness when the coughing subsided. She pushed herself upright and stumbled along the knotted rope to the sickle. "I was wrong. I made a lot of mistakes. I'm ashamed of myself, but I'm going home. I'll set Stephen free right here. Do what you will with me; I don't care anymore."

Alison pulled the sickle out of the ground and raised it over her head, but before she could fling it into the stream, the rope jerked forward. She was dragged along the bank. She cursed the rain, the rope, the darkness, and the gods themselves before she got herself untangled.

She got slowly to her feet and uselessly shook out her skirts. "That's it. I'm done. I'm going home," she shouted at the stream. It didn't answer, of course; it didn't need to. The coracle rested only a few yards away on a small shelf of rock that glowed insolently though the rain.

It did not take long for Alison to turn the white hide boat over and create a cramped, but dry, shelter for herself and Stephen. He was cold now. He certainly didn't care whether he was wet or dry, but Alison would not leave him alone in the darkness. She cradled him in her lap and rocked him gently.

She warmed herself the same way Ambrose did. It wasn't an arcane talent. Once everyone had known how to raise his body temperature, to melt snow, or to dry his clothes. It was a simple exercise of imagination, and beneath the oxhide it was quite effective.

Sheltered in a world where the ordinary was not what it seemed to be, with the rain drumming on the white hide, and her own flesh radiating a comfortable warmth, Alison eased into a trance. She forgot her aching muscles and the tight bands across her chest. She remembered the times she had never spent with Stephen—the moments she had stolen from his fantasies.

Alison touched each image lightly as it passed, returning it to its original form. She wondered if all men concealed such desires in their hearts. He had never known her, much less loved *her*. She was not the gentle, yielding woman of his dreams.

Nor was he the man she had tried to make of him.

They were both impulsive. They both preferred to move swiftly across the surface rather than explore beneath it. Beyond that, they were different. Alison thought she might have come to love him anyway, if they'd met in a more ordinary manner. Now all she could do was mourn while the rain beat furiously against the white ox hide.

Morning came. The rain had ended, and bright sunlight poured through the stretched seams of the coracle.

The blood and sweat had washed away from Stephen's face. Alison smoothed his hair over his forehead, noting that his skin was no longer cold. But then, it was almost hot beneath the boat; even the rock on which they rested was warm. For sentiment's sake Alison traced the line of his cheek and chin with her fingertip and thought of keeping a lock of his hair.

He opened his eyes.

They stared at each other—then sprang apart in an explosion of disbelief. The coracle bounced over the rocks. The white hide had lost its luster; the wood was brittle. The coracle collapsed when it came to a stop in the sunlight.

In the oldest of the sagas it was said that a hero might be brought back to life in a sacred cauldron or wrapped in the hide of a white bull. The sagas were sung by bards, not handed down through the Cymric myths Alison had learned from Ygurna, but she thought she understood what had happened. She thought she'd been forgiven and opened her arms to him.

Stephen reeled away. "Who are you?" he demanded. "What have you done with me? Where am I?"

"Stephen, it's me, Alison! I've brought you back." She came another step closer, but no further.

"Stay away, old woman," he warned, raising his fists before him. "Don't come any closer."

"Stephen, it's *me* . . ." But as she spoke Alison looked at her hands and saw spotted, leathery skin stretched over gnarled bones. Horrified, she touched her face. She didn't feel old, not inside, but she was not tempted to glance down at the pools beside her feet.

She reached out to him with her mind, then drew the thought back. Better to let him go than to pile new tragedy atop the old.

"Crone. Witch. Stay away from me," Stephen shouted. He was still shouting when he escaped into the trees.

He's free, Alison thought, staring at her crabbed hands.

It's over. Everything's over. She didn't doubt he'd find his way. There were layers of magic all through the deep green forests of England. The unwary might take one step off the track and enter an ancient, timeless world, but Stephen wouldn't—not this day.

Magic lingered faintly beside the stream. Alison could see the luminous water of the other world out of the corner of her eye, just as she could see her own hands beneath the twisted ones. The silver sickle lay where she'd left it, but the hide boat had already vanished. When sunlight struck the sickle it began to shimmer.

Alison knew she didn't have much time, or timelessness, left. She took the sickle into the shade, where the magic remained. She did not know what she'd find when she returned to Torworden, but she had to return there now, or never.

Wildecent yawned. She wasn't in bed; she knew that before she opened her eyes, but she was comfortable and, as always, in no great hurry to begin the day. It was warm and spicy-smelling where she was, which, as the night's memories came back to her, was a considerable improvement.

She opened her eyes and looked up at the basket of light. She looked down and saw black velvet—and a man's hand resting lightly over her own.

Ambrose! It was all she could do to keep from leaping to her feet, but she held her breath and stayed still. It was not that surprising, she told herself as she carefully wriggled free. She didn't quite remember returning to the sanctum, but it seemed likely that he'd been waiting for her. She thought she might even have chosen to sleep beside him herself. He might have been asleep and might never have noticed her at all.

He was still asleep when she sat up. He'd slept soundly at Hafwynder Manor after working sorcery, and Wildecent began to hope she'd escape her compromised position without waking him.

"The men return! The men return!" Someone was on the guard-porch. Someone was beating the assembly gong with all his heart and strength.

That was it. Ambrose was blinking, and Wildecent was mortified. She scuttled to the opposite wall, and he made matters infinitely worse by laughing.

Wildecent's hose had clumped around her ankles, and the laces of her tunic dangled down past her waist. He seemed completely clothed and unrumpled—but then, he always did. Wildecent yanked the laces tight and secured them with a knot. She turned around and tried to rewrap her hose without revealing her legs.

"The far side of the vale! They return . . . with wounded!"

The gong clanged again and Wildecent lost her balance. She caught herself, but the strip of dark cloth had fallen to the floor, and her skirts were bunched up. Even her thigh was blushing.

Ambrose laughed all the harder. "Gods' eyes, woman—you're hardly in any danger *now,*" he explained between laughs.

That was true enough—with the men mustering on the other side of the wall—but it was hardly reassuring. "Oh, dear God, the angels and all the saints—what have I done?" she whispered, snatching up her stocking.

"From the beginning? You began by cutting off a man's head. He was condemned and waiting to die, but you got to him before Lord Beauleyas did. I checked. Longsword's lying in a storeroom, not a mark on him, but very dead. Then, you let yourself be carried off by three large green kings. After that you found your sister, I think, and together you moved Stephen. What else you did, I cannot imagine, but I was hardly about to take advantage of you when you crawled into my arms."

Wildecent shook her skirts down. There was no mistaking the good humor in Ambrose's voice. She dreaded what he'd do or say when she told him the truth. "Stephen's dead," she said softly. "He was dead when I got to the grove. I gave his body to Alison and told her to set him free. He wasn't sacrificed, but he wasn't alive—"

She was nearsighted, but she could see Ambrose clearly enough. The exuberance dropped from his face; Wildecent didn't know how to interpret what remained. It wasn't rage, and she was grateful enough for that. She was relieved that they were not enemies, and did not press her luck. Greed was a cardinal sin.

"I must see about Alison," she said quickly, darting from the room before he had a chance to say anything.

Alison sat on the edge of the bed. Her hair was loose and there were tears on her cheeks. She met Wildecent's eyes, then hid behind her hands.

Wildecent's only hope had been that her sister had been able to get Stephen's body away from the interference of Cymric magic. She'd seen the young man's seeping wounds. He was better off dead. Alison's quavering announcement that Stephen was alive and well took her completely by surprise—but no more so than the wail of tears that accompanied it.

"You've wrought a miracle!" Wildecent took Alison's hands and pulled them away from her face. "For heaven's sake—why are you crying about it?" She brushed her sister's hair to one side.

"He took one look at me and called me a witch. He ran away from me. He didn't even thank me—he just ran like I was the most loathsome creature in all England."

Wildecent had nothing to say. She'd ridden away from the grove on a goddess's back; she wasn't head-blind anymore. The Alison who leaned on her shoulder was the Alison she had always known—blue-eyed, golden-haired, and beautiful despite her tearstained face. But the Alison whom Stephen beheld after his resurrection?

They weren't going to get out of this without paying a price, Wildecent knew. There was nothing between her and Ambrose now. Why shouldn't Alison seem like a

crone to Stephen? Any why shouldn't she realize she loved him only when it was too late?

"All that matters," Wildecent said, wiping Alison's tears away, "is that you're here. You'll have other suitors. We both will." She did not add that no love would be like the love they had each felt slip through their hands.

"I don't care. He doesn't love me; he doesn't even *like* me, Wili. I set everything to right, and *now* he thinks I'm a witch."

Alison's lamentations were interrupted by a cough. Wildecent stiffened and tried to block Alison from seeing Ambrose.

"I think it would be more seemly if the two of you descended first. I can appear a little later, and no one will likely notice. But they *do* expect to see the two of you leave this room."

Alison took a deep breath and wiped her face on her sleeve. "Stephen is with them."

"I know," Ambrose replied softly.

"No—Stephen is with them . . . riding . . . alive . . . well."

"I know."

"I did everything you wanted. There's nothing between Stephen and me now—not even the real memories. You can see for yourself." Alison held her hands toward him.

Ambrose retreated. "It's not necessary," he said quickly, skirting the edge of the room to reach the door. "I believe you. I'll leave first." He shrugged and opened the door. "There's nothing to hide, after all. Is there?" He was halfway out before he looked back at them both. "Thank you, my lady."

The door closed and he was gone.

"I think he meant that, Alison," Wildecent said as they heard him join the men already on the roof.

"I thought he was talking to you."

"No, he meant letting go of Stephen. I'm sure of it. I think he understood how hard it would be."

Alison sniffed back the last of her tears. Yesterday's clothes lay on the floor. She picked up her tunic and saw it was still stained a rusty brown. Everything had happened. Somewhere there was a world where Stephen lay dead at the center of an oak grove. And somewhere there might be a world where they could love each other.

"I wonder where we'll get dyestuffs," Alison wondered aloud, trying to pick up the rhythms of mundane life. She failed and threw the garment into a corner. "It's all so strange," she muttered and went back to sit on the bed.

"We did it all, Alison, *together,* just the way we used to."

"When I saw you standing there with Thorkel Longsword's head in your hand—!" Alison shook her head. "I don't know which looked worse: you or him."

"You. You should have seen your own face."

Alison smiled wistfully. "The way it used to be . . . almost."

he sun was high overhead when the weary men rode up to the outer gate of the bailey. Five men were tied facedown across their saddles, another four sat their horses out of habit, not consciousness, and only Stephen seemed fully alert. The Englishwomen had commandeered the kitchen's largest pots hours earlier. They were lifting bandages from boiling, fragrant water as soon as the men dismounted, but Lord Beauleyas would have his say before they could tend the wounded.

"What happened?" Jean Beauleyas expressed his concern the only way he could: with a raised voice and a threatening gesture toward the two young men who had led the expedition.

"The men, Father," Eudo countered. "Let the men be treated."

Eudo's arm was bound with a leather sling, and there was a dirty bandage wrapped around his thigh. He dismounted with difficulty, placing no weight on the injured leg. Stephen waited a moment longer before swinging his leg over Sulwyn's saddle and sliding discreetly to the ground.

"It was an ambush, my lord," he explained. "Lordless men of the forest. They set a trap, and we rode straight into it. The fault is ours that we were blind and careless. There's little more to be said, and nothing that can't wait until the injured are attended to."

Lord Beauleyas regarded his nephew with a mixture of admiration and distrust. Stephen seldom was lost for words, seldom said the wrong ones, and always seemed the master of a situation—a position Beauleyas was unwilling to share. He gave the injured men leave to have their wounds treated, but he did not let Stephen or Eudo go so easily.

Eudo spoke first. He described the fallen tree and the falling net, then he hesitated. Reluctantly he recalled the ignominy they'd all felt, and the chaos of those first moments when his horse had been cut down. He acknowledged that Stephen had ridden to his aid but carefully—almost enthusiastically—pointed out that moments later his cousin had disappeared.

"Disappeared?" Beauleyas asked.

"Into the forest. It was dark before we found him again, and not a scratch on his hide."

Stephen's face was dark and resigned. He allowed Eudo his moment of glory; conceded it because there was no alternative. Now he stepped forward to face his uncle's inevitable questions.

"You ran away?"

The young man forced his tense muscles to relax. There was no easy way to explain what had happened after he'd left Eudo's side, and his cousin was going to make certain it was as difficult as possible. But there was no need to make matters worse by letting his uncle provoke him. Stephen met Beauleyas's stare and spoke in level, reserved tones. "I did not run away, my lord. We were hard pressed and driven into the forest by archers. It was every man for himself. I had just killed a man. When I turned there was another coming for me with an ax. He took Sulwyn in the shoulder—"

His uncle's scar twitched. The chestnut stallion had been as fit as his rider. "We thought it strange, as well," Eudo interjected.

Stephen's composure frayed. He raked his hair and tried again. "I *thought* it struck Sulwyn. I jumped free. I must have struck my head. I remember everything as if it happened twice—"

"Don't leave out the part about the witch," Eudo urged.

"*Deus aie*, cousin, you saw me!" Stephen put his hand to his left shoulder and pulled his hauberk forward. A long tear where the chain mail links had been smashed apart was revealed. The metal was crusted. "Did I do that myself? You found my shield. I can't explain what happened—"

"You said you met a witch and that she healed you," Eudo reminded him with a too-helpful smile.

"I was wounded—badly wounded. I thought I was going to die. The next thing I remember, the very next thing I remember, is running for my life and soul."

Eudo smirked, and Alison, who could hear them from the shelter, held her breath. Jean Beauleyas grabbed his nephew's hauberk. Flakes of rust and dried blood drifted onto his hands. He shoved Stephen away when he let go. "These English forests are strange places," he said, brushing the brown dust from his hands. "Pagan. Go to Lachebroc and see the priest. Tell him what you told me; he'll know what to do."

"There's only one thing to do with a witch's lover—" Eudo began, but his father silenced him with a glance.

"And the next time either of you comes upon a track that's tree-blocked—take the hard way 'round, the branches not the stump. If there's trouble waiting, it's always on the easy path." Beauleyas intended that bit of wisdom to be his final word on the matter, but both young men tried to follow him into the bailey.

"You, to the priest," he snarled, pointing at Stephen. "And you, have your wounds tended."

There was no room for disobedience when the lord of Torworden took such a tone. Stephen headed down the cartway without removing his tattered hauberk. But this time Eudo would not be put off. Gritting his teeth, he put his weight onto his injured leg and hobbled across the yard.

"Father!"

The yard fell quiet. Beauleyas paused. Nobody used that tone with him, not unless he was prepared to die for it. He turned slowly and saw that his son was. It was one thing to observe the rivalry between Eudo and Stephen, to watch as it sharpened both of them, but it was another, less desirable, thing to see a killing rage in his only son's eyes.

Beauleyas wouldn't be the first father to die like this, but he kept his fears well hidden behind a facade of disdain and contempt. A long moment of silence echoed through the bailey.

"You must do something!"

Torworden's lord did not move a muscle.

Sweat beaded on Eudo's forehead. "He's a coward or a witch's lover. If he does not offend your honor, he offends *mine.*"

Beauleyas hooked his thumbs through his belt. "I'll know when my honor has been offended."

"How? How will you know? Will you turn to your devil-worshipping sorcerer?"

Beauleyas unhooked his thumbs and took a step forward. He was unarmored and armed only with a knife, which he had not touched, but his son took a step backward. "I did not hear you," the old man said softly.

Eudo had gone too far, and he knew it. He looked away from his father's face. No one stood near him; everyone was watching. He licked his lips and swallowed hard. "It is a matter of *honor*, my lord . . ."

"When you have honor, it can be offended, not before. Until then there is only my honor at Torworden. And my honor is offended when my men fight among themselves, when two men lead a hunting party and one lays onus on the other for misfortune, while the other does not. *That* is an offense to my honor. Do you hear me?"

"Yes, my lord."

The confrontation was, for the moment, over. Beauleyas pivoted on his heel.

"What about the witch?"

"There is no honor regarding witches," Beauleyas said without turning.

Eudo watched his father climb the motte. He wiped

the sweat from his face and limped toward the stables. Everyone ignored him as he passed.

It was a long afternoon for Alison and Wildecent. Wildecent had been through worse, at Hafwynder Manor in the aftermath of the Black Wolf's attack. Alison had been unconscious then, and this was her first encounter with the wounds of battle.

They had Hafwynder folk to assist them, but each wound was different and, after almost two days' traveling untended, each wound was difficult. One man slipped into unconsciousness as they removed his mangled hauberk; his wounds opened and he was dead before they got the bleeding staunched. That was the curse and the blessing of chain mail: it protected a man from minor wounds, but serious wounds were worse. The women couldn't stitch the chain mail wounds closed, only cauterize them and pray.

The sun shone orange through the open sides of the shelter. It was over. The last wound bandaged; the last man sent on his way to heal. The sisters sent their helpers to the stables with the discarded hauberks. The chain mail would first be cleaned in sacks of sand moistened with vinegar, then mended, then returned to the men so the whole cycle could begin again. Alison blew her hair out of her eyes and set about restoring order among her herbs.

A shadow fell across the powders and ointments. Eudo was finally ready to have his injuries looked at. Wildecent sighed and pointed him to a table. Alison cut through the leather sling. Wildecent grabbed the shoulders of the hauberk and pulled the heavy shirt off.

"Can you take that up to the stables?" Eudo asked politely. "God knows it needs cleaning—even I can smell it—but I don't think I'll be able to manage it myself when your sister gets done with my leg."

Wildecent looked at her sister. Alison shrugged. "Go ahead. Why not?"

"You're sure?"

Eudo had shed the sweat-stained cloth and leather tunics he'd worn beneath the hauberk since leaving Tor-worden. Huge bruises were visible under the layers of dirt on his skin. Finally freed from the weight of the hauberk, his shoulders sagged and he seemed to have fallen asleep where he sat.

"I'm sure," Alison said.

Wildecent gathered the dangling straps of the chain mail. She and Alison had seen, but not heard, the confrontation between the young man and his father, and could feel a reluctant empathy with him. He seemed thoroughly chastened, and not even Eudo could be foolish enough to cause trouble while his wounds were still bleeding. Wildecent trudged toward the stables.

Eudo's arm wound wasn't serious—a clean gash that was already crusted over and cool to the touch. Alison left it alone. His thigh was a different matter. When she'd soaked the dirty bandage free, it was revealed as a dark honeycomb of smaller wounds from the mail surrounding the larger bite from an ax.

Alison considered the task before her. "I'll wash it first," she told him, fishing a cloth out of the cauldron. "The water will burn because of the herbs in it—but the iron will hurt less afterward."

She didn't look at him when he grabbed her tunic. Any number of men who could face naked steel without flinching cowered like children when it came time to tend their wounds. But not Eudo. He pulled her backward to the table. All signs of weariness had vanished and there was malice in his pale gray eyes.

"Heal me like you healed my cousin, witch."

His mouth was over hers before she could scream; his free hand was digging between her thighs. For an instant Alison was too stunned to resist; then she groped for the hot cloth and ground it hard against the bleeding wound. Eudo released her, but backhanded her as he did.

"You'll regret that," he snarled as Alison recovered her balance and put her hand to her face. "You'll beg for mercy—"

He was in no condition to follow her, though, when she ran from the shelter and collided with Wildecent and Bethanil returning from the stables. Alison didn't need to say anything; the blood streaming between her fingers told the other two all they needed to know.

"I'll kill him," Bethanil growled as she started forward.

Wildecent clung to the beefy woman's arm. "We don't dare. Not here," she explained. "He's Lord Beauleyas's son. We can't kill him and hope to survive ourselves— but we can make him hurt so he'll think again before bothering any of us."

All her life Bethanil had listened to the noblefolk of the manor and, though she had her doubts, she listened again and followed Wildecent into the shelter. Eudo was mopping the blood from his leg and didn't hear them until it was too late.

"Hold him!" Wildecent commanded.

Bethanil was only too happy to obey. Wildecent pulled a wide, flat knife from coals beneath the cauldron. She had it against his skin while the metal was still red-hot and held it there while he howled. He was shaking when she lifted the blade, and slumped heavily to the table when Bethanil released his wrists.

"Bleeding's stopped," Wildecent remarked as she cooled the knife in the cauldron.

For three days Eudo was confined to the long barracks. His wound healed but his pride, the other men said, was festering. Jean Beauleyas said nothing, but the fact that Wildecent went unpunished was taken to mean that Torworden's lord was not pleased with his natural son.

Alison shared Bethanil's misgivings. A man who had tried to force himself on her from the bandaging table was not, in her opinion, likely to be deterred by pain. She stayed in the donjon unless she was with Hugh de Lessay, Guy, or one of the Hafwynder men. She kept the door barred and thought of asking Beauleyas for a night

225

guard. But one whose protection she most sought, Stephen, did not volunteer.

The priest at Lachebroc had found no blemishes on Stephen's soul, but Stephen himself had not been reassured. He could abide his shattered memories, but the image of Alison—a skeletal Alison with a sickle in her hand—haunted him.

"I must have hit my head—I was sure it was her," he said to Ambrose when they met at the hermitage.

"I'm sure it was, too," the sorcerer replied calmly. He had waited for Stephen to ask the first questions. He'd begun to hope his friend's memories were so vague the questions would never arise, but, on the proverbial third day, they had. "Alison was there when you got killed, and then she brought you back to life."

Stephen landed hard on the stone seat. He shook his head and laughed nervously. "No . . . no, this is a poor jest, Ambrose."

"It happened the way you remember it—all the ways you remember it."

The young man stared into his hand and struck his fist against the wall. "I don't know what I remember—don't you understand that? She's there; she's not there. She was in every dream, every memory, and now . . . nothing. Nothing but that nightmare beside a stream."

"Alison *did* restore you, Stephen."

"Why are you taking Alison's part now?" He jumped up so quickly that Ambrose retreated involuntarily. "You never had a good word to say about her before."

"My 'good word,' as you call it, is simply that Alison did restore you and she did remove her glamour from your thoughts. And, in honesty, I played some part in it."

"What part?"

Ambrose cleared his throat. He'd made his decision to tell Stephen everything before the hunting party had ridden up the hill. What had seemed right and rational then seemed much different here in woods above the Windraes. "I lent my power to Wildecent." He chose his words with the utmost care. "And Wildecent persuaded Alison that she must undo all that she had done."

"*Deus aie!* God aid me! Am I some gaming-board for all of you?"

"You know better than that," the sorcerer snapped, his own temper rising. "I do not interfere with your honor or your sword, but this was different. I could not leave you to the magic of this land!"

Stephen raised his arm and made a fist. He kept himself from lashing out, but he could not unclench his fingers. "I'm alive," he said, speaking as much to his trembling hand as to Ambrose. "I'm alive. I've lost nothing. The priest says it was a dream from God—a warning that I am too proud, too quick to battle. I didn't confess I've lived for ten years with a sorcerer who talks to the dead because *I didn't think you were involved!*"

The fist jerked closer to Ambrose's face.

"Go on," Ambrose said. "If anyone has a right to be outraged, you do. It might be the most sensible thing either of us has done in a long while." He let the tension flow from his face and made no move to defend himself.

Stephen tried, and failed. He gathered his fist against his chest and held it there. "Why can't things be simple again?"

"Perhaps if we left this island—"

"I can't leave. I can't go back to France, or Normandy, or Sicily, or anywhere else with you."

A new wave of despair had entered Stephen's voice. Ambrose came a step closer but backed away when he saw Stephen's hand clench again. "Why?" he asked. There was no answer. "If I said I would stay, would you leave then?"

"No. Yes. I don't know. You tell me. I was a dead man, Ambrose. A corpse. How am I supposed to feel? How do I know if anything I feel truly belongs to me or if any of my memories actually happened? How do I know?"

"Do you still love Alison?"

A strangled growl escaped from Stephen's throat. His fist shot forward. "I'll kill you, Ambrose." His punch went wide. "Get away from me, damn you. Leave me alone!"

Ambrose took a step backward, then another. He had his answer, though it wasn't the one he'd hoped for. He stopped in the day-village, where Bethanil had set up a provisional kitchen, and asked for bread and wine. They gave him bread fresh from the oven and ale that was left from the previous night's supper. The ale was flat and bitter. He drank it all before taking a horse from the stables and galloping it until Torworden could no longer be seen over his shoulder.

Ambrose was absent that night at supper. Jean Beauleyas stormed from one end of the bailey-yard to the other, as distraught over the missing horse as he was over his missing sorcerer. Bethanil was questioned, but as Ambrose was a sorcerer and known to do things sane men scorned, no one went looking for him. Including Stephen.

It was late the following day when Ambrose rode back. The men at the gate sent him to the donjon where he remained with Lord Beauleyas until the tables were set for supper. His reappearance was overshadowed by Eudo's return to the donjon.

The young man made a point of walking steadily to the high table. He greeted his father, leered at Alison, and gave Wildecent a look that was pure poison. No one noticed when Ambrose took his usual seat.

"You have made a bad enemy, Wildecent," he said to the pale and trembling woman.

She stared at their plate and nodded absently. "Bethanil wanted to kill him. I should have let her do it."

"I am leaving for Normandy tomorrow. Lord Beauleyas has released me from his service once I deliver certain messages to Duke William. I'm going to go back to Byzantium, and I'd like to take you with me."

Wildecent swallowed the hard lump in her throat. "Is Stephen going too?" she asked, concealing her emotions. Not that Ambrose's announcement came as a surprise. Now that Stephen was free from Alison's influence it was understandable that they would both leave England.

The sorcerer shook his head. "I don't think so. After all that's happened, he seems to feel his place is here. After all that's happened, I guess I have to agree. He doesn't need me anymore." His voice revealed his bitterness and Wildecent took his hand in hers.

"Perhaps if you waited a bit longer—"

"For you?"

"No. My place truly is here—in England if not Torworden. But Stephen . . . It's strange to say, but I think Alison would be happier if you could convince Stephen to go with you."

Ambrose smiled and shook his head. " 'Why can't things be simple,' he asked me, when the wonder is, it's simpler than it was before. Stephen cannot accept what has happened. She took herself out of his memories, but he loves Alison as much as he ever did. As I—"

"Alison and I have made our peace with each other," Wildecent said, squeezing his hand and looking away. "I wish you well, but I do not want to go to Byzantium."

"We can search for your family along the way—"

She closed her eyes and brought his hand to her lips. It was tempting. She imagined traveling with him, unraveling the mysteries of sorcery and her birth. But Wildecent had experienced all the magic and sorcery she thought she'd ever need, and she doubted whatever family she had would be particularly overjoyed to find her again. So it would just be running away. "No," she whispered as she pushed his hand away. "I don't love you"—which was a lie—"and I've got my own life" —which was not. "Let's talk about something else, if this is the last meal we will eat together."

But there was nothing more that either of them had to say. They ate in silence, oblivious of the shouting, boasting and singing around them. When the last of the food had been served and the more sober of the men had begun to leave, Ambrose escorted Wildecent to the stairway where they stood in a corner while others moved past them.

"I will talk to Stephen. I'm sure he'll agree to see Alison—and once they're together, I'm sure everything will be . . . simple. I will send someone up for her once he's agreed."

"I'll tell her. She will be glad to know you have forgiven her, too."

Ambrose looked away. "Once they are together, Wildecent. Once everything is *simple* for them, there will be no need for a third—"

"No."

He shrugged and looked much younger than he was. "I'll send someone anyway," he said and headed down the stairs.

Ambrose remembered the bright sun of the Mediterranean when he stepped out of the donjon into a misty English night. He tried to conjure its warmth as he descended the log steps, but all he could recall was the smell of the garbage in the alley where the magi had found him. He was deep in his own morose thoughts when he reached the gate. He decided to walk along the river before he sought out Stephen for the final acts of their friendship.

Something whirled close behind his ears. Ambrose brought his arm up to deflect it, but the flat of a sword caught him across the temple and dropped him, unconscious, to the ground.

230

hy is Ambrose doing this?'' Alison asked.

Wildecent sighed and set down her mending. "He's leaving England and he wants Stephen to be happy after he's gone," she replied for what she hoped was the last time. "I trust him."

Alison warmed her hands over the brazier. "I want so much to believe you. When I saw Eudo in the hall, I almost asked Lord Beauleyas to post a guard outside our door; now I'm glad I didn't." She picked up her needle and continued fitting a band of embroidery to the sleeve of a tunic first intended for her father.

They worked quietly, pausing now and again to warm their hands or add more charcoal. Each time they heard the lower door open they would look up, but it was always someone leaving the hall, never the men Ambrose had promised. The evening stretched on until there were no more outbursts heard from the great hall.

Though neither woman said anything, each had begun to have doubts. Alison wanted desperately to make amends with Stephen, to erase the horror she saw each time their eyes chanced to meet. Her most secret hope was to start over, beginning with friendship this time, not obsession. And since all her hopes were fastened on Stephen, her questions grew there as well. She did not doubt that the sorcerer had approached Stephen, nor that he had pleaded her case in good faith; Alison doubted that anything would persuade Stephen to speak with her again.

For her part, Wildecent doubted Ambrose. They were alike, or so he'd said; so much alike that they could have become one soul if they had succumbed to their passions. And now she had rejected him. If they were alike, Wildecent knew she'd wounded him and he'd never openly reveal the pain. If they were alike, he'd have his vengeance, sooner or later. Wildecent could not imagine a better vengeance than the one he got by sending her to raise Alison's hopes in vain.

The latent tension was dispelled when voices and feet echoed up the stairway.

"I'll get your cloak," Wildecent said, dropping her work to the floor; Alison flashed a relieved smile as she headed for the door.

Alison opened the door and hailed the men from the landing. She wondered why they seemed so startled to see her, and then, more soberly, why Hugh was not among them—nor any of the men she knew. Her cheerful greeting was aborted as they began to race up the stairs. Alison retreated—but not fast enough.

There were three of them, and they knew exactly what they were about. The first shoved Alison against the wall and put his hand over her mouth to keep her quiet. The second did the same with Wildecent, though she threw Alison's cloak at him and put up a fight until she was cornered at the far side of the bed. By then the third had lashed Alison's wrists behind her back; he did the same with Wildecent. They gagged the women with the linen Wildecent had been mending, and carried their struggling but silent captives out into the fog.

The trio of abductors turned the other way at the base of the motte, heading around the practice arena, past the stone yard, to the small postern gate. Torworden expelled its most noisome refuse through the insignificant gate, sluicing it down a steep slope so a small tributary of the Windraes might eventually carry the stink and filth somewhere else. It was not a coincidence that the gate overlooked the steepest part of the natural hill, nor that it was kept carefully stripped of every tree or shrub that might provide a handhold or cover.

The guards on the donjon roof could see the entire slope by daylight. They saw less by night, and animals often came up the slope to root through the garbage, but a torch would have called forth a general alarm, whether it was headed upslope or down. The abductors did not need to move silently, but they did have to carry the women down the treacherous sluice in the dark.

Alison and Wildecent each knew where they were. Almost involuntarily each became still and quiet. Each could imagine the fate toward which they were being carried, but neither was so suicidal as to fling herself down the slope to the foul, swift waters of the creek.

Two more men were waiting on the far side of the creek. The women were quickly shuttled across and then into the forests where torches were lit. Now that they were on level ground, Alison began to struggle again. She thrashed herself loose and thudded to the ground. Before she could catch her breath or get her feet under her, they caught her again. This time they bound her legs at the ankles and carried her slung between them like an animal.

Wildecent saw her sister's fate and was more careful. She draped across her captor's shoulder like a sack of onions and lulled him into a sense of false security while they wound deeper into the Wychwood. They had begun to climb again when she put all her effort into grabbing any part of his neck or face with her bound hands. Digging her fingernails into his ear, she was ready when he let go, and kicked hard as she came free.

There was no way Wildecent could outrun five men. Her only hope was to vanish into the night in such a way that they would not consider pursuing her. She tucked her head down and her knees up while she was still in the air and began rolling downhill as soon as she hit the ground. It was what Lord Godfrey had taught both girls to do when they were learning to ride their ponies, and the saints knew Wildecent had learned the trick very well. It was harder with her arms stiff behind her back, but her hair and heavy clothes protected her somewhat. She had the breath knocked out of her when she finally came to a halt and had no trouble staying dead still, praying no one would come down the slope looking for her.

"Leave her be," a man shouted from the top of the

hill. "We can come back for her. This is the one he really wants."

"If you say so—"

"I say we're late and that she's probably dead already."

The man carrying Alison kept moving, and took the torchlight with them. The men who had carried Wildecent turned around and ran to rejoin the others. There were three men guarding Alison after that. Wildecent knew her own escape had sealed her sister's doom.

Alison sought protection in her magic, hoping that if she could not sway the minds of the men who held her prisoner, she might at least dull her own mind to what was sure to come. But she had never been good at finding peace deep within herself and was unable to do so when she was terrified. She called upon the powers of the forest, though she doubted they would hear her.

The short hairs on Alison's neck and arms stood up as the men began climbing another hill. She had no sense of where they were but she sensed the blood of sacrifices made long before the Cymry. She prayed they'd keep on going but was not surprised when she was dropped before an oak. Nor was she entirely surprised when she'd squirmed around and gotten a clear look at the torchlit grove. Eudo Beau-Bastard sat atop a flat sarsen boulder. His face held the same pig-eyed leer she'd seen from the high table.

"It's appropriate, don't you think, for a witch?" he said with an evil smile. "The peasants in Lachebroc told me about it. They say virgins were sacrificed on this very stone. Personally, I think killing virgins is a waste, don't you? Besides, you're plight-trothed and not a virgin anymore."

Alison was more enraged than frightened, but either emotion was enough to make her choke on the rag they'd shoved into her mouth. She hunched forward and fought to control her retching.

"My men tell me your sister flung herself down a hill.

Too bad. I'd meant to give her to my men. Now they'll just watch until I'm ready to share."

Alison was breathing evenly again and stared at him with all the hatred she could push through her eyes. He still favored his injured leg, she noticed, and though she had no hopes of escaping his men, she was determined she'd hurt him before she died.

But Eudo was taking no chances. "Tie her to the tree."

He stayed well out of harm's reach while his men dragged her to one of the smaller trees. They untied her wrists, hauled her arms above her head, and tied them around the trunk. Then they laid her on her back. Eudo pulled off his tunic and loosened the laces of his braes. He knelt beside her. She tried to kick him but froze when he held his knife just above her eyes.

"I do so want to hear you beg," he purred. He slipped the knife beneath her gag and sawed through the cloth.

Ambrose rolled over and wrapped his arms over his head. His ear still rang from the sound of the sword smashing against his skull. But he was alert now, and the nausea that had wracked him when he'd begun the climb to consciousness had subsided. He moved too fast getting to his feet and lurched forward, clinging to a pile of stone to keep from collapsing again.

At least Ambrose knew where he was now—in the stone yard. He didn't remember being carried there, or how long he had been unconscious, but he doubted it was much past midnight. The sorcerer cursed himself for a fool and took an unsteady step toward the donjon. He'd need the drugs he kept in his room if he were going to rid himself of his headache. It took forever to climb the log spiral.

The donjon was quiet, as it should be at that hour. No one greeted him as he pulled open the door. No one questioned him either. If anyone had noticed his absence, they'd thought nothing of it. Ambrose put his shoulder against the wall and shoved himself up the stairs to his chamber. He hoped the women were asleep.

The door at the top of the inside stairway was closed, but not latched from the inside. He pushed it open and knew something was wrong when he fell across an overturned stool. Moving slowly through his own room, he found a lamp that hadn't been broken and lit it from the brazier. He blinked dumbly at the wreckage. Alison and Wildecent were gone—the fact hammered in rhythm with his headache, but it made no sense to him.

There was a chest beneath the washstand. Ambrose withdrew a wax-stoppered flask from its disordered depths. He broke the seal and held the glass beneath his nose. The fumes burned his nostrils and made his eyes water, but his head began to clear. He shook a few drops onto his tongue and tucked the flask inside his tunic. The drug hit his blood with a jolt.

He saw the smaller details of the struggle now. A half-sewn tunic lay on the floor, the outline of a muddy boot across its sleeve. Alison's cloak trailed from the bed, also marred by footprints. Both women had been carried off.

Gods knew, he'd been careless, making promises to Wildecent without looking to see who might be listening. He'd seen the looks on Eudo's face; he knew the sisters had an enemy who would stop at nothing. And because Wildecent had trusted him—had left the door unlatched—they were both in mortal danger.

Ambrose took a step toward his sanctum; he'd need sorcery if he had any hope of finding them alive. His next step was toward the outer door; Stephen should be here—he owed his friend that much. Another step toward the sanctum; the next toward the door. The drug he'd taken set his mind racing, and with what was left of his rational self he knew he'd need to hear another voice before he could trust his judgment.

Delving under his bed, Ambrose retrieved his sword and slung it below his waist. He didn't expect there was anyone lurking in the darkness between the donjon and the barracks where Stephen slept, but this time he was taking no chances.

He clamped his hand over his friend's mouth. "Get your boots and sword."

The younger man's eyes were huge and white-rimmed in the dim light of the barracks, but he obeyed quickly and without questions until they were outside.

"I expected you earlier. You said we should talk—"

The drug made the sorcerer reckless. "Not now," he said, grabbing Stephen's sleeve and pulling him toward the inner gate. "We've got to find our ladyloves."

Stephen jerked free. "*Ladyloves?* Are you drunk?" he demanded while stamping his feet into his boots and knotting the laces of his braes.

Ambrose related the events of the evening as he knew them in a few short sentences. The recitation sobered them both.

"You didn't sound the alarm?"

"I . . . I thought it would be better this way. If the world doesn't have to know about it. I wasn't thinking clearly," Ambrose admitted. He turned away before Stephen answered, and headed up the motte.

Stephen paused, agreed, and caught up with Ambrose just outside the gate. "You're right you're not thinking clearly. Why're you going back up there? You've got your Greek sword—we should be on our way."

"I'm thinking clearly enough. They could be anywhere. We'll never find them without help—and help is in my chamber."

Stephen reluctantly agreed. He swallowed his aversion to sorcery and followed Ambrose up the log steps.

"We'll need something personal. A piece of their linen. A lock of hair would be best if we could find it." Ambrose pulled the blankets back and shook the pillows. He found two long strands of golden hair, but nothing of a deeper brown.

"We're in luck," Stephen called from the doorway,

where he'd found a half-dozen golden strands caught on a splinter.

They had enough for the sorcery Ambrose had in mind, though he'd hoped to have hair from both of them. But the women had been abducted together. Finding one would be the same as finding the other, or so he told Stephen as they entered the sanctum. Stephen stayed pressed against the wall while Ambrose made a loop of Alison's hair and used it to suspend his talisman in the basket of light.

Ambrose pointed to the geometria. "That is Torworden. I've been building it since we got here," he said with evident pride, though Stephen saw no resemblance at all. "Now watch!"

Stephen didn't want to watch, but it was Alison they were looking for and, as Ambrose had learned, Stephen's love for the English heiress wasn't rooted in his memory. "Can I help?" he asked, as he had never asked before.

Ambrose looked away from his sorcerous engine. "Just watch," he said compassionately.

The crystal hung motionless for a moment, then began to rise along the wires. It drew its power from Ambrose's drug-heightened senses. It moved so quickly the wires began to glow and there truly was a basket of light in the upper room of Torworden's donjon. The wires sang, a diminishing chorus until only one clear tone remained and a single beam of light descended to the geometria.

"Do you see it?" Ambrose asked, and Stephen said that he did. The sorcerer stood up and the room went dark except for the oil-lamps.

Ambrose studied the place Stephen indicated and unhooked Alison's hair from the wire. He wove the hair loop through a longer loop of silk and pulled both taut between his fingers. He'd created a cat's cradle, save that the hair loop moved along the silk, and when it stopped the crystal began to glow.

"Out past the day-village," Ambrose said, collapsing

the figure. He snapped the talisman, silk and hair still attached, onto the gold torc he wore around his neck and led Stephen back down the stairs.

Wildecent had remained crouched below the path long after the forest had become silent. She'd scraped her face against the hard earth until she'd loosened the gag, but she didn't try to unbind her hands or find her way out of the forest until she heard Alison scream. Her sister was far away, which made the sound that much more blood-chilling. She found a jagged stone and rasped the rope across it. When that failed she knelt down and caught the thickness of her skirts with her teeth. It was like being gagged again, but at least she could walk—after a fashion.

There wasn't anything she could do for Alison except survive and return for vengeance. She set off in the opposite direction, continuing to scrape with the stone as she did. Wildecent's goal was the day-village, where Bethanil slept close by her pots. She'd trust only folk from Hafwynder Manor now that she and Alison had been betrayed.

She had fallen more times than she could remember when the rope frayed loose. Walking was no problem then, but direction was. She'd climbed several hilltops and discovered that at night all hills looked like Torworden. She didn't even know if she was walking in the right direction. Nor would she appeal to magic. If the greenwood could protect anyone, Alison needed it most. Sorcery was out of the question.

Some sort of luck remained with her. She found the cartway between Lachebroc and Torworden. Wildecent belted up her skirts again and found the strength to run up the hill. Bethanil's suspicious face, peering out the window, with a cleaver in one hand and a lamp in the other, was the most wondrous thing Wildecent had ever seen. She stumbled across the threshold and threw herself on the cook's mercy.

* * *

"It was Alison he wanted all the time. I heard the men say so," Wildecent said as she concluded her tale of horror.

"Aye," the Hafwynder woman said, nodding as she slapped the cleaver flat-bladed across her hand. "I heard the sorcerer go by a bit ago. But he wasn't alone. The other one, Stephen, was with him. I never forget a voice." She set the cleaver aside and bustled about the makeshift kitchen. "I'll find Eodred. He'll have an idea what to do. You drink this while I'm gone."

Wildecent took a cup of heated honey wine from Bethanil's hands and stared into it. *Stephen?* She sat down on an overturned kettle. Suddenly nothing made sense. Stephen's complicity was harder to accept, and there was certainly no reason for him to carry Alison off into the forest. Even the timing seemed wrong. Bethanil had heard the pair "a bit ago," when it had been hours since the three men had burst into their room.

Her hands began to shake. She took another sip and set the cup down beside her. And yet Bethanil *had* heard the two of them going by. There was no good reason for them to be out unless they were involved.

Wildecent repeated her story when Eodred, still barefoot and his braes billowing wide around his knees, followed Bethanil into the room. When she finished, the old hawkmaster said that Jean Beauleyas should be awakened.

"For what?" she snarled. "It's way too late now."

But Eodred was adamant. "He's lord here. He must be told. It's the only right thing to do," he insisted.

Wildecent looked into their faces. They both believed, even Bethanil believed, that men were wiser than women, and that lordly men were the wisest of all. It didn't matter that Jean Beauleyas was a Norman and a foreigner, or that his nephew and his sorcerer were the ones who stood accused. It was enough that he was a lord.

"All right," she conceded. "Go. Tell him. But I don't want to talk to him or see him—make certain he understands that. Tell him I've fainted or that I'm overwrought. Better yet, tell him I'm already mourning for my sister."

"You should pray that she's safe," Bethanil whispered.

Wildecent remembered the screams and shook her head. "They didn't mean for either of us to survive. I just hope she hurt them—cursed them—before she died."

Both Eodred and Bethanil were aghast at Wildecent's heresy, but the dark-haired woman stared them into silence. She'd started to change the night she'd worked sorcery with Ambrose; the night she'd offered Thorkel Longsword's head to the Cymric gods. The change was complete now, and there was nothing of meekness or timidity left in her.

"I'll go tell Lord Beauleyas now," Eodred muttered.

Moments later he was racing into the bailey-yard, shouting that the Englishwomen were missing. Bethanil put another ladleful of warm wine into Wildecent's cup, then stropped her cleaver with a whetstone like any warrior. Her eyes never left Wildecent, and it was clear she, at least, had no difficulty believing the dark-haired woman was dangerously overwrought.

It was not long before the assembly gong clanged into the night and Eodred came running back.

"He's waking them all to see if anyone else's gone missing," Eodred said softly once the door was barred behind him. "Lord Beauleyas was wondrous angry when I told him what you said and what Bethanil had heard. He means to see justice done. He's promised gold to the man who finds 'em and death to 'em once they're found."

The hawkmaster had taken time to get his boots. He paused to pull them to and to bind the loose cloth of his braes. "Lord Beauleyas said I could ride with 'em too. Says there's a priory not far from here, and it's there he wagers they're taking her. Says if we ride hard we can be there first and bring her back—"

"Don't you fools understand! They weren't planning to marry us!" Wildecent raged.

The hawkmaster looked to Bethanil, who shook her head slowly, then he rested his hand gently on Wildecent's head, as if she were his own child. "Don't worry, little one. Lady Alison's a beautiful woman with property and fortune; no real harm will come to her."

tephen and Ambrose made slow, sure progress through the forest. They followed no easy path, but moved in straight lines guided by the crystal talisman suspended from a loop of Alison's golden hair. Then one time the crystal glowed red and Ambrose put it quickly away.

"We're close, now," he said to Stephen, pointing in the darkness. "Over there a bit, I think." He tossed his torch to the damp ground and stomped it out.

Stephen extinguished his torch as well but put a hand on his friend's shoulder before they continued. "Why did it turn red?" he asked.

Ambrose was grateful for the darkness between them. "She's hurt . . . bleeding."

"Alison?" Stephen asked, though he knew they had only golden hair in the loop.

The sorcerer grunted and started moving slowly uphill through the fog. Like Alison, he could sense the power of the place they approached. It was older than the oak above the Uffington chalk carving; perhaps older than the carving itself. Ambrose couldn't guess how Eudo had found the place, but he had, and now he was abusing it and the last Cymric priestess at the same time. Alison was bleeding, but it was the hill that made the crystal glow.

They went more slowly without the torches and with the need for quiet. While they had been searching, Stephen had been content to listen to Ambrose. They had their goal now, and Stephen took command effortlessly. He chose their pace and their approach once they saw torchlight spilling out of the grove.

Alison wasn't screaming anymore, but when they heard her moan Stephen charged up the hill. Ambrose dove for his friend's knees and wrestled him to the ground.

"You blundering oaf!" he whispered loudly. "Do you

think he's up there alone with them? Do you think his men will stand aside and let you run him through?"

"I'm sorry."

But the moans continued and fueled Stephen's rage. It was Alison whom his cousin had brutalized. Not the leering crone Stephen had beheld by the stream, or the fey maiden of his dreams, but the flesh-and-blood Alison whom he had promised many, many times to protect. When they'd left Torworden Stephen had thought only of rescuing her; now there were two thoughts: rescuing her and killing each man who had hurt or touched her. Stephen said nothing of this to Ambrose. It didn't particularly matter if his friend agreed; he'd prefer to spill their blood himself.

Four men lingered at the edge of the grove. They stood with their backs to the scene and well away from each other, though they were not guarding anything. Their clothes were disheveled and watermarked, but they winced when a woman's moan reached their ears. Belated guilt would not be enough to save them. Stephen grasped Ambrose's arm, then drew his finger across his friend's neck. He felt Ambrose nod and released him. Taking his knife from his belt, Stephen approached the nearest man.

Ambrose removed the silk loop from his talisman and threaded it through a wooden toggle. The magi did not approve of killing, but the gutter-rat they'd brought into their community had survived by tooth, claw, and knife. The child would not purge himself of violence, but clung to it with a stubbornness that unnerved them. So Masianos, first among the magi, hired a tutor to teach the boy the ways of death; a magus could never be too well educated. It was true that Ambrose could not couch a lance or fight encumbered with a helmet and hauberk, but only because his Saracen tutor considered Western ways unrefined, and had taught him the civilized ways of the Orient instead.

Ambrose slipped the strong silk around his victim's neck and jerked it tight around the toggle. The man clutched his neck, but the silk bit deep. He made no sound; not even a death groan could leak past the pressure on his throat. His body spasmed once, then relaxed. Ambrose lowered him quietly.

Stephen had also been successful, but slightly less skilled. His man thrashed the grass as he collapsed with Stephen's dagger shoved high under his ribs. Alarm was shouted and the two other men had time to draw their swords. Eudo and his last man abandoned their raping and looked about for their swords.

The Beau-Bastard did not fight. He met Stephen's eyes but once, as he knotted the laces of his braes, and quickly descended into darkness on the far side of the grove. He was grinning as he left.

His men outnumbered Stephen and Ambrose; he had no reason to fear. Stephen was a worthy opponent with a sword, but not so the sorcerer. The knights had little respect for a curved, watermarked sword, and less for a man who shrieked like a demon while fighting with it. Eudo's three cronies divided themselves two and one, with Stephen facing the pair—which was just the way Stephen and Ambrose wanted it.

Stephen had fought with Ambrose against his back before. Like Eudo and the others, he would not touch a sword that could not be thrust deep into an enemy's gut, but he was confident nothing would strike him from behind. He took a step forward, giving Ambrose and his manic sword a bit more room, and met each heavy thrust with a solid parry of his own.

This night, however, Ambrose had the advantage. His sword was best suited to long, deep cuts through cloth and the muscles around a man's ribs. The man he faced wore nothing more substantial than a woolen tunic. The sorcerer did not waste his strength absorbing the mighty swings with the steel of his lighter sword, but swept them aside. Ambrose waited until the man grew careless and enraged by a handful of small gashes, then he drove in for the kill and proved that the point of his sword was as sharp as its edge. When Ambrose's shouts turned jubilant, Stephen knew only his pair was left—and his cousin.

"Finish them," he shouted to Ambrose. "I'm going after Eudo."

Dark steel swooped in from Stephen's left. There were small notches set along the back of Ambrose's sword. He could make the sword sing as it sliced through the air. Stephen's opponents pulled back a fraction, suddenly convinced they faced a demonic blade. Stephen had the moment he needed to escape the combat, and Ambrose drew his knife left-handed to parry the second blade.

Stephen looked down as he ran across the clearing. His eyes saw her clothes torn to either side; her bloody, glistening skin; the dark, splotchy bruises—but his mind did not. He slowed only enough to sheathe his sword before charging into the brush.

There was little light beneath the forest's canopy of new leaves. Stephen stumbled a while before he found the path Eudo had used to bring Alison to the grove. He paused, and listened, and heard his cousin's heavy stride not far ahead. Eudo's thigh was far from healed. Stephen made haste as he followed the overgrown path, but not recklessly. He'd catch up with Eudo soon enough.

"Put up your sword!" he shouted when he could see the black outline of his cousin moving against the grays of the forest. His own was already drawn.

"Is that you, little cousin?" The sound of metal scraping as Eudo cleared his sword. "I did not expect you so soon."

"You did not expect me at all, coward."

They swung at each other. Darkness undercut their skills, and the swords did not touch. Stephen stepped in and swung again.

"I hardly expected you to pass so tasty an opportunity," Eudo called from just beyond the range of Stephen's sword.

Arm braced for a mighty thrust, Stephen lunged to-

ward Eudo's voice. And swept an armful of leaves from
their branches with his efforts. He'd lost his cousin in the
darkness. He froze, knowing the next move could come
from anywhere, but the next sounds he heard were
Eudo's stride retreating along the path.

Only a fool would charge through unknown forest with
three feet of honed steel at the end of his arm. Stephen
resheathed his sword and followed. Twice more he caught
up with Eudo, and each time his cousin goaded him into
a precipitate attack. Finally, when Stephen stood alone
and panting, he realized Eudo had no intention of fighting him but was simply luring him farther away from the
grove—and closer to Torworden.

The next time when he caught up with his cousin, Stephen shouted no challenge but drew his knife and sprang
at Eudo from behind. He plunged his knife deep, but
Eudo had a coward's luck and a coward's defense. The
Beau-Bastard squirmed at the last moment, and the blade
sliced through the soft flesh of his upper arm, scarcely
hurting him at all.

They wrestled on the ground a moment, then broke
apart, Stephen without his knife and Eudo with his hand
clapped over his naked shoulder. This time the heavier
man did not retreat down the path.

"Why fight with me?" Eudo asked the darkness.
"She's a witch—you said so yourself. I've done you a
favor; you should thank me—"

"Shut up!" Stephen barked back. He'd drawn his
sword again and was crouched forward. He'd forgotten
everything he'd ever been taught about keeping his mind
clear when there was steel in his hand; all he wanted was
more of Eudo's blood.

Eudo knew it—knew his younger cousin was incom-
petent with rage—and goaded him again. "A sorry plight-
troth you made," he said with a sneer Stephen could hear
rather than see. "I had the virgin's flower from her, Stephen, that she wouldn't give to you—"

Stephen's sword was not properly raised when he

leaped across the darkness. Eudo parried it effortlessly, spinning the weapon out of Stephen's hand. But the younger man had not been thinking with his sword when he began the attack; he scarcely noted it was gone. He pushed Eudo off-balance with a flying tackle, and brought his knee hard into his cousin's crotch as they fell. Eudo gasped and released his sword, then got a handful of Stephen's hair and rolled on top of him.

He smashed the back of Stephen's skull against the ground. The younger man seemed properly stunned, and Eudo reached for his knife, only to have Stephen's hand lock over his wrist. They rolled through the dirt, the single knife braced four-handed between them.

Stephen was incoherent with a rage that would have shamed him at any other moment. Eudo was fighting a madman, and fighting for his life. The Beau-Bastard poured all his strength into the arm that still held his knife, and slowly forced it around until the steel pointed down to the hollow of his cousin's throat. He drained himself and the point began to descend.

Eudo was prepared for almost any counter-assault, but not for his cousin to rise into the attack and bite down on his wrist. He blinked. It was over for Eudo—but not for Stephen. The madness that had been rising within him since he first heard Alison's moans was not sated by simple death. The young man withdrew the knife and plunged it back into Eudo's chest not once, but again and again.

Stephen stood up, gasping for air and sanity, his hands hot and wet. There was no honor in what he had done. Then he thought of Alison, and Ambrose's crystal glowing red with her blood, with her pain. An anguished, unwilling cry came from the depths of his soul. He fell to his knees. The knife began to rise and fall again.

It was not long before the madness faded. A shaking young man got unsteadily to his feet. He surveyed his butchery with disbelief and revulsion. The knife fell and he staggered to the bushes. It had been a madness, like

the *berserkerang,* and his remorse was blunted by the certain knowledge that it had not truly been him wielding the knife. And yet he could not return to the grove. He could not face Alison, even though it was her rapist's blood that soaked his clothes.

Stephen wiped his hands on the grass and wished for a stream to wash the blood and bile away. He retrieved his sword and knife; they'd had no part in his madness and he put them carefully away. Before he could stare at the corpse or sink into despair, the forest revealed the sound of a stream not far away.

It was knee-deep and bitter cold. Stephen laid his weapons on a rock and stripped to the skin. He splashed into the stream and let the icy water cleanse the bloody heat from his body and soul. He dragged his clothes in and pounded them against the rocks, then he climbed out and, shivering and shouting, put them on again. He was cold, but he was clean, and he started back up the path to the grove.

Ambrose had killed the last of Eudo's men. His sword—which was black Damascus steel and had never been in Greece—sang as he whirled it clean of blood. He replaced it in its scabbard, but he did not bind the scabbard shut. He trusted Stephen to do what he'd sworn to do, but Ambrose took no chances on trust alone.

The grove was quiet as he stood by the sarsen stone and glanced over every part of it. He'd already seen Alison sprawled beside the oak; he looked for a second woman, and could find none. His desires urged him away from this place in search of Wildecent; then Alison moaned.

It was not easy, but he forced Wildecent from his mind; he would not leave this place until Stephen returned. Bile rose in his throat when he saw what they'd done to her. Alison was still conscious: battered, bleeding, almost naked but able to see that yet another man walked toward her. She had screamed herself hoarse an eternity before. She moaned, and tried to writhe away from him.

Eudo's tunic lay where he had discarded it. Ambrose almost scooped it up, but he could not bring himself to cover her with the Beau-Bastard's clothes, so he loosened his belt and pulled off his own tunic instead. He did not consider the effect this would have on Alison. She kicked the cloth away after he draped it over her, and he had to wait until she'd exhausted herself again before he could replace it or unbind her bleeding wrists.

Ambrose folded her arms beneath the tunic and tried to ignore the wild hatred in her eyes. He could not comfort her. She was like an injured animal that must be terrified further before it can be helped or healed. He turned away and Alison became quiet.

He was not always gentle; it was not natural to his childhood, nor to any later part of his life. The women who gave themselves casually to warriors and other travelers were seldom gentle in either birth or manner themselves. Taking a woman cooled a man's blood; it had nothing to do with the exotic emotion called love. In the most tortured moments of his forbidden love for Wildecent, Ambrose had never once considered *taking* her.

It came to Ambrose that he'd been wrong about love, and that it was the *taking* of a woman whose mind meshed with his own that was dangerous. Sorcery was only indirectly involved. Ambrose swallowed hard. Accepting what he felt for Wildecent seemed far more frightening than resisting it.

Ambrose looked down at Alison. Her eyes widened and she held her breath. The sorcerer resolved that Stephen would never see his beloved like this. He would do the one thing he had sworn he would never do; the very thing Alison believed was the heart of sorcery. He unhooked his talisman and held it before her eyes. They both stared into it, and it built a bridge of light between their eyes.

The shafts of light had faded, but the crystal still glowed

when Stephen raced across the grove. The younger man fell to his knees and spread his arms to embrace her, then pulled away. Alison did not writhe or moan as she had with Ambrose; she did not seem to see him at all.

"Oh God—no-o-o," he cried, unashamed of his tears.

Ambrose reattached his talisman to the torc. "Wait," he counseled.

"What have you done? What did you have to do?"

"I—I entered her mind."

"You made her forget?" Stephen's voice was almost grateful.

The sorcerer shook his head. "I dulled her memories, but I could not remove them." Ambrose saw the questions in Stephen's face and smiled sadly. "You, of all people, should understand. Love and hate have very little to do with mind or memory. She'd go mad if I took her memories away completely, because her heart will always remember. But I think she might begin to heal if you stay beside her until the sun comes up, and carry her home gently."

Alison said nothing but lifted her hand so Stephen could hold it.

Ambrose stood up. He saw his friend's wet clothes and did not ask what had happened to Eudo. He stripped the tunic off the man he'd garrotted and draped it over Stephen's shoulders. Then Ambrose picked up Eudo's tunic and pulled it on. He wrapped his belt below his waist and hung his sword from it. "Take care of her," he admonished, when Stephen finally looked up. "There's someone else I must find."

efore dawn Alison began to shiver. With Stephen's help, she put on Ambrose's charcoal-colored tunic and wrapped the remnants of her clothes around her. She let Stephen hold her in his arms until it was light again in the grove. When he lifted her up and said he'd carry her home, Alison leaned her head against his shoulder.

"I have no home," she sobbed in her cracked voice.

He set her down and knelt beside her. "You have Hafwynder Manor."

Alison made a strange sound that might have been a laugh. "Do you consider I might be with child from—from one of those—" But she couldn't bring herself to complete the thought.

"I could not love such a child," Stephen admitted, having considered the matter while he'd held her during the night. "Male or female, I would give it to the Church, but such a child does not change my love for you." He paused and took her hand between his. "Not even *you* could change my love for you," he chided, not knowing if she would appreciate the irony. "My memories cannot tell me if we have known each other forever or if we met for the first time by a stream. But my heart knows . . ."

She looked away from him, but her fingers closed tightly around his. "There will be a stream around here," she said after a moment of silence, a faint glimmer of her old self in her eyes when she looked at him. "I would like to wash myself."

Stephen grimaced, though he knew there was. "A stream?"

"I feel water beneath this grove. There will be a well, or a stream somewhere nearby."

Stephen shrugged. Alison would always be Alison, and if he would live with her and love her, he would have to accept her magic. He set off and found where the stream came closest to the hill, then he carried her to its banks. He waited with his back to her while she bathed and tore her clothes. There were flowers on the bank. He picked a handful and held them nervously.

"I am ready to go back."

He held the flowers out to her and stared.

Alison's hair was damp, but carefully rebraided. Ambrose's tunic came only to her knees, but she'd made an underskirt out of what remained of her linen, and was decently covered as any honorable woman ought to be. Her lip was cut and swollen, and there was a cut beside her ear where Eudo had slipped while removing the gag. All other signs of her ordeal were hidden until she took a step toward Stephen. Pain tightened her face and showed in each slow, cautious gesture.

Stephen handed her the flowers and lifted her into his arms. "I'll carry you."

"It is a long way—"

"We're in no hurry."

He carried her along the stream until the grove was far behind them and there was no chance she would see Eudo's mangled corpse where he'd left it sprawled beside the path. They had to stop often, and at each resting place Stephen shouted Ambrose's name.

"They'll be all right," Alison would whisper each time the forest birds alone answered Stephen's call.

It was midmorning when another voice shouted back to them—not Ambrose, but Hugh de Lessay. There'd been little doubt as to what had happened once Beauleyas's muster had shown both his nephew and his bastard son were missing. The only question was who had survived, and de Lessay was unabashedly happy that it was Stephen.

Hugh offered Alison his horse, but she could not ride alone. Stephen held her before him in the saddle and suffered Hugh to lead them. The other two men with Hugh were sent ahead with the news that six men were dead—including the lord's natural son—that Alison was safe, and that Ambrose was still searching for Wildecent.

Jean Beauleyas was waiting at the outer gate when Hugh led them through the day-village. Stephen would have fallen to one knee before his lord, but the sight of so many people—so many men—had frightened Alison, and he could not entrust her to any other arms. Then Bethanil came forward, and Stephen's problems appeared solved.

There was so much natural emotion in the cook's plain face, no one would have thought to look for guilt. She took Alison in her arms. Stephen knelt before his uncle.

"I have killed my cousin," he began, reciting the words he'd chosen in the night. "He took the lady I would call my own from your protection and assaulted her with no thought for her honor—"

"Or mine," Beauleyas interrupted wearily. "Get up. Nothing more will come of this at my hands. I've lost my son; I'll not lose you as well."

All those who believed from the beginning that Jean Beauleyas was biding his time to see which of his possible heirs proved strongest could not tell that day or any other if the lord was happy with the outcome. He ordered Stephen to lead another party back to the grove to reclaim the bodies, but when they came back Beauleyas did not descend from the donjon to view his son's remains.

Alison had been put to bed in Ambrose's room and given one of her own sleeping draughts. Bethanil sat beside the brazier when Stephen entered the room. Guilt was now more evident on her face and in her knotting hands.

"She's resting, Lord Stephen," she said as he pulled back the bedcurtains.

He winced at the unaccustomed title. Alison lay curled on her side with her hands beneath her cheek. She sighed when he touched her cheek, but there was nothing fearful in the sound and he let the curtains fall back.

"Have they found Wildecent, or Ambrose?"

It seemed a perfectly natural question to Stephen, but it brought the cook to her knees in tears. She grasped the hem of Stephen's tunic and pressed it against her lips and forehead. Her wailing awoke Alison, who got to her feet unsteadily.

"It be all a terrible mistake, my lord," Bethanil said many times. "She came to us in the night—to Eodred and me. She said it was your witch-friend who'd carried them off—"

Alison blanched and clung to the curtains, fearing the worst now that she'd heard the beginning; Stephen didn't notice.

"I'd heard you go off earlier with him—" Bethanil let go of Stephen's tunic and sat crying on the floor.

"What happened to Wildecent?" he asked, firm but calm and squatting down beside her.

"We said Lord Beauleyas must be told, and she agreed. She wasn't herself and we did not argue when she said she'd have naught to do with the lord once he was roused. She gave little hope of finding Lady Alison alive. After Eodred returned saying the priory was empty, she turned away from us completely. Toward dawn I fell asleep myself . . ."

"And?" Stephen encouraged.

"She must have wakened Eodred, and persuaded him that they must leave. Hafwynder horses were gone from the stables, and bread from the hearth. I'd hoped she'd taken him to search for her, but now I think not. There was an anger in her like I'd never seen before . . ."

Stephen tried to coax the big woman back into the chair. "It is unfortunate, nothing more," he said. "She'll be found. She may have found Ambrose, and they may not be ready to return."

He stood and noticed Alison for the first time. Now there were two distraught women. He despaired of calming Bethanil and tried his luck with Alison. "Wildecent was safe, but it seems she ran off this morning," he said, feeling foolish when the concerned expression did not fade from Alison's face. "Well, she must be looking for us—one of us, at least?" Alison shook her head.

"It is not so easy," Alison said, seating herself gingerly in the chair. "Wildecent thinks Ambrose betrayed us—"

"A mistake. A simple mistake." But he noticed that Alison's face did not lighten at all. "Alison," he said more seriously. "It was Eudo's men who attacked Ambrose as he left the hall. I'm sure of it. You don't think—"

She shivered and shook her head. "No, not once I saw . . . *him*. I was afraid when Ambrose came out of nowhere, but . . . no, I know I was wrong about him from the beginning. I—I shall have to find words to thank him—but Wili knows only what we knew last night, and what she heard from Bethanil."

"But once she knows," Stephen said, still thinking it was simple. "Surely she'll forgive him. I mean, there's nothing to forgive him for—is there?"

"No." Alison stopped and put her hands to her face. In the end it had been Wildecent who made the sacrifice. Now it would be Wildecent who paid the price for being used by the gods. It wasn't fair, but it seemed inevitable. "It was all a mistake," she whispered and began to cry again.

Bethanil laid her head in Alison's lap and they sobbed together. Stephen stood up and glowered at them both. Women and simplicity didn't mix well. "You!" he shouted at Bethanil. "Put your lady to bed!"

Faced with a sharp-voiced man and a simple task, the cook got to her feet. She carried Alison to the bed. Stephen went off in search of his uncle.

Wildecent woke up on the hard dry ground where she'd fallen asleep shortly before dawn. Sunlight made rainbow shapes as it penetrated the tree branches far above her. She raised her arm to block the light and squinted. For a moment she did not know where she was or why it seemed so strange, then everything flooded back. She let her forearm fall back to cover her eyes again.

Too much had happened. In the passing of a few days she had gone from betrayed to betrayer. What else could Eodred think when he awoke and found she'd run off with their supplies during the night? Yet it seemed she had no choice. The path of vengeance was all downhill and very steep; it allowed no deviation or escape.

With a loud, unappreciated sigh, Wildecent got to her feet. Her pony and the donkey were cropping grass near where she'd left them. Her saddle and the donkey's pack were heaped on the ground, also where she'd left them. In the predawn darkness, she'd told herself that she was too tired to make a proper, secure camp; the fact was, though, that she really didn't know how. All her life there had been menfolk and servants to take care of such things.

She'd gotten the bridles off the two animals, but she knew she'd have the devil's own time getting them back on. It had been years since she'd groomed her own pony. For that matter, Wildecent could not remember being so totally alone before in her life. Not even her nightmare journey through the realms of magic and the Cymric gods had felt so strange as knowing there was no one at all to talk to.

Reflexively, Wildecent reached up to tuck her braids behind her ears, and touched instead the tight band of a peasant's cap. Her hand dropped to her side and she stood, trembling, beside the tree. In every sense she was not the person she'd been just two short days before. That timid, anxious young woman had been replaced by someone who trekked alone along the cartways and wore a young man's clothes.

I had to do it, she told herself again. *There is no one else who can avenge the wrongs done to Alison . . .*

Digging through the packs for bread, Wildecent considered her plans—such as they were. At their core was anguish; her heart could not yet accept that Ambrose had betrayed her love and that Alison was dead—raped and, no doubt, sacrificed to the darkest aspects of sorcery. Her heart counseled grief and the rituals of mourning; but her mind counseled vengeance and drove her onward. In the middle of nowhere, in borrowed clothes and with only the animals for company, Wildecent clung to the strident demands of her conscience.

The sorcerer must be made to pay the highest price for his treachery. Without his now-broken promise, she never would have opened the door. His henchmen could never have broken through that door without arousing the whole donjon. Alison would still be alive . . .

Wildecent thought of Alison's glowing face as it had been, moments before betrayal—and, later, as she had heard of her, upside down in torchlight with a dirty rag tied across her mouth. Cold hysteria closed over Wildecent's heart: she had to believe that everything was Ambrose's fault, lest the burden of guilt descend upon her own shoulders. She had been Ambrose's willing dupe. *She* had opened the door; *she* had allayed Alison's rightful suspicion of the sorcerer; *she* had made her sister's horrible death possible.

This realization of her own culpability had burst upon Wildecent the previous afternoon while she and Eodred were riding east toward King Harold. She had been rehearsing her impassioned pleas, painting a detailed portrait of Ambrose's misdeeds, when she heard the echo of her own thoughts. What justice could a Christian king mete out when he heard such a tale of sorcery and magic? What justice that would not condemn her and Alison as surely as it damned Ambrose?

Indeed, as the crystal voice of Wildecent's conscience pointed out, Harold's justice could *only* fall upon her. Ambrose was a deacon of the Church. Any and all of his crimes would be judged in the bishop's cloisters—and, though vengeance thrilled to the thought of what he would endure in their hands, there was much it was best the Christian Church never suspected. So, Ambrose could never be *brought* to justice; justice—vengeance—would have to find him in some out-of-the-way place.

Wildecent finished her bread and picked up the pony's bridle. Her notions of what must be done were much more sharply defined than her notions of how to accomplish it. She had to kill Ambrose, she was sure of that, and he had to die in full knowledge of his crimes, but Wildecent wasn't ready to plunge a cold dagger into his breast. There was still the anguish in her own heart to deal with.

She would have to make herself heartless before she could become vengeance's weapon. It wouldn't be easy, and it would certainly involve a measure of black sorcery—but deep within herself Wildecent knew that she must suffer almost as much as Ambrose, if she were to redeem herself at all.

And so she had left Eodred while he slept and turned southward toward Hafwynder Manor. There were things there that she needed, and a place—the abandoned chapel where the Black Wolf had made his camp—where she could stay while she purged herself of softhearted feeling.

Ambrose returned to Torworden as the sun descended into the treetops. He was tired and dirty, but paused to cast Eudo's tunic into the mud before opening the door of the sunken hut.

"She's safe," Stephen said, springing to his feet as soon as the door was open.

The sorcerer reeled backward. He hadn't expected to find anyone waiting for him; the good news took a few heartbeats to settle in his mind.

"Wildecent? Here? You found her?"

"Not here . . . but safe, I'm sure," Stephen began. He told his friend the story, as it had been pieced together during the day, concluding, "And you're to see my uncle, once you're presentable again."

Ambrose went to the table, where Stephen had thoughtfully provided wine.

"I'll ride out tomorrow—"

"He's sent riders out, but he also said you were already planning to ride out tomorrow." There was a note of hurt accusation in the younger man's voice.

Ambrose pulled his braes. Standing naked in the center of the hut he poured a ewer of cold water over his head and wiped away Eudo's smell. Then he answered Stephen. "Yesterday. Yesterday it seemed the wisest thing to do. By the Two, it would still be the wisest thing, but I won't be going. Not until I find Wildecent; not without her." He sat on the edge of the box bed mopping himself with the castoff linen, wincing when he probed the sore spots on his temple and neck. "I tried to convince her to come with me. She wouldn't—no more than you would. And she told me how miserable Alison was, thinking that you no longer loved her. I thought I might at least set *that* to rights before I left.

"More the fool I was, I stood in the stairway pleading with her and promising I'd send for Alison once I'd talked with you—"

Stephen swallowed Ambrose's words and thought on them awhile. "Alison says 'thank you.' "

Ambrose let the shirt fall to the straw. "How is she?"

"I took your advice; it worked, as usual. Just as you were right when you said I still loved her. I think I shall become the lord of Hafwynder Manor when all this is over, and I think I shall like it very much. But I think I would like it even more if you didn't need to leave."

"I should leave," Ambrose said as much to himself as Stephen. "If I listen to my mind, I should leave because, my friend, magic's not done with this land. If I listen to my heart, I should leave because I've made a fool of myself with Wildecent, and I doubt she'll forgive me—"

"Even Alison has forgiven you, as if you needed it. What happened wasn't your fault."

"Ah, but I made a fool of myself before that—"

"It is not a fatal affliction, Ambrose. Most men are

fools. I've heard you say that dozens of times. Stay at least until we're back at Hafwynder Manor?''

The sorcerer sighed and stood up. "Secretly, I'd always hoped I wasn't like most men. I'll stay."

ABOUT THE AUTHOR

LYNN ABBEY was born in Peekskill, New York, and earned her undergraduate and graduate degrees in history at the University of Rochester and New York University, respectively. She spent several years working as a computer programmer and systems analyst in New York City, before moving to Ann Arbor, Michigan in 1976 to pursue a full-time writing career. Lynn is the author of the historical fantasies *Daughter of the Bright Moon* and *The Black Flame*, and the fantasies *Jerlayne*, *Out of Time*, and *Behind Time*. She is perhaps best known as the co-creator and co-editor (with ex-husband Robert Asprin) of the *Thieves' World* anthology series.

ABOUT THE ARTIST

ROBERT GOULD made his name in the 1980s with a series of groundbreaking covers for Michael Moorcock's fiction, and for several years his haunting paintings graced the covers of books by Louise Cooper, Mujica Lainez, and many others, for which he won a World Fantasy Award in 1989. He founded Cygnus Press to support works of a Fine Art nature, publishing high quality prints and portfolios by such artists as Alan Lee, Barry Windsor-Smith, Jeffrey Jones, and many others. In the late 1980s, he moved to Los Angeles, where he started Imaginosis, devoted to "bringing magical worlds to life" through books, media and merchandising; his project partners include fantasy artist Brian Froud and *Star Wars* designers Iain McCaig and Terry Whitlach, among others. He is also Vice President of Education First, an innovative children's charity based in Los Angeles.

ALSO AVAILABLE

ROGER ZELAZNY'S THE DAWN OF AMBER
by John Gregory Betancourt
ISBN: 0-7434-5240-2

The FIRST ORIGINAL NOVEL IN A NEW TRILOGY, FULLY AUTHORIZED BY THE ZELAZNY ESTATE!

In the final novels of his ten-book *Amber* series, the late Roger Zelazny rewarded readers with several startling revelations about his fantasy universe. But with his passing, many important questions about Amber and the Courts of Chaos were left unanswered.

The Dawn of Amber is a prequel trilogy, exploring events that precede the first novel in the series. Here, you'll meet the young soldier known as Obere as he's whisked away from the kingdom and world he has known and defended his entire life, and placed on a knife's edge of turmoil, intrigue, domination, and death.

To achieve his legacy of power and become a player rather than a pawn in this deadly game whose rules he has yet to discover, Obere must journey into the serpent's lair, the home of his enemies: the Courts of Chaos.

BLACK UNICORN
by Tanith Lee
ISBN: 0-7434-4512-0

It was big and beautiful and so black that it was like a hole in space, and it was completely impossible. Unicorns didn't belong in this world except in legends. But there it stood, radiating magical power, in the shattered wreck of the party.

Nobody knew where it had come from, or what it wanted. Not even Jaive, the sorceress, could fathom the mystery of the fabled beast. But Tanaquil, Jaive's completely unmagical daughter, understood it at once. *She* knew why the unicorn was there: It had come for her. It *needed* her.

Yet she was the girl with no talent for magic. She could only fiddle with broken bits of machinery and make them work again. What could she do for a *unicorn*?

ILLUSTRATED BY CRITICALLY-ACCLAIMED FANTASY ARTIST HEATHER COOPER

"Unlike most fantasists who wish they could write magnificently, Tanith Lee can actually do it, and so naturally that you begin to wonder why nobody else seems to remember what real English sounds like."
—Orson Scott Card, *The Magazine of Fantasy and Science Fiction*

NIGHTWINGS

by Robert Silverberg

ISBN: 0-7434-4474-4

THE HUGO AWARD-WINNING NOVEL

Only at night, on the winds of darkness, can she soar. And it was Avluela the Flier's ebony and scarlet wings that led the Watcher to the seven hills of the ancient city from which, in a moment of weakness, the watcher failed his vigil, leaving the skies and deep space unguarded.

The invaders came and conquered.

With Avluela lost in the turmoil of the conquest, the Watcher set out alone for the Holy City—home of the Rememberers, keepers of the past, and where the secret of Earth's salvation lay hidden in antiquity. On his journey, the Watcher hoped to recapture his youth and find the soaring, beautiful woman he loved. But Avluela held more for the Watcher—and Earth—than love. Her wonder stretched beyond flight, for she knew the riddle to free all men. . . .